DEVOTION
and the
DEVIL

The Borderer Chronicles

MARK MONTGOMERY

DEVOTION
and the
DEVIL

First published in Great Britain in 2013 by ruffthedog.com

Front cover; Stańczyk by Jan Matejko, 1862 (National Museum of Warsaw)

ISBN-13: 978-1-494-88557-1

For my father, who did his very best for me.

THE BORDERER CHRONICLES

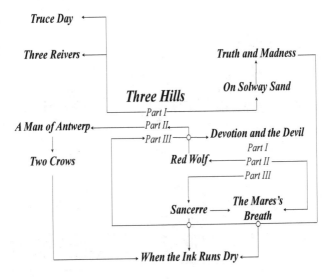

Truce Day

Three Reivers

Truth and Madness

On Solway Sand

Three Hills
Part I
A Man of Antwerp — Part II
Part III — Devotion and the Devil

Two Crows

Part I
Red Wolf — Part II
Part III

Sancerre — **The Mares's Breath**

When the Ink Runs Dry

The German Ocean

+ Leith
EDINBURGH ✚

Scottish East March

BERWICK ✚

✤ Flodden Field

Scottish Middle March

English East March

+ Hawick

Scottish West March

Langholm +

The Debatable Land

+ Dumfries

English Middle March

Caerlaverock Castle ✚

✚ Solway Moss

Orchardton Tower ✚

NEWCASTLE ✚

✚ CARLISLE

Kircudbright ✚

The Solway Firth

+ Allonby

✚ The Traquere's Tower

Workington ✚

+ Cockermouth

English West March

The Borders
The world of John Brownfield

Introduction

Devotion and the Devil, is the second volume written for the *Borderer Chronicles* series. It continues the saga from part three of the first volume, *Three Hills,* and sends four of its protagonists on different journeys; each driven by their own commitment—their own devotion.

Originally two separate novels, *The School of War* and *The Black Merchants' Guild,* they have been abridged into one volume, *Devotion and the Devil,* because although they are separate stories, they have common underlining themes of devotion and narrative threads that are intrinsically linked by shared circumstance, characters, beginning and outcome.

The Borderer Chronicles, as a whole work, is a creation of fiction set in history, touched by actual historical events and real historical characters. It is a chronicle based on the fragments of a chance-found history; scraps of insight into a life only defined by the contents of the last testament of a man, John Brownfield, dated 1601, and his few torn and charred journal pages.

His writings were in archaic, rhetoric text, and although cryptic in its form, it demonstrated a man's deep understanding of his own life and perhaps his twisted view of the world around him. The will declared John Brownfield, '*A Border Horseman, from birth to death, neither Scot nor Englishman,*' and this together with the absence of any other record of a life led, steers the *Borderer Chronicles* to search beyond John Brownfield's own sense of himself as a Borderer, and to tell a fictional story about a man who was, by his circumstances, unsure about his own identity.

It is a text, a fragment of a journal page, which forms the foundation of the second chronicle, *Devotion and the Devil.*

As the light dims and the day grows old, I recall the morning of my life and all those journeys undertaken for pleasure and for profit. Journeys from north to south, and to the east made difficult via the west. Those journeys corrupted by the devotions of strangers encountered, and events that curtail and divert journey's reason. Journeys on paths made through high wall and closed gate; by circumstance transpired by fate and not by design.

I recall my travelling companions, and those I met along the way, from start to finish; people loved and liked and lost. I recall my lessons learnt, battles fought and wonder if the journey worth it after all.

John Brownfield MDXCV (1595)

Devotion and the Devil, imagines one such obscure journey John Brownfield may have taken. It looks to the east, from his likely home in the Marches, situated between England and Scotland, and then looks back to the west, to the well-travelled routes and the triangle of trade that existed between the major towns and cities of Sixteenth Century Europe, including; Newcastle, England; Edinburgh, Scotland; and the second largest city north of the Alpine barrier, Antwerp.

So from John Brownfield's intended journey east to Antwerp, John travels back westwards by unforeseen circumstance to Leith, port of Edinburgh, into the turmoil of the Scottish Reformation and the conflict that existed between the anti-French Protestant Scottish Lords and the sitting Catholic Regent, Marie of Guise, French widow of James V, King of Scotland, and mother of Mary, 'Queen of Scots'.

The conflict culminated in the *Siege of Leith*, dubbed by chroniclers of the age, *The School of War*, because this was the first military conflict of Queen Elizabeth I's reign, barely a year old. Elizabeth at this time was twenty-six years of age. Marie of Guise, forty-four.

From Scotland and his own school of war, Jack returns to his journey to Antwerp and into the intrigue of another man's story, shaped by *the Black Merchants' Guild*.

So the story's time is set, as are the locations. It is 1559, and *The Borderer Chronicles* continue. But a warning, this saga is not simply John Brownfield's chronicle. Because a single life is never completely governed by the actions of a single person, or even a single event; it is rarely shaped by the person who lives it, but by the devotions and interventions of those people; family, friends, antagonists, and agents who work, either in the best interest of their charge, or in the best interests of themselves. So how could the story of one man be told without telling the tales of those whose allegiances twist and turn a life into, not the aspiration of the individual, but the life as fate perhaps dictates. Where lives are defined by the nature of their *Devotion and*, of course, *the Devil*.

Devotion and the Devil

One's own devotions are a fundamental condition of one's soul. They can exist in the psyche in many forms; loyalty to one's sovereign and kingdom; to faith and family; comrades; to the spiritual virtues and even sin; one's employ, whether it is by a master's bidding and the protection of all that is dear to him, or a vocation of one's own choosing; to dreams and aspirations; to power; or to wealth. But with so many fundamentals competing for one's moral application, dilemma is brought to the fore again and again, as one devotion yields to another. So one must be true to oneself and set precedence over one's own devotions. God is, for many, the ultimate devotion and therefore those obediences appointed by God follow as duty. However, I, who have not been nurtured in the Church's fold, do not hold God to heart, therefore I am without true faith or belief that any personage, whether king or queen, pope or preacher, is truly appointed by God to set to man's devotion to the fore. I believe such a heavenly wonder would not conspire with such base temporal man, with all his failings and deceits, to rule over men's minds; this may make me a heretic, and so condemned to eternal damnation. But as lesser devotions are comprised, in favour of greater loyalties; as parts of the soul are destroyed until there is so little soul left as to maintain a quiet mind, it matters little if the pious call me heretic, because I am already in damnation.

John Brownfield MDLX (1560)

Prologue

Kalibrado was said to be a man in another place. They said only his body dwelled in the present, his mind spent its waking hours in the future. They said his thought of the future was, for him, a predetermination; a reality not yet reached by time. And therefore he would not suffer to have his aspirations called a dream of fancy, for he lived his destiny real in his thought every moment of his life, and when he rested, it was perhaps only to dream of that future, as if time had already elapsed, and he was already walking its Arcadian fields.

So it was reported that all his actions, all his breath, existed solely to make all—all that secretly dwelt in his mind, simply preparation for that reality. And his evil put to those peoples who placed any obstacle before him and his aspirations was absolute—absolute corruption, absolute odium, and absolute brutality. He could be the cruellest of men, and his cruelty was without measure.

And so it was. People with lives to protect and property to safeguard; those with royal warrant, those with family in his way, sought out Kalibrado to kill or imprison him. But he was also a man with a dozen titles, all carefully hidden from each other. So whom would they imprison; *Kalibrado; Gabriel de Limeuil; Malin, the monster of Galicia; or Jan van der Goes, the Master of the Black Merchants' Guild?* Although, it would be very hard to find any foolish soul wishing to have that particular devil brought behind their walls and put into their prison.

෨෬

Peppo was hurried in his approach to the library door. He was in no mood to be halted by questions from the servants and soldiers that gestured for his attention as he scuttled down the corridor. The guards at the door saw Peppo approach, his speed dictating they open the large doors that guarded the enormous library. Peppo entered, but his journey was not complete, his new route flanked by a hundred bookcases, a hundred learned oak sentinels standing guard in front of their master's desk and their master of the moment, Kalibrado.

A breathless form stood before the desk, and although his news was of the utmost urgency, he waited. He waited for his master to acknowledge him. He waited, because to interrupt his master would invite his irritation, and Peppo avoided irritating his master at all costs.

Finally after four or five minutes, which seemed like five minutes more in Peppo's distressed mind, his master raised his head from the book he was reading, and Peppo made his report.

'Guild Master... *Giovanni* approaches the monastery. The scouts report him ahead of a thousand riders.'

Kalibrado thought on the number, and nodded. He liked even numbers. *One thousand*, he thought. He loved numbers he could express, written as a single numeral. He thought on it some more, and his mind's eye saw him write the letter *M* down, bold and large. But he disliked approximations; inexact numbers applied to matters military, and he asked, 'And our scouts, Peppo… are they exaggerators or understaters?'

'They are all good men, their report will be true, Guild Master.'

'Then all is well, Peppo. It would worry me to face one thousand… *and one.*'

Kalibrado was a master of the understatement, and he did not share the urgency in Peppo's voice. For all of Kalibrado's science and learning, enhanced a little more courtesy of the monastery's great library, it was not at the expense of his military prowess. He was an able strategist, and an enemy in greater numbers only placed a more interesting conundrum to be defeated. Kalibrado simply closed his book carefully, and took a sheet of paper. He selected a quill from an oversized jewelled gold pot that sat on his desk. He examined the nib and returned it to the pot. He selected a second quill and repeated his action. Then a third. The fourth quill he deemed satisfactory, and began to write.

Peppo thought him calmer than a man should be, with so many men riding towards him, all riding to take his life perhaps. To see him hanged, or worse. To rot in prison—to be tormented a little while he was allowed breath.

Kalibrado carefully penned the order; signed and sealed it with his ring. Then he handed it to Peppo, his loyal secretary. 'Take this to Captain Risano, and then sail away, Peppo. Take my book-boxes with you.'

'What of you, Guild Master? Without the ship, you will be trapped here,' declared an anxious Peppo.

'I am afraid I shall have to stay a while more…' Kalibrado looked towards the lines of bookcases, unconcerned with the threat, more concerned with his reading task at hand. Then he threw Peppo a rare smile. 'Unless of course, Peppo, you have a book-box big enough to fit me? *Well do you?*'

'But, Guild Master…'

Kalibrado could hear the concern on Peppo's lips, and see the fear in Peppo's eyes, and if Kalibrado hated his fellow man for their avarice, he admired Peppo for his unquestioning devotion; Peppo, whose generosity of self put Kalibrado's needs far above is own.

'Worry not, Peppo, the Guild's ships will arrive shortly… But they must not see you leave, so go quickly. It is important you deliver my book-boxes safely to my agents in France… The Guild must not be aware of my purpose here. Then from France, travel on to Scotland and retrieve the documents as we discussed.' Kalibrado handed Peppo a letter, sealed with a bull emblem—*a snorting bull.* 'I have encrypted the message to hide its contents from casual eyes. Our man in Leith should have wit enough to decipher it. Now go… Risano will need his orders.'

Peppo simply nodded and smiled, happy to be of service to his master—happier still, that out of all Kalibrado's retinue, kinder words were reserved only for him. And so Peppo ran as he could, with limp and shuffle, a present of a deformed foot and an aged body, to find Risano, Kalibrado's guard captain.

Kalibrado returned to his book, so he could read a few pages more to help him decide if he wished keep all the volumes of *Magia Naturalis,* to read on at his leisure, and add them to his own library. But after a dozen more pages, he shook his head and closed the book to leave it on the desk with its companions. His critique voiced only for the empty library room to hear.

'Too many of *Della Porta's* concepts are out-of-date. The sciences within these poorly conceived volumes are fit only for schoolboys… *Do not you agree?*'

Kalibrado then raised his head to the long line of flanking bookcases—to the endless lines of books, volumes, tomes and pamphlets and asked them louder, 'He should stick to writing plays… *Do you not agree?'*

Not hearing an answer, he again repeated his question, with voice loud enough to be carried by an echo, the first the room had ever known.

'Do you not agree?'

Kalibrado stood up from his desk annoyed that the books, such eminent knowledge givers, should remain dumb to his observation. He surveyed the ranks of books sitting silently on their shelves, and the volumes that had wasted his hours whilst he searched for worthy insight into unfamiliar subjects. He again shook his head. A reprimand directed at those leather-clad deceivers with design only to entice the reader into their authors' conjecture and prejudiced opinion; aimed only at glorifying the writers' own eminence in a world of ignorance. Kalibrado shook his head again, but this time at the hours spent, never to return.

He stretched a body long seated and confined by his reading. He rubbed tired eyes, and pulled his hand down his face, as if the act would draw out a hundred pages of unwanted fact that had invaded his crowded mind.

Kalibrado was a handsome man; his cruel features conspired to make him so. To take his eyes, his nose, his chin or his mouth individually, and place them on another man's face, would render that man ugly. But in union, all the facets created a physiognomy of such striking mien, that all who saw him could not help but know his nature, but at the same time they would see and stare at a man more attractive than a man should be.

The library was his office; a magnificent library created over five hundred years. The monks who created it were the finest librarians in all of Spain. Their translations included all great works: theological, scientific, the arts, the classics and philosophy. The library's shelves were said to contain one hundred thousand books, pamphlets and transcripts. Some did not believe the number was possible. Some even did not understand the number at all.

The monks for all their care and commitment to the library, however, were criticised. The Pope censured their Order, because it was said they put their acquisition of knowledge before their contrition before God, and thus were endangered by the serpent that led Eve; that led Adam into temptation. But the monks who maintained the great library were past worrying about such mortal condemnation, because they had answered to a much higher power when Kalibrado had visited them to make their library his private office, and their monastery his home for a while.

೮ೲ

Peppo hurried to find Risano marshalling Kalibrado's guard at the entrance to the monastery. And in the midst of men and torches, burning bright against a clear night sky, Peppo handed his master's orders to Risano—six foot of pure soldier; warrior through and through. Free from scar, no blade had touched him—none would dare. He was full of menace and authority. Veteran. Commander. Charismatic. Holding all attention, as his men surrounded him.

Risano worked quickly and without hesitation. Orders were given. Men took their positions without flaw, without fear.

The monastery was without good walls. Simply a group of buildings, huddled so close as to give the appearance of a much larger palace, with peaks and plateaus to complement the surrounding mountains of the northern coast. The monastery was deficient in many ways; narrow lanes once thought defensible, were as much a difficulty for the defenders. But Kalibrado had seen two benefits of this poor bastion, outside the benefit of a

8

grand library to make him an office. The first, was a long manmade bridge that hugged the cliffs between the road to the coast and the monastery doors; the only access, a wooden bridge on stone piers conceived over a thousand years ago, half a league in length. The second was its dock to the sea. Kalibrado knew no one would approach him from the sea. They made their mistake to ride at him from the land.

Thirty of Risano's musketeers waited at the entrance to the citadel. They waited for the mounted horde to reach them. They stood their ground well, even against the anticipation of the overwhelming numbers of horsemen. They were comforted that whilst their master stood behind them, and their captain directed them, victory was assured.

Within minutes, the attacking riders had reached the bridge and had strung out over the walkway. They were riding so as not to weaken the pavement beneath them, but their speed was not suppressed. The mounted men, with their lighted torches, were as a lava flow spilling down the mountain. Across the bridge they came, hard and fast.

Risano with sword in hand, lighted torch in the other, raised his blade and the musketeers readied their weapons. And the horsemen came on and on. Risano's musketeers waited patiently. Waited for the horsemen to cross the bridge. Waited for them to come into range.

And they came. And they rode past the first range marker placed by Risano's musketeers. But no order was given to fire and the musketeers took their eyes off their targets, to look in panic towards their captain. But Risano ignored the silent pleas from his men. He was waiting for the first group of horsemen to reach the end of the bridge.

As the first horse's hoof crossed onto the rock from the wood, Risano tossed his torch high into the air, the flame

9

spinning in the night. And before the torch hit the ground, a greater torch ignited—the world before them exploded.

The bridge disintegrated. Half a league of timber, men and horses sent down to the rocks below, as gunpowder ignited under each support in turn—louder and more magnificent that any volley of cannon—more destructive than any volley of anything known to man. An age passed from the first to last explosion. One hundred and twenty detonations, all bathed in smoke, littering the air with timber. Some riders had crossed the bridge, but not enough, and they were easily cut down by Risano's musketeers, and finished off by Risano's halberdiers holding the rear in support.

Only one had the best view—Kalibrado. He was at a high window. He could not miss his creation. He needed to view his art in action. He looked upon the gap where once an ancient bridge stood—long stood because of Roman engineering excellence and its care and renewal by generations of monks. He stood at the window and looked into the distance. He examined the scene on the other side of the chasm as the smoke cleared. He looked at the disordered riders remaining on the other side of the bridge, and for only the second time that evening, he smiled. His smile formed by two pleasures; his mind sharing two ethereal satisfactions; the success of his trap, with the glorious skill of his demolition; and the erasure of so many enemies, so absolutely.

The noise of footsteps behind him did not draw his study away from the hellish masterpiece he had created, framed, he thought, exquisitely by the window. He inhaled the air, its perfume thickened with smoke and carnage. But as he tasted the delicious aroma on the back of his tongue, he detected an overtone of lavender and roses, and without changing his view he said, 'As usual your perfume overpowers. Even sulphur cannot overwhelm it.'

A voice replied, 'My apologies, if my fragrance offends you.'

'No, Hueçon, it does not offend me. It protects me… because a blade from you will never come from behind. Your fragrance *will always* announce it.'

Kalibrado turned to face Henri Hueçon, dressed well, as was his way, standing better, as was his manner. But Kalibrado was not impressed by such shows of elegance, and he asked, 'What matter brings your odour into my nostrils?'

'Three ships await, Guild Master.'

'Then Hueçon, we shall go before the *Marqués* sends ships to blockade me.'

'*Excusez-moi*, may I ask… how many of his men did you remove from the bridge?'

'Four hundred and fifty perhaps. It would have been more, but ten barrels at the far end of the bridge failed to ignite. Two in the centre failed too, but they did not upset the overall composition.'

Henri looked impressed, and asked, 'Did you count them?'

'Of course my dear Hueçon. Why would one compose such a fine tune, and not tap along to its beat?'

༄

Three ships left the protection of the cove. Three of the Guild's vessels—former galleasses; oared galleys converted to ships, so that their ordinance could be increased, and holds improved. Each carried forty guns. Each ship travelled with the other, as was the Black Merchant Guild's way, so that opportunist privateers would think carefully on attack. The ships were laden with Kalibrado's personal guard, retinue and belongings. All heading out to sea without direction or purpose, other than to put distance from the land, and the well-travelled trade routes that ran the coast, past the monastery.

Kalibrado was on deck. He looked to the open sea as though a complex view of land and activity was to be seen, but the horizon was empty of everything except a sea irked by light winds. He stared not at the sea, but what lay beyond it. He looked deep into the distance, and into his mind's dream of what lay beyond his sight—to a place that, for now, could only take its form in his imagination, and not in his memory.

The captain of the lead ship was not a happy man. No clear destination unsettled him. He liked only the seas he knew, and not the strange waters outside his charts. He stared at the back of Kalibrado's head, as if his thoughts may prick the man's conscious into revealing to him a destination, and thus a safe course he could set.

Henri Hueçon was uncomfortable too. He disliked sea travel. The odours of the world were bad enough, and on board a ship there was little chance to escape them. But he noticed the captain's unsettled stance, and knew his problem. So Henri walked up to Kalibrado, with little regard for Kalibrado's meditations.

Of all Kalibrado's subordinates, only two dared approach him like an equal. His master of arms, Captain Risano, who feared nothing, and Henri Hueçon, a man of such high regard for himself that his ego would rather fight to the death than yield to anyone born better than he, or even anyone with rank or a design to belittle him.

'Our fetid captain is anxious for a destination, Guild Master.'

Kalibrado, irritated to be drawn away from his mind's view, turned to Henri, annoyance clear in his words. 'Then give him one.'

'But I don't know your intentions,' replied Henri.

'And you never shall, Hueçon, but tell him, Antwerp.'

Kalibrado looked about himself. He scanned the deck for his

master-at-arms. The men were busy and it was strange for Risano not to be close by.

'Where is Risano?' Kalibrado shouted.

Near the ship's rail, stood Risano's sergeant; a powerful figure wearing fine etched and embellished steel, and rich cloth beneath. He bore a leather harness about his shoulders that dropped into two leather saddle holsters, filled with two oversize wheel-lock pistols. Both man and pistols were enormous in their form. But for all his impressive presence, his fidgeting and hesitant manner demonstrated a man who was frightened to approach Kalibrado. He had news, and news was usually Captain Risano's duty to give Kalibrado. What was more worrying to him—it was bad news.

Kalibrado's search of the deck for Risano brought his eyes to the uncomfortable sergeant, who was obviously waiting to interrupt with a report.

'What is it, Sergeant? *Speak*.'

'It's the Captain, sir… urm…'

'*Speak*.'

'It's Captain Risano, Master. He's gravely wounded, bleeding badly. I've put him in your cabin.'

Kalibrado's travel was purposeful, and the sergeant moved very quickly to clear a passage to Kalibrado's cabin, opening any door that stood between his master and his wounded captain.

In the cabin, on Kalibrado's allotted bed, Risano was lying still. There was no movement from the captain, and signs from Kalibrado's surgeon standing close by were not promising.

Kalibrado leaned over Risano, to study the man with his eyes only. 'Is he dead, Master Surgeon… he looks dead?'

The surgeon was rubbing his hands clean in a bowl of water, keeping his eyes clear of Kalibrado. 'Sorry, Guild Master. I could not keep him alive. The wounding was too severe. A lesser man would have been killed on the spot.'

The sergeant, keen to report the detail of Risano's wounding, as if it would better his position with his master, spoke, 'It were splinters from the blown bridge, Sir. They caught him in the head and chest. He were too close to the bridge. He stood careless, clear of cover, so the men could see his signal, so that he could face the enemy headlong. Brave he was. Feared nothing he did. He seemed fine, but keeled over on board—bleeding.'

The surgeon shook his head. 'I am sorry, Guild Master. I am told he was a good soldier... I understand he had occasion to save your life more than once.'

'Yes, he was dedicated to his commission, and did his work well enough,' replied Kalibrado, stoically.

The sergeant interpreted Kalibrado's unsmiling face as remorse, and keen to further improve his standing, offered comfort. 'Do not worry, Guild Master. I'll arrange for burial at sea, with the ship's crew standing on... to afford a proper honour, fit for your captain.'

Kalibrado studied with interest the poor man's mortal wounds. His blood spilled out over his chest, staining his costume and the sheets of Kalibrado's bed. After Kalibrado convinced himself his man was truly dead, he declared, 'Yes sergeant, we must see he is buried. Leave us, Surgeon... I need time to say goodbye.'

The surgeon excused himself and left through the open door. The sergeant turned to leave also, but Kalibrado stopped him. 'Sergeant, make sure Captain Risano is disposed of without fuss. I have too much work to do... to be distracted.'

The sergeant looked in horror at the instruction. Risano was the finest soldier he had ever encountered—a man amongst men. The thought of losing him to the sea without ritual was totally abhorrent. But he dared not complain.

Kalibrado stayed his gaze on the blood soaked Risano, his face solemn, as he took up a sealed flask of wine. He drew out his knife, tapped hard the neck to break the top, and poured out the contents into a large silver goblet. He raised the cup to his lips as if to toast the fallen hero.

The sergeant was confused at the sight of Kalibrado's toast, and then began to doubt Kalibrado's instructions, as if they were a test, or a sick joke that he should have found funny. So the sergeant smiled weakly, and reached for an empty goblet, expecting to fill it for the toast.

Kalibrado took a mouthful of wine, rinsed it around his mouth repeatedly, and spat the contents back into the goblet. He then looked at the sergeant, and speaking softly, in the manner of telling a secret or a confidence, said, 'Sergeant, if you ever soil my sheets again… If you ever debase my chamber with blood… I will open you up like this wine bottle, and pour *your* blood out… so not a drop is left… *Do you understand?*'

The sergeant swallowed, his dry mouth making the act difficult. He knew well enough that his master, Kalibrado, did not make idle threats. So he bowed his eyes in earnest contrition and removed himself quickly from the cabin, running his hand over his throat to ensure Kalibrado hadn't already slit it. So powerful were Kalibrado's words, that the sergeant could already feel his knife cutting into the skin.

The sergeant ran the short corridor from Kalibrado's cabin to the ship's deck, and Kalibrado pondered a moment. He thought on his own anger and his inconvenient loss. He rubbed his hands down his jacket, as if they were sullied and required wiping. He then picked up Risano's bloodied, violet silk sash from the table next to his own cot, filled with corpse, carefully avoiding the blood-staining. He stared at Risano's former badge of rank and authority, and then he quickly exited the cabin to find a guard at his door. He looked the short man up and down, seeing only dirty face and frightened eyes, in clean livery and tarnished steel. Kalibrado drew a poor conclusion with regards to the man's soldiery prowess. But regardless of the man's poor appearance, it took only a moment for Kalibrado to decide.

'Soldier, what's your name?'

'F-Ferdinand—Ferdinand Bure, Guild Master.'

'Well, Ferdinand Bure, you are my new captain... *How do you say?*'

The solider looked towards the direction of the retreated sergeant, still visible in the distance on the deck, caught in discussion with four ladies dressed in dark blue mantles, ciphered with a large cross in white—*Sisters of Avalon.*

Bure was hesitant, fearing his giant sergeant as much as Kalibrado, and with the sergeant's vile temper large in his thoughts, he stammered, 'I-I'm n-not sure, Guild Master. S-Surely the sergeant is Captain Risano's second, and thus the new captain?'

Kalibrado was quick to put the soldier down, his voice direct and harsh. 'I say who is second and first. And in the interim you will be my first—my captain of my guard...or would you prefer a term in the Guild's galleys as oarsman?'

The soldier was quick to consider the merits of accepting the promotion, if not entirely convinced of its benefits. 'Er... n-no sir. I'd be pleased to be Captain.'

'Well said, *Captain* Bure. Now be sure the sergeant carries out my orders regarding the former captain here. And as your first test, as my new captain of my guard, ensure the Sergeant's face does not *ever* befoul my view again... He has offended me gravely... *Do you understand?*'

The soldier needed no further words, and as newly appointed captain, Bure scurried off to attend his new commission and Kalibrado's test of commitment, and to find the courage to follow it through.

On deck, Henri, seeking an enlightenment the sergeant had been too shaken to deliver, blocked Bure. But Bure, although a brother in fear with his sergeant, differed and was all too keen to inform Henri of the events that led to his new rank and responsibility. Henri had heard all, and he wore an incredulous smile.

Henri sought out Kalibrado, and was only a few steps into the corridor before he found him.

'Guild Master, surely you jest. Prudence is a mistress to court—you need more than an armed rabbit as your captain.'

'Hueçon, rabbits are easier to find… and lose. He will do until I find a wolf—a more suitable candidate.'

A secret smile formed behind Henri's outward show of concern. Opportunity was Henri Hueçon's stock and trade, and there was always opportunity.

'*Excusez-moi*, if you will permit, may I suggest a candidate?'

'Is he a Guild man, or *your* man?' asked Kalibrado.

'He is a good man, a capable man with men of his own to bolster your guard. I believe he is presently in the Scottish Marches, recently returned from France—from a commission well carried out.'

Kalibrado thought briefly on Hueçon's proposal. For Henri Hueçon rarely made suggestions that did not in some way benefit Hueçon. But curiosity directed Kalibrado to agree to Hueçon's recommendation, if only to see Hueçon's man, and mark him accordingly as a danger better seen, than one remaining hidden from view.

'No, I will pick my own captain, but I will still take him into my guard, as sergeant-at-arms.' Kalibrado looked to the direction of Bure's travel, and his hesitant pause at distance from the big sergeant. 'I am soon to be in urgent need of a sergeant.' Kalibrado paused, and saw more opportunity for profit from his decision.

'See to it Hueçon… *personally*. Go and find him as a matter of urgency, and send him to me in Antwerp.'

Henri protested, 'But I myself have an urgent requirement to be in Antwerp.'

Kalibrado raised is hand to dismiss Henri's protest. Then countered with a smile. 'Antwerp will have to wait to receive you. The Golden City already shines bright, *Henri*—your light will not be missed… *Do you not agree?*'

Henri replied with only a fallacious smile, a thin veneer covering his irritation. However Kalibrado's smile in reply was genuine, fuelled by the thought of Henri in danger and discomfort, transferring by boat in an unsettled winter sea to one of the trailing Guild ships. He also held an exquisite contemplation of Henri Hueçon's journey into the dangers of the Scottish Marches, where robbery and murder were to be his likely travelling companions.

Yes, all these thoughts provided the delight that fuelled the fire behind Kalibrado's smile.

PART 1
'four travellers'

Four Travellers

Once, at a junction in a road, four travellers, from different beginnings found themselves journeying to the same end. All four were different men, with different credos and lives led, different demeanours, clothes to wear and status held.

The four new roads before them all took different routes to the same place. Some would join up further on, some easy on foot, some harder to traverse, some routes were longer, and others were shorter.

The travellers asked each other the purpose of their journeys, and each replied, 'To declare our devotion and defeat the Devil.'

The first man was a steadfast man, although he did not acknowledge it. But he was constant in the sacrifice he made for his kith and kin. His devotion was to the protection of all those peoples that were dear to him.

The second was a noble man, of noble birth, although he did not acknowledge it, and therefore was perhaps nobler in his modesty. His devotion was to unwavering deliverance of his duty, without thought of glory, or want for gold.

The third was a man of God, although he did not acknowledge it. His abstinence of earthly pleasure and earthly sin made him a godlier person, even more so than the most devout priest. His devotion was to the reverent observance of his vows made to God, long ago.

The fourth was a vain, sinful man, dedicated to all the earthly pleasure and self-glorification he could achieve. He acknowledged all that he was, and lived all his life for his own kingdom on Earth, too impatient for his rapture in Heaven. His devotion was only to himself.

All four men would face the Devil, but who would be the man to defeat him? The steadfast man, the noble man, the godly man, or the vain, sinful man? I ask you, who best could play the Devil's game and win?

New-Castle

Chapter I

As the coast approached and landmarks came apparent, it was the sight of a castle and its church; signposting the mouth of the Tyne River and its channel to Newcastle, that brought a missing smile back to Henri Hueçon's lips. The thought of land's freedom and its wide-open spaces, away from the confinement of wood and sail, raised Henri's head in jubilation. He breathed in the scent of earth and trees carried on a seaward wind, and anticipated his escape from the poor company of an unremarkable ship and her unwashed crew. A return to the land to save his ears from the ship's endless fractious niggle and irascible creak, and his nose from its foul stink, which tainted his fine clothes and rendered his pomander beaten and useless against the crushing stench of tar and rot, and all a ship's damp bouquet.

Indeed, a welcome sight it was to Henri, Tynemouth Church. A church that was once enclosed within an abbey, now dismantled under King Henry VIII's edicts. But mercifully, the church still stood for the spiritual benefits of the people, although many a good and bitter Catholic simply thought it was left to stand as a monument to the wilful nature of sovereign power, and the mercenary ambitions of its royal agents.

The church stood within the castle's walls. It stood its blessed guard, to give the fortifications eminence, but all was poor. Scaffolding marred Henri's view, and improvements, started fifteen years previous, did nothing to impress Henri's eye. *But there again, building to defend rarely speaks art, only dour purpose.*

As Henri recalled his memories of the church and castle, he took comfort in favours he had attained for the Black Merchants' Guild, from an English Crown and its agent, Sir Richard Lee. Favours he held, in lieu of payment, for his *invaluable* procurement of Italian engineers to make the improvements to the castle, and for the inclusion of new guns and a Spanish mercenary garrison to man them.

After he watched the castle pass by, and his memories faded, he turned his attention to the ship's port side. He watched a string of boats making their way out of the channel and onto the open sea. He watched the merchant ships and the fishing boats, because the land no longer held an interest for his eye. As always, Henri's celebration of the first sight of land was a mere fugitive thought in an acutely critical mind. Because his delight at reaching land was, as always, replaced by his disdain at the sight of it.

The scene was a poor one for Henri, but with a way to go before Newcastle was reached and blessed disembarkation, he thought it might be as well to pass the time on deck, and reacquaint himself with the deficient sights of the riverside. The sea gulls also had a poor regard for what they saw, and one, perched on the ship's mast, took at shot at Henri's suit. But the sorry bird missed by an arm's length. Henri looked at the guano, rich and fluid on the quarterdeck, and thought on the tragedy of his suit, and the horror of his tailor if the gull had hit. He thought to look at the assassin, but refrained from raising an eye to the monster in case more was to come. He thought ill of the gull, but more so of the noises behind—the chattering of idle sailors.

'The bird thinks to add his own jewel to the glittering crown.'

'Aye, Sam… He's a jewel alreet.'

'A shinier man, I've never seen afore.'

'Aye, Sam, I've niver seen the likes of him afore—*shiny*.'

Henri turned to the sounds of inanity. He saw two sailors; two in the Guild's employ, on a Guild ship; two that should know not to tongue-taunt their better, *a Guild Overseer*. Still they continued to mock; one sailor picking at a biscuit, the other picking his nose with equal indifference.

'D'ya think he'll lend me his clothes? I could wear them to ma sister's weddin'… But thinkin' on it, I fear the groom would mistake me for his bride.'

'Aye, Sam, if ye wore his suit, yer sister's man would likely bugger ye in error, thinkin' ye was his new wife.'

Henri kept a distant uninterested gaze, so as not to provoke the sailors' poorly composed humour into greater insult. Insults too hurtful to go unpunished.

Henri's weapon was his wit; his words better aimed than any pistol point, sharper than any sword. But if the target had no wit to understand finely crafted rebuff—*why waste it?* But Henri's previous assassin had turned ally. The gull swept down to take a seat on a hatch at the centre of the quarterdeck, at a fair distance, but close enough for Henri's suit to take offence at the beast's raucous taunt. Henri had his rebuff and revenge—*no words, but demonstration.*

Without shift in his gaze, Henri brought his right hand to his left sleeve, as if to pull a handkerchief from his cuff. He cocked his left hand, but instead of linen, a slim ivory handle presented itself. Henri gently held the ivory handle, as if indeed it were a delicate silk square, and closed his eyes.

Behind closed eyes, Henri thought on the gull struck. He visualized the act of killing. The knife deep in the gull's body, its head twitching for a moment, eyes open, feet in tremor. But then its eyes would close, and its feet would withdraw tight into its body—*death to the destroyer of good clothes.*

Henri's right arm was fluid and graceful as he released the stiletto from his sleeve. His hand directed the knife perfectly towards the gull. The gull reacted to Henri's sudden arc of movement, but Henri had allowed for the bird's travel... *or so he thought.* The knife missed, and the gull flew away in a wide arc, leaving the knife imbedded in the deck.

Henri looked to his miss and the knife well sunk into the timber. He angled his face away from the sailors, and rolled his eyes at his poor demonstration.

One of the sailors spoke, the mocking tone in his words checked a little by Henri's act of violence. 'It's lucky ye missed. Bad luck killing a seabird it is.'

'Aye, Sam... bad luck killin' a bird... gud job he missed.'

Henri placed confidence on his face where disappointment briefly dwelled, and slowly walked past the sailors. He cast a smile to catch the two men and announced, '*Mes amis*, I think I'll take the view from the forecastle... The air might be more agreeable.'

The sailor with the biscuit replied, 'What about yer knife man? Ye're no leavin' it? Are ye?'

Henri smiled, 'If I wanted the knife, would I have thrown it away?' Then, as Henri turned to walk on to the forecastle, and was no more than an arms length from the sailors, he reached out to pull the remainder of the biscuit from the sailor's hand. He tossed the hard biscuit high into the air, never to return to earth, but to be caught by a swooping sea gull—*the assassin*, Henri's inept accomplice.

❧❦❧

Newcastle and its quay arrived later than Henri desired. The Tyne River was pinched beyond the busy fishing port of *South Shields*, and Henri's ship was made to wait, whilst ships came on out of the depth of the Tyne, to join the others on the *German Ocean*. Henri's patience was tried, but he buried it from his staff, his assistants and his servants. Henri maintained his own dictum well; *having an economy of spirit is a poor gift to share with those who toil in one's name.*

Henri witnessed a town in growth, seeded by coal and corn, textiles and wool, and nourished by the trade that flowed from the Tyne and into it from overseas. Every time Henri brought his trade to the town, he saw the signs of greater maturation. He saw the extension of the quay, and the expansion of the great tall merchants' storehouses, running behind the town wall up to the bridge and beyond. He saw the many-arched bridge, a viaduct to carry people and property across the broad Tyne from *Gates-head* to *New-castle*. The bridge was a barrier against tall ships, and it underpinned the chaos of buildings reaching out from each bank—from each opposing town, like two armies in melee.

Not changed however, was the detritus floating in the river, and the poverty of the hovels built along the banks of the Tyne and even into it. And overall, the townscape viewed from the river was poor, with building on top of building, and naught but poor smells to sniff, toil to hear, and poor scenes for Henri to forget. But above it all, Henri searched. He examined the view through squinted eye; to give the unsightly scene good grace, and he spied the spire of the Church of St Nicholas, standing sentinel over the religious care of its inhabitants, merchants and pilgrims.

Disembarkation was met by men sent to assist the boat and others hoping to profit from its arrival. Foremost was Stephen Liddell, appointed to host the ship and the trade it brought. He was always first to greet the ships placed in his care. And his sight on the quayside was a pleasure to Henri's eye, because out of all the *Hostmen* in Newcastle, Stephen was one to owe the most to Henri.

'It is good to see you, Henri.'

'And it is good to see you, *mon ami*. Although there seems to be far more of you to see these days.'

The man held his hands over his fat stomach, courtesy of plenteous eating, rather than the generous cut and padding of his doublet.

'I've a new French wife, Henri. She adds to my girth.'

'I see she is a generous cook. But I suspect she starves your purse to feed your belly.'

'Far from it, Henri. She has a substantial inheritance, courtesy of three older siblings taken by sickness.'

'Ah… God moves in mysterious ways. Someone always benefits from His plagues and trials.'

'But I must report she is not so much a skilled cook. But she brought her cook from her family home in *Anjou*. He cooked for the King of France once.'

'Then you are truly blessed, Stephen, to have such a royal cook to roast your meat, a rich wife to fatten your purse, and a French woman to warm your bed.'

'Thank you for your blessings, Henri, but I'm sorrowed to report not all is well. She is a cold bitch in my bed. One who does as she pleases, without thought of my position, or the duty of her wifely responsibility. But I am in hope she will settle down, once the French air leaves her head.'

Henri thought on the poor man's delusion with regards to French women and their Gallic virtue, and Stephen's ignorance with regards husbands who do not take their French wives' fancy. In intimate matters of the bedchamber, their abstinence is usually because another already has their interest.

With regards to this factum, one should tell oneself the truth; only a fool would lie.

Poor man, thought Henri, and he enquired, 'Is your cook an able man—young?'

'Why do you ask, Henri?'

Henri dwelled a moment on the lascivious direction of his questioning, then thought ignorance a better strategy. *Mon ami*, let me gift you with my wisdom. A man should only tolerate disobedience from a servant once, his children twice, and his dog three times. In terms of your spouse, either live with it, or do without her. For if disobedience is already displayed, obedience will never follow.'

Stephen laughed. Then he composed himself with a smile remaining on his lips. 'When my assistant informed me a prince had arrived at the dock. I thought it might be you.'

'A prince? You insult me. No prince has either the purse or presence to dress like I. A king maybe… but there again maybe not.'

Stephen laughed again, but this time he arrested his smile quickly, in alarm, in case Henri's quip was not jest, but just offence at an insult taken in earnest. Stephen thought ignorance to Henri's possible wounded esteem, a better policy than apology. So he remained quiet, and not contrite. He did not know Henri Hueçon well.

'Have your servants seen your belongings off the ship?' As Stephen asked his question, and waited on a reply, two handsome men approached from the direction of Henri's ship, exquisitely dressed, poised and perfect in their stance. Their young heads held high in noble haught. Stephen interrupted his discourse with Henri to address the two men, keen to ingratiate himself with any men of substance not known to him.

'My sirs, may I introduce myself… I am Stephen, host of this ship, merchant and eminent town burgher. A man of business, a man to do business, an 'ostman in the know—and a man to know. Whether pleasure or commerce is your fancy… I'll fancy I can see you in profit.' Stephen caught Henri's eye, and immediately felt the shame of his self-declaration of importance. It sounded hollow against the presence of Henri Hueçon, and he thought it better to introduce Henri, the true enterpriser.

But Henri interrupted, 'Stephen, these boys are my servants. They have the blood of *Domenico da Ferrara* in their feet; dancing is their art. They are both called *Luca*, so I have renamed them *Romulus* and *Remus*, to avoid confusion.'

'Such grand names. Founders of Rome. Are they noble Italians? Sons of nobles—sons of a god even?'

'*Non*, I am merely the wolf, and these are just two babes who suckle at my teat.'

Stephen smiled at Henri's boast, and lost for a worthy reply he returned to business. 'What brings you to Newcastle, and what do you bring… wine, spices, silks… goods from the East?'

'On this trip, only myself, on an errand. But I am sure my ship will be well laden for my return to Antwerp, with goods procured with your help, *Master Hostman*.'

'You can be sure of that, Henri. Is there anything I can do for you now? There are players from London in the town. But good seats will be hard to acquire. But if you wish, I will acquire them.'

'*Merci*, but no… Instead, I would like a message sent to a man in the Scottish West Marches. His name is John Brownfield. Could you arrange this?'

'Of course, I will see to it as soon as I return to the offices of the Fellowship—*The Fellowship of Merchant Adventurers*.'

'Ah… the Fellowship. How goes the town's elite?'

'We have a new governor, Sir Henry—Henry Anderson.'

'And does he profit the Fellowship?'

'He continues to build grandly on religious sites stolen by the Reformation. And he preoccupies himself with ongoing issues surrounding our southern gate, Gates-head, and failed legislation to annexe it. He believes prosperity for Newcastle would be better supported by the direct control of that which lies over the bridge—*coal*.'

'An old tale,' replied Henri, 'Do you assist him?'

'In a manner, as I have ambition to be an assignee in the Fellowship, and Governor myself in the future.'

'Then I will do my best to help you in your ambition.'

'And how would you help me, Henri?'

'A better Governor would look to secure control over new trading routes, and new goods to trade... My clients' thirst for wines has expanded to more exotic flavours; treasure from the East; black gold from Africa—slaves for the New World, black skins to add interest to their own households—variety to enhance their own peculiar carnal pleasures.'

'You always look to your clients' benefit, Henri. You work hard for their profit and their pleasure.'

'Yes, I am a *simple* man, *selfless*. My reward is the smiles on my clients' faces.' Henri winked, and smiled wickedly. 'Their smiles, after all, mean they are unaware of the grossness of my profit.' Stephen laughed loudly and Henri was forced to check his surroundings for those who may have overheard, either by design or default, before he continued. 'Returning to your thoughts of Governor. I will say this... Placing profit in your peers' purses is a far greater inducement to secure one's own promotion, than simply seeking to remove an irksome itch, or building a comfortable seat on godly land within the town walls.'

Stephen smiled. Henri Hueçon's sponsorship of his own ambitious intent was better than any heap of gold. More so, he felt comforted in the fact that Sir Henry Anderson's devotion to his dispute with Gateshead and coal, and his indifference to the influence of the rich merchant companies that Henri fronted, would ally his goal. 'I will offer a prayer to your good health and success, Henri.'

Henri simply bowed his head in recognition of Stephen's gratitude.

Stephen was a good *hostman*. He saw well to the needs of all the merchantmen that he received and entertained. He saw to it that all, and any, merchant strangers made good their purchases and their sales whilst they visited the town, and made sure, as he could, their easy passage beyond his own town walls. His adherence to his own guild, *The Fraternity of Hostmen,* was all to him, and because of it he was assigned as host to many of the ships of greater value—those with richer cargos. His devotion to hosting was always well received by visiting merchants, and the rich gifts they left in lieu of trade well made, made his home in turn, well furnished and thus better appointed to receive esteemed strangers and estimable friends—even guests such as Henri Hueçon with extensive entourage.

'Now while you stay in Newcastle, you will be my guest and sample my hospitality. How long will you stay?'

'My trip was not planned, but while I am in England, I will tend affairs. Four or five weeks shall see business satisfied.'

'Good… It will offer you ample occasion to taste my food.'

Before Henri replied, he took a long look at the hostman's belly. Long enough for the hostman to observe Henri's stare. The hostman smiled, waiting on Henri's quip.

Henri did not disappoint, and he replied, with a smile

delivering his words, 'I will taste all, but eat less. Otherwise my poor overworked tailor will surely disown me.'

Chapter II

'Per aspera ad astra.'

Henri Hueçon nodded his head in recognition of the words and of the man sitting at the table. His eyes saluted the handsome face before him. He even found a guilty pleasure in it. But he quickly pushed it aside, because for all of Henri's sins, envy was not amongst them. Although it would still visit him fleetingly from time to very occasional time, when he found favour in a face that wore its years far kinder than his own. Instead, Henri looked around at the inn scene, and judged the noise in the room busy enough to hide any discernible words, before he replied, 'I hardly think the password is required between us, Edward, but if it pleases you... *Semper paratus, semper fidelis.'*

'I think the password is always required. It is a more fitting greeting between spies.' Edward threw an arm to indicate the empty stool at his table. 'Please sit down... Share my wine... or share my ale... your choice.'

Henri looked at the two pewter jugs, one with ale, and one with wine. He lifted the one with the darker liquid to his nose, only to withdraw it immediately, recoiling sharply, face contorted.

'*Merde!*' Henri quickly returned the jug to the table. 'Edward, I would bring out my glass for wine, but this is vinegar.'

Edward dropped his eyes disapprovingly. 'Do not worry, Henri, it is not poisoned.'

'Poison, my dear Edward, would improve this wine.'

'Share it with me, Henri… Believe me, it is palatable.' Edward raised his hand, and almost immediately a serving girl was at his side. 'Annie, a cup for my guest.'

Henri shook his hand at the girl. 'Forget the cup my dear, but take away the ale jug. Its poor origin and odour can only mean poor flavour.'

The serving girl bobbed a curtsey to Henri—for by his dress and manner, she could only think she was serving nobility. But even so, her admiring eyes remained on Edward, holding his lustful gaze on her.

Henri Hueçon reached into a leather bag attached to his elaborately studded sword belt, and drew out a small purple velvet covered tube, tied at both ends with red cords. He carefully untied one end, and slid out a small, etched glass. It contained a small piece of black linen cloth, which he removed to wipe the glass carefully. Only then did he sit down to pour a small fill of wine— barely a drop.

Henri's show always fascinated Edward, but the spell he cast only held Edward for a moment; for it gave way to Edward's anxiety—he was not happy to receive Henri, or any agent of the *Black Merchants' Guild.*

'How did you find me? We have no appointment,' enquired Edward.

'It is the business of my host, Stephen Liddle, to know all who visit this town. Especially those who have a fatter purse than the common traveller or pilgrim, or those without good reason to be here.'

Henri reached for his pomander, worn on its gold chain around his neck. He held it under his nose, delicately drawing the gold filigrane bottle under his nostrils, to both hide a contemplation on his lips, and mask the odour of the inn stink around him. He thought on Edward's appellation, 'spy', and uneasy at the tenor of Edward's remark, set out to counter it. '*Mais non*... I am no spy, and you, Edward, have not held true to your covert watch for many a year.'

'I have been placed poorly,' replied Edward. 'I have no intelligences to report to the Black Merchants' Guild, and now no reason to hold my counterfeit commission. I was misplaced, and my years have been misplaced too.'

Henri's words held sarcasm, fuelled by his disbelief. 'So you do not have *any* intelligences to bind our English Deputy Warden of the Marches, Thomas Wharton, into scandal. No bastards to cause him shame. No suspicions to cause him discomfort. *Nothing* the Guild can use to hold his attention on our whims and desires.'

'No.'

'I find that difficult to believe.'

'He is, by his own actions, no longer a force in the Borders. His once lofty position is in decline with his age... But still, it matters not to me what you believe.'

'Then it is true, Edward, you *are* a poor *spy*... Time to let you go perhaps?'

Edward said nothing. Henri's words would have been welcome, if they did not hold a whisper of finality.

'Edward, you have been two persons. One useful to the Guild, and one only tolerated because of the other. Now you wish to be one again. Consider carefully which one you wish to be.'

'My place at this table is not by choice, but because I have no other table to sit at. My time in the Western March is over. I have no position, or ear on those of interest to the Guild. My only question is— —do I have a new commission, Henri?'

Henri said nothing, and the long pause that followed said more to
Edward than a hundred words delivered in deceit by his Guild
overseer.

Henri, after his period of contemplation, simply said, 'And how is
Jacques?'

Edward's unease was little quelled by Henri's question—his own
question unanswered and his good friend, John 'Jack' Brownfield
brought into Henri's response. *Foul threat, or friendly enquiry*, Edward did
not know. Still he responded, 'All I know, is that he is recently home
from France, but I am afraid he will not be enjoying a happy
homecoming in the Marches. Why do you ask?'

Henri paused again, and Edward's concern grew to fearful idea.
Edward threw back his own wine, and looked on Henri's glass
untouched. Henri was smiling. His smile seemed warm and friendly—
a smile from an affable man. But Henri Hueçon was good at his
show. He was a fine painting, created in colour and form. But like all
great art, he was a figment of an imagination, not real at all. And
despite the smiles and the happy sounds of the inn, Edward thought
harm seemed close by. Fear harried him. So Edward thought to end
the conversation with Henri, to avoid further discourse about those he
loved with a man of dubious intent. He scoured his mind for excuse
to leave the inn. Reason to withdraw from Henri's attention. And
fortune smiled. Opportunity entered the inn—in the menacing forms
of two armed men, searching the room with their eyes.

Edward shot a glance to Henri, and placed a hand on his arm to
hold his attention. 'Henri—men with foul intent. Ones better not to
meet. You'd better melt away.'

Henri did not turn to view the men, he simply tipped out his glass
and nodded to Edward, and slipped away.

⊱⊰

It took Edward six weeks to plan a quiet passage to Spain. Two busy weeks to make fictitious travel arrangements known to all, and two more to arrange hidden travel to his monastery, where he hoped to find sanctuary from poor memories and a pernicious Guild. Six weeks wait in all, delay, because of bad winter storms at sea. Six weeks worth the wait, because he had opportunity to meet up with Jack Brownfield, a friend more than a friend, a man more than a man, neither Englishman nor Scotsman, but born a Border Horseman.

Edward had found few blessings in his recent obligations to the Black Merchants' Guild. But he was blessed to have lived and laughed, and grown and grieved with some estimable souls—none more than Borderers. Those peoples who dwell in the Marches between England and Scotland. Those who define a people made strong by the suffering inflicted on a land caught between two opposing sovereigns. Borderers, whose only certainty was family, and the comfort they could preserve for their own kin by strong defence, or baleful act. Borderers—where honour is the name you carried, and your name was the flag you followed—an allegiance far greater than to any king, or any faith.

Jack Brownfield was such a Borderer. Born in the Scottish West March, his young life tied by way of pledge—a hostage kept within its English counterpart. Jack had been Edward's pupil, while Edward was tutor to an English gentleman, and thus Edward had known him as a boy, and seen him grow into a man. They had shared life for a while—a time longer than mere acquaintance, but time less than kin, from birth to grave. There again, they were closer than kin once upon a time. But the trials of life and lengthy separation can often erode bonds born out of friendship, and reunion itself can be a trial. And Edward wondered whether the verdict of reunion would be indifference to a bond broken by time and circumstance, or tied tighter because of it.

Edward received Jack Brownfield at his lodgings within the *Herded Goose*, and those men that stood at Jack Brownfield's back, with their own pledges of loyalty and swords to protect their captain, stayed from the two men so a private reunion could be held within Edward's first floor room. All Jack's men knew of Edward. They too had cause to call him friend of sorts––more so because of his association with Jack, rather than any amity by their own design. They knew enough to stand well back, to allow the two men to clear the air dulled by deception and events now well past. To stand guard, in order to hide any act of retribution that may be lodged against the perfidy of a friendship damaged.

It was Robert, Jack Brownfield's deputy, who remained on careful watch on the inn. Limiting his drinking, so as to keep a clear head and a vigilant eye on the stairs to the lodging rooms. His ears strained against the chatter in the inn, in order to pick up any alarm from the meeting between the two men.

But Robert's concentration was broken by words from across his table, and he returned a frown to meet them.

'Drink Rab, or get yerself a lass… if ye can find one. There's nowt ye can do sittin' and fretin' the night away.'

'Nah, Tom. Go and find a skirt yerself, or a jug more of beer, or two, to give ye solid sleep… Make it three even, and award yerself a poor heid t'morrow and excuse from yer duties.'

'Aye, I'll do that, but I'll still drink better wi' good company… Join me, Rab.'

Robert thought on Tom's proposal, championed by Tom's smile and ever-affable Cumbrian manner. But then Robert turned his head back to the stairs.

Tom, sensing he had lost Robert again to his concerns, offered more words to ease a troubled Scottish mind. 'They're either embracin' or bleedin'… In either case, Jack doesn't need you to hold his hand.'

Robert kept his eyes on the stairs, but his voice replied back to Tom, 'Jack's nae himself… His temper is poor these days, and more cuttin' is nae a right route tae right reason.'

Tom swayed a little on his stool, well on his way to inebriation. 'Give Jack his poor temper. A little melancholia is a man's reward for his sins. Jack's done what Jack's done… and that was *Three Hills* ago.'

Two hours passed, and eventually Jack and Edward appeared at the bottom of the stairs. Robert let out a deep breath, and sank a long anticipated mug of beer. Jack and Edward were embracing. Affection shared by two friends, well loosened by good humour… and copious spirit.

'We are alike you and I… As if we are the same person… twins born of the same spirit, rather than the same womb.' Edward was slurred in his delivery, only upright because Jack held him so.

'As your student…' maundered Jack, '…I have been moulded in your ways of thought and action. We are the same, because you have taught me… *my tutor*.' Jack finished with a feigned curtsey.

'No, no, John. A tutor cannot mould the spirit of a man—only direct him.' Edward's emphasis of his words with wild finger, flaying the air, unsteadied him and Jack had to hold him tight, to prevent him falling. Edward continued, reacting to Jack's embrace with harder hold and a lusty kiss to his lips. 'No… We are too alike you and I in our thinking… Seduced by the Guild. Robbed of our true identity. Beclouded to our true fidelity. Lost because we refuse to accept who we are… and unhappy because of our actions of hurt. Yes we are kindred spirits, twins of soul—not of earthly woman.'

Jack smiled at Edward's drunkenness, but dismissed his

words as foolish jabber. 'Edward, it pleases me that you have decided to return to your monk's habit. May you find better peace out of your scholar's robes and in your godly attire. But I know you, and you will always have a book in your hand. Books little to do with your godly devotion. Books of new idea… Because I think books are your true dedication.'

Edward shook his head wildly, which made him totter and fall against the wall. 'If books are my ruin, duty is yours, John. For you hide behind it like a frightened deer hides behind a tree.'

Robert thought to move forward, to aid the two before they collided with other drinkers, and into fight with strangers. But Tom held him back.

'Let them have their kinship, Rab—*undisturbed*.'

Jack tightly held Edward's head, to keep it and his rolling eyes steady and focused on him. 'Whatever we do,' offered Jack, 'I think our destinies are linked. Let us hope deceit and the Black Merchants' Guild are not the only chains that bind them.'

'Yes, John Brownfield… I think I shall see you again, someday. In better circumstances for us both… I hope. So for now I say goodbye, but one last favour can I ask?'

'What is it my friend?' replied Jack.

'May I ask one of your men to see me to my bed. For I think I'm needing a soberer man to find it.'

⊰⊱

Two days passed, and the quayside at Newcastle was full of activity, with a stink that Henri Hueçon's pomander could not mask—its fragrant herbs and spices blown on the breeze, to be replaced by the thick acrid smell of tar, wet hemp, fish and the odour of hard work. A lesser man would have wretched up his guts at the smell of it, but not Henri, he was not man to appear less than perfect before others, unless of course he wished to feign a plausible excuse for a rapid exit from vacuous, but distinguished company.

Four tall ships stood against the quay and spilled out their goods, while a further two, taller and broader, sucked them in—all served by many men loading and unloading, dirty and work worn. Henri felt wretched to be amongst such sorry beasts of burden, working the foul landscape, and he raised his face from it, to seek a new vision, one less busy, one less dirty. But the sky was no help. It was as grey as the quay landscape—as grey as the imagined sea that lay beyond the grey river.

Henri had sent his message to Jack, via the good hostman, asking him to secure passage to Antwerp for him and his men, with promise of commissions in the Guild Master's guard. Jack to replace the sergeant-at-arms, his men to replace the few men lost at Galicia. Henri of course omitted to report on the terms of the sergeant's retirement, simply writing, *'The former guard captain's health failed through illness to the chest and maladies of the head, and the guard found further deficit when the sergeant fell from the ship carrying his master.'* Henri had no doubt that Jack would accept; him without a home to set his fire, or family to see him employed.

In the distance, a familiar figure stood clear amongst the maze of grimy men, stacks of goods, rope and barrel; a man distinctive from the workers around him; a man better attired, and a soldier by his stance. Henri squinted eye to see a little better—to fog the scene around him and focus on his target. He was pleased to see Jack smiling, a good sign of a goodly welcome. And, as he picked his way through the crowded scene, he tried to maintain a fair distance from those around him that might soil his suit. Henri thought on his poor new shoes; the soles scuffed and blackened by tar and grease; the soft white leather soiled by the puddles of dirty water that stood around his passage. So he took his time to reach Jack, to lessen the damage to his attire.

Jack was a man formed in his Scottish father's image, but tutored by a different life, so he stood better, wore his face kinder, and clothed his lean body better. Dirty blond hair topped a face wrapped in auburn beard. A thin nose marked his family origins, and his blue eyes pierced the scene before him, seeing far beyond mere picture, into a deeper sense of the view presented.

Henri Hueçon had also been Jack's tutor in youth, and Jack had good reason to thank Henri, for he had gifted his knowledge of the world outside Jack's own; outside those subjects taught by dry scholars and pious priests.

'No gentleman should be allowed in such a place. *Mon dieu*, my stools are cleaner and smell far sweeter than this foul stench.'

'It is good to see you, Henri.'

'And it would be good to see you, *Jacques*, if my eyes could see. My poor peepers are watering with the pain of stink in this... *Mais non*, I cannot describe it!'

'After all these years, Henri, is it not fitting for you to drop your French veneer? I have known you to be a Dutchman since I learned the nature of your true tongue, and recognised the words you used at Wharton's dining table when I was boy. When you were not my paymaster.'

Henri Hueçon smiled. '*Mais non, Jacques*. Like my clothes, my word is my show. I'm beautiful in both sight and in sound.' Henri then moved to stand alongside Jack to share his view, and to hide their conversation a little better from their surroundings. 'Have you passage to Antwerp? It is *très important*... your new commission awaits, and your new master is not a man to be kept waiting.'

'My men are arranging it as we speak.'

'*Bon!*'

'Will you be joining us?' asked Jack.

'*Non*, I have duties elsewhere. Responsibilities to the Guild, which regrettably press me to leave you.' Henri shook his head mournfully. 'My heart grieves at so short a reunion.' But Henri quickly relocated his smile, as he looked around at the dirt and bustle of the quayside. 'Although I know one who will not be sorry to see me leave you here.'

Jack looked puzzled. 'Who be that, Henri?'

'My suit of course.'

Henri turned to walk away, but as he did, he cast a disapproving eye down at Jack's baggage; two meagre leather bags with weapons attached, wrapped and tied in woollen cloth. 'Is this all you carry, *Jacques*? Have you learned nothing about gentlemen's baggage?'

Jack replied the gentle scold, 'I'm afraid I cannot afford the excess of a trunk to carry my clothes.'

'Excess sir, is travelling with three chests for one's clothes. I of course have four.'

Jack smiled, as ever, in response to Henri's wit, and raised his hand in salute to Henri as he walked away. But within six paces, Henri turned again for another last word.

'*Jacques*... what does your tutor plan?'

Jack replied, 'He says he will be a monk—join his order in Spain.'

Henri nodded, and returned Jack's salute with words too low for Jack to hear. 'He will be sorely disappointed then.'

⧉

Standing alone, tied to the quay, was an eighty-ton ship. It was named *Devotion*, although it had many past English, French and

Scottish names placed upon it. From a shipwrights' birthing in Southampton Sound thirty years ago, through a hard life of storm and harsh sea, capture and rebirth, sale, resale, new crew and new purpose—to its current berthing place, via a million miles of sea, through two hundred thousand hours of sail, and a thousand hours of war.

The Devotion's crew had loaded all that was needed—all that was required to make the crossing profitable in terms of goods and men requiring passage. Other loaders and luggers had left; their labour finished and other ships to service—much of the day left to toil. But for some of the Devotion's crew, time was left for rest before tide was right, and the still of the land was lost to the sway of the sea.

As Jack approached the ship, he could hear through the crowds of men, the sounds of a sea shanty…

…In Amsterdam there dwells a maid,
mark well what I do say;
in Amsterdam there dwells a maid,
and she is mistress of her trade.
I'll go no more a-roving with you, fair maid.

Closer still, he could see some sailors gathered around on the quay, around the gangway to the ship, singing the chorus…

A-roving, a-roving, since roving's been my ru-I-n,
I'll go no more a-roving with you, fair maid!

One man was playing a hearty jig on a viol, another sailor singing the verse, another dancing to the pleasure of his shipmates…

I took the maiden for a walk.
And sweet and loving was her talk.
I put my arm around her waist.
Says she, 'Young man, you're in some haste.'

Then all sang heartily, and tapped their feet, because no hands were free to clap a beat, whilst there was beer to quaff...

A-roving, a-roving, since roving's been my ru-I-n,
I'll go no more a-roving with you, fair maid!

Jack hesitated awhile, seeing his men enjoying the song. He picked his way through the crowd so as not to disturb their pleasure...

I took that girl upon my knee.
Says she, 'Young man, you're rather free.'
I put my hand upon her thigh.
Says she, 'Young man you're rather high!'

Then at the ship, Jack stopped short of four men and two boys squatting, tapping hands on knee to the beat of the music. The six were not sailors. They dressed for the land, in heavy jerkin, steel cuirass and helmet, riding boots, cloak and cap—all Border style, wear and worn, donned and dented as befitting clothes on men well tested in their fighting craft. All the six looked on to Jack, as the music rang on...

A-roving, a-roving, since roving's been my ru-I-n,
I'll go no more a-roving with you, fair maid!

Seeing Jack before them, distracted the men from the shanty, whilst opposite, the ship's crew continued to bob head, and tap toe to the music…

She swore that she'd be true to me.
But spent my money both fast and free.
In three weeks' time I was badly bent.
Then off to sea I sadly went.

'Good tune these sea-lads spout… makes you want to dance, eh Jack.' announced Tom, still half tapping a beat.

Jack smiled, then taken by the music, skipped on his spot, a jig of sorts—a poor mimic of the sailor's steps, announcing, 'Does the dance suit me lads… do I not make a canny sailor man?'

A-roving, a-roving, since roving's been my ru-I-n,
I'll go no more a-roving with you, fair maid!

The four men reacted; Robert was stoic, Tom smiled, Francis scowled and Finn laughed. Thus the men assigned their particular natures to the arrangement of their mouths; their demeanours each apparent in the inflection of the sounds they made, or silences held.

The four were Jack's men, more friends than subordinates, older than he, but not wiser, because wise men would not so easily serve with a man without clan, or guaranteed commission to pay. Four Border Horsemen; two Cumbrians, a Scot and an Irish Kern; horsemen devoid of mounts. But all with armour and a warrior's skill, taught from life in the Marches, where husbandry and craft had been displaced by the need to bear arms to defend the land from their sovereigns' vanity. To their rear were two apprentice boys, adopted to act as squires to give the men ease from their leaden burdens, and a feigned importance beyond their status.

Francis was the first to reply, vinegar words, 'You be no dancer and no sailor, and you have said little about our future in Antwerp. Instead you carry-on like a jester… a fool, daft or drunk… what is it… you finally lost your mind?'

Finn shook his head at Francis, and countered in an easy Irish drawl, 'Leave the lad alone, he's a merrier man than he's been… let him have his mirth and pleasure.'

But Robert interjected, 'No, Francis is right… Ye need tae know what ye sail to… Fortune, or fortune 'n' ruin.'

Jack smiled at Robert, and turned to answer all. 'It is all confirmed… We've a soft commission in fine livery as personnel guard to a merchant in Antwerp. We have…'

Tom interrupted Jack's announcement. He needed little detail. 'Pay, bed, food… Is all well?'

'All's well, Tom,' replied Jack.

Tom rose from his squat, walked over to his captain, raised a hand to Jack's hair, giving it a tousle. Smiling broadly, as his fingers danced in the weather worn locks of blond hair, he said, 'Then all is alreet, lad.'

Robert then rose and walked over to join Tom, putting an accepting hand on Jack's shoulder and a confirming hand on Tom's.

'Aye, Tom… all is fine. Now let's all get aboard. If Jack, oor captain, has negotiated new contracts that's good enough, especially a new post wi' canny clothes tae wear.'

Francis and Finn both stood up and beckoned the two boys to collect their gear and join the men. The boys were tardy, and Finn's boot caught one of the boys called Jamie, hard on the buttocks, causing him to whelp like a kicked dog.

Finn fired Irish instruction at the boy, without humour or respect. 'Jamie, anticipate when it's time to move lad, and move yerself quicker than the men… ye'll live longer if ye use yer speed… a child has little else to call on in a fight… use yer haste.'

Jamie recovered quickly from the kick and picked up his half of the bundles, still carrying an affront at being called child, him being fourteen. Tip, the other boy, was already heading for the ship at the run, to avoid similar cruelty to his own seat.

Jamie wanted to rub his sore cheeks, to draw out the sting from Finn's boot, but he dared not bend down to drop his bundles, especially with Finn bringing up his rear—still an easy kick away. Despite the threat, Jamie still complained—the only weapon he possessed to counter Finn's harshness.

'Uncle, why d'ya pick on me… Tip never gets a scold.'

'Yer boy Tip, is no my kin to be chided, and I'm no bothered if he's a slack lad. Yer daddy sent ye to me to become a fightin' man, and I will make it so, even if I wear out ma boots on yer arse in its makin'.'

Robert and Jack waited at the gangway to see Finn and the boys aboard. As Finn climbed the gangway, Jack patted him hard on the back; hard enough to mimic, in some measure, the force Finn had applied to the boy's backside.

'Finn, your tutelage of your nephew may be better applied with more praise and less pain.'

Finn smiled back at Jack. 'Never… A Kern uses his pain to draw his anger… Anger boils the blood, and the blood fuels the body to bloody his enemy. It's a Kern's way—run not walk, fight fierce not fair. Boys are like dogs. They may respond better to kindness, but a good kickin' learns them quicker. After all, there's no kindness in what we do—it's better Jamie learns that. Kick yer man hard and kill him harder.'

Jack shook his head, a demonstration of his displeasure, and he turned to follow Finn, but Robert held Jack's arm in check.

'Jack, is this commission given by a Frenchy of your acquaintance perhaps?'

'*Given* is the word, Robert… and you don't look a given horse in the mouth… or for that matter ask its name.'

Robert held onto Jack, and drew spittle into his mouth, and fired it on the floor of the quay—his eyes following its path to the pavement, and kicking up immediately to stare out Jack.

Jack waited for Robert to push him, to reveal the commission's source, but instead Robert smiled.

'Ach… any commission that pays, is a good commission… soft or otherwise.'

There are days—and there are days. Days to wish away for want of a smile, or for laughter found in the moments that make up a day. There are days that bring soft and restful sleep, and there are days that twist the soul into unstoppable hurt. Hurt not to be felt in terms of cut or wound, but in the mind; where darkness does not yield to dawn each day; where sleep alludes and waking pain is thus prolonged.

Melancholia sticks to me like mud on winter's war ground, and I wonder when spring will come. When sun will dry the land, and blue sky allows the sun to warm my face and drive out the chill.

Men are oft born with weakness in the mind. Women less so, or perhaps they wear their melancholia well. I have never asked the question of mortal being lest they judge me harshly. For melancholia is seen as a weakness of the spirit and often declared from the pulpit as self pity. Instead I feign a steady mind, with false smile and hearty gesture. It is fallacious, all an actor's show. My kith see through me I suspect and hold their tongues for fear of my shame.

John Brownfield, MDLX (1560)

Chapter III

The German Ocean (the North Sea), January 1560

Jamie could not help but notice the ship's cat. A great silver-grey cat of such swaying belly, as it ran the decks, that it must have had its fill of rat ten times over each day. He thought it a poor ship to have so many rats... there again... *with such a cat, would there be any rats left? And if there were no rats left, how was the cat so fat?* The conundrum screwed his eyes and hurt his brain. So he turned his foolish notion to the ship and its hard-pressed crew. He watched the sailors busy about their tasks, barefoot on the slippery deck. Dressed in tarred doublet and breeches tucked into footless socks. He looked to his own boots, and was glad to have his feet warm against the cold. He compared the sailors to his own comrades scattered around the decks. All in finer attire—better clothes for a worthy occupation—soldiery.

A poor life it was to be a sailor, he thought, *who would want to spend day and night in a jouncing coffin, with naught but empty horizons and gut churning seas to turn a sober man's gait into a drunken man's totter? Splinters in soles... Frostbite in toes...* His thinking drew a smile on his face—his own wisdom pleased him, and his own situation pleased him more. *Rather he be a soldier like his uncle, like his fellow fighters aside him; all with sword on shield, steel with staff, dag and dagger.* Jamie's mind's eye looked into the future to see the muster roll; *Finn McCuul, Robert Hardie, Thomas Kemp, Francis Bell, and Jamie McCuul. Not just fighters—Border Horsemen...* And Jamie's smile grew wider.

'What yer thinkin', *La'al Irish?*

Tip was to his side. Jamie did not care for his company, or his poor epithet. It nettled him that Tip had issued him a sobriquet in lieu of his lesser height. Tip, in Jamie's view, being a mere whisper taller, courtesy of a year extra maturation. He was more nettled that it had stuck with the men, and thus naming him foolish in their company, rather than brave or fearsome. Jamie therefore was not in a mind to share his true thoughts with Tip. Instead he drew sputum from his throat, filled his mouth with spittle, and fired it onto the deck in his own show of manliness. Giving all around a demonstration of his maturity. He smiled. He was pleased with his product, and the placing of his discharge.

The boatswain however was none too pleased with Jamie's display, and he stopped in his tracks to remonstrate with the boy.

'Hey there, *child...* belay that spittle, or I'll have you scrubbing the decks... Mind my ship... Place your snot over the side.'

Tip shook his head in righteous condemnation at Jamie's misdeed; even appearing embarrassed to be sitting next to him. Jamie's greater humiliation showed red. And seeing the shame on the face of his brother-in-arms, Tip's face showed his true colour—disdain's satisfying shade.

Jamie hoped no one from his company had seen the reprimand. He looked to his betters—to Tom and his uncle, leaning on the ship's rail. And to his dismay, Tom and Finn's wry smiles, the remainder of laughter on their faces, said they had. Jamie sought out his captain and his second, Robert, to see if his humiliation was complete. He found his captain looking out to sea, standing firm against wind's blow. He was without jacket, or cloak, and he wore his face serious. His captain's bearing and his likeness, reminded him of his priest back home in Carlow. And it took his mind from his chagrin to sad remembrance; back to nine days of mourning prayer, devoted to the departed. A *Catholic novena of mourning* for the many taken from his village by fever, including a departed mother, a departed brother, and a sister left in endless sleep by malady. Nine days of solemnity devoted, and ninety days of sorrow felt.

A dozen steps beyond his captain, Robert stood by. Not looking to the sea, but to his captain also. Jamie studied both men. He wondered his captain's mind. He wondered Robert's action, as he stepped forward to wrap a cloak around his leader.

The sea was busy pitching the ship and Jamie found his stand difficult to maintain. All comfort had deserted him, so he thought to find a seat somewhere in the hold, to find shelter from winter wind, to hide his shame and sadness, and endure the ship's inner stink alone, as his toll.

But as Jamie lurched towards the hatch, a call rang out from above.

'*Ship ahoy!*'

'*Ship ahoy. Ship ahoy, on the port beam!*'

Within moments the ship's captain and crew were about the deck, and within the next instant, Captain James Small had his hands to his eyes, to focus his attention on the dark shadow on the horizon.

The words of his boatswain were fevered in anticipation of a possible target. 'French built merchantman, and a big'un, Captain.'

Captain Small presented himself atop an iron port-piece; a gun in Devotion's suite of enhanced ordnance, to better see the distant shadow.

'Aye, Poppy, a big'un she is. But what is she, merchantman or warship? Low in the water she sits. Down low. Full of prize perhaps, or laden with too much cannon. Let us hope it's gold, and not iron and powder, eh?'

'She's a galley, Captain. I swear it… Oars, I wager, where we have guns.'

Captain Small strained his eyes, to better see the distant vessel. He shifted on his feet to walk the port-piece hall, four feet of barrel, to lean hard out against the ship's rail. His words to Poppy, breathless, as the rail winded him. 'Your eyes have better range, Poppy… Is she French, Spanish, Dutch, or one of our own?'

Poppy pushed his eyes to the distant shadow, to refocus his stare. He held his gaze, until colours could be discerned in the grey.

'French!'

Captain Small's face showed unease. The nationality of the target displeased him. England was not at war with France, only discomfort. But ten years of an uneasy peace, created little charity in a bitter memory; a mind scarred with past slaughter of brothers by a French army. Time did not remove those memories of losses so easily.

Then Small's face changed with new thoughts of profit and he smiled, and offered, 'But the question, Master Boatswain, is…'

The boatswain turned to his captain, waiting for him to finish. But the captain simply winked.

The boatswain knew his captain. He knew how to finish his sentence, and he returned his captain's wink, and replied, 'Aye sir… The question is… Is yon ship a pirate; a ship with foul intent on honest ships, making an honest living?'

Captain Small winked again, and smiled at his boatswain. 'So you think she a pirate ship, eh Poppy?'

The boatswain found it difficult to hold an earnest face as he replied, 'Aye she is. I've heard tale of a terrible French pirate operating this sea. It would be God's pleasure that we see it stopped from its thievin' and murderin' ways.'

Commands given. Commands delivered. Men ordered and men responded with haste and purpose, and within minutes, ship and crew were sailing towards the French shadow in the haze.

'You had better ready your men, Captain Brownfield.' The companionable English sea captain slapped Jack's back hard, adding, 'They will be none too fond of our amorous advances, eh Brownfield? They may even decide to slap us, as we raise her skirts and take our pleasure.'

James Small was an opportunist. A merchant sailor authorised by his masters to commit acts of convenient theft. To plunder ship, and harm those who would prevent such a commission. He was a man of ambition—an ambition that lived beyond the sea and into a dream of ease on the land, with a smart house and smarter wife, land and status. His lowly patrimony hindered his goal, but prize money, reward and the stolen treasure he could acquire (and hide from his employers) would buy his dreams. His spoils had made his masters rich, and his prey, mainly the French and Spanish, poorer—especially if their ships were unfortunate to find themselves alone at sea. He cared nothing of inter-nation treaties and alliances, because there would be always be a nation, or faction, happy to reward him for the prize of a ship.

His men loved him. He made them rich enough to drink and whore mightily in the port towns, whilst providing financial comfort for their bigamous collection of wives and families. And although he contributed well to his masters' wealth, it was not to the detriment of his own growing fortune.

Skilful piloting brought the English ship behind the stern of the French galley. Running to catch the juggernaut as it tried in vain to outmanoeuvre, to meet the Devotion broadside, to bring what cannon it had to bear on the smaller English ship. The Frenchman was clearly a fat merchantman and no warship, for her gun provision was only adequate. Running was no option for her. The three-masted Devotion, at around eighty tons, was much faster than the three hundred ton, two-masted French galley, running at about six or seven knots at her top speed under sail, or oar.

In only twenty minutes since first sighting, the two bow guns of the Devotion reached the stern of the galley, scarring deep her transom.

As the Devotion chased the galley, the call came to ready the men to board the French vessel. Jack steadied his men, checking on their readiness to brawl alongside the boarding crew of the English ship. All were ready. All but Tom, who had announced to Jack, as he curled up to sleep out the excitement, 'If ma Daddy wanted me t' fight at sea he would've taught me t' swim.'

Jack had too much admiration and thanks for Tom's past bravery to call him coward, and order him on to this expedition. Instead Jack took to his own readiness.

As the noise of men grunting and growling on the deck grew, with the increasing shadow of the French ship, four of the Devotion's crew brought out barrels full of weapons; cudgels, axes, poleaxes, spikes and other dull rusty blades. Jack pulled out his sword and dagger, and felt their weight in his hand. He considered their effectiveness for the forthcoming fight. He judged the restrictions of space and balance he would have in the fray. Better strategy saw him return his own blades to his sword belt. He took off his belt, cap and jacket—just donned, and thrust them into the lap of the sleeping Tom. Jack, in his shirtsleeves, walked to the barrels of weapons and lifted from them two axes, dull of blade, but with sufficient heft to satisfy him of their effectiveness as weapons. Thrusting the handles of the axes down into the tops of his boots, he returned to the head of his men, to calm them

59

before the fight.

Robert too, had abandoned his blades for two axes. But his choices were double headed and weightier than Jack's, using the leather lanyards on their handles to affix them to his wrists.

'Aye, here we go again, Jack. Blood afore breakfast.'

Jack placed his hands on the sides of Robert's head, and squeezed hard. 'And I will see that ugly face again afore dinner.'

Robert pulled away from Jack, filled his mouth and spat hard and full on the deck. 'Filthy work my ma would say. Filthy work killin' is.' Robert portrayed a man who was not looking forward to the action, but Jack knew Robert would be the first in, and the bloodiest fighter on the English side.

Finn and Francis stood by Robert, Tip and Jamie at their side, looking to the direction of the French ship. Listening for orders from the older men.

Jack instructed, 'Francis, take the matchlocks to the tops. Take the boys to load the weapons. Fasten yourselves well… it's a long way back down to the deck.'

Jamie complained, 'But Captain, I'm wantin' to fight at yer side.'

Francis was the one to reply, 'You will be Jamie… We'll be their watch. Your uncle's a wild beast when his blood's up. He'll run hard in amongst the enemy, cutting. Careless he'll be. We will be watching his back from our firing place. Mind you do your jobs. Keep me in fresh musket… And keep your foolish heads down.'

Following the track of the galley's process in the sea, the Devotion came alongside the behemoth, with a terrible sound. The thunderous thump of timber on timber. A barrage of cannon rang out from both ships. Thunder, smoke and splintered wood filled the air. Ropes flew from the English ship, as English grappling irons sank into French timber, and even French flesh.

Captain Small gave a rude shout, which held its bloody note against the racket, and led his men over the side to melee with the enemy.

Soldier and sailor climbed the boarding ramps, their voices screaming louder than the English and French handguns—all calling death and comrade to strike hard their target. Jack's men joined in too, voices louder.

Jack followed Robert up one of the ramps pushed against the gallery of the French ship, while English crossbow and gun kept French heads down—whilst the Devotion's company climbed aboard. The sing of bolt and bullet flew overhead, as they climbed. Robert reached the French ship's gallery, to be met immediately by a dark skinned French sailor. Robert welcomed him with a head butt, and, as the sailor recoiled, the bold Scot leapt from the gallery to bring one of his axes down hard on the sailor's head, splitting his skull. Robert recovered quickly. Another French sailor ran at him from his left with a poleaxe, forcing Robert to push out his axe to counter the blow. The force of the strike against his axe unbalanced him. But Robert did not need to recover well to meet this second opponent, because Jack had already reached the top of the gallery. With axes in hands, Jack jumped down from the rail, and sunk dull metal blades into the back of Robert's attacker.

In his great pain, the French sailor dropped his poleaxe, but there was no great wound. So Robert finished off the falling second French sailor, with another blow to the head, removing an ear and rendering the sailor unconscious. Both men recovered quickly and stood together. They scanned the scene, Robert volleying spit from his mouth onto the French deck.

'They're big bastards on this boat, Jack.'

Jack looked at the melee around them, and then smiled at Robert. 'They are at that, Robert. As big as this boat, and twice as foul.'

Both friends threw each other a broad smile, and ran into the scrap shouting slaughter. Jack low with axes at French legs; Robert high at French heads.

Atop the mizzenmast, Francis had a good view over the French deck. He placed his shots well. With Tip and Jamie furnishing loaded musket, he had hit four men out of six shots taken. Two dead, he knew; one in retreat, nursing his wound; the fourth swimming in the sea, or drowning in the cold.

Jamie kept a close watch on his uncle, as he swept the French deck, spotting targets best placed to ensure Francis's shots were laid in the name of his own kin's safety. But Francis had his targets marked, and he ignored the calls from the boy. He sighted French officers, and those French with ranged weapons that were covering the assault.

Two French sailors, under direction, were at a *sling*—a swivel gun, set on the French ship's forecastle. They swung the hand-cannon, to point to their own deck, looking for a concentration of attackers. Shrapnel to see them killed. Francis traced the lie of the sling, to see their point of aim. Jack and Robert were at the end of it, thumping their axes with vicious frenzy into their enemy. Francis knew the range was long, but still he aimed. He allowed for the swell on both boats, the wind's blow. *But who to hit?* One shot, three targets. He selected the man directing the gun crew. He fired. But the shot was well wide.

'Another matchlock!' Francis barked.

None came.

'Pass me a matchlock… or a bow.'

But the boys were in difficulty—fumbling against the swell affecting the boat, and distracted by the shots and bolts flying past their ears.

Francis turned to Tip and Jamie with fire in his eyes. 'Bastard boys… can you no load a weapon!'

Tip managed to finish loading a matchlock, and passed it to Francis. Nerves breaking his reply, 'S-Sorry.'

Francis grabbed the weapon and scowled at Tip. He brought his aim to the sling, and fired, hitting the sailor with the match. But his shot did not kill, or even disable the sailor; it simply distracted him from his action. And Jamie gasped, as the wounded sailor brought the match back to bear down on the sling.

But a fourth had joined the firing party—Finn.

Jamie watched his uncle, unrelenting in his attack against the three French sailors. No hesitation or fear did he show. No thought of self-defence—only of frenzied attack. He hacked like a man possessed, and none could defend against his blade, or lay hurt on him. It was his unrelenting assault that overwhelmed the three.

The last French sailor standing, fastened by the point of Finn's sword fell beneath the forecastle's rail, and Finn followed him down—a moment later to rise, swordless. Jamie looked on his uncle, his hands well bloodied. He watched him bathe in the rich red fluid, to paint his face redder than his hair—redder than the beard he wore to frame it.

Then the sling was in the hands of a mad Irishman, and he brought it around to a new target, and touched the match. It fired.

Jamie looked to the point of his uncle's fire, and saw the bloody mess of a hand cannon fired close-range on a group of French sailors on the other side of the ship—laid bloody and broken on the deck. Jamie then turned his head to see his uncle, triumphant at the gun. To see him return to the fallen gunners, and run a knife across any throat that still had breath.

Francis, relieved at Finn's intervention, noticed the great silver-grey cat easing his way across a rope holding fast the two ships, and pointed it out to Jamie. 'I see even the ship's cat joins in the fray.'

Jamie laughed nervously. 'I think he goes more in search of fresh meat. His own stock of rats must be running low.'

'Dedication to its belly,' replied Francis, as his head moved quickly, scanning the fight for the next direction of attack, or any comrades in danger. The fray was well choked, and Francis saw little opportunity for safe shooting. 'Boys, I'm going to join the fight… Stay here. Keep watch. Take only those shots you know are clear of our lads.'

Tip and Jamie nodded, but Francis was gone. Jamie returned his watch on the cat on the rope. He watched the line slacken and tighten, as both vessels rocked in the swell. The cat made poor travel, as he continually stopped to sink his claws into the bucking rope.

Jamie was not alone in his observation of the cat. Forgetting the fight, the boatswain dropped his sword and ran to the rope.

Then the cat seemed to lose his balance for a moment, his tightrope prowess failing.

Jamie gasped fear for the four-legged buccaneer. But with one hand on the rope, the boatswain stretched out to grasp the cat. Fat cat in hand, he had poor grip on the rope, and suddenly the boatswain was, himself, in danger of falling from the ship.

'*Save the boatswain!*' came the cry from the fray.

'*Never mind the boatswain, save the cat!*' came the reply.

The grappling hook, attached to the rope, had a poor hold of the French ship. It slipped free, sending the boatswain heading down, still clutching the cat. But the rope was short, and the boatswain and cat were swung hard into the side of *Devotion*, only inches from the sea and wave's grasp.

Jamie looked on, aghast as he lost sight of the boatswain and cat. But the boatswain was strong, and he maintained hold of the rope and the cat. The cat ran up the boatswain and up the rope, to appear atop the ship's rail, triumphant. The boatswain, with two hands free, also climbed the rope to safety, shaken.

Jamie brought his attention back to the fight on the French ship, looking for safe opportunity to fire. But amongst the action, bloody and swift, there was little chance for a safe shot. But it was clear to Jamie and Tip that the French crew's fight was waning. Even so, some still had fight in them. Some had even enough fight to see Jack laid to the deck.

'Arête!'

The call was clear and loud. It was heard. And all understood.

A halt had been called to the fight by the French Captain, kneeling in submission at the feet of two of the Devotion's crewmembers, under the direction of a breathless Captain Small. Men and tools abated their actions. There were no jubilant shouts of victory. Only a mass of men, recovering breath and poise as they cooled their blood, looked to their wounds, and either took prisoner, or were imprisoned.

Robert, who had received a bloody nose, courtesy of one from his own side swinging a cudgel as he scrapped, spat out blood and mucus as he cleared his throat. He moved along the galley's deck, scanning for his men. Finn, red with other men's blood; Francis, sour; Jamie and Tip aloft the mizzen, signalling praise for the victors. Even Tom, awake from his slumber, stood smiling at the ship's rail; bow in hand and an empty quiver. A moment of relief met his mind, as he counted them all—all without major wound or injury—all but one.

Chapter IV

The instruction was well shouted amongst the men. They were to be underway in less than two hours. It had been three since the last blow had been struck. Wounded men still required tending. Repairs were needed to Devotion's main mast, so she could take sail. There was also considerable damage to the French galley—too much for Captain Small to take pleasure in the Devotion's gunnery. Urgent repairs were now required, so at least the galley could make her way under oar; its oarsmen mercifully spared from the fight, for reasons of their criminality and enforced confinement. Neither ship was immediately seaworthy for heavy winter seas.

It was no wonder Captain Small was anxious. He needed more speed on board. He needed to remove his bounty from the danger of retrieval by the French. Warships perhaps, sailing the German sea to Scotland. Haste indeed required. Haste not aided by the sorrowed loss of members of Devotion's crew by French fire and blade. Taking the galley was harder than Captain Small had thought. Its merchant sailors had fought more like war men, hard and resolute. His own price paid, costly.

Robert was also brooding. Some of the last blows were placed upon his own captain; bringing deep wound to head and arm, long sleep and shallow breath. He blamed himself for his lack of guardianship.

Robert's concern was easily apparent. There was poor room on the Devotion. There were too many men cramped within suffocating wooden walls, and too little comfort for an injured Jack. Robert looked around at men wounded; at those too badly to return to duty; too badly to find places better to sit and lie.

Robert wondered whether the captured French galley would offer Jack better, more comfortable accommodation. With most of its captured crew interned in its dark hold, the French ship would be running only that crew which Captain Small could spare; bolstered by those sailors from the French ship, who thought turncoat an easier choice than prisoner. Also, the French ship's principal cabins would be vacated, whilst their former, higher ranked occupants took the *kinder hospitality* of an English captain, onboard an English ship. So Robert sought out Francis and Tom to help him move Jack out of the dirt and danger of infection, and into the light of the deck—to seek transfer to the French ship.

Robert hurried Tom and Francis to move Jack before he woke, to save him the discomfort of difficult travel. But as Tom, Francis and Robert carefully carried their unconscious leader, they encountered Captain Small, flanked by two of his men.

Captain Small blocked Robert's travel, his question harshly delivered. 'Scot, where do you take your captain?'

Robert boldly replied, 'On board yer prize, and a better bed tae find him.'

The tone of the Captain's reply was no better offered. He was a man with the weight of his losses, undermining his joy of a valuable prize won. 'I should be vexed you do not think to seek my permission first. I suggest your man be better placed in my cabin.'

Robert distrusted Captain Small's offer. *Kindness offered in poor temper, was often a gift that came at a dear price.*

Robert, Tom and Francis, threw the same look of concern amongst each other. They each tried to read the other. But then they returned their eyes to Captain Small, as he spoke again.

'Boys stop frettin'', and bring him to my cabin. I'll set my surgeon-barber to his wounds and any broken bones. I'm needin' a word with yer man when he wakes.' Captain Small stooped to take a closer look at the unconscious Jack, his head well bloodied and skin deathly pale. He shook his head mournfully, and spoke in softer tone, 'When… or if he wakes.'

Robert started to protest, to keep Jack in his care and free from any interrogations. Normally his protests would be well heeded, him being a strong-willed man, with a considerable presence amongst any crowd, but Captain Small held his hand against Robert to still his mouth.

'Scot, hold your concern. Your man will be comfortable enough in my cot—for a while at least. I need his wits.' Eyes on Robert, and pointing to Francis, he continued, 'Your boy here tells me Captain Brownfield has good learning and a keen wit?'

Francis was quick to reply, 'Yes, he is as quick with his mind, as he is with his blade.'

Francis' offer of confirmation regarding Jack's intellect drew astonishment from Robert. Amazed he was, at an alien compliment from an acid tongue. Francis, after all, was a sour man, one who had long enjoyed the benefits of favour and admiration amongst his soldier kind, by the way of his better education. All of which waned in the wake of Jack's superior ability to understand and relate the science of the world.

෨෩

Jack was in pain as consciousness arrived, and distress formed a grimace on his face. 'What the...?' Jack questioned his surroundings, but not his discomfort. He remembered well the fight; the shot and blow that he thought had killed him.

Jack's movement to sit up brought a searing pain, which forced his teeth to clench and his jaw to bind—holding in a scream desperate to seek release. His full awareness of his sorry state came upon him quickly; announced by sharp pains, then dull aches and discomfort in his ribs, arm and head.

Jack's focus had returned and his head had cleared enough to recognise his environment. To see Captain Small, sitting at his desk, pen in hand, and the ship's cat sitting with him; enjoying the comfort of a quiet place after a world of war and disturbance.

'Ah Captain Brownfield, you wake. I wish to make my gratitude to you and your men known. So I have mentioned your contribution in my log. I must also record, eight of my good crew taken into God's care by the way of the French fight... My lady Devotion will sail poorer for their passing, and music on board will be less sweet... for my better voices have been added to God's choir of angels... my cousin amongst them.'

'What the...?' Jack's words were still hiding in his damaged head, struggling to form a voice for his questions. So he took a while longer to gain a proper perspective, and a better-cleared mind.

'I think that piece of French oak knocked your brains into the sea, Brownfield.'

Jack did not look at the captain. He was still too busy drawing in sights and sounds of the cabin, in order to clear his mind of mist. He controlled his breathing, taking in long and slow breaths, filling his head with good air to soften the ache, and exhaling gently to control the hurt in his side.

As Jack scanned Captain Small's quarters, he tried to form the nature of the man from his personal belongings scattered around the cramped cabin. But it was more of an exercise in recovery of his wits, rather than curiosity regarding the sea captain's character.

'I... I think my men enjoyed the exercise,' offered Jack, his words screwed around the pain that issued from his body's side, contorting his head and mouth.

'I think they did. I saw them during the fray. I think they laid many more Frenchman to the decks than my own good ship's company.' Captain Small's voice was highlighted with a humoured tone—the beginnings of a man becoming pleased with the day's work and his prize. His loss softened by his dream of his future better secured.

Jack saw little of interest in the cabin—nothing of the man. No hint of a personal life outside the paraphernalia connected to sea craft. His eyes left the walls and surfaces of the cabin to rest on the back of Captain Small's head, still bowed to his journal. His scripting frequently punctuated by recharging of a quill, long past its best.

Captain Small cleaned the nib of his pen, placed it to the table, and turned to face Jack. 'Captain Brownfield. Do you know of our French prize and her mission?'

Jack shrugged his shoulders, and used his eyes and expression to confirm his ignorance, for his head was not for movement—it hurt too much.

'The French ship was on route to Scotland, carrying supplies to support the French garrison at Leith. You may not know that England's ships blockade the harbour. We have also discovered hidden within the ship, despatches—one in *Latin* we think.'

Jack was still forming cohesion in his mind and shifting his body to find some comfort from his ribs and arm.

Captain Small, seeing Jack's distraction, picked up a folded paper from his desk, and travelled to the oak cot where Jack was sitting. 'I am told you have learning and speak Latin. So I would like you to look over this despatch. Tell me if you can read it.' He placed the folded paper into Jack's hand—the one on his good arm.

Jack studied the writing and seal upon the paper before he unfolded it to read the letter contained within. An unruly hand had written the script upon the envelope, and Jack read aloud the French text. *'La première lettre doit être livré avant le 9ème. La deuxième lettre après le 11ème.'*

Jack looked to the sea captain to confirm if he had understanding of French, but his face was hard to read, so Jack translated aloud to save the captain's embarrassment. *'The first letter is to be delivered before the 9th. The second letter after the 11th.'*

Jack then turned his attention to the contents of the message, but it was not Latin, it was encryption—a cipher.

IJ VCKPY VQ ASL SLKTLD VQ HGHWVY, ASL IPHCLC VQ ASPD SPAELC OLZ HWS YTNSAD VGLC KZJFTPUEZ

Jack's re-examination of the broken wax seal offered little more illumination, as the device of a *bull* upon it was unknown to him.

'Was the seal intact when you found it?' enquired Jack.

'Yes it was. Can you read the message, Captain Brownfield?'

Jack refolded the paper ready to hand it back to Captain Small. 'It is not Latin. The message is encrypted and of little use—unless you have the key to the cipher.' Jack held the paper aloft, towards Captain Small. 'Who was on board to carry such a message?'

'French sailors, French soldiers, their wives and children. A few bookish men, lawyers' runners, a Dutch merchant who throws curses at his bonds, a Spanish cripple who babbles in Latin—*about the stars,* I think, even a few French gentlemen running from ruin in France, for favour in the Scottish court. The carrier of the message could be any one of them.'

Jack nodded in agreement, but as his eyes fell on the paper to read again the instruction on the letter, questions began to push out the cloud of mayhem from his battered mind.

'What date is it, Captain Small?'

'It's the fourth day of January.'

Jack read over the bearer's instructions written on the message again. '*The first letter is to be delivered before the 9th. The second letter after the 11th.*'

Jack asked, 'Is there another letter?'

'There was no other letter like it.'

Jack voiced his thoughts aloud, 'Possibly destroyed, or one delivered… Yet…' Jack re-focused his eyes on the paper… but his head hurt too much, and he gave up his nagging question, and gave the letter back to Captain Small.

'Do you have *any* thought on the message, Brownfield?'

'Only a poor one, Captain. The instructions seem strange. Surely separate letters should have upon them separate instructions regarding delivery. Also, why have you only found one letter? Why were both letters not destroyed?'

'Perhaps the first letter has already been delivered.'

'Perhaps.'

Jack dismissed further thought of the cipher, and lifted himself off the captain's cot, to stretch those parts of him that could be eased without pain. All whilst Captain Small opened the paper, to re-read the cipher.

'The third word, *VQ,* is repeated… three times. What does that mean?'

'Probably a preposition,' replied Jack. 'For example; in, to, on... and so on. But do not be fooled. First and second words may use different encryptions, so they may be in fact different prepositions.'

'So this is a complex cipher?'

'Ciphers usually are. Which makes it stranger that the delivery date be included on it. Why place such information directly on secret letters? The date may give clue to the contents of the message. And why is not the month included in the date?'

Jack felt poorly. There was a sickness forming in his stomach, and sleep forming in his mind. And for all the reasoning that remained in Jack's knocked head, there were understandings that fell away. So Jack revisited the conundrum of the cipher and re-applied himself to the puzzle—to help his mind fight his malaise.

He closed his eyes and became his long past mentor, Edward. He thought on him and his method. He thought on him and begat his seeing eye. He left John Brownfield behind, and stood as his beloved tutor, with all his wits and learning in matters of logic and science. He thought, and thought... Dismissed idea, and formed better hypothesis. He applied mathematics taught well by his friend and he ran through all forms of ciphers and equation he could remember. He thought on the process his tutor used to deduce events unseen to the untrained eye on that *Truce Day*, so many years ago. How he enquired and eliminated—read evidence and cleared his mind of prejudicial thought, so as not to drown new and better explanation.

A rich enlightenment caused Jack to raise an arm in jubilation.

'First and second letter.... *Yes!* He forgot his ribs and his wound and raised his sore arm to form a fist. But unbearable pain brought him to his reality, and he screamed and swore at the stab to his side, and pain in his arm.

Jack held down his arm, and still grimacing, resumed the

Tutor's psyche. It took him two good minutes to return to the Tutor's mind. Long enough for Captain Small to swear a little in complaint for the delay.

'Do you know Brownfield, or do you bluster and delay because you're as dull-witted as me?'

'A moment, Captain.' Jack returned to the questions in his mind.

After a few more moments to ponder the cipher, and the facts surrounding its recovery, Jack spoke again. 'The month is not mentioned because the month is not relevant.'

Captain Small, turned parrot and repeated Jack's last words, 'Not relevant?'

'Yes, not relevant... because...' Jack's last word trailed away and he screwed up his face. *Pain.* He dismissed the discomfort of hurt from his mind and he squeezed his thoughts together to find again his enlightenment—and it came like a wind fuelled breaker on the shore.

'*Yes, yes...*yes. Not relevant, because the instructions are not for the deliverer, but for the receiver.'

'That makes no sense,' added Captain Small.

Jack had recovered composure enough to declare his thought. 'Perhaps there is no second letter. Perhaps the instructions for delivery are actually the key to the cipher.'

'That still makes no sense—to place the solution to the puzzle in plain view.'

'Perhaps the recipient does not have a cipher key, but wits enough to work out the key, if clues are given. Think on the instructions; '*The first letter is to be delivered before the 9th. The second letter after the 11th.*' What number comes before nine and after eleven?'

'Eight and twelve,' replied Captain Small.

'Correct. Now what if the first letter in the cipher reads as the eighth letter and the second letter the twelfth.'

Captain Small's eyes darted over the cipher as he tried to comprehend Jack's meaning; looking at the eighth and twelfth letters in the cipher, and trying to make sense of them in French, a language he could speak, but not write.

Jack saw the Captain's confusion and interrupted. 'What is the first letter of the alphabet?'

'*A*,' replied Captain Small, fearing more tests of his poor learning.

'And if you were to deliver *A*, as the eighth letter?'

Captain Small struggled awhile to recount his alphabet. Struggled and failed to get past what came after *F*.

'It's *H*... *H*... the letter *H*.' Jack fired his words at Captain Small, because his continuing pain and the discomfort of a full bladder, reminded him that he should be urinating then resting, and not twisting his mind with puzzles.

Jack grabbed his ribs, and squeezed them tight as if he could replace broken bone with good bone. As if it would hold back the discomfort, but he only managed to squeeze more hurt from sore ribs, and force a curse from a sorely head. He breathed deeply to arrest his suffering, but the act only brought greater sharpness to the pain. So he continued with more measured breath, shallow, low and quiet.

'So *H*, would be start of our new alphabet for revealing the first letter of each word, and similarly the twelfth letter *L*, would be the start of our new alphabet for the second letter of each word.... and so on. Repeating until the true meanings of each word are spelled.

Jack took the letter from the Captain and laid it out on his desk.

'So the first letter in the cipher reads not *I*, but *B*, and the second letter reads not *J*, but...' Jack counted twelve letters back from the letter J. '...*Y*'

'So the first word is *BY*. And the second word is...' Jack took up the captain's pen and loaded it with ink, and scribbled two long lines of letters on a clean piece of paper. He applied his mind to the paper and deciphered the second word. It read perfectly. It took a while to draw out the next few words, and then as he relearned a new alphabet, he could read most of the words within the alien text, without reference to his key.

'I think Captain Small, you may wish to pass your cipher on to those in dispute with the French in Scotland. Either the English agents in Edinburgh, or the Protestant Lords of the Congregation—*The Faithful Congregation of Christ Jesus in Scotland.*'

'Why?'

Jack hesitated. A sickness formed in his head that he could not ignore. He held himself still for a moment to quell the rising nausea. Then taking a deep measured breath, he said, 'The cipher is written in English, not French… so perhaps…' Jack put a hand to his mouth, '…so perhaps it was not meant for the French garrison there.' Jack's rising nausea now made concentration on his words difficult, and his breath became laboured. 'It is a… strange affair of language… considering the messenger was on a French ship… sharing a French captain's hospitality, destined for a French encampment.' Jack was now sweating profusely, deathly pale and rocking gently.

'Thank you, Brownfield. It seems a better route with damaged ships, is one to Scotland. I have a French ship captured, and a spy somewhere among my prisoners, either belonging to the French, the Scottish Lords of the Congregation, or even the English fleet… Either way there is better profit to be had in Scotland… Antwerp, for now, will have to wait.'

Jack was not in a position to argue, or even care. Because his world had, once again, turned to black.

PART 2
'the school of war'

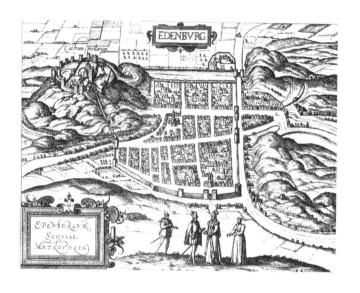

Edinburgh

Chapter V

The Firth of Forth, Scotland

The Devotion's skiff had been gone half the day. Robert cursed it. He cursed Captain Small for being on it. He cursed any member of Devotion's crew that failed to give him news on it. And all he could do was pace the deck and throw eyes to the sea to look for it. He kept steadfast vigil for Captain Small for the remainder of the day. He looked towards the English flagship. He looked towards the shore—to the sandy beach at *Figgate Muir*. He looked for Devotion's skiff amongst the boats ferrying men and supplies between ship and land. But half a day turned into a whole day and more.

Robert's eyes scanned the extent of Sir William Winter's fleet as it sat in Scottish waters, against the precept of a treaty signed between England and France ten years past. Sitting so as to blockade the firth. Sitting in numbers enough to threaten the French-born regent, Marie of Guise, defender of the Catholic faith, who sat on the Scottish throne, in lieu of her daughter, Mary—the Scottish Queen by birthright, already married to the King of France.

Robert was not surprised to see the English at anchor in the firth of the Forth River. They had been there thirteen years ago, and three years prior to that; bringing mayhem and murder to the peoples about. Some sailors said it was another bout in the old fight. Some claimed a state of war had returned between England and France with its 'auld alliance' with Scotland. Some were even told the fleet was there by misadventure, or mischief; sitting at anchor only by the will of Sir William Winter, against the will of the Queen of England. But many knew Winter from old—he was no maverick, no pirate.

But Robert and the sailors were not to know. England had already signed a treaty with the Protestant Scottish Lords against their now unwanted and unseated regent. English fear that Scotland would become merely province of France was all too real in wary, English political thought. More so, it was a fear well rooted and well despised in the Scottish nationalistic mind—especially amongst some antithetical Protestant Lords, with ambition for rule and not mere subjugation. And although England viewed the Scot as an irksome raggedy fox, capable of stealing her eggs—it was better the fox than the French cock, who some believed would gladly steal away the whole henhouse, to return it to heel, with proper faith and proper tongue.

Finally, after many hours on deck, Robert returned below to check on his ailing comrade. Jack was not well. He had fallen into deep sleep. He needed better care; another surgeon. But Small had ordered, by threat of arms, no one leave his ship until he returned. All Robert could do was look on his ailing friend and curse Captain Small some more.

The Devotion's surgeon had made, best he could, bindings to Jack's broken ribs, set rigid his broken arm and dressed his wounds. But he was short on skill and would not treat Jack's broken head.

Robert had tasked Jamie and Tom to rouse Jack continually, to check his condition. But each time Jack woke he puked, and complained of deep and blinding hurt in his head and failing vision.

Robert was right to be concerned. *Blood on the brain,* he thought, *he needs bleeding.*

※

It was not until dawn before the skiff returned—short its cargo of the captured; those French officers and passengers deemed important enough to present to the Protestant forces for immediate bounty or interrogation.

Tip, seeing the returned skiff, roused Robert, but Robert was forced to pace an hour more before he was allowed to see Captain Small.

'My captain needs better care—a better surgeon,' demanded Robert.

Captain Small yawned and sank into his chair. 'I will send the skiff tomorrow, to ask for the fleet's master-surgeon.'

'Nae enough… My captain has a malady o' the heid, and needs treatment now. I want tae take him off ship, tae seek better care ashore.'

'The Devotion is ordered to stay with the blockade. Sir Winter orders all my crew, passengers and prisoners to stay aboard.'

'I ask tae leave, only oot o' courtesy. Ye can either give me yer blessin' and yer permission tae leave… *or find fight instead!*'

'Captain Small disliked threats. He stood up and barked, 'Do you wish to join the French sailors in the hold!'

'Call yer watch, Small. But they'll find yer neck broken, and me and my lads hard tae take. More of yer crew tae see a watery grave I imagine. But ye dinnae need to imagine it, because ye've seen what we can dae.'

Captain Small was tired. He cursed Robert for his menace, and cursed again Sir Winter for putting him in such a position. He thought on his Devotion's new commission. Both his ship and the French galley were interned. Bounty owed and promised. But he knew Sir Winter. He was no pirate perhaps, but he was also in no position to pay. Captain Small disliked requisition without proper contract, as it was inevitably without reasonable likelihood of proper compensation.

He thought on the consequences of letting Robert go. And he thought again about making him stay, *reprimand and heavy fine perhaps on one hand, antagonism and possible death on the other*. But he was too tired to care—already too little profit to protect, too tired to fight. 'Go where you please Scot… But you'll need to travel to Edinburgh to find better care. The French soldiers and their Catholic Queen are hold up in Leith. The Scottish Protestant Lords inhabit the roads right into Edinburgh, although they far from control them. I am told the French troops sally out of Leith at will. Edinburgh Castle stands neutral, and rumour tells of an English army on the march from Berwick. Denial is steadfast, but I think Sir Winter is not here for the view.' Captain Small again sank back into his chair. 'Do you think your man will last the course on a litter?'

'I dinnae ken. But I agree there are better surgeons in Edinburgh. Jack has well-placed friends there, courtesy of a French coxcomb. And I have kin enough in these parts tae see us safe into Edinburgh's walls.'

'Then good luck to you, *Scot*. Take care. Scotland lives its life in war. But it never learns from it. Mind well you do not get caught up in another deficient-born Scottish enterprise. For I am poorer already than I was this morning... and I've only been in Scotland little more than a day.'

&)(&

Robert was a happier man to have Jack awake. Happier still since Jack ordered himself unstrapped from the litter so he could walk. A better policy, as the roads were not kind, and the litter did little to soften the discomfort of the ruts, running long stretches of well-travelled roads.

Free from the litter, bump and shock, Jack's ribs shouted relief. His legs were well enough to carry a broken head and broken arm. But Jack was not blind to his injuries. He felt sore and poorly. His head was on fire and his arm ached. The bindings around ribs and arm were loose, and he needed better attention. But pride dictated he kept quiet as they travelled carefully through deceit, suspicion and danger towards the gates of Edinburgh; past cordons of men in conflict with the French and their Scottish Catholic supporters; soldiers, peasants and papists, all determined to restore a Catholic regent back into her Scottish palaces.

'Promise me, Robert.'

'What, Jack?'

'Promise me, as soon as you deliver me to the merchant's house, that you and the boys retire far from trouble.'

'Aye, Jack, dinnae fret. Me 'n' the boys will take a drink, and then take oorselves away from Edinburgh, and oot of harms way. Although, with ye recoupin', there'll be nae commission in Antwerp fer a while. No pay fer me 'n' the boys.'

Jack leaned in to Robert, to hide his words from the others. 'That seems to be the way of it. I am sorry Rab, to see you and the boys poor.'

'Nae harm… We'll get by. I suspect yer own funds are light too?'

'Gold is nothing to me. I would sacrifice it all for a quiet mind.'

'How says you Jack… ye want a quiet mind? Ach ye be a fool. Your conscious will be the death of ye. I fear it. What is past is past, done is done, all gone *Three Hills* ago. Forget and move on. Dae not let foul rememberin' taint the now and colour the future grey. Money may not remove ill-thought, but it still buys pleasures enough tae stifle it.'

At Edinburgh's walls, the men rested. The western gate stood large, an ornately decorated port in the city's *new* wall; erected in defence after the Scottish defeat by the English on *Flodden Field.* But, that was a lifetime ago and the wall had become more constraint than comfort for its inhabitants, for the wall merely served a purpose to control goods coming in and out of the city. So a lifetime on, the wall's security was routinely breached as the city's inhabitants sought an easy path for their goods to escape the city's tax, fee and toll.

Entering the walls was easy; Robert knew the way. Smugglers' routes were aplenty, and the placement of some coin by Robert in the proper hands saw his comrades steal into the city without question or inspection. Soon they were on their way unchallenged, walking through a long forgotten jousting ground, burnt Catholic yard, chapel and college, and through to the market square, where dealings in horse, cattle and execution were routine. Except there were few cows and fewer horses that day, as the Scottish Lords took all for a Scottish army, leaving Scottish people in deficit.

To unhelpfully announce their arrival, a madman, a wretch in rags, dancing an insane jig, accompanied them on the way. Insane utterances in Latin issued from his mouth. Wide eyes mocked and flaying arms threatened. Robert claimed he was a murderer, hanged, who later emerged from his shroud alive and so escaped his sentence, only to live in the market square all his days to taunt the gallows and the law. Robert calmed his party as he guided them through the city. 'Pay nae heed tae the loon… Nae one takes a care aboot him. He's but mair noise, and another fool in a busy market.'

Past the *Grassmarket* they walked, steeply down a street of tall stone, open gallery, thatch roof, and a thousand and more folk, towards the merchant's house, and the merchant Jack knew would give him comfort and care, and deliver a good surgeon to tend his wounds. He knew, because he had a name to give the merchant that was greater than gold—*Henri Hueçon*.

The merchant was once a clothier like his father, selling homespun. But he had long since moved on to finer wares and better customers. He worked long hours to see his trade grow. His enterprising hand was in many other businesses and they all profited by his association. He was one owing to Henri Hueçon; his debt hidden from his ledgers, so it was not one for his auditors, but one for his confessor. Henri Hueçon acquired many such debtors. He enjoyed their shame and the interest they repaid. Henri Hueçon traded in favours, it was his strength—it was his riches. Henri understood the science of a man's ambition. It led to the accumulation of many such debts, and all were valuable; regardless if it were a noble man or lady with secrets that would see them treated not so nobly by their peers; or a bishop with a fancy for boys; or a timid man wishing to procure and maintain a mistress without the knowledge of a jealous wife; or even a merchant wishing to procure greater profit by trading in illicit goods. Yes, Henri had many such debtors all over Europe and there was never a man better at acquiring such debts, with full assurance that he would be reimbursed when he required it.

The merchant was not a member of the Black Merchants'

Guild. He was far too lowly to be included within that hidden union. He did not even know of it. But Jack was a man declaring to be Hueçon's *good* friend. So the merchant welcomed him into his home as an honoured guest, to recover in more comfortable surroundings, if only to lessen his debt to Henri Hueçon. Jack's boys meanwhile, found an inn. Not one far from the troubles, but one closest to their thirst; the loudest one on the busy streets of Edinburgh.

There is nothing like it. Few cures bring out the man locked within himself; that draw out the poet, the philosopher and the minstrel. Nothing is so perfect at breaking the stolid man, vanquishing placidity and bringing delight before discernment. Its influence can make sense out of war, and relight warm memories gone cold. It can make the meekest brave, and the bravest humble. It can banish sorrow, and return enemies to friends.

I would sacrifice a warm bed, a comfortable fire, a woman's welcoming embrace for it. I would risk cut, bruise and chide to find its intoxication. Liquids of the spirit—ale, liquors and wines.

John Brownfield MDLX (1560)

Robert raised the empty blackjack high into the air. 'Innkeeper, a new jug fer another round. Another drink fer absent friends.'

Finn looked around at the unfamiliar faces in the inn, at the poor company about, and clamped his hand on Robert's back. 'Aye, there's too many good souls not here tonight.'

'Aye, Finn... Too many boys gone afore they had time to drink their fill,' replied a grim Francis, woefully shaking his head.

'Francis is sour when he's sober, and dour when he's drunk... there's no winnin' with that lad,' said Tom, smiling. 'Besides, I know one boy dead afore his time. One who drank his fill twenty times over, and his neighbour's twenty times more.'

Only Jamie and Tip looked at Tom, lost to his meaning, then to each other, then to the newly placed full blackjack on the table.

'Come on Jamie. Come on Tip. Serve yer betters,' instructed Finn, 'Fill up the cups. Mind ye leave yer own to last.' He raised his hand to Tom, to beckon his words. 'Come on, Tom... tell the boys which drunkard ye are meaning.'

'*Bendback Bob*. He drank twenty lifetimes of ale before he was cut down.' Tom raised his beaker. 'So a cup to Bendback.'

All raised their beakers and drank to the memory of a long departed friend, and several more, in dedication to all their compeers cut down on the field of battle.

Francis stood up to address the table. Swaying. Well intoxicated, he raised a toast, 'And let us drink to those long forgotten. Best forgotten... because they were bastards and dungbags all.'

'Who are ye meanin'? Ye sorry, sad man.' asked Finn.

'I have news of our former master, *Walter Traquere*,' announced Francis.

There was little enthusiasm for Francis' news, but Robert cocked a ready ear and a receptive eye towards Francis to encourage him to continue.

'He has been made an auspicious captain of the field—a camp-general no less.'

'So Jack's former gaoler, finally lives his ambition tae be greater than he is,' said Robert.

'Aye, Robert… but I hear it is a price dear, for he pays for the comfort of his commander's camp whilst he campaigns,' replied Francis, falling back onto his stool.

Finn lifted his beaker and drank down its fill without break, bringing down hard the pewter cup on the table. He drew his hand across his mouth, to rub the spillage into his thick red beard. 'Never mind the gossip regardin' a master long forgotten. Or *news* that Francis forgets to tell his comrades when he hears it… until that is, beer loosens his niggardly tongue.' Finn turned to Robert. 'I've never questioned Jack's command afore, but…'

Robert interrupted, swaying slightly, 'Then dinnae now… *Red-Irish.*'

Finn threw his hand to cover Robert's mouth and pressed hard to hold it steady. '*Wheest, Scot,*' Finn countered, then continued, 'As I was saying. Why are we seeking employ from that French lady-man—that coquet?'

Robert pushed Finn's hand away. 'Aye. Finn, I'm often wonderin' that too, fer I dinnae like the man. But Jack knows best.'

Francis shook his head. 'That Frenchy is a coquet that flirts with himself, such is his fondness for his own shadow. They say he bathes every day, and he sends his water to his brew house to be turned into beer—which he serves to his guests.'

Finn returned his hand to Robert, but this time it alighted on his shoulder, as a gesture of solidarity. 'It seems that egotist Hueçon, in his conceit, thinks his stink produces nectar, eh Rob?'

Robert nodded, his head bobbing uncontrollably, dancing to the drink. 'Aye, it's a tale I believe. It's the kind of s-show… that F-Frenchy would present tae his… a-adorin' public.'

Finn smiled at Robert's increasing insobriety, his own deep drunkenness not far behind. 'I agree Hueçon's show is unbounded, but I doubt even his...' Finn hesitated. 'No, forgive me poor tongue. It deserts me...' Finn took another drink, as if it would clear his mind, then he continued, 'As I was saying, I doubt even his self-devotion, extends to his effluence. The truth more like, he pisses in the water and serves it up as contempt for his guests to quaff.'

Francis, nodding in agreement with Robert and Finn, took a mouthful of beer poured from a newly filled jug, and immediately spat it out—wiping the remnants from his lips. '*By gow!* Seems Hueçon's brew is on general sale here in the town.'

Tom laughed. He passed his own cup to Francis, his words kindly offered, 'Here take mine lad it's not tainted.'

Francis took Tom's cup and, without thanks, sank the brew in a single mouthful.

'Francis, I think you drink too much,' said Tom.

Francis slammed the cup hard on the table, and looked straight ahead towards the door of the inn, expecting someone to enter. 'As Captain Jack would say, *it calms my pain.*'

'Ye'll be worse for it in the mornin',' said Tom.

'But tonight I'll be smiling,' replied Francis, with only the hint of a smile on his lips.

'We'll at least it's gud t' see ye smilin', *m'lad.*'

'It's good to see you smiling at me, Tom my man,' replied Francis.

Tom stole Jamie's cup and raised it to Francis. 'I add my salute to ye, Francis. I raise ma cup to ye. What shall we toast?'

But Francis did not reply. Drink had stolen his tongue, and his rare display of good humour had emptied away with his last drink. So Robert stepped in, drunk, but with a briefly found clarity and feigned sobriety, to offer a good sentiment—good words.

'One can only hope fer a strong heart, powerful resolve and an unerrin' faith.'

All that could, said, '*Aye*.' All raised the cups to it. All except Jamie who hoisted the half full jug to his lips, only to spill its contents down himself.

'Ach Jamie ma boy, ye waste the liquid,' said Finn in a scold, before he turned to Robert to applaud him. 'Fine words, Robert, they are. I think the drink makes you a good sage. Ye must have the Irish blood in ye. Fer only the wisest words come from my Isle.'

Robert bobbed and swayed under the spell of the beer, smiling at his incapacity, his lost perspicuity, his drunkenness. He laughed. Then he tried to refocus his eyes, as if clarity of vision would help him issue his words better. 'I'm no wise, fer I'm always fightin' another man's war.'

Finn slapped Robert hard, and then embraced him like a brother, for he was a brother—a brother-in-arms. 'Steadfast yer are Robert ma boy. In Carlow we would call ye a great man, because ye wear yer steel so well. Keen is yer blade, keener yer honour. Yer charge is yer treasure, and yer treasure well won, because the sweet Irish angels know yer name, for yer place is already earned amongst them.'

Robert's eyes closed and his head dipped low. His words lost their fire, and were sadly spoken, 'Ye were always a gud'n wi' the words… *Gud Jack*…'

Finn raised his eyebrows at Robert's misnaming, but thought better of correcting him.

Then Robert's head came out of his stupor—his sadness. Eyes open. Eyes wide, declaring, 'Words to good fer me.' He looked to his comrades, and his pride in them was evident. 'Good soldiers ye all are… ye fight with ye brains… keen 'n' sharp.'

Francis then sat to attention. Bolt upright. Eyes forward.

Recovered from his silence—his mind also escaping the numbness of the drink, the chains of insobriety. He held a none too steady hand against the talk. He held his position until some kind of clarity filled his head and he could speak all his bitter words clearly. 'We are not paid to think, only to act on order. Like dogs... Yes dogs of war we are, and like dogs, we can only expect a place to sleep, meat to eat, and a bitch or two to shag.'

Jamie, long quiet in the company of the older men found courage to speak strong and bold, 'I'm a dog too.'

And all the men in unison, shouted, '*Woof!*'

After all had laughed at their jest, at their stab at poor Jamie's pride, and the wound they left on poor Jamie's face, Finn countered the boy.

'Na a puppy ye are... so no so much yappin'. Leave the barking to the men.'

Tom butted in, smiling broadly, as an intervention to save the pride of a wounded boy, to blunt the bitterness of a sour friend, and the unfamiliar melancholy of a Scot. 'Are we salutin' or sermonisin'?'

'No, Tom, we're salutin',' replied Robert.

Robert raised his cup, and the other men did too. All offered the same salute.

'A strong heart, powerful resolve and unerrin' faith.'

Robert fought back the sadness that dwelt within him, and, newly roused by the stirring salute and his pride at being at the head of such fine friends, he felt another salute was in order. But he was impaired, courtesy of the beer, and he clumsily jumped up off his stool and raised his beaker to his men, spilling most of its contents. 'Spoken like soldiers. No, like true warriors.' Then Robert raised his beaker again, losing the last of his beer. 'Tae the best o' Border Horse. Best o' men in this sorry kingdom.'

Finn then clumsily brought the beaker to his mouth to

discover his vessel empty too. 'Who steals my beer?'

Finn launched the heavy pewter cup across the room, meaning to bounce it off the wall. Instead it made firm and painful contact with a head. And the head was amongst a group of heads, all-sitting around another table. The head was none too pleased, neither was the group of heads, already peeved with the words of Robert's loud salute. All stood up from the table, and turned to face Finn.

The inn fell silent.

The beer did not remove caution from Finn, or help an apology to his lips. Nor did it temper his action towards the angry drinkers—nursing one of their number, holding a head wounded by Finn's cup.

There were no kind Irish words or gentle apologies, only mock and jibe. 'Ah some boys jealous of my good looks. Some boys wantin' a lesson in fightin'… Foolish fellows.' Finn's words, his contemptuous smile, did nothing but irk the angry men. And his own befuddlement did nothing to help the odds against him. As he saw, in drink, double the adversary.

Finn stood ready, swaying, and he lifted a spoon from the table in lieu of his sword; left with all other weapons outside the inn—as was required under the rules of the house. He held out his foolish weapon to the angry men, losing none of his soldiery art, but much of his clear vision, as he strained eye to see the direction of his multiplying foe.

The hand on Finn's shoulder was not well received and Finn turned to face its owner, his spoon held at the ready to strike a foolish blow. But Finn saw Robert and he rested his spoon at the sight of a friend. But Robert landed a hard blow on Finn's jaw that sent him crashing to the floor, unconscious.

Tom looked on at the felled Irishman, raising his observation with Robert. 'I hope ye didn't hit him too hard.'

'Just hard enough—the drink did most of the work.'

'Aye, a good jug of beer is the best sleepin' draft,' agreed Tom.

A spokesman walked from his angry comrades, leaving them to tend to their injured ale-mate.

'Yer man will pay for the insult.'

'He meant nae harm,' answered Robert, sobering up and opening his arms to the spokesman in an act of contrition.

'But harm was done… Done tae the Laird… and the Laird will see yer friend lodged in the Tolbooth for his violence.'

'*Laird!*'

The word was heard throughout the inn in hushed tones and thought by many more, who wished to keep the quiet within the inn. Some recognised him. '*Laird James,*' some whispered. Others whispered other names.

Francis, hearing the whispers, looked away to put his head in his hands. Tom placed his hands on the two boys, catching Jamie displaying foolish intent—evidenced by his hand searching his belt for an absent sword and a missing knife.

'Come on friend,' pleaded Robert, looking at Finn on the floor. 'I've punished him fer ye.'

'Saved him from a bigger beatin', I suspect. But ye'll not save him from a hangin'.'

From behind the spokesman, the wounded lord stepped forth. 'Are ye soldiers with the *Faithful Congregation of Christ Jesus in Scotland*? Are ye? Or does yer fealty lie with the English, the French, or the Catholic. Fer the sake of yer lives, I hope it is the Lairds of the Congregation… Dae ye serve us?'

'My Laird, we do not,' replied Robert humbly, eyes lowered.

'Then what do ye dae here?'

'We have arrived from the sea, with intent tae travel tae calmer waters.'

The Laird looked at the men. Even without weapons they

were clearly soldier class. 'Ye're soldiers. And ye have a good look aboot ye. And good soldiers are always seekin' a fightin' war. But fightin' fer who?'

'Fer those that pay,' replied Robert.

'Then pay fer yer friend's poorly aim.' The Laird put his hand up to his head to feel the hurt and draw down some blood from it to show Robert. 'Or his good aim—depending how ye see it.'

'The charge; attempted murder wi' a cup does ye nae honour. But what would be the price if yer verdict be accidental and not mal-intent?'

'Hmm, lets see if I can give the hangman some respite… fer he has been busy of late.' The lord rubbed his hand over his face, his beard's growth—his mock contemplation transferring the blood from his hand to his cheek, reinforcing to all the injury against him. 'Fight fer our Protestant cause against Catholic Marie and her Frenchies. I could press ye into it, but a debt may be better incentive tae see ye fight harder, and stay the course… especially with yer friend kickin' his heels against a gaol wall. Let's put a bounty of say… a dozen French heads… nae, lets say twa dozen, tae see your friend released withoot charges being brought against him.'

Francis placed a hand on Robert, and placed his words in his ear, 'Remember what Captain Jack said… *retire far from trouble.*'

'*Wheest, Francis.* What Jack disnae ken, will nae disturb him from his rest.'

Robert turned his attention once more to the Laird. 'We will fight far better with oor boy on the floor at oor side. He makes pleasure oot of seperatin' heads from men… He'll make the count up himself, that's fer sure.'

'What's yer name, and his?' asked the lord.

'Mine is Robert Hardie, of Edinburgh. His; Finn McCuul, of Carlow. I'm formerly servin' George Gordon, the Earl o' Huntly, who can vouch fer my true word and honest character.'

'I am pleased tae know the Earl, he is a fellow Laird o' the Congregation, so his reference will see ye 'n' yer sleepin' friend in good stead.' The Laird rubbed his wounded head. 'Perhaps one more boy applied tae fighting would gi' greater profit in terms of dead Frenchies… Besides the gaols are already emptied of wicked lads, forced intae fightin', and filled wi' only foes pressed into dyin'… Ye'll have gud company in the fight; the worst of Edinburgh's scum and the best of Scotland's soldiers.' The Laird found a smile. 'My crown is hurtin' a little less…' and then he pointed to his own table. 'And I'm wantin' tae return tae my drink 'n' my friends.' The Laird beckoned one of his companions still seated at his table. 'Talk tae my man here. He will see ye placed well tae fight with yer friends… and yer boy on the floor.' The Laird smiled at the unconscious body of Finn, before throwing a wink at Robert. 'I will see yer Irishman has a gud supply of cups tae throw at the enemy. I suspect he'll do mair hurt tae the French than all oor musketeers put together.'

Chapter VI

The merchant's home was perfectly kept. A credit to a man who provided it, and to his wife, and of course to her servants, for its keeping. Many of the people in the City remarked on it. Visitors were grateful for its hospitality and comfort. Even the merchant's fellow traders envied him for his home, including the poorer people that walked the poorly streets past its doors; jealous of the finer goods delivered through its portals.

Much expense had been laid on the merchant's property. Expense hard earned by a man with a tireless devotion to his trade of buying and selling. Accumulating profit from importing those goods better conceived and better made than his native country could provide; fine goods and furnishings for households, including those with royal connection, or even royal pretension.

The merchant had covered the inside of his cold, stone walls in decorative wainscoting, removed from a house far nobler than his. His hard work had clothed it in fine tapestries—fine, but perhaps not quite fit for a palace. The floors were well swept and softened with rugs from Persia and the Low Countries. The ceilings and the beams painted with naive religious depictions to please a pious young wife, by an artist perhaps reimbursed in terms of quantity, rather than quality. His wife was given finer furniture than her neighbours to soften her nest; foreign furniture gilded, and in lighter coloured woods to brighten sunless rooms, darkened by low ceilings and the shadow of tall buildings that surrounded her home. Fresh and colourful blooms filled the vases in the spring and summer seasons, winter greenery and dried flowers in the colder months. Drinks were served in glass rather than base metals, food on silver rather than pewter and wood. In all, it was perfect—as perfect could be, in such an imperfect city.

The house was free from children, and was laid out over the first three floors, with another three storeys above set out as tenements. The merchant's shop occupied the frontage of the dwelling and all the upper floors were accessed externally by a turnpike stair.

With its size and meagre household, unusual in a choked city, it had ample room to house Jack without too much inconvenience to the family and its servants. A household that included the merchant, his wife and her aged father, who would spend his days by a fire that kept old bones comfortable, whilst his daughter occupied herself as mistress over his lodging.

'Don't sit so close to the fire, *Daddy*. With all the spirit in you, you'll catch ablaze.'

'Dinnae scold daughter. The spirit is all I have.'

'You make me sad, *Daddy*, when you use yer words so.'

'What has an auld man got, but his memories, coloured better by a dram or four?'

The old man stood up, feeling the stiffness in his joints. He shuffled the oak settle closer to the fire, and punched new life into an old cushion. It was his way. He would be contrary. He would nettle his child whenever he could. He thought he had no respect from her. She treated him like a child to be fed and scolded, never to be seen or heard.

The merchant's wife looked to her father, shook her head and bit her lip. The old man annoyed her. But she loved her father, although she never told him so in a house where she was no longer merely a girl to take comfort in a father's arms, but instead the mistress of the house, and her father an old man in her keeping. Too many of her declarations of affection had long since been met with an indifferent response from a bitter old man. Yes, she loved her father, and her care was constant, and her own sacrifices to maintain his care, continual.

The old man gave his daughter a look. He studied her response to his actions. Studied, because no stinging words came at him, so he could only judge the success of his action by the signs of anger on his pretty daughter's face. There was nothing but vex on her smile. The old man's eyes smiled too, but no smile ever issued on his lips. He was pleased with his action. He did as he was regarded—an irksome old fellow. But his nettling had its humour, and he added, 'Besides daughter, I make it my dedication tae be so full o' the spirit, that when the English burn Edinburgh, I'll go off like an incendiary, and take one or two of the arsonists wi' me.'

'You old fool. Drink any more and you will not see the sunrise, never mind the English marching into the streets.'

'Ah leave me alone and tend t' yer patient.'

'He'll be fine just left alone.'

'Aye, he'll find this a lonely hoose.'

'Stop your moaning, *Daddy*. If you are feeling neglected find yourself a puppy.'

The old man wanted to find a pithy response to his daughter's chide, but his humour took an absence from his wit, so he remained silent. Instead, he watched his daughter at her desk, sorting out yarns and threads from a wooden box—materials to apply to a linen cloth. He had watched her do this a dozen times lately, but still she was yet to start another needlework task. Her intention was clear, but her application found wanting. It was much like her life; a series of perfectly coloured threads that were present, but would never form a perfect picture.

The old man sighed at his daughter's sadness. He knew she was sad, even though she never shared her feelings with him. She had the pretence of a woman in her place, and he pondered whether her sadness was the want of children, or a husband that would provoke her heart to flame, instead of lukewarm regard. So he thought to break her sad thoughts.

'Child. This Brownfield? Is he kin o' yer husband tae be housed here?'

'No kin, and I'm annoyed that my husband puts up a stranger in my house. Worse still, a soldier, with a soldier's disregard for courtesy.'

'Ah well, with all the unrest in the City, and fear o' the French, it'll be safer tae have a man aboot the hoose—even an injured man.'

'We need no foul fighters under our roof to see us safe. Your son-in-law has provided well for our safety, *Daddy*. He contributes generously to the City's council. Eighty pounds. They tell him it's enough to see twenty men fight for a month.'

The old man thought of a petty soldier's wage, barely a shilling a month, so it was clear to him, even with the disbursements applied to waging war, the captains and the Council were making profit—there was always money to be made. 'Naive child. It'll take twenty times twenty… and twenty times more, tae kick the French oot o' Leith. They've already plundered oor City. They merely spar wi' oor sham warriors—shopkeepers' boys 'n' pressed men, who can only wag their dull blades, whilst the French swagger and display proper soldier skill tae their women, watchin' from their cosy walls.'

'Your son-in-law believes we will win this holy war.'

'I suspect lass, he tells ye only that ye find sweeter tae hear. I doubt there's profit fer him in this fight.'

'Your son-in-law…'

The old man interrupted his daughter. '*Son-in-law, son-in-law?* Whit's wrang daughter, can ye nae bear tae call him husband?'

'Hold… hold your spiteful auld tongue! My husband deserves better respect from ye.'

'And from ye too daughter.'

෨൦෨൦

Both time and meals were taken in Jack's room, which formed the third floor. It was a condition of the merchant, wishing to keep his *honoured* guest away from other visitors that would call and dine with him and his wife from time to time. Mostly his visitors were customers, best kept ignorant to the presence of a man unknown to the merchant—a stranger, whose occupancy would raise questions too difficult to answer honestly. The merchant was gifted, both in embellishment in order to sell, and feigned ignorance to his goods' dubious origins, but he was completely lacking with regards to outright deception.

But as Jack's health improved, and his room became a cell more than a hospital, the merchant's wife invited Jack to walk the house and take meals with her and her father. Her husband mislaid from the house for days at a time, as he troubled over his trade, badly affected by the unrest in the City and the blockade of Edinburgh's port at Leith, by English ships.

The merchant's larder was well stocked, and meals were of fine invention—tools of hospitality to impress upon the merchant's guests. Jack enjoyed the breakfasts; not a meal familiar to him, but he became accustomed to the sweet omelettes, herrings, finely made breads and watered wine. All were a taste of the morning to

103

welcome. Similarly, dinner served every day at least an hour before noon was varied and wholesome. Beef, veal, mutton, pork and pigeon, all well roasted, seasoned, and an embarrassment to a man who had lived lean many a month on field fare; rabbit, fish caught and stolen beef cooked rare; all on the run from its owners. But Jack welcomed the fat growing on his sore bones, and the respite from field rations and inn food of poor creation. Indeed, he had not eaten so well since he left his home some seven years ago, when he left his wife, whose command of her kitchen was as capable as the merchant's own cook.

Jack's first supper, shared with his hosts, was laid out in the large kitchen; one of two in a house that was once two houses back to back, made one by a man with ambitions to impress all with a large home to house a large family.

A servant presented Jack with a bowl in which to wash his hands before he sat at the table and he cleaned his hands thoroughly. He acknowledged the merchant's wife and her father and took his place.

'Will you give grace, Captain Brownfield?' asked the merchant's wife.

'Forgive me madam, for it is a long time since I offered a thanksgiving.'

'Then sir, you will be grateful of the practice.'

Jack smiled at the woman's wit, bowed his head and began:

'O Lord, thank ye for this table and its food.
Praise thee for this wonderous offering.
Foods and wine to do us good.
Thank thee for thy blessing.
May we praise thee all days to come.
And to thy love we succumb.'

Jack raised his head, to catch the head of merchant's wife still bowed and eyes closed in earnest thanksgiving—her own prayer made longer than the devotional offered by Jack. Within a minute more the merchant's wife raised her head.

'Thank you, Captain Brownfield. Where, may I ask, did you learn your thanksgiving verse?'

'My wife, madam.'

'You are married?'

'I am a widower. Although to give myself such a title dishonours those husbands who have lost a wife to grief, for I was an unworthy husband who left his wife long before I lost her.'

'How so… *unworthy*, Captain Brownfield?'

'I put myself before my husband's devotion.'

'Is that not the way of men? Is it not the women who devote themselves to their husbands, parents and their children, whilst the men devote themselves to themselves?'

'You have a poor regard for men, madam, to think of us so.'

'If my husband was devoted, he would not be absent at this table, and he would not have put a stranger to it in his stead.'

'I think your husband works hard to give you this table. My presence is a consequence of his hard work, and not by his choosing. But if my presence causes you discomfort, I will remove myself from it immediately.'

The merchant's wife dialogue irked Jack, and he thought to leave the table to prove his point, but the old man interjected to bring civility back to his supper.

'Lass ye needin' kinder words for yer husband's guests, and better words aboot yer husband afore them at his table.'

The merchant's wife bowed her eyes to affect recognition of her father's seniority, although she thought ill of his unwelcome chide.

Jack's temper too, was cooled by his words, and he was sorry that the lady was reprimanded so publicly. Jack thought on his host's kindness and resolved to be more understanding of a woman excluded from the facts of her husband's commitment to Henri Hueçon.

Jack nodded his acknowledgement of the old man, and turned to the merchant's wife. 'My apologies, madam. I am a stranger put at your table. But I wish to call myself friend of this household. I am grateful for your kind keeping, your hospitality and the warmth of your home. Your husband is a good man to offer me such wealth, and you are a fine woman to care for me so well in his name.'

The merchant's wife smiled. 'I am sorry to speak badly of my husband and apologise for my discourteous behaviour.'

'*Gud!*' The old man clapped together his hands. 'Now we're made up, we can eat afore supper goes completely cauld.' The old man lifted the lids on two large pots. 'What dae we have here? Ah capons in wine and salt sauce, and... breast of mutton... Fine and wondrous fare in a city surrounded by siege 'n' war, and another twenty thousand extra mouths tae feed... *Remarkable!*'

After an hour, Jack's consumption of the food was complete. Nothing that was put on his plate was left, except bones and gristle. It was not so on the plates of his hosts.

'I am pleased you find the food to your liking, Captain Brownfield.'

Jack looked to his own platter and at the merchant's wife's smaller plate, still with food. 'I am afraid you did not find it as palatable.'

'It was a fine supper. It is just...' Discomfort showed briefly on the merchant's wife's face, but it was only a moment to be thrown away and replaced with found disdain. '... in this house we do not clear our plates. The leftovers feed the servants better, and the remainders are distributed to the poor.'

Jack felt contrite and drained his cup, and so that the liquor may help ease his conscience more, he sought more wine, but the jug was empty. He looked to the ale jug, but it too was empty. All consumed by the old man, who had quietly succumbed to its sedation, and found himself sleeping upright in his chair.

'You are a good woman to care for the poor so.'

'It is God's desire, is it not?'

'It is how it is written,' replied Jack. '*The Good Text* sponsors charity.'

The merchant's wife seemed pleased with Jack's words, her eyes directing Jack to a small table behind him, where a Bible sat. 'You will see this is a protestant household. And what of you sir, how do you worship?'

'Poorly.'

'Do not soldiers and armies have priests aplenty?'

'On the field of war, yes. But I was born a Scot. Born in the Borders where church and priest are deficient. And although my later boyhood was with benefit of tutelage by both priest, and a man with a godly leaning, I am afraid I have a poor regard for faiths designed and directed by men.'

'I shall pray for your lost soul.'

'Better you pray for your countrymen. Those who fight to remove the French from Scottish soil.'

'My husband says the Scot are merely at arms because their masters are overlooked by a French Queen, favouring Frenchmen in positions of power within our government.'

'Then your husband is a discerning man.'

'I think he worries that he loses trade. The Queen's Court is a good customer.'

'Then your husband is a wise man. Business is best served if one overlooks petty differences regarding faith, foreignness or family.'

'I believe greed directs my husband, and so he has a deficient soul like yourself.'

'Then your husband is a fortunate man to have you to pray for his soul.'

Jack stood up from the table, and his ribs squealed pain. He looked on the old man still sleeping, and then at the merchant's wife, waiting for Jack to excuse himself from her table. They exchanged a look without words, and it was longer than was proper between a man and a married woman. But without witnesses to assure correctness, their action could be assigned by their feelings, and not by the protocols dictated by propriety.

Jack was caught by the look of her, and he became embarrassed by his thoughts. *She is pretty... She is more than pretty... Retreat John Brownfield, lest my improper thoughts taint my face an unworthy pennant to wave before a virtuous woman.*

'May I be excused from your table?'

'If you find my company dull, then you must find better company.'

Jack did not want to offend, again, the merchant's wife. So feeling the hurt in his ribs, he excused himself as politely as he could. 'It is only I have not eaten so well as I have at your table. So much good food has fatigued me. My ribs, head and arm hurt, and I think I need rest and sleep.'

'Then you must rest... *John.*'

Jack took himself to his room, to rest on his bed, so as to seek respite from the ache in his ribs. And as he thought on the pleasing face and form of the merchant's wife, and his ardour grew, he sought relief of a different sort.

Chapter VII

Days came and days passed slowly for Jack, nursing the discomfort of his hurt. The enervate inactivity of his body led to an unrested mind running thoughts better ignored—brooding. The nights were particularly uncomfortable, even with a bed more comfortable than he had known of late.

Some nights the pain in his ribs and his restless mind would dislodge him from his soft bed to sit in the box-seated oak armchair in his room; its hard embrace kinder on ribs better left undisturbed by a cuddlesome mattress. A solitary candle would illuminate his world while he sat and penned thoughts coloured by the lateness of the hour and the frustration of his confinement. The draft from dying winter winds, forcing its way through poorly fitted window shutters, would make the light bounce on the velum as he tried to control the neatness of his script. The dancing flame moving shadows around his room and in his mind.

His writing was lamentable, badly conceived, and poorly directed by his weariness, rather than the sharp recollection of a fertile mind. He tried not to disturb the household while he waited out the night. He was always quiet with careful movement. Yet still, at some point during the dark hours, a light would appear at the bottom of his door. It would rest awhile, as if its owner was contemplating the scene inside Jack's room in their head. Listening for sounds, Jack would watch the light, sitting silently, and he would snuff out his own light so it would not encourage the visitor to announce their concern regarding his nocturnal unrests.

My tutor once told me, there are things to question—the essence of the stars, the cause and effect of nature, the fundamentals of the sciences, and the word of men. He also told me there are things to accept and never to question—those horrors and the trials of life that cause us hurt; the unerring challenges of life that are designed to strengthen our faith before God.

He told me not to dwell on these things that cause us discomfort. Those thoughts and memories that make little sense in our understanding of the goodness of our Lord, because addiction to them will cause us a suffering greater than hurt to the body. Wounds to the body will heal, or will be the end of our body, if God wills it to be the end of our suffering on Earth. Wounds of the mind though, twist us into men unrecognisable; men who will find no joy in life, and will either seek to end it, or continue in suffering.

My tutor told me, the sword to wield against the evil of wounded thought—the unquiet mind; was to dwell only on proper action and good deed.

I am afraid I was a poor student, and so I experience melancholia. And at times the suffering in my mind is unbearable.

John Brownfield MDLX (1560)

Conscious of his disability and melancholia, Jack spent much of his days sitting alone at the window overlooking the wide busy street below. Because the merchant had extended the upper storeys of his home well into the main street, Jack had good view of the largest fortified entry into Edinburgh, *Netherbrow Port*, its arch and towers separating the city from the growing suburb of *Cannongate* beyond.

Poorer views altogether were the heads and limbs of criminals displayed above the port. But the merchant's wife claimed fewer criminal and more Catholic heads were finding their way aloft the spikes. Heads from sorry souls loyal to their Queen and their shared faith; those who dared challenge the Protestant Lords' control of the city, whilst the mere delinquent were allowed their heads, and instead pressed whole into battle-service against the French garrison ensconced in Leith.

So when Jack was not using the light of the window to illuminate his dour writings, he was watching the street, assigning lives and stories to the folk passing by; people, and people with their animals, either labouring up the bank, or carefully making their way down the slope with their burdens and goods. All stepping carefully on the slippery pavements, made treacherous by the dirt and detritus covering the stone and cobbled way.

For all the comparative richness of the merchant's house, the sight in the streets was a poor one, with little interest outside to feed Jack's mind searching for relief from its own disquiet. A poor mix of tradesmen and poorly costumed townsfolk, dirty and crude in their demeanour.

But over the days and weeks, through the wet and cold days of spring, the early morning sun and afternoon gloom, the mood outside changed. People stopped to talk in greater numbers and their discourse seemed to be animated by more than mere routine gossip and the woes of war on their doorstep.

One day, outside the merchant's house, a speaker in the street had gathered a good crowd.

'*Neighbours!* One can choose to say one or the other. One can choose to feel one or the other. But no one can deny them when they come. For love and hate are passions driven by the heart's desire—actions without adherence to sense or thought of consequence. Both are the war cries of Heaven... *or Hell*.'

The sounds from the street coming through the open half-glass window, pricked the attention of a wearisome Jack writing at his desk, and he pulled the shutter further open to hear better the street preacher's oration.

'Our lord, and the Devil are the same suit in different colours. Each cover our nakedness, each mark us out to our enemies and to our friends...'

The other sounds in the street, and the noises from within the house, conspired to deaden the clarity of the oration. So Jack put down his pen, and swung wide both the lower double wooden shutters. Sitting himself down on the window seat, with his flask of spirit and horn beaker in hand.

'*Thou shalt not kill!* God punishes you for your actions. Your weapons of war are deficient against your brothers... Yes neighbours... *Brothers!* For we are all descendant from Adam and from Eve. You build your weapons under Christ's banner. You sing war in His holy places... But Christ laments as you laud. Your weapons only make him bleed. Your cannon make him suffer. Mark my words, your weapons of war against your Christian brother will be deficient. Christ will steal them from you... He will take your cannon. He will blunt your steel. He will cut short your pike and your scaling ladder. He will hold up his hand to stop you.'

'*Catholic! French lover! Devil!*' came a woman's shout from the crowd, then agreement from some, and silence from others.

But the Orator countered the insult with kindness in his voice––pleading, 'No brother—sister. I'm no Catholic. I'm no heretic. I speak only as a peaceful Christian soul, wanting your soul saved by peace, not conflict or war… *or murder.*'

The crowd quieted. But parts of the crowd were not convinced by the Orator's plea. One tall man, put down his box pack, to stand on it for even greater height, to address the growing crowd himself. 'What dae we dae to protect oor city and families from the French? From the English, who pretend to be oor friends, and who now sit in oor waters and likely march on us, as this fool speaks his… *love 'n' peace.*'

The Orator replied the man, in a shout, '*Kill the enemy. Rape his women. Murder his children. Burn down his home and defile his Church.*'

The crowd looked puzzled by the Orator's words—words of pillage and rape. Then after a deliberate pause, the orator continued. 'Yes, but that horror which we heap on our enemy today, will visit us ten-fold and more tomorrow.'

'But we are strong. John Knox says God is wi' us against the papist… *and we will beat the enemy.*' shouted the tall man, followed by agreement and cheers from the crowd.

The Orator looked to the direction of the tall man—the heckler, to counter his support and growing accord. 'You say that, but it is because you are young. But age weakens even the strongest. Ask this of the Greeks, the Egyptians and the Ancient Romans.'

'*But they did not have oor God afore them carryin' their banner,*' shouted the tall man. Again the crowd cheered, louder and with greater accord.

'No—they had a hundred gods, and what good did it do

them? Believe me, the Holy Roman Empire may live in strength today, but it will grow weaker tomorrow. And yes… a new strength will replace it, with new banners to wave. But that strength in turn will suffer the same fate. *Do not let Knox lead you down another sorry path.*'

'Whit faith are ye?' came a dissenter's voice, loud and clear in the growing throng.

The Orator looked to his shoes. His eyes cast down. His head shaking in discord. His voice deliberately lower. 'I have faith in God, and not in man. Not in Knox.'

But the tall man countered, 'Knox is a gud man o' God. He leads oor Protestant Church tae righteous victory.'

Again the orator cast his eyes down. Then he lifted his hands slowly to the crowd, with eyes following, and his voice strong and measured, 'When you taste pork, it is a flavour to savour… it begs you to eat more pork. But if you try to consume the whole pig, it will sicken you until you can eat it no more…'

A voice shouted out, in interruption, 'Ye dinnae ken *Wee Jock McCallister* then?'

The crowd erupted in laughter.

The Orator smiled broadly and beckoned quiet from the crowd with his hands raised against the amusement. 'Yes brothers, sisters… there are hogs amongst us who eat whole pig and more… but please bear with me… When the rest of us taste pork, it is a flavour to savour; it begs you to eat more pork. But if you try to consume the whole pig, it will sicken you until you can eat it no more… But men who taste power, rarely spit it out and banish it from their diets. When men taste power, they wish to taste it everlasting… But it gnaws at their souls until it consumes them.' The Orator paused, sensing he had the crowd, quiet and compliant to his words. Then he started again, slowly, earnestly, rising in tempo and force. 'Knox is no man of God. He is a man of men, wanting them to bow to his notions… He was a Catholic once… He challenges and changes—to suit his own will, and his own hunger for lofty position… *Leave him to himself, and let history set him and the zealot on their own path to destruction—a path without your blood staining it.'*

There was accord and there was discord, in equal measures from the crowd. And the tall man, seeing the nodding heads, and discourse of assent with the Orator, spoke again, 'You speak badly peacemaker. Knox leads oor fight… he saves us from damnation.'

The Orator shook his head. 'He leads you to disaster. What will you do when you fill the trenches around Leith with your dead?'

'Dig new trenches!' replied a loud voice.

The speaker could not reply. Four men, not from the crowd, mounted his dais, roughly grabbing his gown. They laid a vicious fist or two on him—before they dragged the poor man from his stand and wrestled him to the floor. He tried to speak. Jack heard some words. But a fist, and two more to his face, quieted the Orator. Then, he was removed from the street. But there was general dissent in the crowd and a fight broke out between factions, and even the tall man was toppled from his stage.

Jack found the spectacle worth watching—men fighting men. But so much more diverting, were the women laying their fair fists soundly on the menfolk—men who would then retreat from a worse hurt and indignation. Jack smiled, and filled his cup to salute his quarrelsome entertainers.

Jack's attention was pulled away. His door opened. The old man appeared in his room.

'Lad, does the noise ootside yer window disturb ye?'

'Yes. There appears to be much unrest on the street.'

The old man walked over to the window to look at the fight still raging. 'Aye, the Scot has a wilful nature. He'll find conflict whar'ever he is.'

On the street, through the window, the old man recognised friend fighting friend, sister beating brother, and the tall man thumping hard a protestant layman. The old man took Jack's cup and poured himself drink. He looked at the half filled beaker, gauged its fill, and then drank direct from the flask instead, long and eagerly.

Breathless from the deep drink and the strong spirit's debility, he continued to speak, a little slower and more measured than before. 'Even wi' regards tae family… he serves them poorly. He has fickle care fer his religion, country 'n' king. He'll show up tae fight under their banners, but leave his heart by the home's fireside. He'll bawl Scotland, and fer the English coin, turn coat as easily as a woman's smile turns tae frown.' The old man sighed. 'He only has dedication tae himself… and tae his family of course… but only if it suits him. His purse comes first, and his progeny second.'

Jack drew a knowing smile on his face to accompany his reply. 'True. It's not the other man that's his enemy. It's himself.'

'Aye, reet enough. Mind ye, the Scot can fight, and be bonny aboot it.'

'He'll even fight himself, if there's no one around to fight.'

The old man laughed. His laugh leaving the residue of smile on his lips, which in turn grew into a broad grin that lightened Jack considerably.

The old man's cynical discourse and poor opinion of his fellow Scot suited Jack's mood; Jack being long plucked from any notion of maintaining nationalistic pride or allegiance to the Scottish flag. Jack, a man of the Scottish Marches, born of Border folk—clan before king, clan before nation, and clan before God—*if it suited*.

Jack smiled at the old man and took back his beaker, sweeping his hand across the flask, indicating to the old man that he should retain the flask for himself. The old man nodded his thanks and drank again, only a sip, for the flask was now his, and its contents for him alone. He held the flask and settled on a chair close to the fire, to feel its heat.

'Brownfield? I knew a Brownfield once. From Exeter he was. English bastard he was. Should o' cut his throat. Ye from down there?'

'No… And stay your knife, old man. Brownfield is not my name by birthright, but by way of a name given to me by the English in internment, and given to myself in the name of protest.'

'Ye a prisoner?'

'A hostage.'

'A hostage. Therefore gentleman born be thee. Yer words are better bred, but a Border tongue still forms them… but which Border name?'

'One who fought and lost against the English on the Solway Moss. One given by my father, who lost two sons that day.'

'Aye, I was there. Marchin' under Laird Somervell's banner. It was a sorry affair. The Laird himself was taken prisoner… But ye could not say he was hostage, because his keeper, Thomas Curwen o' Workington, was gud tae him. The English King, Henry, give him two hundred pounds fer his troubles, and set him back on a nag far better than the one he took tae battle… I think even the poor English soldiers that took him didn't get their ransom… Aye it was a sorry affair. Commitment was lackin' that day—on both sides.'

'That it was,' replied Jack.

'Pride is nae guarantee tae victory. It's not tae be mistook fer devotion tae a cause.' The old man took a long drink, and saluted, 'Tae absent friends.' Then another drink. 'The sight of English ships in the Forth brings bitter memories tae an auld mind. Foul remembrance even the spirit cannae quell… I fought at *Pinkie Cleugh*. Many thought I was too auld tae carry ma pike. But I held

Meg proud against the English horse. She even kissed an English captain full on the mouth. Poked well she did that day... but lost she was... in the bog... as I ran away. Foul times. The English cleaved many heads that day. Many limbs were lopped. Bodies lay in parts. So many parts of men... it was hard tae tell how many were slain.'

Jack felt a pang of hurt, recounting his first time in battle, him too caught in a bog and running away. He felt humbled in the presence of an old soldier. He felt sorrow for a man's soul cut and scarred. Not by war, but by defeat. Then Jack held a guilt that his own meagre service had been for pay, and not for a country's honour or faith's call. Jack recalled memories long past of a father's stories, of a man who fought and fought again at the call of his country's muster. A call only once Jack attended, and never again submitted.

'Yes, my daddy too talked of fearful sights of a battlefield left. My daddy fought at Flodden. He said he had never seen so many kin and kith carved like beasts on a butcher's table. Even the sight of the English cut and bloodied did his soul no joy. Even though it was thirty and more years ago, I suspect that butcher's table still runs red in his sleep.'

The old man closed his eyes and nodded deep in agreement, enhanced by the strong liquor. 'Aye, it was a sorry affair... but it was'ne all blood 'n' death.'

The old man's stare was distant, and Jack thought he had succumbed entirely to the spirit. Old eyes were glassy, his sitting infirm—swaying. Jack thought the old man might tumble from his chair and fall head first into the fire's grate. So Jack stood up to distract the old man's slumberous gaze, wincing as his ribs complained. But the old man's eyes re-focused and returned their stare to Jack.

A bony finger waved the air to conduct the old man's prose.

His eyes followed it as he directed boldly spoke words to Jack. 'War was a time fer men tae be wi' men. I remember oor own lads were bold and good company. But the food served us was'nae fit for heroes.' The old man drew his finger to his mouth, to indicate a secret to be kept. Head swaying more and eyes blinking. His words softer in hushed tones. 'So me and Will 'o' Weasel, that butcher's bastard I called a friend, sneaked in tae the English camp tae find a better meal.' The old man clamped a hand hard to his chest. 'We'd sewn on the English badge—bold tae oor suits.' Then he suddenly stood up, bolt upright, pointing firmly towards the fire. 'We marched reet intae the English camp, drunk their ale, and were handed a meal by their cooks.' The old man smiled, and the smile grew into a laugh, until another drink of spirit killed the laugh, and he continued, re-seated. 'It was a canny night, it was, and tae remember it we stole one of their banners tae take back tae sit beneath oor own.'

Jack thought to help the old man to his bed, for his outburst seem to fatigue him more, and spirit was fast taking him to sleep. But the old man's story continued.

'We fought under the *Blue Blanket*. A bonny pennon given tae us by the King, thirty years afore Flodden. Aye, we were proud o' that flag. We, who marched, fought and died for the guild of tradesmen 'o' this town... I remember it bore an inscription; *Fear God, and honour the King with a long life and prosperous reign and we shall ever pray tae be faithful fer the defence of his sacred Majesty's royal person till death...* Aye bonny words... often poorly applied and rarely realised.'

The old man's head sank into his chest, and Jack waited for it to return upright and his recollection to continue. Jack waited and waited, but it was clear the old man had succumbed to his drink. But a fearful notion took Jack, and he walked over to the old man to put a hand on him to ensure he was still with life.

He was.

Jack left his room and the old man hunched up in his chair, and found the merchant's wife on the gallery of the floor below, talking to a servant girl. He excused himself as he interrupted their discourse, and quietly informed the old man's daughter of the old man's condition. She beckoned the serving girl to fetch two male attendants from the shop below, to help remove her father, from Jack's room, to his own bed.

All was done like it had been done countless times before, without discretion.

'I am sorry for my father's condition.'

Jack smiled at the merchant's wife. 'Don't be. We've all sought spirit's blessed sleep before.'

She returned Jack's smile, thankful for his understanding. 'I think you are being kind sir. I see it in your eyes.'

'You are a kind lady. But don't be hard on your daddy. It is hard for men to see the sense in life—the good of it. Sometimes the drink helps them see that which they are fond of, and banish the hurt of life for a while.'

Chapter VIII

The following day the old man had a heavy head. He wished it away as it was a head too heavy to carry. His senses were impaired. The pain of it dulled even his nettlesome ways and made him quiet for the most of the day. But he made the mistake of nursing his ills in a poorly-picked chair—one in front of the kitchen fire. Warm it was, but a place of peaceful refuge it was not. It was a busy house. And as his day wore on, he ignored prudence whispering within his battered brain to better pick a dark lonely corner of an empty room—a place better for quiet and for his head.

'You disgrace this house, *ye drunken auld sot.*' His daughter's voice was loud and hard.

'*Wheesht* girl... have some charity.'

'*Charity! Charity! Whit charity d'ye offer me?*'

'I'll be a good lad if you leave me alone daughter. That's demons in ma heid, and they are makin' such a racket. Give me yer silken voice and nae yer screechin'.'

The merchant's wife took a long breath to quell the brute Scot within her. To calm her face, worn red like her hair. 'You'll be at Church the morrow... to give thanks, because a good protestant

English army has arrived at *Restalrig*, and now do battle with the French. Yes you old fool—you will be with me at Church… to give thanks.'

The old man did not show surprise at the news, for rumour of it had ran for days through the city.

'Why child? D'ya think the English Queen cares aboot yer faith? D'ya forget whit the English did tae my daddy at Flodden field? Tae Edinburgh? Tae yer own daddy sittin' here in front of ye—*sufferin'*? Why d'ya think we suffocate within these new city walls? Because, its the English ambition tae have us as a neutered dog at their border.'

'John Knox says Elizabeth, the new English Queen, is not like her father. He says she is a good and devoted Protestant. She sends troops to help our Protestant Lords remove the Catholic threat, the Catholic Queen. Elizabeth removes Scotland from the French hold, and saves it from being a mere Gallic province.'

'Naive ye are lass. She's still a child, governed by great men. Bastard born tae a woman separated from her heid, fer want of a boy bairn. Everything she does nae doubt is tae save her own heid.' The old man leaned forward and grasped a poker from its stand, brandishing it like a sword. Then to plunge it deep into the fire's embers, stirring them into fiery flame. It was if he was stabbing an enemy. 'And daughter... even if she is a queen wi' a free hand tae rule, like ye, she is her father's bairn, with all her sour father's nettle 'n' fettle.'

The merchant's wife shifted on her feet, rocking with agitation. 'You are wrong, *Daddy*. I'm no like you, and she is not that cruel English king.'

'Ah lass, lift yer head oot o' the clouds. Elizabeth aids us only because of her fealty tae her royal name and the *Tudor* taste fer power. She nae doubt fears France and all the Catholic princes will take it away. She has much tae lose. Much like ye daughter, if the

English decide tae turncoat and make, by force-of-arms, Scotland into a mere English burgh and rob yer bonny home, and tax yer husband merciless fer the pleasure of it.'

'Whit d'ye know? Ye spirit fuddled auld sot.'

'I have seen enough nae tae be trustin' 'n' thankin' any sovereign fer ma freedom.'

'Ye're a bitter auld bull. D'ye thank no one? D'ye think no one does right by ye?' His daughter's face wore red again, and her brute words returning, resounded around the kitchen sending servants, not already gone for sake of tact, scattering.

'Ye're a… a… *bitter auld bull!'*

'And ye're a sorry coo, without a bull tae mount ye. Just a foolish ox tae toil fer ye, and fill yer world wi' pretty things, so ye can fill yer mind wi' fanciful thoughts.'

ഇൗരു

That night, after supper, when servants were no longer at their masters' needs and about their own business, finding what comfort they could in a corner of their own, or on a bed shared, or in front of the kitchen fire's last embers… When the shop was shuttered two hours past its closing, on the eight of the clock… When the house was finally quiet… The merchant's wife knocked at Jack's door, and Jack invited her in.

'Forgive me intruding into your evening, and the lateness of the hour. But, I wish again to apologise for my father's behaviour. And thank you for not raising his misbehaviour at the supper table.'

Jack shook his head gently. 'There is no need to apologise. His bothersome manner belies his heart's thought. He is simply a good man wounded. He is hard for you to bear, because your love for

him is a heavy burden. Do not take his actions to heart, good lady.'
Jack swept his hand to present the lady with his chair.

The merchant's wife smiled at Jack and his well-meant words,
but refused his gesture given to her to sit.

'I will say it again. You are kind sir, but an earnest prayer would
do him just as well. He would do better to devote to God—to
accept life's pains as a lesson, and to praise God for it.'

Jack smiled, but it was to hide his indifference towards prayer,
and the lady's notion that suffering is a lesson to be thankful for.

'Prayer yes, but the drink helps dull the pain whilst God thinks
on removing it.'

The merchant's wife lost her smile and found a harsher tone to
her words. 'Prayer is the proper way—the path to Heaven. God's
divine path is not necessarily scented with roses. Drink is the fool's
tool to easier thought.'

'I accept those with faith are comforted by their beliefs in the
face of adversity. But those who have fought and saw kith and kin
butchered often need more tangible understanding of the horrors
of life. Drink may fool them, I know. But sometimes better is the
foolish answer that arrives in a flask of liquor. It can lift the spirit,
without the need for a hundred listless hours of prayer.'

'You have no faith, Captain Brownfield. You obviously do not
listen to your heart as you pray… *If you pray at all that is.* God always
fills the heart of those who pray earnestly. Good men pray. Good
men have conviction and do not scorn proper devotion. They
fight now on the fields around Leith for their faith.'

Jack looked away to hide his rising contempt, and to swallow
his scorn, but he turned back to parry the lady—*his pride dictated it.*

'My *good* lady. Men may fight for their faith. But those who
truly love God perhaps should not fight at all, lest they break his
commandment regarding murder.'

'I did not realise you were a dove, sir. I fear, in boredom, you listen too much to the ranting of the misguided preacher outside your window. Listen to the hawk instead—to John Knox. Our bible permits killing in time of war, or for punishment—to hold our laws safe, and rid our realm of the Devil's creed. I know you not to be Catholic, are you not a soldier even?'

'I am no dove. I do not shout peace. I am a soldier, yes. It is my craft. I fight for pay, as honest a reason for murder as I can get.'

'War is not murder.'

'War is man's excuse for murder. On the battlefield as you hold your opponent hard and stab him to death. Until his flesh is soft and his bones are broken. Until all his blood is spilled out on the ground. Then to see his kith and kin—his women and children lay killed, because he is not there to protect them; it does not ring justification to kill a man because he fights for reason of faith or fealty—only foul murder sings in my ears.' Jack's anger with the merchant's wife and her piety, was openly apparent. He drew in his bile and swallowed it hard. 'Now if you please, I will ask you to leave. I leave zealots to murder in the name of the Church, and it is not polite to argue with a kind host.'

'I will pray for your soul.'

'Save your prayers for the good. I am a man with poor virtues and a proclivity to sin.'

The merchant's wife flushed red her cheeks, and Jack wanted to blame the fire's blaze. But there again he thought, *perhaps his words were too harsh.*

The merchant's wife bowed her head. Jack frowned, disappointed that his retort caused embarrassment to his host. But he misread the flush on her cheeks and on the roundness of her bosom. He knew nothing of her secret smile, and her excitement for his words.

'Do you not believe in God... do you not have faith, John

Brownfield?'

'I do believe in God… it's just… at times… I wonder where He is.'

'He is with us—*always*.'

'Then, madam, He holds blind sentinel over His flock.'

'You hold a common view amongst men who carry pain in their soul. They do not give it up to God, so they suffer so.'

The merchant's wife appeared smug to Jack. Pious. And her words poked at a grief, a disconsolate Jack was holding; a seed of atrabilious discomfort to grow into blind, enraged thought.

Jack shook his head disdainfully and wore a cynical smile. He resented those who chose to offer glib answers to another's melancholia. And his resentment shaped the form of his reply.

'Words so easily said by those who have not endured pain. They so easily assign it away with a prayer.'

The merchant's wife took offence at her kindly offered words, and her offence was easily seen and heard. 'How dare you assume I have no pain, sir… *How dare you!*'

Jack just smiled in return, which turned the merchant's wife anger into hurt as she continued. 'I have suffered loss. A mother murdered in war. A good father's kind nature lost to me—now bitter and lost in his past youth.'

But her wounded words did not soften Jack's resentment, instead his scoff continued. 'Sounds like it is *you* that is bitter, and still carrying hurt… do you not offer it up… *in a prayer?*'

Jack's derision of her piety bit hard. She fumed. She clenched her teeth and spat her Scot's anger at Jack. '*Oh how it is. Oh how it is!* Fer those who revel in melancholia—who think their pain is deeper than another's. Who think someone's hurt o' the heart 'n' mind is any less or greater, because the cause is different by degree.' The merchant's wife's face grew redder, and she pulled and tore at the handkerchief in her hand. She chewed hidden words violently in her head, until she could not hold them any longer. 'I am married tae a man nearly three times my age— married by arrangement tae secure business fer a greedy brother, and a home fer a spiteful father. *My husband,* who is too auld tae secure his issue, disgusts me when he crawls all over me… tae apply his… *wedded love.*'

'And now we have the hurt, and the Scot that hides badly within; the principal distress that you carry, *my lady.* My heart bleeds for you... You who *rots* in this silken prison; who **eats** poorly and *labours* each day telling her servants what to do. My heart is sorry for you… and your only hard labour… lying on your back beneath an old man's wizened prick.'

'*Ye durty pig!*' snarled the merchant's wife.

She raised her hand to Jack, to slap him, but held it short of his cheek, as she checked her anger. Jack did not recoil, his eyes hard and fixed. Instead he grabbed her raised hand, and kissed the palm hard and full. She tried to remove her hand, but Jack held it firm until he had finished with it.

Free of Jack's grasp, she drew back her hand to lash at Jack again, but Jack moved forward quickly and forced his head close, delivering hot breath and spittle with his words.

'Save your strike madam for a worthy insult.' Then he took a lusty kiss from the merchant's wife, pressing hard his mouth onto her lips.

Her resistance was there, but so was her want.

෫෮෬

'*Do not release. Do not release… Please do not release in me…*'

Jack thought on it. But lust had well taken him. And as he thought on her and her entreaty, he justified his need, his want— his lust expunged in a moment of ardour, by turning it into a grand love. And for that moment and moments after, Jack had true intentions of devotion to the lady. But moments after that, when the pleasure in his bed grew cold, he did not ponder on the truth of it. He did not think of love, or even care if he had left more than mere memories of himself within the woman—lamentable seed to grow within the corpus of the good merchant's wife.

'I am ashamed.'

'Why?' asked Jack.

'Because I have thoughts best not belonging to a married woman.'

'Then throw your thoughts away.'

'I wish I could,' she sighed.

Jack understood the merchant's wife's coyness. She was a woman who had made up her mind to be unfaithful to her husband. Her presence in his bed declared it, along with words designed to draw out sympathy from him that may give her infidelity justification.

Jack held his eyes deep on the lady, until he caught her eye and fixed her stare. 'Thoughts you wish to keep and not declare. Thoughts… let me think… carnal thoughts?'

'Please sir, do not embarrass me.'

'It is I who am embarrassed. I wish you would say it plain. If you wish to let me know you would like to take me as a lover, and not merely as a casual tumble… just say so.'

'How dare you!'

'I dare woman, because it suits me to lie with you. I have not enjoyed woman's flesh for some considerable time. And you take my fancy.'

'How dare you!'

But no apology came from Jack. No contrition to appease a lady's honour.

The merchant's wife sat up sobbing, and swung her legs out of Jack's bed. 'I am wicked.'

Jack felt pity for the woman, and he pushed honesty aside, and wrapped his deceit in words of love. 'No, my lady… Not wicked. You are with me… and I am glad of it. I will leave your house if it suits your honour. I will stay in it if it suits your love.'

The merchant's wife turned to Jack, and smiled meekly. 'Then stay.'

Chapter IX

Antwerp, March 1560

Every day, whilst in his palace, Kalibrado walked the halls. He walked a circuit that he designed. He walked it twice a day for exercise; not only for his body, but also for his mind. He had a route—the same route every day. He counted the steps. He counted the stairs. He totalled the slabs in red marble that lay on the chequered floor. And, as he walked the circuit again, he replaced his count with the white marble slabs just as before.

He was assured of quiet on his walk, because the household servants and clerks would avoid his circuit—avoid the eye of Kalibrado and his unkind attention. His guards would stand by along his route and assure his safety on his walk—out of sight, but always in earshot of his particular staccato stride. But Kalibrado never usually walked in solitude. Usually Peppo, his loyal secretary and Risano, his bold captain, would be five or six paces behind for his directive and for his protection. He was not a man calmed by their absence; he was the opposite in fact.

And so today his pace was quickened, hastened by his own disquiet. His mind, usually ordered by the numbering of his steps and sights along his route, was wrestling with disorder and disquietude.

His mind questioned, *Peppo should have returned by now. What was the problem? One, two, three, four... red slabs five, black doors four.*

His mind took control of his body. His concern removing the steady pace he normally adopted and replacing it with an agitated gait. It was a foot-sound that concerned his guards. He found himself in corridors sooner than usual, catching servants who thought they had moments longer to linger, and guards who had failed to reach their position in time.

Three arches, four windows, ten pillars, nine sconces... thirty-two steps... Where is he?

In matters of the Guild, Kalibrado was always calm and assured. He had managed the Guild's affairs well over his years as Master. No problem had been so great as to unsettle Kalibrado, and as a result Guild resources had multiplied five-fold. But with matters concerning his own aspiration, he was less than measured, less than calm. He had applied himself carefully and perfectly to its construction. But as it progressed from a form in his mind to a form actual; as it emerged close enough for him to touch, smell and see it real, he became less restrained. His passion clouding those skills in which he had long possessed—patience and ultimate proficiency.

Kalibrado turned over the issue in his head, *Where is he?* He had not heard from Peppo since Galicia.

Where is he? No message. Delay... Dead... must be. Twenty steps more, then fresh air to free the mind. Where is he?

Peppo had hid well his departure and route to Scotland from all—from the Guild, even from his master.

Where is he?

At the end of his second circuit within the palace interior, Kalibrado reached the great stone canopied door leading to the courtyard garden, and the last part of his daily tour. Outside, on the landing, was a series of dog-leg stairs that led to clipped and ordered green of yew and box hedges—all set out in ordered perfection, with no comprise to the natural world. Man's discipline applied to nature; refinement given to God's unruly environment. All the order was confined within a perimeter of a red and white chequered stone flagged walkway.

This point of the walk was usually the highlight of his meditation. When any puzzle still without solution was resolved within ten laps of the large courtyard garden, protected and enclosed by the substantial red brick palace; its walls highlighted and enhanced by white stone and marble detailing, mirrored by the shapes and squares formed by the clipped green, sitting on the white gravelled earth.

On one side of the courtyard, where the palace was a storey shorter, there ran a long ivy-covered walkway, interspaced with dome topped gazebos, all in yew, all shaped and clipped. Even the ivy covering the walkway was ordered––testament to Kalibrado's wife, who directed her gardeners to tame even the most unruly of God's creations.

The day was lit by a sunless sky. No threat of rain. Not that a little wet bothered Kalibrado, especially when there was a conundrum clouding his mind. And, as he walked, he put his voice to his mind's words, uttering his thoughts for himself to hear in the hope he would tell himself the answer before his turn around the courtyard had been completed.

'Where is he?'

But Kalibrado had not noticed Henri Hueçon standing in one of the gazebos as he passed.

'Where is who, Guild Master?'

Kalibrado turned quickly to see the source interrupting his self-discourse.

Henri repeated, 'Where is who, Guild Master?'

Kalibrado was caught, but recovered to maintain his private thought. 'Your man of course, Hueçon... *Your man of course.*'

Kalibrado looked Henri up and down and thought he had again overdone his costume. Of course Henri thought different— his presentation inspired by the latest Italian style; a perfectly executed array of finely detailed green-silk jacket, overlaying a fine gold embroidered white silk shirt that had a strangely fashioned small stiff collar that elevated his head to its heights. To this he had perfectly matched green-silk breeches in the Venetian style, trimmed and highlighted with gold brocade. All overlaid with a stylish cut, short-sleeved coat in bright red leather, ending just short above the elbow. He wore his long hair tied up under a black velvet cap to give the appearance of cropped hair, which would be far more fashionable for Antwerp, if not other places. His hair concealed, perhaps to hide the realisation of age; where once luxuriant hair has thinned and removed its virility from parts of the scalp; an age that his vanity proclaimed as thirty-two; an age he had not seen in actuality for ten years plus three.

Kalibrado looked at the green hues in his garden, and then again at Henri, who blended perfectly with his surroundings, as if the painter of the scene had only a limited colour palette, but absolute skill in the execution of the landscape.

'Well, Hueçon, what brings the tailor's demonstration to my door?'

'I have news regarding the replacement for your sergeant.'

'I doubt whether he is fit to be called a replacement. Let us just call him, *a new sergeant-at-arms of the guard.*'

'As you wish, Guild Master,' replied an apparent biddable Henri, lowering his eyes in a show of respect, or disguised contempt.

'*As I wish. As I wish, Hueçon!* Kalibrado's temper flared at Henri's mollified words. 'If the state of the world was as I wish, I would not need a new sergeant and my walk would not have been interrupted.' Kalibrado counted five in his head, and calmed. 'Well-well, is your news for you alone?'

'Your *new sergeant-at-arms of the guard*, Brownfield, is in Scotland, wounded. Caught in a fight between an English privateer and a French merchant ship.'

Kalibrado looked to the walls surrounding the courtyard, seemingly scanning the windows. 'Seems your man is a poor choice, if he wounds so easily. A poorer choice still, since he does not know his east from his west. His commission is in Antwerp, not Scotland.'

'I am informed it was a hard fight. A one well-won by Brownfield and his men. I am told the French ship was well loaded with Frenchmen fit-for-fighting. The French ship was captured and taken as bounty to Scotland, where Brownfield…' Henri paused and smiled as he continued, '…*your new sergeant-at-arms of the guard* recovers his health.'

Kalibrado's mind pricked a thought, *French Ship and Scotland*, and he asked, 'Do you know of the ships and their destinations?'

'The English privateer; the ship carrying…' Henry paused again to emphasise his next words, to poke again at his Guild master, '…*your new sergeant-at-arms of the guard*, was the *Devotion*, bound for Antwerp. The French merchantmen; the *Saint-Clair* out of *Le Havre-de-Grâce*, bound for Leith.'

Kalibrado was a happy and unhappy man in the same body—happy to have a possible answer to his conundrum concerning Peppo, unhappy to have another problem to solve, and irked at Henri's badly hidden impertinence.

'Was the Saint-Clair with passengers?' asked Kalibrado.

'My report says, yes. It also says… *your new sergeant-at-arms of the guard*, deciphered a secret dispatch, sealed under a bull emblem, whilst under the duress of his injuries, and he…'

Kalibrado arrested Henri's report with a hand held against him. 'Yes, yes, Hueçon, I get your gist… Your man must have some wit, if not the wits to stay his sword whilst under my commission.'

Although Kalibrado was irked by Henri's answer, it proposed a theory to why Peppo had not returned from his commission in Scotland. He had possibly never reached it. The Saint-Clair may have been his ship, Le Havre his most probable port of departure. But many seals carried bull emblems. Kalibrado said and shared nothing. Instead he weighed out probability in his mind. Displaced fancied thought with good reasoning. Dismissed dubious connection with likely event.

Henri waited on Kalibrado, but Kalibrado maintained his silence as he mulled over a new conundrum. Instead he beckoned Henri to walk with him.

They had walked a full circuit of the garden, under the gaze of the palace's windows and a dozen pair of eyes that watched from the deep shadow of the rooms, before finally, to Henri's relief, Kalibrado spoke again.

'Hueçon, regarding your man, is he fit enough to return here?'

'His wounds are inconvenient only.'

'Then as soon as they cease to be an inconvenience to him, I want him here.'

'I will send the message.'

'Good… And Hueçon… Tell him to bring my secretary with him from Scotland… *if he is alive*. I suspect him to have been a passenger on the Saint-Clair. And if he does bring him back alive, although I suspect him dead… I will make him captain of my guard, and place all his men on sergeant's pay.'

'Peppo… in Scotland?' questioned Henri, surprised to hear of the secretary's location. But Henri immediately regretted his response. Because whatever Peppo's mission was, it was one for Kalibrado, and not for the Guild. He knew not to ask further. Any questioning would raise Kalibrado's hackles. So he feigned a cough, and when his throat was clear of enquiry, he continued, 'I will send a message directly.'

Henri turned and walked away without being dismissed, because he knew he could not hide the questions on his face, or the other questions in his mind from his voice.

But he knew his feint was poorly delivered, because Kalibrado's voice called him back.

'Oh, Henri. It is a gross coincidence to find your man on a ship intercepting a ship perhaps carrying my secretary to Scotland. *Do you not agree?*'

'That it is a gross coincidence, *yes*.'

As Hueçon left the garden, past three tied hounds and a chained monkey urinating on the steps leading to the palace entrance, he was unsure what these new intelligences meant. But as he studied the cleanliness of his hands, and straightened his rings on his fingers, he considered Kalibrado and Kalibrado's secrets. And then he talked low and measured to his fingers, as if they were his men waiting on his instructions. 'I think our master Kalibrado holds more and more concerns not of the Black Guild.' He then smiled at his fingers, waggling them gleefully. 'I think your decoration is looking tired. I think I will seek out the *House of Cellini* to furnish you with new rings to wear.'

Kalibrado returned to his circuit of the garden, re-counting the circuits he had already completed to ensure he completed his ten laps.

On his eighth circuit, as he passed the shadow of one of the gazebos, another voice interrupted him once again.

'The garden is at its best at this time of year, before gaudy colour mars its simplicity.'

Kalibrado halted; irritated to have his count interrupted once

137

more, and his daily walk disturbed a second time. His voice was underlined by a growl, which kept its volume low. 'I am beginning to think the garden would be better without the gazebos. Too many crows nest in them. Their chattering spoils the garden's quiet and the peace of its promenade.'

'My regrets if I disturb you.'

Kalibrado stayed his position, not turning to acknowledge the voice, in case he reveal its owner, skulking in the shadows.

'*Furet*, I doubt you possess the ability to regret.' Kalibrado raised his eyes to the windows around him, to the walls, roof, anywhere and everywhere except to the gazebo. But all the while he concentrated his thought on the direction of the voice, and his contemplation of its owner. 'I take it you wish to make your report, otherwise why would you disturb me? But I must tell you, it irks me that you do not make appointment, but instead choose to ambush me.'

'I prefer not to have an open association with you and the Guild.'

'I assume you have been here for some time, whilst Hueçon paraded himself for his own pleasure… So what is your view?'

'Hueçon seeks to magnify his own sense of glory. I suspect he would see you unseated as the Guild Master. He seeks out your true devotion and he knows your allegiance to the Guild is to be questioned. His man, Brownfield, will certainly be a poor choice to assure your safety.'

'I do not need you to tell me that. Hueçon has glorified himself since he was old enough to wash away the sin of his birth. He wishes me misfortune. My problem is, he is well respected. He ingratiates himself very well with the Guild Council and wins their favour. I would sleep better without him, but my position would be further endangered if I was *even* slightly suspected of his death.'

'Do you wish me to design a fitting death for him? An artful one, free from suspicion?'

'Perhaps. If it could be done, you would be the best tool. But for now I will keep him close, so I know which of the Guild Council I can truly count as friend or foe.'

Furet remained in the gazebo away from prying eyes, and Kalibrado, uncomfortable to be seen standing in open discourse with himself, joined him there.

Furet stood grey; a man without any feature that would mark him different in a crowd. His anonymity was his disguise, and he held as many names as a crowd. He was relaxed and easy in his hide, even in front of a bigger monster than he. And Furet was indeed a monster—a monster without evil feature, or corrupt form. He could stand next to the man in the street without giving alarm, or causing fear, and take his life away in less than a breath. Assassination was more than his skill, it was his vocation, and the Guild Master carefully employed him only on matters of stealth and necessity.

'Do we have the priest for the Guild?' asked Kalibrado.

'Yes you have him,' replied Furet.

Furet reached into his jacket and pulled from it a paper, which he unfolded and passed to Kalibrado.

Kalibrado saw it was a public notice, and he started to read it aloud, '*Cum gratia et privilegio Imperiali ~ der allmächtige und unbesiegbare Ferdinand der Erste, und das heilige Römische Reich…*' But Kalibrado grew conscious of prying ears, as well as eyes about unseen, so he continued to read on in his head.

…Ferdinand the First, and the Holy Roman Empire, has upheld and enacted the punishment this day by the City of Ausburg, on the body of Katherine Lachner, who was found most guilty of a murderous act upon her baby. The courts, observing her own penance for her sinful act, demonstrated by her cutting out her own tongue, do agree to benefit the peoples of Ausburg, by her body being given over the Society of Physicians for dissection. Her remains to be

taken after, to be sacked and hung in the Perlach market for all to know her heinous crime... Kalibrado did not finish the notice—he turned his eyes to Furet instead.

'So what of this. What is this to do with our priest, *Father Freke?*'

'The girl was his delinquency, his mistress. The baby, his bastard. I made myself available, *as a good friend,* to help him solve two problems—to rid him of two embarrassments that would see his ambition bruised. I offered myself as an intermediary to end his affair. He thinks his rejection drove the girl to madness and murder her own baby, and then cut out her own tongue and thrust her hands deep into fire as penance. But she needed a little help on all counts.'

Kalibrado smiled. 'The hand of God perhaps to kill her shame?'

'No, the hand of Furet and his sharp blade.' Furet's eyes shone. 'The priest is consumed with guilt... I have worked hard and long to ensure his mind is twisted by the foul outcome. His illustrious connections will disown him if his involvement is known. The girl well liked. Well connected. Freke knows *his secret* is safe with me.' Furet smiled.

Kalibrado's face was illuminated too, by the thought of a task well executed. It mattered not the odious nature of its threads. And as he thought on, it glowed brighter with further thoughts of gain for the Guild, via a coerced priest with intimate access to politician, spy and prince.

When Kalibrado's satisfaction of a commission well carried out was complete, and his expression of delight stilled, he said, 'Of course Freke will honour his debt to you for hiding his shame... a debt we, the Guild, will grow as we twist him to our way.'

Furet nodded in understanding.

Kalibrado studied the ivy carefully, tracing the path of each sprig in turn, and he asked, 'The girl, was she pretty?'

Furet replied, 'Katherine Lachner, called in fondness, *Kate*, was a beauty from a wealthy family, much sought-after for marriage. Many would be her suitor, but alas her heart was, in secret, with Freke. It was her father's generous, but foolish heart that failed to dictate her marriage in good prudence, and instead let her seek her own heart's desire. He is now half a man without his... *Kate*.

The poor girl could not speak or even write her pleas of innocence. She was even dumb to questions that might see her saved. The authorities thought her mad, they did not know that I, Furet, had pricked deep inside her ears with hot needles to see her deaf. Her father offered much to the authorities and the courts to save his daughter from the hangman. I had to pay much more to ensure she dangled.'

'Is this your way of telling me to expect your expenses to be extravagant?' said Kalibrado, pulling away a rogue shoot of ivy trying to escape from his wife's perfectly pruned display.

'My purse was well lightened by the affair, and my lady *Angeline*, expects only the very finest of everything.'

Kalibrado thought on *Angeline Schräll*, Furet's courtesan and his chief expense. 'She expects everything of everything. She is one who will not rest until she has all.'

In the distance the sound of children laughing was clear. Furet needed no instruction to melt away. He was gone in moment, and even Kalibrado, with his intimacy of the garden layout, was lost to know how he disappeared.

Kalibrado's reception of his children was as warm as any good father's embrace. Each child in turn received Kalibrado's smile and his kisses. Only kind words for his children had he. Beatrix was four years old, Hans was six.

'Can I play with the dogs and the monkey, *Papa*?' asked Hans.

'One does not play with animals, one teases them. They permit this for reward. But without reward the animal will resent you. Have you a reward, Hans, a bone perhaps for the hounds, or a piece of fruit for Henri?'

'No, *Papa*.'

'Then leave them well be, especially the monkey.'

'Why the monkey, *Papa*? He is only a little monkey. My teacher tells me of giant monkeys that live in Asia. They sound frightening, but Henri is only small.'

'Animals are just like people, my little Hans. The more stature they possess, the more strength they can display. This will be enough to instil fear, and that, with loud vocal warning, will be defence enough. However, the little animal, without these attributes of strength, must attack without warning to kill its opponent. This is its only defence. Therefore never trust a small animal, or a small dog, for it will give no warning of its attack. You will never know if it feels threatened… and its bite, although small, can still bring great harm.'

'I think I see, *Papa.*'

'Good, now run along to your music lesson, it must be time.'

Beatrix ran on with joy in her skip, but little Hans stayed his ground, and looked on to the dogs tethered about the balusters leading to the entrance steps of the palace. He looked at the monkey, higher on the steps, looking down on the dogs as if they were its subjects. He knew not to play with them, but this still did not quench his interest in the beasts, the monkey most of all.

'*Papa*… why is the monkey called Henri… and the dogs have no names?'

'The dogs have no names, because they are mere servants who's only worth is to support me in my hunting pleasure or, as guards. The monkey, however, is a fool to entertain my guests as they arrive at our home. And you must always call a fool by his name, and what better name for a fool than Henri?'

'Oh I see, *Papa*.'

Kalibrado smiled at his son, and, as he waved him off, he asked, 'Hans, what would you do with a dog that bit you?'

'Beat it, *Papa*.'

'And what would you do if he bit you a second time?'

'Short chain him, *Papa*.'

'And a third time?'

'Drown him, *Papa*.'

'A wise child you are.'

Chapter X
Siege Works, Leith, April 1560

'T'was a bonny fight today.'

Finn was exuberant, and he strutted the trench to display it. He held his sword aloft, and his eyes examined the blade as it caught the sun. He smiled as it winked at him. He smiled at its bruises, and at the bloodstains upon it.

'Aye, that it was,' replied Robert, seated, spitting his agreement full on the earth, whilst his head shook disapprovingly at Finn's display.

Francis sat on the firing step, drawing a whetstone slowly over his blade, and he muttered to Robert, 'Finn's reputation grows… The cock knows it. That's why he struts.' Then he shouted down the trench in Finn's direction, to abet Finn's braggart display and nurture Robert's disfavour with it. 'How many French today Finn?'

'Not enough to see me happy, Francis. Those Frenchies fight hard to keep livin'. I suspect they like to stay alive to enjoy the fightin'. They're men after my own Irish heart. Men worth the killin'. Men worth the sweat on my beautiful brow.'

Francis feigned a smile, and replied, 'I heard the French shout a name at you. A name with a bounty on it no doubt.' Then he turned to his comrades sitting about, to Robert and Tom, with Jamie and Tip close by, announcing, 'The French call him *Loup Rouge—Red Wolf.*'

Jamie, hearing his uncle's new epithet, stood up excited and moved to the middle of the men—to have a better view of his uncle, now strutting out of ear-shot. 'Is it because he his fearless and savage?' he asked proudly.

'Nah,' replied Tom, 'It's because he bites when he's shaggin'.'

Robert laughed, and Francis' smile was real on his face. Better for seeing Jamie's proud face blunted by Tom's wit.

Tom found a barrel to sit upon, and he stretched limb and neck, to ease the discomfort of muscles well tasked. 'I have bruises that never heal. New bruises on old. My skin is black 'n' blue all over. My jack's cut bad. My blade well blunted. My pistol failed me… *again*. And I've lost ma dagger… stuck in a Frenchy's eye.'

'You are getting too old for the fight,' said Francis.

Tom looked to the insult, badly made, and dismissed it with a frown. He was forty-five and still resilient. 'We've been fightin' badly, and runnin' away wi' the Scots for the best part of two months. Now, wi' the English here, we'll be sittin' in the ground on our arses for a dozen months more. I don't know what is worse.'

Jamie looked at Tom's tired face and thought to offer some comfort, to help him locate his lost Cumbrian charm. 'Well at least the French will no longer have it all their own way, with us well entrenched around the town, and English cannon aplenty. We'll soon be in the midst of them, cuttin' 'n' killin'.'

Finn, who had returned to the men, heard his nephew's boasted words. He looked at Jamie, and thought no longer on his own fight that morning, but remembrance of his nephew's reckless action during the fray. The cock and swagger of his gait changed to a march, as he strode up hard to Jamie, scowling.

'The French will be havin' their own way with you my lad, if you don't stay yer distance in the fight. These Frenchies will shag women, beasties and boys. It matters not to them where they dip their wick. Do as you're told in future lad… or I'll be asking Captain Jack to write a letter to your daddy, in my name, to tell him that you're only good enough to work the plough and nothin' else. You're still a poor squit of a soldier Jamie McCuul, remember that.'

Tom interjected, to save the discomfited Jamie from further scold. 'Finn, I hear the Frenchies cleaned all the whores out of *Cannongate* to fill their lodgings in Leith.'

'Aye, I suspect Marie of Guise makes a bonny bawd,' replied Finn, losing eye contact with Jamie.

'It's a sorry affair. I've a day's wages and not a tupenny whore to spend it on,' added Francis grimly.

'Save yer money, and keep yer pleasure from the pox. It's nae called the French disease for naught,' said Robert, 'Besides Marie's moved tae Edinburgh Castle. Seems she's mair scared o' the English than the Scot.'

Tom turned to Tip, who was chewing on a piece of stale bread. Tom was keen to include the lad in the men's discourse. Too often Tip remained quiet and outside the men's fellowship. Tom always had a kind thought for diffident boys, and their difficulty mixing within the company of hard men—if not a heart's held pain for his own absent children.

'Tak ma boots off lad… and tak ma sword to be sharpened. Find the camp gunsmith and have ma bonny wheel-lock pistol repaired… I'm afraid it's too delicate for this hard campaign.'

Tip nodded as he tore and tugged at the bread, but he remained seated.

Robert grew agitated by Tip's tardy response to Tom's request, and shouted, 'Come on lad, put a fire under ye. I'm thinkin' a keen blade and a true pistol is goin' tae be Tom's best friend on this sorry field. Yer own greedy belly can wait.'

Robert shook his head, stood up, and walked the boardwalk that lined the lee-side of the earthwork, until he left the trench all together. He walked away from the siegeworks to find a pleasant repost, with good green grass rather than viscid earth, and a tree to shelter only from sea winds, and not from French shot.

Robert liked his own company. But he was a man amongst men, often at the centre of other men's lives, so solitude was a rare thing, but a treasure he much desired.

He who has responsibility over men, is rarely alone, but forever lonely.

And so it was with Robert, forever responsible for his comrades, second to Jack Brownfield, but forever the man to direct the men in action—the man to receive their questions and gripes. And the men of his charge never let Robert forget he was once their troop leader, long before Jack ever was.

Robert counted himself fortunate to have good men by his side and Jack, a friend, at his fore. But for all that, to be alone was a pleasure he loved, and one he planned to devote his winter years. That is if he ever survived his autumn years, to a time when his sword grew too heavy for his arm, or when his eyes were no longer able to tell enemy from friend, and he could retire with his pride whole and his duty done.

So when solitude came, he sat in its quiet pleasure, drawing in its air and breathing out his inquietude. He could think and ponder without his thoughts being questioned, and he could sigh openly without fear that his sadness became shared. War was a hard world, and one's own miseries were always best kept hidden, because a misery shared with a neighbour, simply drew out that neighbour's misery, and misery begets misery until morale is diminished and the war is lost.

Robert found himself comfortable for once, seated on the ground. He was pleased he had found a sheltered spot against the trunk of an oak tree. It gave him good vantage over the camp, whilst being protected from friendly eyes, and unfriendly fire.

The day was clear, and whereas the sun was hidden, the light was good and the weather still, peaceful and kinder than days past. Yes, he thought he would like to stay there a while, and a while longer than that—longer than his duties as a soldier allowed.

Robert Hardie had always been a soldier, like his father before him. Except his father was mutilated at Flodden Field, less than fifty years prior. They said at the time, God's hand must have been upon him, because his wounds and losses were so grave that his death was assured. Yet, against all the understanding of fatal wounding, he survived. But the half of him that survived was a poor share; any good in him cut away by the English broadsword. What was left could not work to make an honest purse, so he took the beggars' badge and worked the streets of Edinburgh. Beggary was a poor income, especially when its profits were turned into ale and spirit to feed a crippled mind.

Eventually, from within a house ruined by a bankrupt soul, cruelty and dearth, Robert's mother abandoned her husband, while Robert was still attached to his mother's breast, to ensure her own meagre hard earned income was directed to feed a son and his two older sisters.

Devotion to her children however, was skewed towards the girls, and his mother despised Robert. He was a living reminder. A boy begat by a butchered soul, cruel and terrible in his wretchedness, and a wife too terrified to refuse coitus from a husband once loved. So neglect was his childhood's mantle, and

Robert left as soon as he had age enough to satisfy recruitment as a soldier. At first he entered into service with George Gordon, the fourth Earl of Huntly, securing his appointment by applying long established family connections with the Gordons and his father's service and sacrifice under the command of the Earl's grandfather at Flodden Field. But pay from this Scottish Lord was unreliable and forever deficient, by way of application of spurious fines and fees. So he sought service into the only standing army in the South-West, travelling to Carlisle, and despite his nation, into English service he went for better pay, and to fight his brother Scot more times than not.

Robert's vantage from his tree was good, and there was a great deal of activity to be seen amongst the camp. Life was busy. Camp life was busy, always busy. War was hard work. For every thousand men to be fed, armed, camped and maintained throughout the ardour of war and siege, there was another world of work for another thousand souls. Work bore heavily by the women folk, boys and deficient men too old to fight, but never too old to labour to their deaths for the sake of the glorification of younger warriors and embittered princes.

Robert thought fighting was the easy part, *a canny game o' ball, with a better prize fer victory and harsher wounds fer the vanquished.* And he thought he would not exchange his game of war for a life of weary work. Even if it meant a comfier bed, and an older age better assured.

Robert looked beyond the men and soldiers labouring on the siege embankments and the soldiers grouped around, resting, gaming and debating. He studied the women tending the men, walking the trenches and embankments, with their baskets and pails.

Suddenly without warning, further down the line, the English guns opened up and the French guns returned their shout. Their terrible sound, carried on a light wind, rang loud in Robert's position, to make them sound close and threatening. Some women scattered. They ran to take cover. And as Robert looked before him, he drew a puzzle into his head, a conundrum of sorts— –the science of a person's psyche.

It was easily apparent that men maintained courage, often bolstered by pride—a base manly need to be admired and accepted amongst their fellow man; to show strength, and to maintain a strong desire to hide their own fear. Whereas women in the field of battle tending to the men, displayed their fear openly, but still maintained courage by their actions.

He recalled the orgy of the fight in the morning, as man laid relentless weapon on man, steel on bone and blade through flesh. He remembered two women who, without thought of self-preservation, ran onto the field of battle to help the wounded. Those same women now cringed and bolted at the sound of cannon fire, and now cowered below in the trench for fear of hurt.

He wondered who were the brave. Men, who held their fear inside and acted bravely to take life when it was required of them, or the women who were fearful, yet who displayed such bravery to save life when it was not required of them.

Robert thought on it awhile, as the French guns pierced the quiet enjoyment of his rest—an inconvenience to his ears. But his stomach complained to his head to stop it thinking. So he took his brooch that held his mantle, and used the pin to pierce two holes in each of two eggs, produced from his bag. He took each egg in turn, and made one hole larger and sucked out the contents. But his stomach still complained to his head. And he reasoned that his thoughts would be better applied to finding better food—meat. He stood up and walked calmly towards the camp, through the sounds of the guns to find Francis and Tom—his boys, who always seemed to have a full larder in their packs; obtained through petty larceny, or in Tom's case, his well applied Cumbrian charm on the ladies of the cook house.

❧❧

For the all the days that skirmish broke out between attacker and defender, there was many a day more with little to do—even with the siege works surrounding Leith continually extending and improving.

For some, siege was either endless toil or endless waiting. And even when the construction of new earthworks took precedence over all, some captains still could not be bothered to assign tasks to keep idle Englishmen and their mercenaries busy.

The work was never issued fairly, and even though the English pioneer outnumbered the Scot three to one, it was the Scot who found himself more with pick and spade, and earth to move. Materials too, were commandeered and robbed from the Scottish peoples about. Their trade brought to a standstill. Fields, the daily battleground, left untilled. The farmer's horse commandeered for troopers, or yoked to the labour of siege.

Hard times were everywhere. Even Captain Small's French prize-ship was stripped of timber to line the trenches and the mine-workings that struck forward to Leith. His prisoners, the French sailors, were put to the task of dismantling their galley; their own captive oarsmen, who unwisely thought themselves free, remained in the bonds of hard labour for purposes of digging.

The English commander did all to save his army's purse. He drew many a note of restitution, never to be repaid.

❧❧

In siege, for some soldiers, action is respite from inactivity. But for Francis there was never respite in his querulous spirit. He was, as he always was, entrenched in his own bitter nature—vinegar to Tom's honey.

Francis could not sit, and he walked up and down their appointed place in the trench, between two siege built fort-emplacements, *Pelham's* and *Somerset's* mounts. He walked back and forward along the line of their position until he stopped short of Finn, sleeping, his steel bonnet over his eyes, his body propped against a wall of timber.

'This is no way to fight a war,' was Francis' protest.

Tom moved his head from his sentinel watch to look at a dour Francis. 'Never mind it Francis, this is easy fightin'. Sittin' on yer arse.'

Francis closed in on Tom to prick his ear with misdeed. 'Tom why don't we gather Jack and get ourselves out of the mud, and into the green of the Borders?'

Tom smiled at Francis, and shook his head. 'I dinna think Rab would be too fond o' yer plan. Desertin' is not his way.'

'Ach, Robert's a fool, with a fool's adherence to principles that will see him killed afore he's forty.' Francis climbed the firing step to peer out over the earth and timber rampart. 'They'll not miss six… let's go… tonight.'

'Get it out of yer mind, Francis. Robert gave his word to the Laird in exchange for Finn's freedom.'

Finn, who all thought slept, spoke, pushing his steel burgonet up from his eyes so it sat back high on his head. All his face wore a smile. 'Ah Francis, my bitter boy. At least there'll be one amongst us with a life o' good years to recall. Years where he devoted himself to his honour, and did not compromise his principles for an easy path. Ye should know better than to plot such dishonour wi' Robert at our fore.'

152

Francis did not welcome Finn's observation, and he whipped his words back at Finn. 'Hold yer tongue, *mad Irish*. We wouldn't be sitting in this muck, if ye could hold your beer.'

'*Mad I may be, sad I am not. Bitter be thee, better be me,*' sang Finn.

Finn's deranged ditty did little to sweeten Francis. 'Be you, mad Irish? I'd rather be gelded with a hot iron than wear your foolish face.'

'Ah me boy, Francis. Keep yer balls, and admit ye love yer Irishman, don't ya?'

Francis kicked Finn's boot hard, and Finn repositioned his steel bonnet over his eyes. His smile broader than before. No kind words or embraces from Francis would he receive, but his friendship he had. His smile knew it, and Francis, though he would never admit it, knew it too.

Tom returned to his watch. From his elevated position in the trench, he looked to the walls of Leith; to any activity that may indicate the French garrison was preparing to sally out against them, or repositioning of troops and guns to indicate a shift in their defences. But nothing was of interest, and Tom's gaze fell away from Leith to his own lines and a young green soldier standing different from the Scottish volunteers forming the musket line. Different, because he was better attired in bright new armour amongst the poorly dressed and equipped Scottish musketeers. Tom looked on at the Scots, with barely a lighted match amongst them to apply to their muskets. He chastised their unpreparedness in his head.

Robert appeared at his shoulder, offering words to accompany Tom's observation. 'Aye their guns are na better than sticks, without a lighted match cord tae set them firin'.'

Tom threw Robert a glance and responded, 'Aye no wonder the French are havin' an easy time comin' and goin' out of Leith.

Wi' nowt but butchers' boys, labourers and ne'er-do-wells, wi' sticks pretendin' to be guns, and shiny Scottish gentlemen at their front commanding nowt, but offering a tasty target for French marksmen.'

'Then it is well the English army are here, tae supplement this sorry siege wi' seasoned soldiers.'

⁂

The morning of the sixth day of May was strangely lit, and stranger still it was quiet, after days of cannon fire aimed at the western walls of Leith, after a dozen skirmishes with the French to test their defences.

The sky was alive with the colour grey—greys of different hues; held into great dense billowy clouds—rain clouds. The clouds held back over Leith, and Robert was wetted by light rain, whilst the bright morning sun, raised behind him, projected a rainbow that connected the ramparts around the town to his own army's trench work that fronted it. The sight of the rainbow lifted Robert's heart. He took in its sight, its colour and its remarkable form—the perfection of nature. But in his own isolation of thought and consideration, he did not notice Jamie standing to his side. And in turn, Jamie did not see past Robert's examination of the rainbow and into his quiet mediation. And so Jamie, instead of holding his tongue, rudely interrupted Robert's quiet pleasure.

'Rab, it's God's bridge… He points our way to breach the town,' Jamie raced his words, his excitement misplaced in Robert's world.

Robert turned to look upon the unwelcome intrusion into his thoughts. Towards the boy, who had removed from him a sight more welcome than the usual drab and grey that coloured every morning badly. So Robert closed his eyes to fix the remembrance of the rainbow in his head, lest it be the last beauty he saw before God willed him dead on the floor of that sodden war field, and he threw a sad look at Jamie to show his disappointment of a moment of delight interrupted; spoiled by the selfish and unschooled gabbling of youth.

After a moment, Robert answered Jamie, his tone measured and his words formed by nobler thoughts, planted by the beauty of the morning. 'Methinks we all interpret wonders from God different, and we give them those meanin's that best suit oor own ambitions. A peaceable man may look upon the rainbow and say God connects men... He disnae disinherit men because they're French, or Catholic... But Jack tells me learned men fer hundreds of years have known the truth of that wonder. Simply science... and nae God sent, but God made regardless.'

Jamie responded, 'But God controls all... including rainbows... is it not a sign?'

'Aye, there is a power at work that's fer sure, but God's miracles are reserved for trials grander than this fight, fer this is nae holy war. It is but a petty squabble between princes, and a shameful parade of man's ignoble ambition.'

'So does it mean the rainbow is not connected with the assault planned for tomorrow?'

Robert looked around him to the growing activity—to the men, and to the flags dotted around the fields and earthworks surrounding his position. He considered the pennants and standards laid with armorial devices and mottos; some richly embroidered; some ragged by the ravage of campaign. He thought on Jamie, the boy's youth and his sateless fervour for battle. Then he took a last look at the rainbow still painted by the sun, and with a smile placed on his face for the boy beside him, said, 'Perhaps it simply makes a better banner than those poor rags that fly in God's name.'

Chapter XI

At the appointed hour before daybreak, Robert gathered his men in the gloom ready for the assault. They left their position and travelled to the first line of soldiers that had formed ahead, to the section that held the greater numbers.

Robert looked on at Tom, Francis, Finn, Jamie and Tip, armed to storm the western walls with blade and shield—all except Tom, whose stick, *Knocker,* was at his hand. Tip and Jamie carried the men's ranged weapons on their backs, as was their duty, with instructions to follow on close behind. Then he looked to his assigned captain, Master Sutton, a confident fellow who held himself resolute, as a good captain should.

Robert was proud of his boys. His, because Jack was missing, which promoted a comment from his mind to his lips, loud and clear. 'Shame the party is nae complete. Jack'll be grievin' tae know he's missin' a proper fight.'

Francis was the only one to reply. 'I think he'll be happier tucked up in his downy bed, rather than running this cold field.'

'Ah Francis, ye be sour. I've never known Jack choose comfort over his commitment tae his comrades in the field.'

But Francis just shook his miserly head at Robert's wide-eyed notion of Jack's obligation, both to the game of war and to his comrades.

Ahead of the crowd of gathering men, positioned atop the embankment, stood an officer—English by his banner; a banner that bore an evocation to Queen Elizabeth and a quotation from the Psalms; a Protestant banner for an English gentleman. No one knew his name amongst those standing with Robert and his men, but his presence atop the earth spoke loudly. Then a shout was offered and his rank heard.

What's for breakfast, Captain?'

'*Frenchies*—all of them broiled, I swear it. Or I am not by name Randall, a virtuous captain in this noblest legion. Pleased to be yer sergeant-major-at-arms. Proud to be standing with Elizabeth's brave boys.'

The English soldiers cheered loudly. The Scots and foreign mercenaries stayed their tongues, their disinclination to rally behind an English banner obvious, with many a Scots' expression shouting their profanity.

Captain Randall stood with his banner in hand, and he raised his eyes to see it catching nicely in the breeze, flying boldly as he thought his banner should, and he looked into the crowd of men before him. He looked onto the other flags standing; gentlemen's guidons; standards to God, to a Protestant belief; tradesmen's pennons; standards bearing Latin motto; banners of faith and fealty. He looked on to study the men carrying them, and he felt pride to have their eyes upon him, looking to him as their leader. He saw the English face proud; the foreign face reticent; and the Scottish face hostile. And as he scanned noble faces and fine attire, dirty faces and rags, his attention fell on a young boy, poorly dressed, dirty, and carrying the St Andrews Cross ripped and worn. The boy's eyes were red and his nose was running.

Captain Randall took off his helmet so that his men could see him more clearly—see his face, his smile, and see his resolve.

He pointed to the poor young boy and shouted, 'Come up

here lad. Wipe yer nose and bring yer bonny flag to stand with mine. Ye'll be a man before the day is out, I promise. Ye may be wiping blood from yer nose rather than snot, but ye and yours about ye here will be better men fer a good fight, with the French beaten and the town's gold in yer purses.'

All the men lifted their arms aloft, and a cheer was raised. It was a grand acclaim. But Robert, Francis, Tom and Finn stayed quiet. They left the cheering for those who were impressed with boasted words, because they knew the assault would be no less hard met than those that had preceded it.

Jamie saw his comrades had stayed their shouts and adulations for their commander, and he questioned Robert, 'What's wrong Rab? Not looking forward to the fray?'

'Na, Jamie lad. I'm fond of fightin' men, but nae runnin' against shot. The advance against these badly breeched walls is nae somethin' tae laud.'

'But are they not fine words… fit-for-fightin'?'

'Aye, perhaps, but fine men are good with words. Some even have a heart big enough tae share with the disheartened man. But I'd rather have a wee timorous beastie leadin' and nae a hound. These walls won't fall by barking at them, but by creepin' quietly intae them.'

The cheers were relentless as the petty captains thinned out the crowd into a broad line for the advance. At the centre stood Captain Randall. Next to him was the boy with his flag, flying poor against the English pennants.

The throng of men waited for the order. The tension amongst the waiting horde was evident to all. Minutes passed. Minutes more. Then silence fell on the men for a moment as they waited for the signal. More minutes passed, and tension was turning to fear; it was about the men's faces. But not all men showed fear— not all were subject to anxiety. And as Jamie looked along the line, he was impressed. In poor light he studied best he could the men and their armour, weapons, the banners, and those carrying the scaling ladders, interspersed amongst the broad line of men. He envied those in better steel than he—those with better gun and keener blade. He looked on at the older men who wore their armour better, like it was part of them, and he adjusted his own cuirass, his *back and breast*, to sit higher. He placed his shield from his hand to be carried on his back, as others did—to show he was fearless with regards to French arrow and shot.

'Look Uncle. There's an Irish piper, along with English drum and fife.'

'Aye, Jamie boy. But I fear French tunes will stifle his drone and hide the melody of his chanter.'

'French tunes, Uncle?'

'Aye, Jamie lad, the French drones and chanters—*cannon and musket*, except they'll be spittin' a refrain to spill yer blood and no a rousing tune to stir it. Still, the piper be the luckiest man here on the field.'

'Why, Uncle?'

'Because he'll be deaf to the shot that murders him, and his last breath will be holdin' an Irish angel's sweet note, and no death's sour cry.'

Jamie walked forward, to push his way through the line and stand at the front, but Finn pulled him back.

'Stand back m' boy. Let those with fervour and fidelity to this cause soak up the first volleys.'

'But Uncle…'

'Hold m' boy. Prudence will preserve yer life. Yer sword better applied against French flesh, rather than your flesh wasted by French gun.'

Jamie opened his mouth again to protest, but a hunting horn blew the signal, then the sergeant-trumpeter sounded his accord, and clamourous shout was about—the attack was on.

The line moved forward to the beat of the drum—to the music. The shadow of the walls was in the distance, outlined by the signs of dawn—the rising of a sun yet to be seen. Then French cannon sounded. The men returned the thunder by way of a shout that grew into a deafening roar, as men took to the assault—to run at the walls.

When the game is on, all fear can leave the field as the thrill is upon the fight. Men with men rushing the enemy can be the joy of war. No thoughts of falling in the flood, only of reaching the enemy to sink a blade deep into his flesh.

And so it was. Jamie was in shout, and his blade was in the air. Finn to his front was running with such speed that he quickly overtook those men in the line ahead of him, denying his own caution that he had previously counselled Jamie. But Irish Kerns are driven by a blood surge that overtakes all reason, enabling them with fierce countenance that few fighters on the field of war can match.

The horde surged forward against the French guns. At first, smoke only appeared from the walls as indication of their numbers; their fire falling short of the men to burry stone shot into the earth. Then the men overtook the outer limits of the guns' range, and the guns' numbers were felt in the ranks of the men. Cannon and gun cut into flesh and bone. But the horde charged on. Then the French opened up with matchlock, latch and bow, and charging men fell—but not in great numbers.

The sight of the fallen spurred the attackers on with both fear and bloody reprisal. War cry suffocated scream. The men's shout was their weapon against the defenders' stone, steel and lead. Then a defender fell from the walls, tumbling down the steep earth rampart, and his falling raised a victory yell, even though the attackers had lost at least two score more on the field.

Close to the wall, the flanking fire from the bulwarks was fierce—it cut hard into the men. More fell. Then the youngest and fittest reached the base of the French defence. The attackers poured their own shot into the French, atop their rampart, silhouetted in the half-light. But the light was still weak, and fire from the attackers badly directed and applied. Their fire did little to keep the French head down, nothing to spoil French enjoyment of an easy target—the crowd of men below.

Those men far behind, still on the run up to the walls, took heart from the sight of a wall reached, and the scaling ladders now closing on the fortress. It gave them vigour to run hard on—to add weight to the men standing in the sluice at the base of the ramparts. The sluice was deep. The water bitter cold. Stones and shot rained down; bolt and arrow; rock and wood; all from the walls—from French soldier and their women alike. Boiling water was even thrown at the men beneath, but it added no more comfort to the cold bath below.

They all gathered at the wall, and found no cover. They waited to scale the ramparts. Veteran English musketeers tried to keep French heads down—to give their comrades chance to raise the ladders, but the French still had the best of it; they continued to pour fire into the crowd. As the mass of men grew denser, every French shot found a mark. Men dropped, screaming, holding head and wound. Falling in greater numbers now—filling the sluice, so men had to clamber over greater obstacle to reach the ladders; climb over their own wounded men without heed to their hurt.

A bold French soldier raised himself aloft on the rampart, clear of cover. His arquebus in hand, aimed to fell an English officer he had spied bringing up the men to the ladders. He was too keen to show himself, and he fell wounded into the mass below. To fall and die would have been a mercy, but he survived to be torn in two or three by the attackers; his limbs raised on spear and halberd to cries of delight.

But then spirited shout turned harrowing call. It was all around, loud and terrifying.

'The ladders are too short! Too short! Too short by a man's length and more!'

Behind the panic at the walls, still on the field, Tom's age was telling. He could not run at a pace, so had fallen behind the others. But he ran the best he could. He had lost sight of his comrades and he found himself running with strangers, cripples and cowards. But the ramparts of Leith were closing.

As Tom ran on, breathing hard, he saw the young Scottish flag bearer on the ground, his body twisted and broken by cannon; his face still, as if he were sleeping. Tom looked around for his banner, but it was missing. He looked ahead and saw its torn sheet waving in the wind, carried by another.

Further on, around eighty paces from the wall, he saw Jamie standing. Tom ran on to overtake the boy, turning to shout at him to run on. But Jamie's face held shock, his weapon on the ground. He fell. Tom ran back to the fallen lad to help him up, but it was clear he had been wounded, for he clutched his belly and his face was now screwed up hard with pain.

Ignoring the running men around him and the sergeants' shouts to advance on to the walls, Tom knelt down to tend to the young lad.

'It looks like ye're shot,' said Tom, seeing the blood about the base of Jamie's cuirass. 'Shot below yer steel breast… Ye're an inch unlucky lad.'

Jamie inhaled and groaned. Then he took a deeper breath that turned into a terrible scream, ending in desperate words. '…*It hurts bad.*' His eyes flashed desperation as he raised a hand to grab

Tom's arm. '*Tom!*'

Tom leaned in closer and moved the boy's hand grasping at his wound. It was bleeding profusely. It was a bad wound—fatal, and Tom knew he could do little to save the boy's life, so he replaced Jamie's hand to stem the blood's flow. 'Hold it tight lad.' But blood still flowed out rich and fluid.

Tom shook his head, and with broken breath and finality in his voice said, 'I think ye're needin' to make yer peace with God, lad… Yer as good as dead this day.'

Jamie, through his own shallow breathing, had now some measure of control over the pain. He looked down to his wound, and then at Tom. 'Is it that bad, Tom?'

'I'm sorry lad it is,' replied Tom, shifting on his knees to cradle the boy—to give him greater comfort in his hurt.

Through the boy's pain. Through the agonies of a body pierced, and a mind terrified in its realisation of death, Jamie looked on Tom's kindly face. It calmed him a little. And through a twisted face and the backdrop of war, the boy began to question his life, as many do when it comes to its ending. 'I was a gud soldier, wasn't I, Tom?'

Tom smiled at Jamie. His eyes holding a strength which the boy took comfort from. And even though the sound of gun and cannon fire filled the air, and the cries and shouts of men killed the quiet of the scene, Tom maintained his own calm to tend to a boy dying. And he cradled him like he was his own beloved kin. 'You are lad… Ye're a gud soldier. And even though you be Irish, I will call you a *Border* man. And I will carry great pride to have known you, and will speak well of you to kith and kin, and all the peoples who have cause to ask me to recount my knowin' of Jamie McCuul.'

But Jamie did not respond. He smiled instead. Tom knew death was coming. The boy's pain had elapsed. It was leaving his body, as his blood drained away.

Shots rained down, and Tom could hear them falling close to his position, but he stayed his ground. He maintained his charge, and he held the boy, protecting him from further wound and further hurt.

The attack was now a retreat of sorts, as some men tried to press on, whilst others stayed their ground to pour fire on the walls. But those with sense of the futility of the assault were pulling back. Robert, retreating, came upon Tom and Jamie. He stopped between them and the shot coming from the walls. He held his shield up as protection to the two. Nothing was said. And as he crouched, to seek an understanding in Tom's eyes, a hit was made on his shield that buckled his arm. Robert thought to raise his sword—to defend himself from the attacker, but he found a bullet well imbedded in his *targe*—his shield. The shield had done its job well to stop harm.

When life had left Jamie, Tom looked about him, and the attack had now become a rout. He was seeing men run away from the walls with fear in their faces, desperate to escape the reach of the French fire. The air smelled bad. Defeat, a stink in his nose, and Tom, for the first time since kneeling with Jamie, thought to leave the scene and the danger it proposed. But he was reluctant to leave the boy, even though there were signs the French had begun to sally out of their walls to prick and poke at the retreating men.

Robert had his hand on Tom, his eyes pleading retreat. 'Come Tom. Leave Jamie. Time and truce will be given tae collect oor dead... Time now for the livin' tae leave.'

So Tom turned to his own lines, and ran with the crowd, and to safety—not looking back.

The men were breathless, bleeding. The women were about seeking their men and tending to the wounded. More and more men joined the crowd—retreated, dejected, angry.

Robert searched the scene to see if Finn, Francis and Tip had made it safely back, but found none about. He ran the crowd to seek them, but still no one. He climbed the trench's firing step to look over the field, to see if he could see his men—if they needed help, or rescue.

Day had arrived—illumination. The bodies of two hundred men were strewn over the field. The wounded stumbling, crawling back. Others were helpless—alive, but caught immobile on the field, screaming. All at the mercy of the French, still firing from the walls, and sallying out of their ports to cut down their enemy caught lost and alone.

Robert closed his eyes. He bit hard to quell his scream, as he thought of Finn… and Francis… and young Tip perished. He spit hard his hate to the floor, and threw away his shield. Four lost. Four friends gone.

'Ye'll be needin' that…'

Robert turned to the voice, to meet the Irish brogue. Finn was in the trench behind, standing with Francis and Tip.

'We got caught up at the rampart,' announced Finn, 'Francis took a Frenchy off the wall with his musket. I couldn't very well retire until I had one too. It's a long way to run without reward.' Finn smiled. 'My aim was off… too much beer last night. Tip here must of loaded a dozen times… He's a good lad. Steady under fire.'

Robert smiled.

'I've seen Tom about, chattin' to a maid, but where's m' nephew. Where's Jamie?' asked Finn.

₧₧

News quickly came in that no success was gained that morning. All the men learned the true extent of the assault and, the complete failure of it. As well as the main assault, neither the attack from the sea, nor the feint from the south, made their objectives. All were beaten back. The French had held Leith, without much distress to their forces, or their defences. Some talked of a thousand casualties. Some talked of more or less. But everyone had a tale of kith or kin killed, or bloodied that morning.

There was talk of treachery. Fingers were pointed. Accusations thrown at some captains, both English and Scottish. Claims were made of foul allegiance with Marie of Guise and the Catholic cause.

How else could one explain attacks so poorly applied?

❧❧

Finn wore his anger openly that morning, for all to see. His outbursts were loud enough to be heard by all the bitter men standing around.

'Good generals win wars, and good captains win battles. We have neither in this army.'

Finn's words were met with nods, and an undercurrent of agreement from the men around him. But Francis was the only one to articulate the men's muttered endorsement of Finn's displeasure.

'Yes, the attacks are poorly applied. Our cannon fall short. Our ladders too. There's a failure here that's not just deficiency, but treachery. We'll all be dying outside the walls and not dancing inside them, that's for sure.'

Again the men around voiced low agreement. Low, because their petty captains were close by—captains unhappy at Francis and Finn's comments.

Through the crowd of men came a well-dressed soldier; an officer in good steel plate and a feather in his cap. He stood in front of Francis, a foot taller, and pushed the end of the stick he was carrying, down into Francis' chest.

'Hold your dissent little man. Or ye'll be subject to a flogging.'

Robert was quick to intercede, grabbing Tom's stick *Knocker*, and landing it hard on the officer's stick, removing it from its arrest on Francis. Robert then stood between Francis and the officer, and smiled.

'Sir, there has been much death today. Many are still hurtin'. We've lost good friends. Tempers are ragin', because we've been beaten back again. The lads here are mis-firin' off words that would be better used against the Frenchies. A floggin' is nae goin' t' motivate the lads towards better fightin' against this hard enemy.'

The officer's face, beneath its cap, grew red. It matched his feather. For a moment he was lost for words. But then they started to grow inside him, boiling up, loud and venomous, until they could not be contained and were flung from his lips.

'*How dare you!*'

Robert simply smiled at the officer's response, which in turn provoked the officer into greater abuse.

'We would be better placed inside the town… and not be festering in muddy trenches if we had more Englishmen in the fight and less Scottish scum.'

Tom broke in to stand beside Robert, to add his equable smile to bolster Robert's calm against the storm—to add words in defence of his friend. 'Careful lad, the boys here are more Scottish than English. Ye would be a better officer if ye used kinder words about yer troops.'

But the officer's anger was not abated by Tom's words, instead he re-directed his rage towards Tom. 'Yes, too many Scotch, and that's why we're failing. There is never true commitment from a Scotsman, and the Cumbrians are no better. You forget who your Queen is. Are you English, or do ye fancy yerself a Scot? *What's it to be boy?*'

Tom was not unsettled by the officer's rant. It was not his way. He was relaxed, even though the officer had the power of punishment, and even death if he wished it.

'It's been many a year since my pappy called me *boy*. I dinnae call myself English or Scottish. I'm born of Cumberland, proud of it. My devotion is to my kin and to my friends here. If ye're floggin' ma boy Francis, ye're floggin' me… and by the looks of the lads around us here, at least half yer army will need to follow. So think again.'

The officer looked around. He looked on the faces of the men. Violence towards him was worn by many—none more than Finn and Francis, whose stare shone certain murder at the officer. The looks on the men unnerved him, but it was terrible look on Finn's face that frightened him the most, and he bowed his eyes to hide himself from the surrounding hate, and turned to walk back through the jeering crowd from whence he came.

Finn was the first to comment, smiling away the murder from his face. 'It appears the English are not so devoted to their duty, lads.'

But Robert countered Finn, while he pointed a scornful look towards Tom for his reckless intervention. 'Dinnae judge the English by that sorry soul. They wear their badge of allegiance as well as any, and fight as well as most.'

⁃●⁃

It was a terrible sight. All looked to Finn for his reaction. But he was without any show of distress, or anger, or hurt. Tom placed a kindly hand on him, but he was cold to the sentiment. Francis voiced his rage, but Finn was deaf to his rant. Robert stood before him to catch his gaze—to block his sight over *Leith Links*, to the town's ramparts. But Finn turned away to pick up his bowl and walk from his position past Tip, whose sobs were hidden into his hands.

Robert turned back to look towards Leith. The French were out; recording their tally of kills; lifting the English and Scottish dead near the walls; stripping them of armour and clothes worth the taking; lying them on the earth rampart that formed the defences of Leith; a morbid tableau; an insult to the attackers; a salute to their Queen Regent, standing the battlements of Edinburgh Castle. The corpses, a grisly barrier for any attack to cross; bodies left to blacken in the sun, to putrefy in spring's warmth.

Tom sat his place next to Tip. 'Jamie runs Heaven's field, lad… Grieve not for his body.'

೮୬୯ୡ

The evening after the assault, whilst men sat around their fires talking, drinking, eating and meditating on themselves and the fight that had been, Finn appeared in front of his comrades. His appearance halted all friendly discourse, consumption and private thought. All eyes were on him, but tongues were stayed. Each man waited for another to speak, but none had words to speak, although all had questions to ask.

Finn smiled at the silence. He read the enquiry in his friends' eyes and answered some of their unvoiced questions. 'Aye m' lads, I've returned to my fold. Cast off ma civilized clothes to be what I am.'

Still the men stayed silent and some buried their eyes in the fire, whilst some stared at Finn.

Finn had worn his thick red hair long since Robert had known him; tied about his head, braided, with a beard cut and shaped into two points. His armour had changed little since Finn was recruited into fealty to an English lord, to fight as Border Horse under an English captain. His armour had been that of a Border Horseman, simple and light; a cloth-covered brigandine with short mail sleeves, hose, and long leather boots, rolled down at the top. His steel peaked burgonet protected his head, it was battered, but it had kept his red mop dry and bloodless for nearly twenty years.

But the man-beast standing before them that night, was not Finn, Border Horseman, but Finn McCuul; Kern. His name, a bastardization of an Irish myth; a fabled hunter-warrior. Finn howled his identity with his appearance. For he had cut his mop of long hair into a *glib*, a hairstyle once favoured by the Irish Kern; long and thick over the eyes and short and shaven at the back. His beard had gone, but his thick, long moustache remained. His armour was gone, replaced by a simple saffron tunic ending at the knee, laced at the neck, and over-worn by a short doublet, rich with embroidery that was well worked onto large hanging sleeves. His legs and feet were now bare, snow white from being cosseted in wool and leather for nearly twenty years. Over all this, he wore a rough cloak, again of Irish cut and of the same muddy colour as his tunic. He bore no pistols or bow. But he had retained the two short steel throwing darts he carried, fixed in a leather sheath tied at the back of his neck. His Irish sword was free from its belt, but still in its scabbard, which he carried over his shoulder as you would a pike.

Robert spoke, 'I have not seen your kind in yer Irish mantle for some time.'

Finn ran a hand over his cloak and said, 'Ma fine *Sasanach* clothes were smotherin' the Irish in me.'

'Well ye're all Irish now, Finn', replied Robert.

'Aye that be true,' replied Finn, grinning at Robert's endorsement, 'I wish my enemy to see me comin', and know how… I really am… and how I was.'

Francis' muted disbelief at Finn's appearance, turned to scorn and ridicule. 'Ye'll be an easy target for French in your piss-dyed nightshirt. And yer thick red mop will not deflect the blows better than your old steel bonnet.'

But Finn ignored Francis, and announced to all, 'I've been carrying my tote of old clothes for twenty years. Time I returned to my heathen ways.'

Tom put down his beaker and picked up a nearby log to throw on the fire. He stared at Finn until Finn caught his stare and returned it.

Then Tom said with a smile, 'Well Finn… ye be a Kern again, with yer 'Kernish' ways. But be so kind not to start collectin' heads. A severed head does nowt for the appetite.'

Robert laughed at Tom's observation regarding Kerns' penchant for collecting severed heads as trophies, and added, 'Aye, Tom, a rottin' dissevered French heid stuffed wi' garlic, is a poor substitute for a roasted hog's head stuffed wi' a rosy apple.'

Tom smiled back at Robert, and he looked to see Finn's reaction, but Finn did not bite, he only joined in the joke and offered, 'Don't worry yerself lads, I'll be cutin' off only the heads wi' bonny faces. I wouldn't want to frighten ye wi' ugly Frenchies.'

Chapter XII

Jack had, in all, remained in the merchant's house for the best part of three months. Holding the lady's interest in him with a sympathetic ear, whilst holding selfish thought, because the comfort of a pretty woman in his bed was too great to resign to any moral propriety, or respect for the man who hosted him. He promised her much, more than he was willing to give, in order to ensure she was wanting. His words were those she desired to hear; words of comfort and of escape from her wedded bonds. But, in some small measure, Jack's deceits were not entirely founded on his lust, for Jack did love her for a while, and at times fancied to give the good lady release from her sorrow—her internment. But mostly, with regards to the good lady, the evidence of his actions belied the reality of his thoughts.

His ribs had healed in a fashion. A slight discomfort he still carried, but the pain was easily bearable. His arm and head had healed. Strength was with them both, given through good care, in a rich home.

During his recuperation—his time in Edinburgh, he had kept an ear on the news of the battles that raged around Leith, and of the nature of the danger within the city itself. To this end, the old man visited him daily to share the ale-house chatter, and to tell him of the depravations and shortages within the markets—and to also ascertain the manner and intention of the man who had revived his daughter's spirit, and improved her humour.

The time had given Jack writing opportunity, and he had placed entry after entry into his journals. He thought he had good reason to be pleased himself. A comfy nest and much improved, insightful composition. His texts better applied to paper with fewer dispirited thoughts. His narrative clear and concise. His verse invented, free from the distraction of any responsibility that may press on his mind and mar his prose.

However, for all of Jack's contentment with his situation, others may have censured Jack for his poor intention towards his host and his good lady, and his reluctance to face the wider world––for he had no other reason to be there, except his selfish desire for an easy life, and a wanton woman.

∞∞

The merchant, Jack's host, had been absent from Edinburgh for ten days. He had travelled to the Western coast to secure new routes for goods into his depleted warehousing. For no trade was coming into Edinburgh from the East, with Leith blockaded and under siege.

The merchant was glad his unwelcome guest was in better health, and comforted with the thought of a fighting man billeted within his home. Well placed to protect his wife in a time of distress. It was a commission Jack took from the merchant with only the slightest of coercion. Jack was more than happy to offer his skill-at-arms as payment for the merchant's hospitality— happier with the thought of days and nights with his wife not shared.

Whilst the merchant was away, and Jack openly nominated as his wife's escort, the merchant's wife had asked Jack to escort her up to *Calton Hill*, to look upon the siege works around Leith. News of the failed assault three days ago had filtered throughout the city, and curiosity had taken up many more to look upon the battlefield, and the macabre spectacle of death that lined the defences of Leith town.

ഇ൚ഇ

There had been a crowd on Calton Hill since the siege began, even through French assault. People always kept vigil, and there was much news to be had from self-appointed commentators—much of dubious origin and ridiculous speculation.

Some people reported victory with regards to the assault, not failure, with the ramparts of Leith breached and parts of the town fired. Many agreed, fearing any dissent would be judged harshly in the pulpit. But the Scottish soldiers who had deserted, and those too injured to remain in service, told their kin of treachery amongst the Scots captains; those who failed to press home the attack, because of hidden allegiance to a Catholic queen and faith. They told of the scaling ladders that were built a man's length short. Some blamed treachery for the miscalculation; some blamed divine punishment, because the scaling ladders were built in the holy place of St. Giles Church; many more, bending to the will of the Protestant reformation, questioned the repeated failure of the Protestant forces to unseat Marie of Guise, perhaps caretaker for their rightful Catholic queen. A sign perhaps that the *heretic* would never prevail against the will of those faithful to Rome, and that their own reformation was poorly chosen.

From their high vantage on hill's summit, Jack looked

northeast towards Leith, standing a mile away. He studied the fall
of the land to the sea. He studied the English built bastions, the
gun emplacements, and the lines of trenches ringing the town. He
concentrated his eye upon the scattered remnants of an army,
strewn over open ground leading to the walls of Leith—to the
mass of corpses colouring the land peculiar at the base of the
ramparts. The sight was an explicit indication of the extent of the
dead—and the failure of the attack. Jack considered the town's
defences, and he looked beyond to the broad inlet of the firth and
the blockading English ships.

'Are we safe here… are we not too close?' asked the
merchant's wife.

Jack twisted his head to his surroundings—to look upon the
people congregated on Calton Hill. He looked to the walled city of
Edinburgh in the southeast. The suburb of Cannongate stretching
out its fingers from the city's eastern gates to the palace of
Holyrood to the south, and his eyes traced back along towards
Edinburgh Castle at the top of the city—better seen from their
lofty perch. He studied the loch at the city's feet and the boats
upon it, like so many flies on a pond. He turned around to look
upon the high volcanic peak of *Arthur's Seat* behind them, and the
shadows of the people standing there; keeping sentinel on the sea,
and any sign of a French fleet intent on the relief of the hungry
garrison of Leith.

'You are at least safe from the French,' said Jack.

'Are the siege-works well placed?' she asked.

'I am no general, no engineer, but the guns seem to cover the
town well.'

'Good… Then we will win over the Catholic… I am sure of
it.'

Jack sighed, and replied, 'You stand behind your faith well
enough, but in doing so, you talk of sedition against your rightful

queen. Does that not trouble you?'

The merchant's wife stood close to Jack. 'I was three years old when the infant queen was presented to us by her mother, Marie of Guise. It was my earliest recollection. I was eight years old when I travelled to Dumbarton with my father and mother to see her steal away—to marry the next king of France. She may be born a queen of Scotland; born in lieu of a son; born to succeed her father, King James. But Mary is now a Frenchman's wife, with her French mother ruling in her place.' The merchant's wife slipped her hand into Jack's hand. 'No my love, we have no worthy prince of Scotland.'

Jack looked down at her hand tenderly holding his own, and guilt stole his words. For all his intimacies with the good merchant's wife, it was her hand given as a public gesture of devotion, without shame or secrecy that humbled his melancholic heart.

Jack's silence puzzled the merchant's wife, and she asked, 'You say nothing my love. Do you have sympathy with a queen who does not even care to live in her country, or her dowager mother—the regent queen who rules in her place?'

'I have sympathy with a woman.'

'You forget these women have allegiance to France first and foremost.'

'I think on them as women first and foremost. A queen is not born a queen, no more than a baker is born a baker.'

'But surely John, to be born of a baker, dictates that another baker is born.'

Jack smiled at her wit formed words… and her wisdom. He thought awhile to think of a worthy reply, one not to counter her humour, but remake his point.

He looked back to Leith, and then to the Royal Palace of Holyrood, sitting at the foot of the hill. Then he looked back to

Edinburgh Castle, and to thoughts of Marie of Guise watching from the walls—displaced from her royal home and her palaces in Leith and Edinburgh. He looked past her privilege and the malice sponsored by her enemies. He looked to a woman married by the agreement of men. Only to see her husband dead within four years of marriage, and their only two boy children join him whilst they were still babes. He thought on her only surviving child, Mary, removed to France at five years of age, to see an allegiance set between two countries against England; a country now camped on Scotland's shores as friend. He thought on a foreign woman in a hostile country with fractious nobility.

Jack sighed again, and said, 'A queen is a woman, with a woman's frailty. They are only human, with all the complexity of a sinful creature. A prince may be the definition of what they are, but never who they are.' Jack squeezed the merchant's wife's hand. 'Motherhood is a state of nature. Sovereignty is merely an appointment of state. Motherhood may be suppressed, but never subjugated… Perhaps her allegiance is neither to faith nor France, but only to preserve her daughter's inheritance… because it is the only thing a mother separated can give.'

The merchant's wife looked deep into Jack's eyes. 'You are a good man. If only you were a devout one.'

'I am devout, it's just my devotion is perhaps misplaced from a godly calling to dutiful one. If I were long nurtured within the folds of a family, I no doubt would sing fealty to my family name… and live and die in its honour and protection. If perhaps, I were nurtured within the Church's fold, like others around me, my own strong sense of duty would sing loud in the cause of faith. But church care within the Marches—the place of my birth, was sparse. And although I had the privilege of a priest in my boyhood, he was poor and never turned this soul towards God's path. Instead, I only have my duty, neither to kin, nor country, nor credo… So I affix my sense of duty to my commission. At this time… it is awarded to your protection… Tomorrow it will be to something else—my men, or my appointment… So I am sorry if I am deficient in my godly devotions. I know this is important to you.'

'Only because every man needs a proper notion—a Church to build his life upon.'

'I fear I will favour no faith, for it simply divides kingdoms. I will always take faith on faith… whatever is prescribed by the state, because questioning it will only bring misfortune… not enlightenment. My good friend, my tutor, said the truth of God is a lesson temporal man will never learn. I am in no doubt God created the world… and man in it. But every day we discover new wonders, new peoples… How can we hope to know God… if we do not yet know His world created by Him?'

'You paint a bleak picture. But I will pray for your soul, John Brownfield, for it is a soul worth the words.'

'I thank you for your kindness.'

The merchant's wife studied the scene below, her finger tracing the lines of trenches in front of Leith. 'I hope God's kindness protects your men.'

'They will be well drunk, or safely warmed by their wives back in the Marches.'

'Marches John? No… They fight our cause down there, in the trenches around Leith.'

Jack's heart thumped. Panic filled his mind with fevered thought and laid his body with cold sweat. He pulled free his hand from her grasp to clutch his belly, to quell a rising discomfort. But as he looked down on the lines of trenches in the distance, to the ramparts of Leith—sickness entered his mind, and questions.

'What do you mean—*woman?*'

The merchant's wife was hurt by Jack's harsh reply. 'Your

men… My husband says they fight for our cause alongside our countrymen and the English.'

'Why did you not tell me?'

'I thought you knew.'

'*Knew!* Do you believe that if I knew, I would be here, standing with women, children and old men?'

'I thought…'

'Think no more… I should not be here holding hands like a doting puppy. My place is afore my men, my duty is with them. *God curse me!*'

Chapter XIII

Jack knew he would leave despite his fondness for the good lady. He was reluctant to leave, as he had been too long without the sweetness of a body given in love. Coition proffered; not for exchange of money, or duty, or favour, or even safety and sustenance, but gifted without cost. The impassioned want of a woman for a man. The fervid desire to express affection without restraint or coyness—without expectation or agenda.

Yes, Jack was reluctant to leave.

It was good to share his bed with fond affection, as well as the satisfying release of lust. But leave he must. Because to stay would mean to deprive a husband of a pretty wife, Hueçon of good favour; enter into a poor match—into a life not of his wanting, and to renege on a commission made with a man of the Black Merchants' Guild.

He thought on Guild matters—doings not to be dismissed for reasons of trifles of fancy and fond company. Commitments better not replaced by the comfort of passing thought—the possibility of new home and new family.

However, the Guild may have not been so heavy on Jack's mind if he had not received a message that very morning from Henri Hueçon, regarding securing the release of Jan van der

Goes's principal secretary, Peppo, and his safe return to his master—Jack's new master in fact; the master of the Black Merchants' Guild. Or indeed, his compunction may not have been so evident, if he had not witnessed the aftermath of the attack on the walls of Leith and its bloody outcome. Jack's conscience was pricked sore that day. His place was beside his men, and not within the comfort of a woman's flesh, regardless how wanton it was, or how desired it had become.

ഇൽരു

Jack left the merchant's house one early morning in May without farewell. He left notes for the lady, her husband and her father; notes of courtesy and thanks. He ensured nothing was placed within the letters to compromise a woman, whose faithfulness to her husband and her faith had been yielded so corruptly for his own pleasure. His letters were only of his best wishes and earnest thanks, and a promise to commend the merchant to Henri Hueçon for his, *'most bounteous hospitality and generosity with regards to sharing his home and comforts.'*

Robert and Tom were there to greet him as he stole himself away from the merchant's house. Two men, Jack was relieved to find alive on his enquiries. Men he reprimanded for the disobedience of his orders, but whose presence now lifted his spirits, even if sorrow had filled him, with the news of Jamie's passing on the field of battle. Robert may have sounded comfort by declaring Jamie's soul had entered the gates of Heaven to dwell in peace, but his death was left to dwell uncomfortably within Jack's own doleful lamentations.

As they walked the streets leading out of Edinburgh to join the siege works around Leith, Jack's regrets, bolstered by new dishonourable misdeed, bounced in a head sore with wound, and as his mind tried to sooth memories better forgotten—older scars. This new wound gnawed hard his guilt. Jack, looking for amnesty, thought words of regret spoken with friends would give his conscience easement for his desertion of the lady. So he recanted his tale of his affair with the merchant's wife to his friends, respectfully and tenderly, so as not to provoke vulgar mockery.

Tom, who was well schooled in the casual and not so casual affair, was quick to console a morose Jack.

'Never mind, Jack. The lady will have fond memory when her anger abates.'

'I think I only add to her misery,' replied Jack.

'Lasses love to think themselves as moral, virtuous… They love to think they hump in the name of love, and as such they assign romantic intention to it. But take it from me, Jack, lasses like to shag as lads do. Except lads are honest about their base intention.'

'You may apply your principles of love so, Tom, but the merchant's wife's romantic aspiration was fuelled by my deceit.'

'Do not be fooled by women, Jack. They know the truth of it. They know after a man achieves release, when his ardour quickly succumbs to disinterest, what fuels his declaration of love.' Tom slapped Jack hard on the back, with a wink and a smile on his lips. 'But if she's wise she'll stay her tongue, stay in bed, and give the man's love half the hour to return, so he can *declare* again, *eh Jack.*'

'I suppose you always *declare* twice nightly?' asked Jack

'Never on Sundays, but I'll make up my tally come Monday.'

Robert, who had largely remained quiet during Jack's discourse asked, 'Jack, wi' such intimacy between thee, should ye nae use the lady's name proper?'

Jack thought awhile before he replied, 'No, because I do not wish to assign her to a name, and thus to my memory.'

Tom laughed at Jack's strange thinking. 'Fret not Jack… that ye do not love the lady enough to stay. Fret not that you think you leave the lady sad. For I think she will find comfort with another lad sooner than ye think.'

'What make's you so sure?' replied Jack.

Tom ruffled Jack's hair with a mischievous hand, and proclaimed rudely, 'Robert here, shagged her twice within the week, and I shagged her Sunday past.'

Jack smiled at Tom's obvious fiction, designed poorly to lighten Jack's mood, and Jack, who regretted sharing a matter of the heart with his men, joined in the humorous invention to hide his hurt. He decided to colour the lady immoral and show a feigned indifference to her, so his friends would leave him alone to his remorse.

So Jack looked into a muddy puddle. His eyes smiled at it. 'Tom, ladies are like water. Water can look so pure, but it is rarely clean. Dirt is honest, it colours the water foul so you know not to drink it. You expect to get what you get with a dirty whore. I can only hope you and Robert are free from pox. I'll have your company, but not your discomforts.'

Both Tom and Robert laughed, and Jack was pleased to hear it.

Robert was still laughing as he walked the road down through Cannongate. 'I'm afraid ye'll nae find the trenches so comfortable, Jack.'

Jack smiled, still hiding his sadness, and he turned to look back to the city walls—to hold a memory. Then he refocused his gaze towards a new goal, asking, 'Where do we find Lord Grey and his staff?'

Tom turned his head to Jack, wide eyed, and raised again his hand to ruffle Jack's dirty blond hair, but Jack saw Tom's intention and dipped to avoid contact.

Tom, challenged by Jack's avoidance of his affection, kicked Jack in the pants. 'What's yer plans Jack? Are ye goin' to ask Lord

Grey to make us all generals?'

'No, simply to seek out Sir Richard Lee.'

Robert was the one to reply, 'Then in that case we better journey tae *Restalrig* and the deanery there. There's a loch on the way tae get cleaned up, and I hear there's a bonny *doocot* on the loch side—eggs fer breakfast, pigeon fer supper.'

Tom added, 'Ye will be lucky to pluck any birds from that dovecote whilst the English occupy the ground. A rabbit will have to do.'

And beyond my melancholia, I understand. I oft dwell on the notion of finding an ingénue, a sweet maid to be rescued. And in my deep affection for her and her love reciprocated, I would perhaps secure respite from myself, and the quiet mind I have longed for would be assured. But it is all folly, it will never be true love, or will it save me from myself. It will only be a man enjoying the attentions of a woman; to be enjoyed because she draws interest for a while; flattering and fuelling a low-fired ego.

My father once announced to a brother lost; lost to me and once lost in love, 'Infatuation is the consequence of a restive spirit and distracts a man from his responsibilities to God and to his kin. Beware the sin [lust] that hides itself in love's mantel, as it deceives men by burning fiercely in their hearts. But lust burns only briefly. Whereas love in truth is not a fire, for no fire burns forever, instead it is the very ground on which the fire is built, for it lasts forever and sustains our lives beyond mere warm comfort, because it feeds us and gives us life.'

But as I recall the man I knew, the man I have been. I think on what true love is. It is not the affection I bear for a love lost, or the yearning for a love that might have been, because such found fondness is a fiction in the mind that exists only in a moment. It is not even the promise of love, for it has no proven value, and therefore is only a fancy of the heart.

No, the love I know, is the love that stands with me throughout the days of my life. Those kith and kin who have demonstrated their allegiance to me time and time again with little regard to their own best interests. That, and the love of a wife I once renounced, and thus was taken from me.

God forgive me, for my fidelity to her was poorly applied, and my punishment is to live without her goodly devotion.

John Brownfield MDLXXXII (1582)

'Captain Brownfield.'

'Yes, Sir Richard?'

'So… you think to come to me with a letter from Henri Hueçon, asking to release a spy?'

'A spy? No, Sir Richard. The man is a secretary to a Dutch merchant.'

Sir Richard Lee stretched a gloved hand over a large drawing still in the making; a map depicting the siege works around Leith; defences marked, trenches drawn. It covered the best part of his table and was surrounded by pots of coloured inks and smaller sketches. Amongst the clutter, he picked up the letter given by Jack as way of introduction, reading it once more.

'Hmm… no spy… Henri claims our interned Spaniard is merely… as he pens it;

'An honoured member of his employer's household, dispatched for reasons of recovery of personal documents of no regard to the French, Scottish or English Crown.'

Yet we find him, a man from a country no friend to England. A Spaniard indeed, and no doubt a Catholic. Although, I am to understand we have failed to get him to confess to anything, including his faith, or his country of fealty. His silence has been hard kept… *believe me*… as we have applied such tools to the task of unlocking his secrets that would make even a mute find his tongue. Such a silence can only be suspect, and leads one to the conclusion that he is well able to carry such secret ciphers.

So what do we have? A tongue-tied Spaniard on a French ship, bound for a French held port in a time of conflict. It can only lead to one verdict… Yes, Captain Brownfield, I think he be a spy, and a well trained one to boot.'

Jack was unmoved by Sir Richard's biting commentary. He was simply glad Peppo was still alive, and hopeful he was in a condition to return to his master.

'Sir Richard, like the Spaniard, I am only another employee of his master, caught up in a war not of my choosing. I will simply ask you, does Hueçon have your assistance in this matter?'

'Lord Grey is in no mood to release spies. He blames them for our failure to storm Leith's walls. He blames them for all the intelligences passing to and from Mary of Guise. He blames them for the preparations of the French. He blames them for cruel rain and bitter cold… and for the wretched blackbird that sits outside his window each morning and wakes him rudely singing spring's song.'

Jack looked to floor of the deanery, to calm his words. Sir Richard had good cause to be nettled by his commander. Victory points praise at all, and all share in the prize, regardless of deservedness. Defeat points only the finger of blame along the line. Sir Richard was a man accused, *but there again*, Jack thought, *following the death and wounding of a thousand men on the field to Leith—who could escape blame?*

Jack thought on wiser words—those given by his father; *a soldier's temper must be relaxed in the face of his captain's rant in defeat. Save cruel temper as a rebuke for the enemy instead.*

Sir Richard Lee was not Jack's commander, his army not his employer, and Jack was not ready to be dismissed by an irksome captain, licking sore wounds. 'Good Sir. I am here to reclaim favour owed to Henri Hueçon. Not to fill my ears with woes of the defeated—to listen to sour captains sing accusation. If the favour is too great—if the service Henri Hueçon has done for you in the past is too slight to grant him your assistance… then my time here is wasted and I shall leave.'

Sir Richard Lee pondered. He looked sharply at Jack and thought to rebuke him. But then looked about him, to the dark of the sparse room and the short candles burning.

'*Prick them forward to an end*, those were my orders given, but to whose end? I think it is all the noble captains here, whose end is nigh...' Sir Richard paused. 'Is the sun shining, Brownfield?'

Jack replied, 'No, but the day is bright.'

Sir Richard Lee looked to his window, half shuttered. The window light was small, barely casting any brightness into the room. 'It is bad enough to live in darkness when the day is dead, but this room is perpetual night...' He stifled a sigh and squared his shoulders. 'Go... Wait for word in the courtyard. I will talk to Lord Grey. The hour is still early, but Grey hardly sleeps.'

Jack kicked his heels for two hours in the busy courtyard. One hour longer than he found reasonable, but an hour less than he would have given before he walked away. A soldier came through a crowd of men, message runners, captains and sergeants, all standing awaiting the morning's instructions. He came to escort Jack to Lord Grey's door.

The soldier led Jack through the deanery to a once private chapel, long emptied of religion; now filled with tables of maps, papers and half eaten food. A cot, unmade, stood in a corner away from the draught of doors and windows, and more piles of paper and a dozen large boxes stood like guests at a party around the floor. Strange to be seen were helmets and caps of soldiers piled high in one corner, as if waiting for their owners to reclaim them.

Lord Grey sat behind the largest desk, one closest to the window light. He wore a great fur cloak against the cold of the room, and a long thick greying beard, not shaped, on his face. Jack studied the man's beard and thought it left unkempt in an attempt to hide the gross scarring around his mouth. Lord Grey looked all his part—an ancient dog of war. His smile showed it—crooked shaped and gaps to his teeth. His face wore it—hard and unfriendly. But his dark, red ringed eyes told a story of a tired man, one with little sleep and less comfort.

Lord Grey rose from behind his oak desk, the top of it covered in papers, journals and maps, to stand and face Jack. Then he moved around the table, walking slowly as if to conceal his limp, until he was at arms length from Jack. He stared. He did not speak. Actions to intimidate. But Jack was not easily menaced. It would take a far crueller face to do that, and a much bigger man.

Eventually Lord Grey turned from Jack to stand at another table. Several paper stuffed leather folios covered the top. Lord Grey pointed to the folios in turn. 'This pile are orders for today. These for tomorrow. These are intelligences for Lord Norfolk and these are intelligences for Lord Cecil. I dare say Sir Richard Lee and Sir James Croft have similar. I am careful to say only that which my commander, Lord Norfolk, may wish to hear, and pray Lee and Croft do not call me liar.' Lord Grey pointed to another folio sitting separate from the others. 'And this pile contains reports of good English knights and gentleman slain or injured. All died, or received wound honourably according to my captains' own commentary. *All mind you.* Oh how my captains' pens are blind to the truth of men grovelling in the earth—those whose noble name does not always come with a noble heart. Devotion to the fight is a fickle love in the face of likely death. Perhaps they find the cause shallow... fighting for Scotland instead of against it. My Queen; my Elizabeth's treaty is badly drawn. Her allies, the Scottish lords, are greedy to the core... They cry, *'uphold my pride,'* and mutter, *'fill my purse'*... Scotland is not blessed earth, but only land to them—income, and the right to squeeze the last penny from those who work its poor pantry. They have as much land in England... Better land, better bought they are.' Lord Grey stepped to the window to look onto the courtyard. 'Brownfield... nobles, bishops and politicians all see monarchs as nettlesome children to be coddled and paraded for their convenience. The Scottish Protestant lords kick their Catholic Dowager Queen, for no other reason than it suits them to do so, because she does not coddle them in return. They spit nothing but hate, and dream of nothing but gold and power.' Lord Grey turned back from the window to face Jack, '…and hate has no place in war and gold is poor recompense for life lost and a legacy of a hundred years of resentment. Power serves only man's vanity… and vanity is nothing but gross sin.'

Jack waited to reply—until he was sure Lord Grey's oration was completed. A long pause dictated response was required.

'But war is never a kindly act, Lord Grey.'

'Not kind perhaps, but it is a game—to win or lose—a mere solution to disagreement where sober words have failed. Where good sense is trampled by princely pride, or political expediency. No, Brownfield, hate has no place in it. Murder is simply an unfortunate outcome… no more. If I could win the game without a single drop of my enemy's blood being shed, I would.' Lord Grey looked to the pile of helmets in the corner, then to the pile of papers on his desk. 'I loved the game of war…once. War makes men, and magnifies men's names. For history only remembers the war-makers. My dedication to this noble sport was perfect… Now dedication is lost in a pile of paper. My players retired from the field… and one game too many—*lost.*'

Jack looked again at Lord Grey, surprised to hear the old general so bitter, so vocal to a stranger. 'It surprises me to hear your mind.'

'Only the dead have a quiet tongue.'

Lord Grey turned to his desk and opened a small leather covered chest. It was full of papers. He pulled out a good handful of the paper and looked through each sheet, one by one, until he reached half way through the pile. 'All these are all secret dispatches. The French are not good at ciphers, or hiding secret messages. But there again, this campaign goes so badly, I suspect for every dispatch we find, two safely find their way. And I wonder, how many of these are simply placed for me to find in the first place? This one, in my hand, is poorer still. Yet it stands out, because it is different in its form from the others. Sir Richard Lee now declares the possible carrier of this message to be a friend, not foe… and I am in dire need of friends, Brownfield. Our gracious monarch rags me, her good commander. Her first minister goads her, and I am without favour. I am declared a *failure,* and I think regardless of the final outcome of this siege—it will be my last battle… And by gad, I hope it is. For I have seen enough blood soaked fields, and towns run red with ruin and death.' Lord Grey paused, his eyes lifted to the ceiling. 'But there again, it is that very spilt blood that runs through my own heart, and without it, I would surely perish.'

Jack looked on a man, wounded. He wore no fresh cut or bruise. But he was wounded sure enough. He looked at a man, some men called an oak of England, firm and steadfast in his duty to his service and to the Crown, whoever may wear it. But he was no longer oak, but rotting wood. Jack thought to offer some kind words. He chose poorly—*flattery.*

'But the Queen gives you wardenry over the Marches. Command in Berwick, and generalship over her army on this venture. You have an illustrious history. All know it.'

'You are a fool, Brownfield. Elizabeth is but another bitter prince—one who holds me no special favour. Her minister, Cecil and even my once devoted commander, Thomas, the Duke of Norfolk, grant me no favour. I could have finished this before it began… if I had my way. It was a simpler matter to take Marie of Guise from Edinburgh Castle and its noble governor, Lord Erskine. Erskine had not declared his favour to either French Catholic Queen, or Scottish Protestant lords. But no… I am refused this by Norfolk. Now I am chastised for failing to amble into Leith and politely take it away from the French... No, Brownfield, my betters do me no favour.'

Lord Grey took a deep breath and pinched his sore eyes to bring them life. He returned to his seat and placed both hands on the table, stretching his arms across the confusion of vellum sheets and parchment rolls. He again drew in a deep breath, and lifted his eyes to Jack.

'I will grant you a favour, Brownfield. I will give this *friendly* Spaniard to you in good will, and this strange message that he may, or may not have carried. All these gifts in return for your service.'

'If I can grant you service, I will.'

'Good. My Lord Scrope, who owes you no courtesy, tells me that he has heard you to be an able Border Horseman, with a campaign in France to your credit. I am also in a mind to recall an old rival, Sir Thomas Wharton, who had you interned as a child. Who declared you to be...' Grey grabbed his beard and ran it through his fist, thinking his history. 'Can I remember? Yes, I remember now... *a promising exercise in cross border co-operation*... or did he say *coercion*? I cannot remember. But there again, I recall Wharton reporting that his own captain, your gaoler, declared how easily you turned your back on your own kith and kin. Perhaps I am wrong to trust you?'

'That was long ago... I loyally serve those who I enter into contract with. Nation or notion, kith or kin, matters little to my sworn service.'

Lord Grey smiled. 'A true professional soldier—a rare weapon in this sorry war.' He ran his fingers through his beard again whilst he pondered. 'I have a proclivity to trust my first thoughts so, *I will* give you commission. You will command a horse troop in my army, to counter those French raiding parties that sally out to prick our gun emplacements and forage for much needed supplies. The French are too comfortable riding out at will, unsettling our guns, killing crews and pulling guns from their mounts. So you will place yourself in the cordon where you see fit. Stand in support of our firing lines. And you will use the time, as you harry the French, to seek a way into Leith to gather me intelligences from within the town, regarding food and the displacement of men.' Lord Grey returned his hand to rub over his beard, fingering the scarring around his mouth. 'My scouts and agents have had little success penetrating Leith. I will be impressed if you have more success. I have instructed Sir Richard and Lord Scrope to gather your troop––mostly Border men like yourself. I'm afraid they are without captains, because either their masters disown them, or they disown their masters. They are deserters and thieves, murderers and mischief-makers. Many have been saved from hanging, because they renew their oath to this army. What do you say, Captain Brownfield? I think they will make excellent Border Horsemen.'

Chapter XIV

He shifted on his horse. He looked to his right, along his own line, his eyes resting on each of his mounted comrades in turn; Francis, Tom, and at the end of the line, Finn seated bareback, inspecting his hair and moustache through a small hand mirror. Jack thought he must have procured that item feloniously from a man far richer than he, or perhaps by way of a gift, or stolen memento from a rich man's wife. Then Jack looked to his left; to Robert and Tip, flanking a sickly grey-faced Peppo, hands and feet bandaged, and seated on a tall horse of great age. Jack's eyes were searching for recognition of soldiers—a reminder of how war-men looked. But then he directed his eyes away from good troopers to look upon his commission—base and beggarly men; their mounts poor, their equipment poorer still. Pitiable were they; half with spear and steel cap, half with weapons likely recently stolen or borrowed and therefore probably not well practiced. No pistol or latch, few corselets and fewer shields.

Jack muttered low towards Robert, 'I hear one of their former captains broke his neck… Probably by his own hand, or theirs… These are Border dregs.'

'Aye, mounting men, born in the Marches, do not *Border Horse* maketh,' announced Robert, shaking his head and spitting on the ground.

Jack smiled at his comrade's reply. His own dissatisfaction of his charge eased a little at the sight of Robert in the saddle, patting his horse as if it were an old friend. 'Still, I suppose for you, it's good enough to be out of the earth and back in the saddle, eh?'

'Aye, all's well,' replied Robert.

Jack stepped his horse forward, so his voice could be better carried to the men before him.

'If any have seen recent fighting, raise your hand.'

A few hands were seen. Robert counted, and shouted, 'Twelve.'

Jack directed his shout to the twelve. 'All you, with hands high, step forward.'

Twelve horses came through the crowd of sixty.

Robert rode forward to join Jack. Then riding the line, he looked the twelve up and down. He stopped at one man, better attired than the others—one carrying a border lance. Robert pointed, and barked, 'You.'

The man replied, 'I rode behind Sir Wull Kirkaldy, he being shot and wounded by the French at *Tullibody* sees me here under a new captain.'

'And afore that?' Nothing came in return. 'Has yer lance pierced flesh?' asked Robert.

'Aye, I've poked a few hogs wi' ma staff.'

'And man flesh?'

'Na.'

Robert turned his eyes to the next man. 'You.'

'I rode with the eight hundred under Earl Jamie Hamilton, who harassed the French at *Callendar Woods*.'

'Are those the same Frenchies who now sit in their fort here, and won't come oot?'

'Aye.'

'Then my lad, ye job was poorly done… Ye should have cut them to pieces, instead of waiting for the English to do yer job.' Robert rode on a little more, and shouted, 'Is any man here in feud by way of family bond with any other man?'

All the horses stepped forward.

Robert shouted again, 'Is any man in feud with more than one of his neighbours standing here.'

Half stepped forward again.

Robert shook his head and scowled at the men before him. 'I suspect ye're with me, because nae one wants ye… Scum ye be, but that makes nae odds tae me. If any be cowards, fight and ye may live. Shirk, and ye will die, because I'll gut ye. And those of ye who would see ill of their comrades in this troop would be wise tae focus their disharmony against those whose corpses brings bonus. Because there will be nae profit in seeing harm tae yer own kinsmen… Yes kinsmen, because when ye fight under my watch, ye're my family and nae others. Remember that, and keep ma knife from slittin' yer throats. Because I will dae it wi' a smile, because I hate ye all… *Scum.'*

Robert turned his horse and winked at Jack. He wondered if he went too far in his address to Jack's troop. So he looked on Jack and waited for his nod of approval, or a wag of his disapproving finger. A nod came, flourished by Jack's open hand, sweeping his acceptance.

Robert smiled, returned to the troop and continued. 'Are all ye Protestants?'

'Aye,' The shout was loud, yet unconvincing.

'Liars!' shouted Robert in return. 'Are all ye soldiers?'

'Aye.'

'Liars!' replied Robert. 'Are all ye poor in purse and wantin' pay 'n' bonus?'

'*Aye!*'

'Well now we have oor common ground, and a reason tae fight.' Robert wheeled his horse and returned to Jack's side, raising a hand to push back his bonnet from his brow.

'Are you finished, Robert?' asked Jack.

'Aye,' came Robert's mocking reply.

Jack smiled, and cantered out once more to face his troop, to shout his order. 'Disobey and you will be fined. Cut any one other than armed Frenchmen, or Catholic, or even a Leither intent on harm in the name of Marie of Guise... and you will be fined. Bring me a dead Frenchy in his armour and weapons and I'll pay ye twice the bonus.'

The men looked amongst each other, pleasure and satisfaction painted on their faces.

₧₧₧

During the first few days of Jack's new commission, Peppo remained silent. His wounds inflicted to his aged body during torture, slow to heal, his trust hidden, his dialogue sparse. But the Guild password, *per aspera ad astra*, return of the coded message and sight of Henri Hueçon's letter to Jack—requesting him, on behalf of Jan van der Goes, Guild Master, '*to seek out Señor Diego Guas, Peppo's alias, lost with the St Clair on route to the Port 'o' Leith*', slowly brought Peppo into acceptance of his rescue, and rejection that his release was simply a trick to reveal his purpose in Leith. Despite his admission that he was indeed the secretary of Jan van der Goes, he feigned ignorance of the coded message and the strange bull emblem seal upon it. Jack Brownfield may have been a fellow agent of the Guild... But Peppo's mission in Scotland was no business of Guild agents.

Henri Hueçon had let Jack know, in his letters, that he had gone to considerable expense and trouble to investigate Kalibrado's suspicion that Peppo was on the ship, *St Clair*. Henri's contact with Guild informants in Scotland had already identified the presence and role of Sir Richard Lee, within the siege works around Leith; a man of influence owing favour to Henri for procurement services at Tynemouth, and Henri thought him Peppo's best chance of release. He pressed on Jack, Peppo's importance to his master, and no doubt the importance of his mission. Peppo's return was paramount—Jack's new commission within the Guild was dependent on it.

Jack, reading that the news that Peppo's imprisonment, as spy within the Protestant Lords camp, had not been well received by his new master, Jan van der Goes, pricked Jack's conscience and presented fresh dilemma.

Jack deliberated over his responsibilities—his commission within an unforgiving Guild, and his commitment to serve in Lord Grey's army. But with Lord Grey sponsoring Peppo's release, and Peppo needing time to regain his strength before a journey could be undertaken, Jack justified his decision and his priority—*his commission within the siege of Leith would be delivered*. However, he was not ignorant to the disharmony it would cause with his Guild Master and the censure it would bring, and he thought it prudent to omit to inform Peppo that it was *he* who decoded the message on the ship, an event that set the course for Peppo's internment. After all, it was not the contents of the message that interned Peppo, but Peppo's poorly picked name on transit, an uncorroborated alias. Jack thought his new master may be none too fond of a new captain that puts his trusted secretary in peril.

A man who holds another man's secrets is far more important that the man who holds his blade.

What Jack did not know, was that Henri had already reported

Jack's deciphering exploits to Kalibrado, and regardless of that misdemeanour, Jack's poor fate had been already sealed as soon as Henri nominated him to Kalibrado's guard.

⁘

Captain Brownfield's Troop of Border Horse, listed in Lord Grey's orders was omitted from the muster roll and billeted near the village of *Wardie,* two miles west of the centre of Leith. Close enough to support the siege lines, as well as protection for the small harbour of *Newhaven,* but far enough away from Lord Grey's main forces so its contamination of already demoralised troops would not be felt. Despite Lord Grey's orders for the troop, his official censure—omitting them from the muster roll, would ensure their pay could be disputed and so spare the English coffer—their sorry lives spared from capital punishment would need to be reimbursement enough.

The distance and isolation of their posting afforded Jack and Robert time and space to test the ability of their new horse troop, if not their mettle. Open moor to trample. Drills to execute.

All that was seen was poor in terms of discipline, but most of the men had fighting spirit, aggression and some skill with the blade from horseback. But even so, Jack thought it better to equip all the men with musket so that combat may be carried out at distance and on the run; musket training far easier and quicker than procuring steadfastness in the face of hand-to-hand combat with a well-tested enemy. Muskets were easier attained and available to him from Lord Grey's armoury—apparently more so than good men.

Robert studied all the men carefully and he singled out the troublemakers in the troop; those belligerents with a more truculent nature, obvious ring leaders and agitators. Robert held them back for special treatment—a night of hard drinking with Finn and Tom, as fellow subordinates. The party was well attended and two of the subversives came through the night of drinking, and apparent camaraderie, revealing themselves to be men who Finn and Tom thought would lead the others into dispute with their captain; two, who by their actions would only do foul by Jack's difficult management of such a sorry bunch of men. So Robert released them from service the next day, without pay or explanation, only with threats and promises to hang them both without tribunal if he saw them again. There were additional men Robert would fret over more than others, but he assumed the mantle of sergeant-at-arms with the power of life and death over the men to keep them in check.

The rest of the men he took to the fields and put them through musket practice. He lined them up on targets and tested them for their skill with weapons. Even Finn, who still favoured the bow, was tested with a matchlock. He stood the test, intending to shoot poorly and leave the *noisy* weapon to others, but his pride beat his plan and he shot perfectly.

'Yer eye is in, lad,' said Robert.

'To be sure, I've a natural longin' to see my shot well placed, but I'll be leavin' the gun to others.'

Robert thought on Jack's orders. He thought to insist Finn take the weapon. But as he pondered correct action, Finn had picked up his bow and loosed four arrows into his target whilst the man next to him was still loading for his next shot.

Robert laughed, took Finn's musket and handed it to the man standing behind—one waiting on his target practice.

'Tae see a man wi' skill wi' a bow, is a bonny sight,' announced Robert.

Finn simply grinned. Then he suddenly killed his pleasure. He swiftly pulled a steel dart from behind his neck, and without apparent aim, threw it with tremendous force to hit the next man's target. Finishing, by spitting hard on the floor next to Robert's boot. All before his neighbour even had chance to place his own aim after loading. Robert could see it was not conceited show that directed Finn's dart to hit his target—it was his anger. Robert hid his concern. He knew the Irishman's blood was up and instead he thought to ask a question not connected with the practice.

'Where's yer saddle, Finn?'

'Sold it,' was Finn's curt reply, 'To make sure Jamie's body is taken home, safe to his daddy.'

Chapter XV

They stood their ground on the hill—watching. Counting the French horsemen as they rode into the distance, galloping hard along the dense tree line. They kept their eyes on thirty riding the track. And they lost sight of them all as the thirty broke into the trees about four hundred yards along the path.

'Jack, we'd better ride hard if we are to meet the French and cross swords,' urged Francis, glancing a look over his shoulder towards the sorry rabble standing behind him.

'No… The French make good time,' answered Jack, 'It'll be too hard a ride to catch them… and I doubt if our nags have the legs for it.'

Francis kept his eyes on the group of horsemen behind him. Jack's answer did little to calm his worried thought, spoken. 'You will be judged harshly if we sit here and do nothing.'

Tom, alongside, was not so concerned. He simply patted his horse on the neck and tried to appease Francis. 'Jack's reet. Poor *Madge* here will keel over if pressed.'

'You've named your nag after your wife?' asked Francis.

Tom smiled. 'Aye… Mountin' this cuddy mare reminds me of mountin' and ridin' my good lady wife… Sturdy, but no stamina.'

Robert looked on, to fix the position in his mind where the last of the French horsemen disappeared into the trees. Robert then looked at Jack. He studied Jack's face, chewing over a strategy; his eyes narrowed, his brow furrowed with thought and a vision of what the future may hold under different actions. Robert knew Jack's plan before Jack had even announced it. He kicked his horse, and rode down the hill; towards the track the French used to access the wood.

'Where do you go, Robert?' shouted Jack.

'Tae wait fer the Frenchies tae return—catch them as they exit the wood. That *is* yer plan isn't it?'

Jack said nothing. Instead he spurred his horse on to meet Robert. And Francis, relieved, ordered on the rest of the troop to follow on.

'Ambush the plan, Robert?' asked Francis, as he caught up to the lead men.

'I suspect so. There's only one path into the trees. I reckon Jack thinks they'll be returnin' that way.'

Ahead of Jack's troop was Fraser. He was a thin, mean built man with a hundred questions. His round steel skullcap topped his head hard, creating the perfect crown for an unrelenting and joyless face. His broad blue bonnet, worn over the back of his skullcap, did little to soften his visage. He wanted answers to pass along to the other men to earn their acceptance. Fraser targeted Francis, because he was shrewd enough to know it was Francis who was keenest to keep the men favourable to Jack's leadership.

'How lang afore they return?' asked Fraser.

Francis looked to the man, meaner than he, and replied, 'I suspect they will not try to return until dusk or dawn, when they've got a better chance to steal past the cordon. They'll be scouting and foraging till then.'

'What's tae say they'll be back this way by nightfall, or if they're plannin' tae return at all?'

'With food needed urgently in Leith, and their numbers needed on the walls, I suspect their orders will extend to no more than a day or two away foraging. If they don't return... well it's an easy fight for us. After all, we're only ordered to prevent entry into Leith, and not to draw sword against those wishing to leave it.'

Past the single entry into the wood, there were three tracks through the trees. Three tracks easy enough to negotiate in the gloom of dusk or dawn. One path clearly showed the recent French travel on the ground. But Jack rode each and every one of the paths to determine the likelihood of the chosen French return. He convinced himself the surrounding spring green of the wood was too dense for travel to be made off-track, even with a clear night sky and good moon, and he was happy that rapid travel by horse and stolen wagon, through the trees, could only be made on one of the three paths, and only one other path was remotely passable by horse alone.

Jack and Robert agreed ambush deep in the woods would be the better policy, where the tree cover was denser and the paths were constricted by dense scrub and bank. They both decided that a place of attack should be established on the two better paths. To this end, they scouted good ambush points—places where the French could be contained easily, and slaughtered with impunity, even with poor aimed musket fire.

Two places were found deep in the woods, but Jack reviewed the merits of their plan and proposed the division of the troop by three to cover the entry into the woods, as well as providing ambush on the two paths. A contingency in case the French slipped by the ambush on the third unguarded path, or other paths unseen, or even if they managed to break free of the ambush trap.

Robert did not agree. He maintained that division of the troop into three would provide poor odds for the ambush parties, and the men left to defend the exit would have a far harder time of it without the dense cover of the deep wood. But as dusk approached and deployments were required, Jack's proposal to cover the exit was upheld, with a compromise; only one path would be covered, the broadest—the one already travelled by the French horsemen.

The troop was divided—thirty and thirty men. Jack would retain the horses under Tip's charge and command the group covering the exit from the wood. While Robert would lead the ambush on foot, with Tom, Finn, Francis and the better men of the troop.

Robert, unhappy, insisted Jack take Finn, and whilst preparations were being made, he quietly reassigned better men into Jack's company. Better men than Jack was expecting.

෴

An uncomfortable night was spent deep in the wood—waiting. The men did their best to keep their alien sights and sounds hidden, but smouldering match and nerves held ready, did little to comply with the order for concealment.

Francis looked to the east, to the sky not hidden by the fresh green mantle above.

'First light will be soon, perhaps the Frenchies still forage, or lie low and delay their return?'

'Perhaps,' whispered Robert.

'…In which case we'll be spending another day and night in this thicket,' muttered Francis, 'For the sake of my wet arse, I hope there are plenty of empty bellies in Leith to press the Frenchies to return before dawn.'

Robert raised his head and strained his neck to listen above

205

Francis' grumbling.

Francis continued. 'Perhaps they're too busy filling their boots with gold, or wetting their wicks with stolen women… or perhaps they've sniffed a trap and took flight… a day's pay I'll wager on them not returning.'

Robert forced his words through gritted teeth, low and harsh, 'They will sniff us for certain, Francis, if ye dinnae hold yer tongue and maintain the quiet as agreed.'

Robert looked to the shadows. The wood was black dark, but Francis was correct, *day was coming*. He looked ahead at the line of the track from his elevated position on the bank, and imagined the French scouts picking their way along the path, feeling their way carefully over rutted way, and walking through the dense green.

The tension was palpable as they waited—as they listened for sounds of horses travelling. But an hour passed, and there was little noise outside the owls and beasts that dwelled in the trees, taking life and making it in the spring green.

Then sounds in the far distance, the noise of travel. No voices. Perhaps horses.

'It's them. They've stopped ahead,' whispered Francis.

'Perhaps,' Robert replied quietly. He stilled his breath and listened hard for the sounds through the trees. 'Could be deer in the distance… not close… Can't tell which direction.'

The sounds were slight. Then nothing.

Robert held rigid and concentrated his ear, but the sounds did not return.

Francis waited awhile before relaxing back into his hole in the ground. 'It's nowt. Dog foxes fighting… Deer, or other beasties doing beasties.'

But Robert maintained his alarm, and held his head high to the wood, eyes closed, dread fear filling his senses. His worried thought saw Frenchmen passing wide his own position in the distance. Travelling free of ambush and towards the exit and Jack. Jack, at the exit of the wood, sat astride his horse looking into the trees, voicing his thoughts.

'The night is still too black… There is still time. They'll delay to first light, and ride hard through the wood on the broadest path. That's what I would do. Ride hard and fast… Outrun the patrols and guns around Leith.'

But as Jack looked to the horizon behind him, the night was already receding. No sound of fray came through the wood. But through the wait, as day touched the night, sounds did come—men on horses.

Jack quickly beckoned Finn and twelve men, with matchlocks loaded and fuses smouldering, to move forward and enter deeper into the wood. Jack then rode forward with the remaining men to block the exit.

The lack of gunfire, the silence, and the sound of horses made it sickeningly clear to Jack that the French had travelled clear of Robert's ambush. They had travelled through the broad expanse of wood, in the black of night, on one of the poorer paths against Jack's reasoning.

Who else could it be, but the French returning?

'Are these Frenchmen cats, or owls?' muttered Jack. 'Methinks they are men to fear.'

Jack turned to look at the men around him and spied a boy's face—Tip, and thinking ahead to the fray, ordered him back to his position, back to the care of Robert's horses with harsh reprimand. He then called Fraser to his side.

'Stay with me… If I fall… you take charge.'

In the trees, Finn positioned his men with great stealth and quiet along one side of the track. Fuses were covered to hide their glow, as men waited; blowing life into their smouldering matches, hiding best they could in the open wood with matchlock ready and ears listening.

The horses travelled the path, single file, French voices above them, and Finn held his breath as they rode by. He counted their sounds as they passed, one by one, until he counted twelve. He hoped he had counted more mounted men than stolen packhorse, for his attack would be poorly applied if his men behind, on the exit side, had nothing to fire on but riderless horseflesh, and his six men ahead had the whole of the French troop to hold.

Finn's word would be the signal to fire. His men were anxious, but they waited. Then to their surprise, Finn stood up from his cover and ran the open ground from his tree, straight between the line of horses, cutting the column in two. He raised his hands to the head of the nearest mount, and it reared at the sight of him, its eyes full of fear at the sound of his screaming voice.

'Come to me ye French bastards. Red Wolf is amongst thee! Time to lose yer heads!'

All the French knew the enemy were amongst them, and alarm was shouted.

Finn's men stood clear of cover and took aim and fired their matchlocks. Three riders fell.

Finn meanwhile ran past the rearing horse before him, drawing his knife hard across the inside of the rider's wrist, cutting deep his flesh and the artery beneath. The rider screamed and grabbed his wounded arm, his horse to bolt into the trees.

Confusion was about the French. Some riders at the head of the column galloped on to escape the fire, shouting for their comrades to follow. But the ones remaining, now blocked by Finn, and not knowing the numbers of enemy about, thought to turn and flee in retreat, but Finn's men had come at them with spear and sword to unseat those in confusion. A number at the tail of the column retreated back down the path, but a good number rode up to support their comrades in fight.

Finn drew a steel dart from behind his neck and, at the run, launched it at another Frenchman still mounted. But it missed its mark and glanced his horse. But Finn still ran on and thrust his long knife into the French rider before he had time to counter, dragging him from his mount to cut him again and again, until the fallen man was stilled. The slaughter of the Frenchman boiled Finn's blood, and he kneeled down; to thrust his hands deep into his kill's wounds, to cover his hands with the dead man's ichor, to paint his own face wet, blood red. Finn loved the smell, the feel of another man's gore on his skin, and his body shook with pleasure.

Finn looked up from his kill, eyes shining in the half-light, to see his men amongst the French; fighting and winning. The sight of it brought further joy to his lips and he yelled to his men, *'An extra day's pay for each French head!'* Then fearing the kills were being taken by others, he called out, 'Fetch my bonny Irish sword.'

One of his men came close to him to throw him his sword, still in its scabbard.

And Finn was amongst the French again, cutting and running down those who tried to flee.

Ahead, the lead French horsemen, free of the fight, had reached Jack's position. Seeing Jack's men blocking the way, one of the French raised a shout, *'Disperser!'* and the French tried to evade Jack's men, dropping their forage sacks to the ground. Jack saw the lead man, the one who made the call, twist back into the wood. Thinking him the French officer in charge, Jack took after him, calling for Fraser to follow him on. But Fraser stayed his ground.

The French Captain, returning to the wood, saw his own men not already caught in fray with Finn's men, scattering. So he took to the third path, it was his only route of escape.

Jack chased the French Captain, but ahead of him the Frenchman was making a better gallop. So Jack placed his reins in

his teeth, bit hard, and brought up his small crossbow, his *latch*, to load a bolt. With great difficulty he struggled to charge it, as his horse galloped on through the murk—finding her own way over rut and fallen branch—through narrow track—through the trees—
—branches low and forever causing Jack to duck. Jack's eyes kept a desperate watch on the path ahead for danger and obstruction, while he fumbled. And eventually his latch was loaded.

Fortunately, the track through the trees was straight for some distance, the light improving all the time, giving Jack a good shot at the French Captain's back. Jack considered sinking the bolt into the Frenchman's horse, in the hope it would cause it rear and halt the French Captain on the track. But Jack's indecision, the rutted track and poor check of his mount caused him to launch his bolt poorly, and it went hopelessly wide. The French Captain rode on, with only a head turned briefly in reaction to the passing dart.

The French Captain, fearing another shot, took a turn off the straight and narrow track, where the greenery was open, but it only led to thick bush and scrambling vine. His horse faltered in the impassable wire of bramble. The Frenchman, lost for an exit from the twisted barbed stems, dismounted; jumping free the thicket and readied himself to receive Jack, his horse still tied immobile in the vine.

Jack soon reached the French Captain and drew his sword to bring it down on the Frenchman's head, but a French blade was raised to counter the blow. The French Captain then ran at Jack's horse, pushing its flank hard into the bramble. He unsettled Jack's horse and the horse reared. Jack was unseated and fell into the wiry green.

It was the dense green that cushioned Jack's fall and restricted the French Captain's charge. He could not easily reach Jack to trust his sword at him. It gave Jack time to recover and exit the vine, sword ahead of him held against the Frenchman.

The French Captain's sanguine smile worried Jack. The

Frenchman's posture, as he held his sword in mirror of Jack's stance, worried him too. Jack knew this man was confident, and therefore, probably, had skill with a blade; well tried and probably better tested.

The French Captain raised his sword arm higher than his head, his elbow parallel to his ear—the *high guard*. His sword was a rapier, pointed down towards Jack's chest. His hold on it was relaxed and steady. The Frenchman then pushed forward his left hand, as if to offer it to Jack as a greeting. Then Jack knew—he had confirmation; this man was well schooled with a blade.

Jack did not want a duel. Fighting was a dirty craft. War, and not his master's tuition, had taught him to strike hard, strike first, and strike till all life was gone—and then strike some more. Cut and slash, until skin became nothing but blood and tissue, until flesh was chopped soft. But this Frenchman was smiling. He was making sport of it. Jack did not want sport, just a quick kill, so he could count a French captain into his tally, and procure more bonus into his pay.

The Frenchman's stance was learned, but his play foolish. The terrain was not fit for easy movement—the ground uneven, and the thick verdure restricting. Jack knew the rapier needed space and length to its target. So Jack ran on at the French Captain, with a low guard to get close; all the time anticipating the Frenchman's lunge at his own chest. The French Captain obliged, but Jack had anticipated the strike and quickly changed his sword from right hand to left. He parried the thrust away, just, running on to grab the wrist of the Frenchman's left hand to push it away too, following through to head-butt his opponent. Then he raised a knee hard into the Frenchman's crotch.

But the French Captain did not yield, as Jack's head and knee were poorly applied, failing to contact hard enough onto their targets. The French Captain recovered and pushed back at Jack to unsettle him, to regain balance and stance. But Jack too held his footing, and with head up, struck a blow, but it was parried away. As was the second, the third, and even the fourth. The French Captain returned the attack and Jack worked hard to counter the Frenchman's well-placed strikes. Jack answered the Frenchman's attack again with his own, and again, each strike was ably countered. The French Captain came in hard again, running his sword along Jack's blade to its guard. It allowed him to come in close to land his free fist hard on Jack's ribs, causing him to yell out and retreat sharply to save another blow. But Jack recovered quickly, gritted hard his teeth, and used the echoing pain in his ribs to add more fuel to his fight; he brought a blow hard enough to push through the Frenchman's defence, cutting his blade into the Frenchman's steel breast. The French Captain recoiled, his hand feeling the damage made to the leather trimmed edge of his breastplate, cut at the shoulder. When he discovered his arm was free from cut, he smiled.

The French Captain retired enough to regain his stance. His smile shrank a little as he caught his breath—expelling confidence and inhaling doubt.

Jack felt his ribs ache and his strength wane. He knew he could not sustain this fight. His condition was too poor. He was weaker than he thought. So Jack put all the remainder of his strength into assault and threw himself violently at the French Captain. Hitting hard. Ignoring the danger of the Frenchman's sword. He was fearless, and he used the weight of his heavier blade to its advantage—running in, pushing away the Frenchman's blade, to punch hard the Frenchman in the face with his sword's steel basket-hilt. The French Captain, bloodied, fell back into the tangle of vines, hand over face.

Jack should have followed through and thrust his sword into the bruised Frenchman, lying caught in the vines. But he did not.

Instead he stepped back to catch his breath. To quell his bursting heart, and grab his arm and ribs shouting rest from searing pain, and terrible ache.

The French Captain recovered himself from the vines, and spat blood and tooth to the floor. He took Jack's retreat to be a courtesy to a fallen opponent, and he smiled at Jack's chivalry. He brought his sword back into play quickly to threaten Jack. So Jack retreated two more broad steps, to catch his breath some more, and to renew his guard.

The French Captain came on again. But this time his free hand had released a dagger from behind his back. He renewed his high guard, but this time the dagger added greater danger to his attack. Jack knew he had no second blade, or shield, to counter it.

The Frenchman spoke good English, clear and audible. 'I saw you were without dagger, so I kept mine sheathed… But I think I need its assistance… You fight with vigour, though I suspect you carry old injury, *heretic.*'

Jack felt his resolve for combat die; drowned in fatigue. Fear washed over him, and the inevitable sense of the Frenchman's blades piercing his own flesh—sinking into his organs. He dropped his guard. He buried sword tip in the ground's moss. His grip on sword loose. Head dropped.

The French Captain hesitated. He waited to seek his own understanding of the man's condition in front of him. He thought, *fatigue or feign; an easy kill or a wounded animal; a trick or tease to lower my own guard?*

'Be wary', his sword master would tell him. 'A man who has lost the fight has already resolved to die. So he may abandon all his own defence to attack you. He will have no fear. He will give all to kill you, and much more strength he will have—in death's resolve.'

Jack was clutching his side, holding his ribs to keep them steady against his own hard breathing. Feeling the pain in his arm, but not daring to drop the sword to free his hand and rub out the ache.

The French Captain retreated a little, undecided how best to take the fight, the kill, forward. He thought on his enemy before him, seeming breathless. Sword tip resting on the ground, head down, but eyes still fixed on him. He over estimated his opponent; he even feared him, and so misread the signs of a man beaten. The French Captain thought perhaps a knife was hidden. His opponent's distress a deceit to bring him on. A counter-strike planned. So the French Captain delayed.

The scene around the men had changed, as light replaced darkness. Dawn turning more into day. Night retreating in haste. The sounds of English voices in the woods.

A quick kill and retreat to Leith was required for the French Captain, but that was no longer assured. And again he looked on Jack, and his posture still seemed defeat, but his eyes were steel hard.

The French Captain, a prudent man was he; a timely retreat perhaps now more pressing than the effort of a kill. Quarter given to an enemy, an easy agreement between good sense and good grace. So he spoke again clearly in English. 'Our encounter reminds me what it is to fight a warrior. There are too many peasant militias; too many boys in armour… all without skill. Our fight was good. This dawn, my blood fills my veins. It rushes and I feel alive. It is my earnest hope that when I die, it will be in battle, on my feet with sword filling my hand, and fight filling my heart. And I pray that my end is met by a warrior such as you. I sweat at night at the thought of my life being extinguished by a peasant, or a boy with a blade. So I spare you to fight me again perhaps. On another day you might best me, and at least I would concede my life to a worthy opponent.'

The French Captain did not dwell on his last word. He turned and ran to Jack's horse some thirty or so yards away. He did not intend to give Jack an opportunity to rejoin the fight, or allow Jack's comrades, bolstered by reinforcements running through the woods, to catch up and put his prowess to further test.

Relief at being alive met Jack first, then indignity. Being beaten was hard on the pride, especially by a cock of a Frenchman. But as he gathered himself into an order, feeling his arm and wet patch on his breeches—blood from a cut disregarded during combat, he looked on to the path the retreating French Captain took, and smiled sheepishly. Although Jack had thought the Frenchman's proclamation over-blown, his conceit evident, true nobility in these times was rare. Jack had not observed the Frenchman's indecision, and doubt over his own condition in the fight, so Jack only thought the French Captain had spared his life either by issue of his good grace, or by his self-indulgence—to trumpet himself to the living as a champion. Never-the-mind the reason, Jack brought a thought to his mind to return the favour, as a matter of his own honour—if he could. Then he put his embarrassment of being beaten out of his mind, and hacked free the Frenchman's horse. But it bolted, and Jack found himself on foot, as he headed back along the path to rejoin his men.

∞∞

'Open the gate.'

The French Captain waved to the men on the walkway to signify his thanks as he maintained Jack's horse up to the town's defences of earth bank, gabion and timber. Beyond lay the walls and the open gate with twenty French halberdiers standing guard.

Inside the walls, the signs of bombardment were clear. Damage was all around—blackened and broken timber—ruined

215

stone. There was an absence of life that should be abundant in such an industrious town; on a day usually set aside for its largest market. An important port-town, already noted for its dedication to fulsome emporia, copious trade and expanding commerce.

At the checkpoint, within the gates, his hungry men waited to see him safe. All hoped he was without serious wound. They were pleased to see all was well with him, and there were more than a few hands clapped on his back as signs of relief. His men freely displayed love for their man, all in lieu of his own family's affection, and their own absent family care.

'Has my horse returned?' asked the French Captain.

'He has. Sorry to be without you... Lame he is,' answered one of the men.

'How many of my troop have returned?'

'Half, and no food with them,' came the reply.

The French Captain looked to the skies, then looked to the earth to spit disdain from his dry mouth. He looked onto the direction of the centre of the town, and to his lodgings. He thought to quench his thirst, eat a little, for a little was all there was, and rest awhile before he reported to his superior. He looked beyond, and thought again on his commander, who would be quick to discipline him harshly for a tardy report, never-mind a failed foraging raid. And the French Captain thought again. Any unnecessary censure was to be avoided. He hated it.

While he looked, the men around him stared too, but their picture was a sight beyond their captain. It was over his shoulder and onto a man walking slowly towards them.

The man approached slowly, and all the soldiers showed interest. The French Captain, catching the gaze of his men, turned to see what had caught their attention.

The approaching man was carrying a small bundle wrapped in a faded red cloth. Faded in places to the palest of salmon shades, darker in some places from wet or worse, all tied with leather cords.

The man's expression held nothing. His eyes were empty. His pace slow and deliberate, as if he was unaware of the men in front of him, or the makeshift barricades of baskets filled with earth and stacked to form a firing platform, which stood directly in his path.

Moments seemed longer, and time slowed while the man reached the French Captain. Again no expression formed on the man's face. No question or request in his eyes, or on his lips.

The French Captain struck a forceful gaze at the man to push him into acknowledgement, and then he placed himself square in his way to intimidate, but nothing unnerved the man.

'Well what is it?' The French Captain's voice was firm and hard.

The man, in dirty clothes, not poor garments, just dirty from soot and ash, from earth and blood, held out his bundle.

'Speak man,' ordered the French Captain.

Without a change in his manner or expression on his face, the man spoke. 'Yer war has took ma bairn… She were a bonny lass. Bonny nae mair.'

'And what do you want me to do?' asked the French Captain, harshly.

'Yer war has took ma lass… Now ye burry her.' As he said this, he held out his bundle further so that the French Captain could take the sorry package.

One of the soldiers, concerned, moved forward to form a barrier between the man and his captain. 'Go. Take your child away. Burry her yourself.'

But the man stood firm, his expression as before. No anger. No hate. No grief. Nothing one could see and label as emotion. A blank face from a man with no place left in the world, because his world had been taken away.

'Burry ma daughter.' Tears then came to the man in a flood. 'Burry ma daughter... I beg you, *good Christian.*'

The French Captain studied the man's small bundle. He could only imagine the horror within. A destroyed life. A bloodied child. Then he looked into the man's eyes, wet with tears, and it was that, rather than the sorry sight he was carrying, that brought a sadness deep within the French Captain.

'Take his child, my soldiers. Burry her in the graveyard within the church precinct... amongst the bishops, burghers and priests.'

One of his men protested, 'But Captain, they will not allow it.'

The French Captain did not take his gaze off the man. He did not raise his voice to his soldier. He simply repeated his order calmly. 'Take his child, and do as I order.'

'But sir...'

The French Captain turned to his soldier, with a cold and hard stare. The soldier knew his objections were badly placed and foolishly pleaded.

'Do as I tell,' growled the French Captain, 'Otherwise your brothers-in-arms will be digging two graves.'

The soldier carefully took the child's body from the man, and gestured to the other soldiers to follow him, to help with the guaranteed conflict that lay ahead with the priest, as they attempted to inter the body where their captain had ordered.

The man did not thank the captain. He simply walked away, to find a ruined corner of a hurt town, in which to endure his grief until he could live again.

80C03

The French Captain was uncomfortable, tired and aching. He closed his eyes, as if the act would transport him home to France. To once more stand outside his father's house in new soldier's garb. To remember his father standing proud, because he could see his son was now a warrior-man like him.

But he opened his eyes, because the sounds and smells were not how he remembered his father's home to be. Nor should they be in the rooms of the palace of Marie of Guise, in Leith.

'Asleep, Captain Boulliers?'

The French Captain was surprised to see *d'Oysel* walk into the room, to take his report.

'No, *Monsieur d'Oysel*. Just remembering France. I have been away so long I sometimes forget how beautiful she is.'

'How long have you been in Scotland, Boulliers?'

'I arrived twelve years ago with *Seigneur d'Essé*. I have been home only once. Ten years past to attend the affairs of my dead father.'

'Ambassadors and soldiers share the same misfortune. We serve our mistress land faithfully, only, never to see her… That is until we retire, *eh Boulliers?*'

The French Captain said nothing. He only wondered why he was standing in front of *Monsieur d'Oysel*, French ambassador to Scotland and chief in lieu of Marie of Guise, and not his own Captain, *de la Brosse*, or even his military commander, *Vicomte de Martigues*.

'My cupboard is bare, Captain Boulliers. If I were to hold a feast, my guests would need to share one plate of horsemeat—for that is all I have. Even the sea sits on my doorstep, but do I have fish? No… and I only have horsemeat, because a lame horse limps into our walls today, and so is available to me… So I ask you directly. Can I expect food to come into these walls?'

The French Captain's eyes dropped to the floor thinking the horse was his own. Then he gathered himself to report.

'There is little to find. Lord Grey has made certain no food is available… and what we did find would barely feed half the men for a day. And that we found, we lost on the road.'

'The English caught you? You lost men too?'

'They did. We did.'

'We? You mean you. You, Captain Boulliers, lost your men and the food. It is a poor report. It will show badly on your record, and I suspect *de la Brosse* will fine you for the loss of men.'

'As you wish,' replied the French Captain.

'Sit here and write your report, Captain Boulliers. Words for your commander's reading pleasure this evening. Make it explicit. Then tend to the dispositions to the south-west. I am told the trench is poor there. The English will easily overrun the mills.'

'But the mills have no grain to work and the mill trench is a poor place to be with the English musketeers covering it easily from their new fort.'

'Our engineers and intelligences call the new English siege works, *Mount Falcon*, and the new fort they build is simply cover for new mine working. We will do well to sharpen our wits and our defences, do well to dig more sound-holes in the floor of the ditch, to listen for the mine as it approaches.' d'Oysel studied his fingers, and smoothed off a ragged tip to an untidy nail. 'And when you have completed your tasks, go home, you look tired.'

'My home, I left in France with my wife and child.'

'Then to your lodgings, Boulliers, to your comfort… How is your woman here?'

'She tends me well enough. Finds food when I cannot, and her boy is sweet. He reminds me of my own boy in Normandy.'

'Your own boy will be well grown by now—a man. Let us hope he does not need to travel here to tend to his own dead father's affairs. So after your labour, go to your woman for comfort, and to sooth your melancholy, go play with the boy, as if he were your own in Normandy when he was small and sweet.'

Chapter XVI

The boy had a stool. His father made it well. Constructed of five oak planks; two long planks, angled out slightly, forming the legs and notched at the feet, held in place by two shorter planks forming deep stretchers. The fifth formed the seat, cut with a heart-shaped handhold so the boy could carry it around single-handed. All was beautifully carved with representations of ivy and roses. It had a richly embroidered cushion, measured to fit by his mother, demonstrating her needlework craft. It was a cushion ornamented with vivid blue and green dyed threads, depicting the tree of life. No stool or cushion was better conceived, better made, or more lovingly awarded.

The boy, five years born, was small in stature, smaller than the other boys his age. The stool provided him height enough to reach cupboards and door handles otherwise beyond his grasp. It provided access to a mother's waist to embrace, and a father's cheek to kiss before he retired to his bed. His stool was many things—a stool of course, a place to sit, a seat to place in favoured areas of his home, it was a horse to ride and a tower to stand upon, to defend his castle from those enemies he created in fiction. Upside down, it would become a ship to sail the high seas. Placed on its well-stuffed cushion, he would stand within the box formed by the oak boards, and he would become its captain, commissioned to sink English ships. He would rock it to the rhythm of the sea, its imaginary sails catching the blow of the wind.

His stool was his companion, and he carried it here and carried it there. Always accompanied by his comrade on a hundred adventures, his little black and white dog; his father's gift again, rescued from the streets, and brought in from the cold into a warm home to provide a loyal companion for a beloved son.

His father had died a year past. Killed, they said, by robbers as he journeyed home from the tanners. His hides taken. His purse stolen. There were no witnesses to his demise. People who knew the cordwainer thought it strange that he placed his life in peril that way. After all, he was a careful man. Some called him a frightened man, a coward. But he knew otherwise. His skill brought him revenue, and revenue bought security in an altogether insecure world. His trade paid his rent, his taxes and clothed and fed his aged mother, aged father, his wife and his beloved son, better than most of his craftsman neighbours who worked Leith's commerce.

His customers had included many in Edinburgh, the French garrison, and he even had tendered his services to the Court of Mary of Guise while she lodged within Edinburgh's walls. All his endeavours were aimed towards the security of those he loved. He had worked hard and kept himself safe, because in the world he was all they had between assured sustenance and assured poverty.

People thought the boy had the disposition of his father, sweet and gentle. But he was always taking things. His mother would often chide him about it, *'the path to the Devil starts with small transgressions. Taking without permission is stealing. Do not think otherwise my sweet child.'* In spite of his mother's censure, the boy always took small things. Articles that he thought too small to be missed—

objects lying and hiding in other objects. Items he deemed already lost, and therefore, for him to find and keep. He liked shiny things. Those items that he could pretend, in his small hands, to be bigger and bolder than their design. Yarns were rope, a thimble—a goblet, a spoon—a shovel to dig, a wonderfully carved bone-handled awl—a sword to wield as a warrior.

His mother ensured the boy could read. She was forever sewing for greater profit and turning coin into books to fill his world. His mother read with him to fill his maturing mind with a lexicon of new words. And when his eyes were tired, she would read him tales of *Aesop* every night, dressed with pirates, to rest his mind and see him safely to sleep.

The Princess and the Pirate

[Adapted from Aesop's fable, The Eagle and the Kite]

'A beautiful, kidnapped princess, overwhelmed with sorrow, once stood on the deck of a dark and dreadful pirate ship, in the company of the ship's scurvy and unscrupulous pirate captain.

The pirate captain, seeing the princess was unhappy, told her that she should not be sad, and that once the king had paid her ransom, she would be released. But the princess said she was not unhappy because she was kidnapped, but because she was lonely, and despite all her father's efforts, he had not found her a rich prince suitable for her to marry.

The pirate thought on the princess' dilemma, and seeing she was both beautiful and royal, pleaded with the princess to take him as her husband instead of a prince. He declared he was far more able to bring her wealth and riches beyond her imagination. And to this end, he filled her mind with stories of the enormous treasure ships he had plundered whilst at sea. The princess, persuaded by these fine words, accepted the pirate and married him.

Shortly after their wedding day, the princess asked the pirate to sail away and bring her back an enormous treasure ship, like the ones he had told her of. The pirate sailed away, and it was a whole year later when he returned with only the smallest of bags, made from the poorest of cloths, with three of the smallest gold coins within.

The princess, unhappy with her prize, asked the pirate if the shabby bag of three small coins was the extent of his devotion to his promise. He replied in his scurvy pirate tongue, 'In order that he might attain her royal hand, he would have promised anything, however much he knew that he would fail in the performance of that commitment.'

'Do all pirate captains make promises they can't keep, *Mama?*' asked the boy, well tucked within the sheets and blankets of his small bed.

'Not all my sweet, but pirates are often poor in their devotions. They often offer more than they can give, and often give less than they can even offer.'

'I do not understand, *Mama.*'

'You will… *someday.*'

She tucked him carefully into his bed, straightening his bed-makings, and kissed him sweetly before snuffing his candle. She carefully rose from his side, and quietly left the bed-space, cosy, behind its heavy embroidered curtain.

'How is the boy?' asked the French Captain, sitting at an empty table pushed close to the hearth.

'He is fine,' she replied. 'He does not seem to be hungry.' She looked at the French Captain, tired and worn. His face bruised and cut. 'How was your day?'

'*How was my day?* You ask me as if I spent the day making shoes, or turning bobbins on a wheel. As if my day was dealing with irksome customers and foremen, and all the other inconsequences of menial work.'

'I'm sorry husband… I did not mean to make trivia out of your difficulties.'

'Do not call me husband… I do not call you wife… I have a wife, and she is not you.' The French captain looked unto the fire and grumbled to himself, 'Difficulties she says… she mocks me.'

'Again I'm sorry. I only wished to share in your troubles.'

'Then share my mind filled with a dozen of my men dead… Share in my horse, lame, and likely end up boiled… and I not even given the gristle to chew on.'

'I am sorry.'

'Save your apologies. What have you to eat?'

'A stew.'

She walked reluctantly to the fireplace and took the lid off a large iron pot standing close to the flames, and taking a single wooden porringer from a stack of three close by, she transferred all of the pot's remaining contents. She presented the French Captain with a bowl of weak liquor.

The smell of it was poor—the taste poorer still. And the first mouthful brought a sour grimace to his face.

'Any meat in this slop?' he asked.

'There is none. The bones are already boiled bare of flavour.'

'Fresh vegetables?'

'Only the green I could find… weeds mostly, and a little seaweed.'

The French Captain cringed at the thought of it. But a second, third and fourth spoonful was taken because his empty belly demanded it. There was not enough for a fifth spoonful. 'Any bread to mop up this slop?'

'There is none…'

In the corner lay the boy's dog—sleeping. Yet not sleeping, because one eye was open to the world, and his ears forever alert to the noises of Leith.

'No meat… and yet a sack of it lies in the corner,' declared the French Captain.

'You cannot think of eating the boy's dog. *I will not allow it.*'

'*Not allow it. Not allow it!* I am in no doubt the boy ate well tonight… and no doubt he fed his leftovers to that sorry bag of dog-flesh.'

The Captain took a deep breath and quelled his cruelty, coaxed on by a terrible hunger and a tired mind that robbed him of care and kindness. He rubbed his hand hard through his long hair, as if the act would wash away his thoughts and place him back home in Normandy, with a rich harvest picked, and tables full of plenty to feed his good neighbours.

'Come here boy,' he said to the dog, putting his hand down in an act of contrition.

The dog hesitated… then hearing a kind tone, stood up to travel to the seated man to receive a hand of kindness. The dog enjoyed the hand that scratched him well. In places his own two back paws could never reach.

'I am sorry,' said the Captain. 'The siege will end for us in defeat… and all this suffering will be for nothing, except to glorify us in the records of war. For the English have not unseated us, and never will… *by force*. No salvation comes from France… She has abandoned us to see to her own troubles… Revolt makes her poorly and weak. So we are left to parley the end of it.'

The boy's mother put her hand on the Captain's shoulder, and he tenderly covered it with his own as he continued, his words softening with tiredness.

'd'Oysel talks of agreements discussed between Queen Marie and the Protestant lords. But he does not know detail, for the English… *[yawn]*… will not let him leave Leith to consult… *[yawn]*… But new gossip flies like a bird… and it lands to tell us Queen Marie is now sick…'

Sensing his drift into sleep, the boy's mother walked away and thought to bring the French Captain a blanket, in the hope he would stay by the fire and sleep the night out by its warmth. But his words stopped her at the doorway.

'Where do you go?'

'To fetch you a blanket, husband.'

Her address annoyed the French Captain, and he screwed his face at their sound. But she looked comely in the door's frame, and tiredness had stirred his loins and fuelled his want of release.

'Come here woman.'

His eyes declared lustful intent. She hesitated. She thought to

227

stay by the door—to turn and find some chore to do. But prudence dictated a man pleasured may buy a man more inclined to care—a man more willing to maintain his provision and protection. So she walked to him.

The French Captain looked deep into her eyes. But the warmth of her love was not there. Her want of his body, absent, and she was not his long left *Michelle*, his French wife.

'Bitch!'

His hand was hard and she did not find any mercy in its restraint as it slapped her face. And the boy's mother entered into another world—a land of misery and anger, ruled by the hand of the French Captain.

Punishment was given freely by that hand, and on vile occasion, foot. Behind the curtain, the boy heard it all, as he had on countless nights before. His new father's anger and her terrible pain. But he blocked out the noise. He covered his head with his arms to drown out the cries of his mother. And he placed his mind on his dog, wishing it safe, and on his crew aboard his ship keeping watch for pirates in the cove.

છ૪૭

His mother always hid those bruises she could see; hid them best she could. She covered her arms and neck. Bathed out of sight of her son. But she could not hide her face—that unseen to her. She felt the swellings on her cheek, around her eyes, and she knew there were always bruises to mark the French Captain's affections. The boy said nothing. Asked her not for the reason of it. He only went about his childish business. He played with his stool and dog.

His mother stayed her complaint. After all, the French Captain provided security and never a hand laid on the boy. Few women fared so well without a husband's income to pay rent and buy food. So the mother endured. She remained quiet.

Her good neighbours could not help. They were long gone. Removed by the French garrison as they interned themselves in Leith. Ensconced themselves in the port for reasons of strategy and access to the sea. French soldiers, their whores and women, now filled the many homes that once housed honest work. Her once good neighbours now shared the homes of others in other places. And as the siege ran on—as homes were removed by fire and English shot, the townsfolk of Leith suffered loss of home and income. But not the boy and his mother, their home was spared by way of her sorry union with the French Captain.

⁝

The boy was confined to his home for reasons of safety. The house had a stout basement with a stone ceiling—a place of protection whilst shot rained down from sea and land. But the lad was an adventurous boy, and his dog good at finding rat and crow, and even a rabbit or two that were foolish enough to find their way from the green of the land to the disorder of the town. His mother praised God for the bounty that presented itself without reason on her kitchen table. She questioned the boy about the gifts. He kept silent. She questioned the dog. He cocked his head, and stayed his voice too, but his illuminated brown eyes told her truths about the boy—confirmation of his misdeeds. The truth of a devoted dog and his devoted child-master foraging against her wishes.

The French Captain saw it too as he walked the ramparts between the church of St Nicholas and the ruined tower of St Anthony's. He watched the boy scavenging in the empty houses, all amidst the English throwing shot into Leith.

He had assigned sixteen men to cordon off the ruins, to keep

Leithers from the danger of the weak and ruined buildings. But d'Oysel had censured the French Captain for depleting the firing line on the walls. Now the hungry crawled over the ruined homes unabated, and in danger.

The boy's dog was led by a good nose through the gardens belonging to the benevolent canons of St Anthony, through the ruined buildings and houses about. And the boy was led by his dog. The sight of them took the French Captain from his duty as he followed their travel amongst the ruins. But it was not the sight of a little black and white dog, or even a boy that caught the French Captain's eye, but a clay tile sliding from one of the roofs. Then another. And another. The French Captain thought one of the buildings was about to collapse. Then the tiles stayed their travel, and the French Captain breathed.

He studied the house. It stood proud, six storeys high. Largely intact it showed signs of fire. But the Frenchman could not see it all, it being largely obscured by the muddle of houses that formed South Leith.

Then another tile slipped and fell. He heard the houses complain—groaning, then cracking, and the French Captain knew the house was shifting—breaking its timbers. His concern for danger grew into deep distress at the thought of calamity befalling the boy and his dog, and his eyes desperately searched the surroundings for the two, but saw nothing.

Then two figures clad in black habits, ciphered with the blue cross of the canons of St Anthony, could be seen running in alarm; two friars with a closer eye to the danger about and the urgent need to put good distance away from the ruined houses.

The French Captain ran to the nearest steps leading off the walls. He descended at the gallop. He covered the ground to St Anthony's Church at a sprint so he could see better the bases of the houses in the narrow wynds. He eventually came to a house marked by a pile of broken roof tiles on the cobbles. He looked up to the rooflines, to the high peaks and timbered gables. It seemed the houses were already toppled, their roofs leaning in on each other. But it was their ill-conceived construction and chaotic extension, rather than dire consequence of cannon. The French Captain searched, he ran the houses, but there were no signs of people, or of the boy, or even the dog.

The house before him was crying, then groaning, and he could hear ceilings falling inside on the ground floor.

Time to leave, he thought. Then from the door on the forestair a dog appeared, and it ran straight past the French Captain onto the street.

The boy! The French Captain ran the forestair and onto the gallery shouting alarm. He kicked open the door, and his eyes searched the room.

Nothing.

There was dust falling from the door lintel. The walls were weakening. The French Captain closed the door behind him to fill the gap and preserve the building's strength. And then he ascended two more floors, searching each in turn.

Nothing.

He called for the boy. He shouted his name, but nothing was heard except the last calls of the house, breaking.

The French Captain, by the fourth floor, was breathless, and he was relieved that there was no door closed or barred for him to force. There was no one in the main room.

Then sounds—noises in an adjoining space, and he ran to investigate. Part of the ceiling had fallen; dust still in the air from its fall. He looked up and the remaining ceiling was hanging. The sounds around were frightening.

Must get out.

As he turned to leave, from the corner of his eye, there was recognition. On a stool was a small knife with a horn-handle; out-of-place in a modest house, for it was richly engraved and expensively purchased. He stepped quickly to the stool in order to retrieve the knife and examine it. Recognition was immediate. He thought it lost to him these past four days.

The boy!

He called again, but heard no reply. Then he thought to pull at the bed. The bed was heavy. He found it hard to drag aside, expecting either ceiling above or floor below to collapse at any time.

There he was; curled—hiding—afraid.

The French Captain grabbed the boy. He ignored his protest—his screaming, and he ran to exit the building. His escape onto the separate turnpike stair was his refuge, because as he descended the spiral stairs, the roof of the building adjacent collapsed, bringing its weight of tile and timber through each and every ceiling—the tide of dust choking his escape.

Blind, only instinct guided the French Captain to the exit and onto the street.

The French Captain grabbed the boy's arm and he started to scream, fearing the heavy hand his mother endured. The dog took alarm, and bared his teeth at the French Captain, but the Frenchman took no heed, and dragged the boy away from danger. The boy pulled and the dog snarled. But the Frenchman was strong and would not let go, or abate his march along the road to find the safety of the cellar, to inter the boy for his own good. The boy pulled again and rained his fists on the French Captain, but the Captain took the blows with indifference. But the dog was another matter. His bite was hard and his teeth cut deep. The Frenchman kicked hard to release the dog's grip—and he retreated, but only to lunge again.

The Frenchman's boot was well aimed, and he kicked hard the

dog's head. It made a sickening sound—hollow and hard. The dog whelped and fell still on the road. The boy screamed. But the Captain marched on, dragging the boy.

❧❧❧

It took the boy the best part of the night to pull at the planking that covered the basement's small window—to escape and look for his dog. It took him the best part of the dawn to find him; hidden in a gap of a collapsed wall, where his last breaths had took him. And it took the boy all morning to dig the grave for his beloved dog.

The sun was still half hidden when he started to work the ground. But it was high in the sky when he thought his hole deep enough to inter his friend. The spoon was small, his labour made harder for the use of it. There were easier places to dig, but the orchard behind the ruins of the hospital of St Anthony's was a fitting place for eternal rest. And the dog was laid so that no shadow would ever be cast over his grave.

His mother's favourite shawl made a good wrapping for his friend. The material was rich and opulent enough—a fitting shroud for a noble warrior. *Coverings of wealth*, he thought, *fit for a prince*. It was all he could do for his dog.

The English were kind that day. They had shown respect for the passing of a fellow knight, his four-legged sergeant-at-arms, and no shot was fired to drown out the boy's sad acceptance. And when the last prayer was offered. When his hands had finished returning the earth over his friend, he returned to the house, to the place where he stood—a sad shadow in a doorway.

❧❧❧

'By the looks of it the first blow killed him,' announced the French soldier. 'He died where he sat… No defence offered.'

'She surprised him I suppose,' replied the second soldier, fascinated by the wounds. 'I'll get help to remove him.'

As the second soldier turned to leave the room, he squeezed past the boy—a shadow in the doorway. He patted his head, saying, 'Poor sweet boy. Nobody to care for you now.'

The first soldier, hearing his comrade's sentiment, cast his eye from the stilled body to the boy. '*Oui*, the boy will be an orphan by tomorrow.'

'Yes, she'll hang for sure,' replied the second soldier.

The boy stood stolid, clutching his dog's leather collar made by his father. He stood for a while looking at the body on the chair and the soldier standing over it. Then he turned and left to stand in another doorway, far away from the scene and the soldier. The soldier, distracted by the boy leaving, tripped slightly on a five-plank stool close to where the dead man sat. It was placed awkward. Not placed for the dead man's feet, but perhaps for someone to sit next to him. The trip was unfortunate, because it brought the soldier's head close to the dead man's face; horrific in its form. A picture of chopped and punctured flesh, torn and bloodied until little flesh existed to mould features recognisable as Charles Boulliers, the French Captain. And from a wound that once was an eye, protruded a fine carved bone-handle. It was not the handle of a dagger, but of a woman's needlework tool—an awl.

Devotion has many forms and consequences.

Chapter XVII

Tip pulled and pawed at the tight fitting dress. He fingered the cording. Pinched the bodice. He wanted it removed. Free from body, to feel the skin beneath it. He was flushed with the thought of it all, and how it felt.

'Ye're a lovely lass. Stop fidgetin' and let's get on with it. There's precious little time.'

'I don't want to do this.'

'Stop yer frettin', ye're bound to be nervous. But we'll be done afore ye know it.'

'I'm changin' ma mind.'

'Come now, afore we're spotted. Lift up yer skirts and lets be havin' ye.'

Haste was necessary. There was fear that suspicious eyes were on them. So Tip took his hands off the dress and moved carefully forward. He was flushed, not with excitement, but by embarrassment. The tight dress caused it so.

'Could ye have no found a bigger dress, Tom?' whispered Tip, as he picked up his skirts and found his way through the rocks of the shore.

Tom looked to Tip's dress, tight across his chest, and then to his basket. 'Aye, ye look a little flat-chested. Could ye not stuff a little paddin' down yer bodice? And could ye no find any cockles or periwinkles to fill yer creel whilst ye were on?'

Tip's face was red with shame. But the cold wind was biting, so it was well hidden amongst the cold, red faces of Tom and Francis, as they made their way up the beach to join the other women and men, gathering seafood from the rocks.

'Don't mind Tom,' said Francis, picking his feet up, negotiating the soft sand. 'You may be lacking an eyesome bosom, but you look sweet in yer girlish garb. The French will never notice. Come ten of the clock they'll be too busy keeping their heads down.'

Just ahead, men, soldiers, women and the children of Leith were strung out along the coast, picking cockles and periwinkles to feed a starving town. Perhaps two hundred. Perhaps a hundred more. Lord Grey had warned the French commander, Monsieur d'Oysel, that no quarter would be given to those who ventured outside Leith's ramparts to collect food. But an empty belly grumbles louder; it has no pity. The devoted husband will risk his life to save a wife, and a mother to save her child. And men and women will do all to feed the need—hunger.

Tom, Francis and Tip were all dressed as women. All with baskets, and kerchiefs and coifs worn over their heads. Finn was excluded. His vanity decided that he would not lose the thicket above his lip, so broad and deep—his red moustache. *A highland coo hanging on his nose,* Tom would say. A coo to graze on the crumbs missed by his mouth, and catch the snot dripped out of his nose.

Tip and Francis were selected for their slightness of build. Tom, because he knowing a woman's ways so well, feigned a woman's walk most excellently. Although Robert needed to find the broadest brimmed hat to cover his face in shade; Tom not being in the manner of any woman, in either face or form—even with beard shaved and the twinkle bright in his blue eyes.

Jack had first thought to ride with Robert into Leith on the back of a French patrol, hidden in French trappings, wearing French suit and armour taken from the dead. But Finn, scouting the nature of the French excursions out of Leith, thought it too perilous for Jack and Robert to tag onto returning French horsemen. Discovery would certainly be assured.

Jack even thought entry into Leith too difficult to chance. The French too alert to spies entering their citadel, once town. But Jack's orders to enter Leith, for reasons of gathering intelligences, had extra meaning for Jack, as Peppo had insisted he would not return with Jack to Antwerp without the documents he was sent to Scotland to collect. And those documents were somewhere within the walls of Leith.

But an idea for Jack to steal and use came his way. A month past, nine-spirited Frenchman had dressed as women. They ventured outside Leith's walls and caught an English scout. They presented their prize to the English, by way of his chopped head aloft one of Leith's church steeples. A foul act presenting fair idea, because even if Jack's *ladies* were discovered as men, the French may hesitate to act against them, thinking them as their own men scouting, disguised again.

Ten of the clock came. Sir Winter from the sea and Lord Grey from the land, both were good to their word. From the sea came cannon fire, and from the land came English cavalry from west and east to chase down the cockle pickers.

Jack rode with his troop, to both protect his *ladies* from heedless cuts from the English cavalry, and to press hard the Leithers and French running to the gates in Leith's ramparts and walls. The pickers ran. The women screamed. Baskets were dropped. Sea bounty lost. And although not planned, many were still caught fatally by blade and hoof.

The English ships bombarded Leith from the sea. Cannonading the defences as agreed. High enough to avoid hitting people on the beach. Hard enough to keep the defenders low. Shots went astray. And all within ten minutes, the action was completed, and at the end of it, forty or so Leithers and French were laid dead on the ground. Some English too. But Tom, Francis and Tip had ran through gate with the retreating horde, and melted into the chaos of a town under fire.

There was enough of the North town destroyed to find covert shelter. Ruins enough to hide, and Tom, Francis and Tip waited out the day in silence, until night was well in and movement would be well hid.

Tom was the first to break the silence as agreed, as the church rang the tenth hour after midday. 'Well Tip. How are ye feelin' so far?'

'Nervous,' replied Tip.

'Gud. Use yer nerves behind yer sword. It'll push and strike all the harder for a few jitters behind it.'

'Let's hope he hasn't the need for it,' added Francis, eyes peering over a ruined wall.

Tom pulled a paper from his sleeve, unrolled it and studied the map drawn for him by a Leither, fighting with the Protestant lords. He studied it, taking landmarks from around him to fix his position and thus ascertain the direction to the house of John Kerr, the man holding Peppo's documents. His finger traced the route, his eyes following his finger's point. The way to the river was narrow; it followed the line of burgage tenements built behind the better houses of North Leith. Cover was assured, but so was discovery in the confines of the densely occupied tenements and houses that lined the way.

Francis watched the streets for movement. 'Tom, there's much ruin and burnt timber ahead. What if our man has moved on, or flit Leith altogether?'

'Peppo states we will find him in Leith.' Tom joined Francis at his lookout, putting a hand on his shoulder to whisper, 'Question is *sweet Francis*… will we find him restin' cosy in his home, or cowerin' in a hovel… or dead in a hole in the ground?'

'He'll be dead. That's for sure. It'll be our bad luck to get caught. That's for sure as well… It's the way of it… Caught and buggered by the French.' Francis thought on his predicament, then in a panic tore at the neck of his dress. 'I'm taking this dress off. If I'm to die, I'm dying dressed like a man.'

Tom smiled at Francis, his hand clamped hard on his shoulder. 'Put a bonny tongue in your head to match yer bonny dressin'. Ye'll no be helpin' Tip's jitters with defeatist talk. Yer a bigger man than any of us… Even in a dress.'

Francis heeded Tom's gentle scold. If one man could sweeten Francis, it was Tom. It was Tom's way—with all men, women and beasts.

Tom addressed Francis and Tip, 'We need to travel to the south o' the town. It means crossing the river. So we'll either have to brave it out over the bridge, or sneak over the river. We'll no be swimming too much, we'll be walkin' more. It's low tide. Plenty of clarts to stick us in if we're not careful.'

'I'm for the bridge,' replied Francis.

'I agree with Francis,' added Tip.

Tom grinned at the two. 'Aye, better not get our skirts dirty, or the camp lasses we borrowed them from will be none too fond of us on our return.'

Crossing the bridge was easy for the *women*. The French soldiers were too busy manning the perimeter, guarding only the main gates and roads inside the town walls. A few times, people on the street, not recognising the women, would give Jack's *ladies* a second look, but the *women* moved quickly and kept to the narrow dark streets. Their eyes forever being drawn by movement against walls and doorways, and skyward towards windows and to the outline of turret, roof, and tall gable, silhouetted against the background of the night sky.

They eventually reached an area near the precinct of St Mary's Church and Tom rested his friend's minds with the fact they were close to their goal; John Kerr's house. But on the turn of a corner there was a wall that ran for a hundred feet fronting a row of storehouses. It had no cover or lane either side. Half the way along was a group of eight men almost blocking the way. French soldiers by their sounds, alert by the liveliness of their conversation. Worse still, they were gathered around a large brazier, illuminating brightly the lane around them.

'What are we going to do? We cannot just walk past them,' whined Francis.

'Just keep yer heads down and act shy. They may leave us alone.'

'Leave us alone? They're French *damn you*. If a pig walked by they'd want to shag it.'

'Then ye'd better brace yerself for a rough ride, Francis,' replied Tom, grinning.

The three *women* walked the street, close together, heads down, round shouldered, arms tucked tightly in—daggers held and hidden up sleeves. They felt the Frenchmen's eyes upon them as they approached. They kept together as three maids might, not wishing to attract the advances of men with base intent. But the closer they got, the more they heard the talk of the men, and even though in French, it was clear Jack's *ladies* were the subject of their Gallic discourse.

Tom whispered, hand tight on his dagger's hilt, 'Heads down ladies. But if these boys decide to mount these mares, they'll find a sharp saddle, eh?'

But Tip and Francis remained silent, aiming for the only gap left by the French soldiers, quickly diminishing as the Frenchman moved to block their way.

One soldier bent down in an attempt to get a better look at the women, but only Francis' face could he see.

'*Mais non. Ils sont trop laide, mes amis.*'

And the Frenchmen seemed to part, laughing.

The three *women* walked on past to the mocking sounds of Frenchmen. But as they reached the end of the lane, the three *women* could hear the sounds of footsteps following. Then a shout.

'*Francis... revenir, mon ami.*'

And Francis, hearing his name called, reacted a little by turning his head. He saw a French soldier outlined against the light, following close behind. Close enough to see the lecherous intent on his face. But in the distance his comrades continued to call him back.

'*Francis, revenir. Nous vous acheter une pute au lieu.*'

But the French soldier, did not heed the calls of his comrades to come back. He followed the *women* instead. They reached lane end, and all turned into a darker narrow wynd that ran between houses. Now Tip, Francis and Tom, placed a little more haste into their stride.

'*Arrêtez s'il vous plait,*' begged the soldier.

But the *women* marched on, losing a little of their womanly gait.

'*Arrêtez, arrêtez,*' insisted the soldier.

Tom and Tip kept their heads down and marched on, nerves jangling. But Francis showed his worry, and turned again to look at the French soldier hard on their heels.

'Arrêtez. Hommes. Espions!' The cries of the soldier were obvious in their alarm. The *women* had been exposed.

Tom and Francis, hearing the loud calls from the man behind, fearing the alarm, turned without discussion to quickly step hard back towards the French soldier. The French soldier, seeing the purpose in Tom and Francis' step, started to draw his sword. But it was too late. Without hesitation, Tom and Francis ran in, grabbing the Frenchman's arms. With their free hands they punched hard their daggers into the soldier's chest and neck. Punched viciously without abate until the terrible cries of the soldier fell silent—until breath was killed in the man and laboured in his killers—until their dresses were well bloodied, and the Frenchman well bled.

'Have you noticed…?' said Francis, catching his breath and spitting clear his mouth, 'A Frenchy can never die quiet, and their blood has a taste peculiar?'

'It's the garlic. They season everythin' wi' it,' replied Tom.

Tip looked for disturbance beyond the fight. A dog was barking. Then a dog more. Then the sound of men carrying steel filled the air. Then cannon fire sounded. The increasing noise around them brought fear to the men. It rattled their senses. It stopped their breath. Their wits and senses fevered as they tried to detect the direction of the danger. Tom and Francis drew pistols from beneath their skirts to the ready. Tip drew his knife and pointed to the clattering sound. They stood silent. They stood still, waiting for the sounds to show form   for the soldiers to appear. But the clatter of men in steel on the run diminished. Breath was released and a calm of sorts returned to the three.

Tom led Francis and Tip down another wynd… three, four, then five doors, until they stood in a doorway under a lintel inscribed with a blessing, *Christus mansionem benedicat.*

All the time cannon sounded, bringing destruction close their position.

'Are they targeting us, Tom?' asked Tip, cowering in the doorway.

'Us nah, just you, lad,' answered Tom, pointing to the door. 'This is the one we want. Give it a knock, lad.'

Nothing came of Tip's knock, and the three *women* stood quiet. Tip knocked again, but still nothing.

There was a crack in the planking of the door, and Tip pushed his eye up to see through it. He could see a solitary light illuminating the space far behind, and he turned his head to hold his ear, listening for sounds of movement within.

'There's a candle burning… and noises… I think… someone's in… I'm sure of it.'

'Knock again, lad,' said Tom.

This time Tip hammered on the door, with his eye still to the crack.

Francis quickly moved in to grab Tip's hand, to quell the noise. 'Do you want the French on us… be careful, be more quiet.'

But Tip's eye was pushed too hard against the crack in careful examination to respond to Francis. Then he saw the light go out for a moment, as if something had passed in front of the flame.

'Someone's behind the door.'

Tom stepped forward and pulled Tip from his sentry, and shouted, *'Per aspera ad astra.'*

Francis' eyes flashed alarm at Tom's raised voice. *'God damn you,* Tom… Latin? Why not shout it louder, perhaps say it in French… I'm sure there's still a few in the French garrison with mud in their ears who didn't hear it.' But Francis stilled his rant when Tom's words worked like a magic key, and bolts behind the door were drawn.

The door opened, slowly.

'Who's there?' came a gruff voice from behind the opening.

'Three lads come to collect papers. Three lads sent by way of a Spaniard called Peppo, with a message from his master, Jan van der Goes,' answered Tom.

A small lean man presented himself at the doorway. 'Then come in… and be quiet. I could hear ye clammerin' up the street an age back.'

The sound of the cannon abated, and Tip was directed to the door to keep a watchful eye on the street, whilst Tom and Francis followed the small man deeper into his home, a short candle leading the way.

They travelled through a long narrow hallway into a large room at the back of the house. The man walked about lighting candles to illuminate the space. Maps and charts filled the room. They hung on the walls. They covered the tables. And rolled, they sat in a dozen niches built into the panelling under a staircase.

At a high table, strewn with drawing instruments, inks and rolls of vellum, the men stopped, and Tom handed the man the coded message, returned to Jack by Lord Grey.

'Are you a mapmaker then?' asked Francis.

The man looked Francis up and down, disdainfully. 'Are ye a lass then?… If ye are, ye be a durty ugly wee sow.'

Francis looked down at his dress, bloodstained. He thought on his ridiculous attire and the insult thrown at him. His mean temper, rested, began to rise. His nerves, jangling along to cannon fire, brought it to the fore. 'These are dressings to steal into yer town. Disguise to see us in. But there's nothing ladylike about my blade and pistol… if ye have a mind to insult me a *wee* bit more.'

The man heeded Francis' threat, and held the cipher up to a candle on the tall desk. He looked carefully at the broken seal on the message. 'It's been opened.' He presented the cipher to Tom and repeated, 'It's been opened… see… the seal is broken.'

'Aye lad, it's been opened, so what of it?' replied Tom.

'Ye ladies cannot have come directly from Jan van der Goes. The seal is broken... the message is compromised.'

'The message was intercepted by the English... But my captain retrieved it. We are here at his order, via Jan van der Goes, his agent Peppo and the password,' advised Tom.

'Aye, the password... the password.' The man nodded his acceptance. 'Are ye Guild men then?'

'No,' replied Francis.

'Not Guild men, yet ye have the password... The Guild must trust ye, tae give ye the password?'

'Peppo offered it out of necessity,' replied Tom.

'How is Peppo? Still hale and hearty? He's sprightly fer an auld man... isn't he?'

'He's fine,' countered Francis, 'Now, can you apply more haste? And to save your time, my captain has already deciphered the message.'

But the man shook his head. 'Nah, prudence dictates I read the cipher myself.' He walked to a cupboard and drew out a flask of brandy and three silver beakers. 'I was savin' this fer better times... But I think better times may be too far off fer me tae be saving this from my pleasure. Wait here—drink. I'll nae be long workin' oot the message.' The man took his candle and the cipher back through into the other room, leaving Tom and Francis to pour themselves a brandy.

'He's no trustin' us, Francis,' announced Tom.

'Aye... No doubt he's out through the front door to hail the French.'

'Nah. Not with Tip at the door, on guard.'

Francis looked at the brandy filling his beaker. 'You don't think the brandy is tainted?'

'Poisoned?' replied Tom.

'Aye.' Francis chewed his tongue, desperate to taste the liquor.

'Nah,' said Tom, wetting his lips. 'Who keeps poisoned brandy in their cupboard?'

'Aye, you're right, Tom.' Francis mulled over his dilemma. 'Are ye not drinking, Tom?'

'After you, Francis.'

'No… You're the senior man. After you.'

Tom picked up his beaker and studied the liquid within. He inhaled its aroma deep into his nose… and sighed. 'It smells canny… very canny.'

Francis too, raised his beaker to his nose. 'It smells too good to be poisoned… *far too good.*'

Tom looked long and hard into his beaker, loving the very sight that filled it. 'Peppo is hardly sprightly. The old man can barely walk.'

'Aye… barely walk… he has a deformed foot.'

'D'ya think our boy here knows that?' offered Tom.

'Aye, I suspect he was testing us.'

'I agree, Francis… Still if it is tainted. If it is poisoned. It'll be no such a bad way to go… if it tastes as good as it smells.' Tom considered carefully, but the odour was too perfect for his nose to deny his tongue, and he refused good sense. He put the beaker to his lips. 'No!'

Tom returned the beaker hard to the table and wiped his lips clean, even though they had not touched the liquor.

Suddenly the man returned from the hallway with a kinder demeanour and a more courteous voice. 'Aye, sorry lads. My name is John Kerr. I am a mapmaker, of sorts. I have deciphered the message. Ye would'nae ken tae come here, if ye were not who ye said ye were. Only Peppo could tell ye my name, and nae trick or foul coercion would prise information from that old badger. Ye may look foul, but ye dinnae feel foul.' He walked to the table, picked up the jug and poured himself half a fill of brandy, sinking it straight down. 'Ah... never have I tasted better spirit.' He then looked at the two beakers still full on the table. 'What's the matter boys? Nae thirsty?'

Tom and Francis looked at each other and quickly reached for their cups. Tom, the quicker to sink the contents of his beaker.

The mapmaker began to remove the litter of boxes, piles of papers and baskets from a large coffer lining a wall. 'When I was in the other room, I could hear the French soldiers aboot, searchin'. Is it ye lads they seek? Yer boy at the door is fair anxious.'

'We've a dead Frenchman, poorly covered by straw in an empty pig pen to our credit,' declared Tom. 'Ye're not mindin' us cuttin' a Frenchy are ye?'

'Nah. They bring me nae profit, so I spare nae tears fer them.'

'Gud. Then we best away as soon as we can. Give the documents to Francis here. I'll go steady our boy, Tip, at the door.'

The mapmaker continued to clear box and basket off the coffer, to eventually open it. He showed Francis three folios, two in blonde leather and one in blackened leather; all sealed with the mapmaker's badge.

'I was commissioned tae create maps from poorly rendered originals and sketches from a Dutch pilot's rutter. There were coastlines and seas I've never encountered afore, and as they were so interestin', I let my apprentice render them too... only fer practice ye understand.' The mapmaker hid his eyes for a moment, concealing his fear of retribution by the Guild. 'It was my earnest intention tae destroy my apprentice's copies, but his work was so excellent... even better than that by my own hand. His embellishment a joy tae see... I could nae bear tae destroy them. But I cannae keep them either. So I turn them over tae ye— —tae return tae Jan van der Goes. Keep 'em safe. Make sure the seals remain intact. They are very valuable.'

Francis bundled two of the folios into a leather bag supplied by the mapmaker. And while the mapmaker made good the coffer with box and basket returned, Francis took the third folio, in blackened leather, and pushed it into a sailcloth bag, stolen from the mapmaker.

Profit, he thought.

Francis left the mapmaker still burying his coffer and joined Tom and Tip at the front door. Both were standing behind closed portal. Alarm in their eyes.

'French at the doors.... Every door, checking houses. We are cut off,' cried Tip.

The mapmaker, running into the front room, grabbed Tom's arm. 'Back door. It runs straight tae *the Shore*. Ye'll be able tae run tae the *Sandport* along the river. There's nae gate there. But always lots of Leither's holding sentinel on the open sea fer whatever sea-bounty she brings in on the tide. Ye'll be able to hide yerself in the crowd and steal out. The cocklepickers niver give up, not whilst there's bairns tae feed.'

Around one hundred yards from the mapmaker's house, Tom, Francis and Tip rested. The cannon started up again. This time it was cannon from the sea—from English ships. The *women* took cover in a doorway to understand where the shot was landing. About eighty paces away, along their direction of travel, roof tiles were hitting the cobbled street.

'It's close. The ships have found their range... seems like they are targeting our part of town,' offered Tip.

Francis held his head to the sky, muttering blasphemies unheard, then returned to spit hard on the ground. 'Months and more, shot has landed in the sea, sand or buried itself in the turf... Yet tonight those sailor bastards find their skill. Methinks, in this venture, God is not with us, Tom.'

'*Wheest*, Francis.' ordered Tom. 'If God be against us, we wouldn't have got this far. Think of it, as he sends the cannon to make good our escape. Well targeted fire to keep French heads down.'

'Aye, and knock ours off, no doubt. For he owes me no favours.'

The empty streets were now occupied. People sought better places to be—all running from those areas hit by cannon. Panic was about, as husband yelled at wife and child to flee the area. Soldiers were everywhere directing the rout; clearing the area for more soldiers coming in from other parts to reinforce the area against expected attack.

But for all the activity—all was the better for it. Better for making escape. *Three ladies* now had good cause to be running down the wynd towards new places. Towards *the Shore*, the riverside that ran its length to the Sandport, and the interned ships blocking the way to the sea.

The noise was first, a crash on the roofline above—a building hurt. Then a rain of roof tiles came down; missiles to halt the *women's* run, and the three found cover under the house's timbered arch. But the house cried more and Francis looked to see where the damage was. But tiles kept falling and kept him tight to the building side.

Francis looked to Tom. Tip cowered. Tom shouted, but he was not heard. The house spoke too loudly. It groaned around them. Then it fell. Stone, tile and timber hit the floor. The *women* buried.

Tom awoke, blind to the scene around him. Then he felt something tugging at his arm—moving him so the tiles covering his head slid away. He moved leg and free arm to push. Then as his head cleared the tiles, he saw Tip pulling at his arm to heave him free of the timber and tile that covered him.

'Where's Francis?' Tom groaned; his words choked by the dust in his lungs and throat.

Tip looked to where Francis last stood and saw nothing but rubble. Then he spied a foot. He clambered over tile and timber to pull again at the house, to bloody his fingers more and cut his hands deeper—all to free Francis. Then Francis appeared like a shoot from the ground, punching his way clear of the debris that surrounded him. The building tried to hold him back, to keep him fixed, but Francis screamed escape and pushed aside roof timber and stone from his legs to see himself free.

'My dress is well ruined now. Bessie be calling me some *bad* names when I return it.'

Tom was happy to see Francis safe, with nothing but bad cut and bruise, his grateful arm clasping Tip tightly around his shoulders. All three looked around. Fire had taken hold of some of the buildings nearby. But no inquisitive eyes were on them, no French, no garrison guards.

Tip broke free Francis' grasp and moved forward to see the way to *the Shore* more clearly. 'Hold men,' he instructed.

'Look at the lad,' declared Francis, 'He saves our necks from the rubble and now he thinks he's in charge.'

'Men, time to run… Run to *the Shore*,' ordered Tip.

With Tip giving the all clear to leave, all three took to the street; their travel hidden by the sounds of cannon and the cries of people caught in their fire. They managed to run clear the wynd and made haste along *the Shore*, onto the Sandport; the open way to the sea that led through Leith's walls.

Confusion was their cover. Ten score people were running to find shelter, or bolster the firing lines. Cannon-fire cracked from the walls and ramparts, aiming at the threat without. No Frenchman or Leither paid heed to the *women*. Even the musketeers on the ships and boats, covering the Sandport way, failed to target the *women* running out of Leith. Not whilst other woman and Leithers, caught again on the beaches outside the walls, were running in.

Chapter XVIII

It was rumour on the Wednesday. On Thursday it was talk. By Friday it was rumour no more. Marie of Guise was dead. She died 11th day of June 1560.

No one in the English trenches, or on the hills, or in the forts that surrounded Leith knew for certain how she died. Many speculated. No one knew the truth of it, but all were glad she was dead.

'There'll be nae tears fer that troublesome coo.'

With the good news, the men's spirits lifted. An end was in sight. All were sure of it. The English and the Protestant Scot celebrated, even the Catholic Scot and the French held their breath, hoping for an end to it so long as it meant truce and not defeat.

By Monday the following week, a truce was called. And by Thursday, Jack and his troop had joined others, breaking bread and sharing jugs of ale on the beach outside Leith's walls. Ate and supped, joked and laughed with those they tried previously to kill—the French.

Jack walked the victualling. He patrolled the tables to see men with men, all eating and drinking; platters of roasted beef, bacon and poultry aplenty, wine and beer—good cheer. The English and Scottish soldiers were untroubled to see the French gather up more than their share to take back for the children and women in their care; those hungry souls still behind the walls. They applauded the French for their meagre contribution to the fare; one horse pie, sad roast capon, and six roasted rats fattened on decay. All seemed to share, as if they were old friends breaking a fast and enjoying a feast. Some soldiers, heartened by the goodwill, asked Lord Grey to send supplies into Leith. But it was not Lord Grey's purpose to give respite to the besieged, only a taste of it— to lessen their resolve to fight on in the absence of their queen. But the men were already tired of siege, and the most of them were pleased to stop the fighting, forget the harm and forgive—*the most of them.*

Finn walked the tables too, at Jack's back, as directed by Robert to see him safe. But foul purpose was about Finn, hidden poorly behind his Irish eyes. He smiled sourly as he caught the eyes of the French. He roughly pushed Frenchmen aside who stood in his way. He hoped they took offence. He aimed to malign. He wanted fair reason to draw a blade in righteous defence—to stab away his hate and restore his pride. But no one took his ill manners as insult. All laughed it off with wine and beer.

Robert was close by, always having a care for his men. Finn's murderous intent was clear to Robert, and fearing trouble, he stepped up to Finn, placing his hand firmly on his arm.

'Hold yerself, Finn. I'm tired of steppin' in when yer prudence takes its leave.'

Finn turned and smiled at Robert, releasing his hand, replying, 'Ye worry too much, Rab.' Then he turned away.

Robert stepped in closer and reapplied his hand. His hold tighter than before, and growled, 'Keep wearin' yer handsome smile, Finn… and stay yer blade.'

Finn turned again to Robert, but this time he had thrown away his smile and found an unfamiliar scowl instead. 'Look to yer pack of dogs, Rab,' he snarled, 'I'm one hound no longer in yer care.'

'Cuttin' a few Frenchies is nae goin' tae bring Jamie back... *Red Wolf.*'

Finn wrenched his arm free of Robert's strong grasp. 'Perhaps not Rab, my boy, but I'll be able to stand afore my brother, and tell him his grief is shared by a good deal many more French fathers.'

'Ye've killed enough tae maintain yer honour... let go yer murder.' Robert held his stare firm. 'Jamie chose fightin' and not ploughin'. Death and hurt is often the only pay we realise.'

Finn shook his head. 'It takes more than a sword to make an Irish warrior. He is judged by the heads he takes. Jamie's account is deficient. I'll need to be murderin' more to maintain his Irish honour and fill his warrior's tally... Him not here no more to see to it for himself.'

'Then yer next fight will be wi' me... I swear it Finn. And I'll see ye join Jamie afore ye cause any trouble this day.'

Finn held his tongue. Robert's words—his threat, did nothing to ease his Irish ire. He held his face firm—stern, his Irish cheer missing as he challenged Robert's authority. But Robert was not for retreat. So Finn, not wanting fight with his friend, not wanting to harm or kill him, smiled and bowed his head in submission. 'A feast with poor company is still a feast.' Finn rubbed his arm, giving him time to find his sweet Irish manner in amongst his hatred, and bring it back to the fore. '...and besides, Rab, ye've a strong grip... and my arm is now far too sore to be wielding a heavy blade.'

Jack walked on, touring the tables. He had not witnessed the scene between Robert and Finn. His concentration was engaged, searching for the French Captain. He asked around for the French

Captain's name. Many knew him from Jack's description, and were keen to give a name, proclaimed with pride, although they refused to tell Jack where he could find him.

'You look for *Charles Boulliers*?'

'I do,' replied Jack.

'Why do you seek him?'

'He spared my life, so I promised myself to return a favour as a matter of my own honour.'

'How far does your honour to yourself run?'

'As deep as I can deliver.'

The priest was earnest. Thin. Starved. His face wore two months hunger, and his gown hung on him like a shroud. He did not seem impressed by Jack's declaration of honour.

'You cannot repay your debt to Captain Boulliers. He is dead, murdered by his woman.'

Jack was caught, only slightly, saddened by the priest's news, and so he turned away to hide his half-regret. Composure, however, was quick to find Jack and he turned back to the priest, to say, 'I am sorry to hear the man is dead, and sadder to hear of death's cause. For I think he wished to die in battle… and to be killed by a far nobler hand.'

Jack felt sorry for the wretch in front of him, and picked up a loaf of bread from the table closest, to hand it to the priest.

'Save your tainted bread. It is offered as poorly as your condolences.'

'Tainted?' asked Jack. 'And I am sorry if you sense my sympathy is half given, for I only met the man once, and would have gladly killed him to save his woman the chore.'

'Honesty from a sinner is simply half a lie. The bread you offer is tainted, as all heretic offerings are. How else am I to judge alms from those filled with the poison of a bastard faith?'

'Bread is bread, *Father*. Think not on the hand that gives it, but the baker who bakes it, or the hand that planted the seed and threshed the wheat. I'm sure a Catholic hand, somewhere, was in the course of its making.' Jack held out the bread again. '*Here*, take it for the children. God will forgive gifts taken from the heretic.'

The priest thought on, and took the bread from Jack, nodding his gratitude. 'For the children.' The priest crossed himself. 'Does your honour debt still stand to the dead?'

'If it will see him rest easier in Heaven… yes.'

'Wait here.'

The priest was gone for the best part of an hour, and Finn and Jack waited by the table with the most jugs filled, and cups to empty.

When the priest returned, he had with him a small boy, no more than five years old, his eyes black and empty.

'Captain Boulliers leaves the boy he adopted—his woman's child. No one wants him. There is no one to care for him. Will you take the lad?'

'I am sorry. I am not from here, or even there. I am a soldier caught in whichever war prevails on me. I cannot take the boy.'

Finn caught the boy's eye, and he smiled at him. He beckoned him over, but the boy stayed fast by the priest's side. So he tempted him with a chicken quarter pulled out of a nearby Frenchman's hand. The Frenchman objected of course. He stood up to defend his repute and retrieve his bird's leg. But Finn threw him a vicious scowl in reply.

The Frenchman stood his ground, mean and angry. Finn maintained his black-look, held hard his face and stance, and snarled in aggression. The Frenchman was big and battle tried; he was not for yielding—not put-off by brutish show. But his comrade recognised his friend's challenger, and whispered, '*Loupe Rouge,*' and thinking better of challenge with a beast of greater repute, the outraged Frenchman threw away his anger and bowed his eyes in compliance, to survive another day of a bloody campaign.

As the Frenchman gave way, Finn's scowl changed to self-satisfied smirk. He had quietened the complaint. His name had fought his battle. His reputation was now well made, and his smirk turned to triumphant smile.

The boy now stretched forward to take the chicken from Finn, but not to eat it. Then, slowly, he moved to stand beside Finn as if he were family.

'It is the first food the boy has taken since they took his mother away,' said the priest. 'It seems brutish behaviour impresses him.'

Jack looked at the child and Finn's kind attention. He thought of Finn's loss, the child's loss, and his own guilt gnawed at him; it bit hard into his own sorrow and poor thought; into his bitter heart—the heavy armour of his melancholia. His face wore regret openly, and the priest was cold to it.

The priest nodded his head in easy acceptance, both of Jack's refusal and his own confirmation of another selfish man's excuse. He stepped forward to retrieve the boy from Finn, in order to return the boy to the orphanage.

'I will take the boy.'

The priest looked at Jack, surprised.

Melancholia had its grip tight on Jack. It rendered him weak in spirit—selfish in nature. But as Jack looked at the boy—into his eyes, it was not selfless charity that changed his view and pressed him to say *yes* to the priest, but the notion that his own melancholia would find it hard to thrive, whilst he had cause to live for something greater than himself—a devotion grander than his dedication to his own sorrow; the care and nurture of a child. He thought a sacrifice of care for the boy, neither kith nor kin, could be atonement for his sin, and see his spirit healed by the beneficence of his action.

The priest said nothing. He simply walked away and left the boy behind. He felt wretched in his doing. He knew nothing of Jack Brownfield, his true faith, his piety, or if he was a better man to care for an innocent child, or if, indeed, he was a better man than Charles Boulliers. For a fair Catholic, Boulliers may have been, a heroic soldier perhaps, but a kind man to a boy's mother, no.

He kept his head from turning back. He blocked out sight of the boy in case he weaken, and thus reclaim him from a stranger and a life shaped by another's faith, and the boy's damnation because of it. He held his resolve by means of his mental discourse with God and his company on the walk back to Leith and his ruined church.

Can a man have two faces? It is my knowledge that women only have one, rarely completely innocent, but often free from evil in its form. But as for men, I have known many men who carry both the faces of good and evil. It is the way of it. It is such that men are rarely completely good or are evil absolute. War would be noble if man wore only one face, wholly good or wholly evil. Then the badge of evil would be clear. It would be marked on a man's face, and the good could feel comforted that their cause against evil was clear and just.

Only God and I, his priest and confessor, know the truth of Charles Boulliers. Men may hail the warrior, but God will judge that man harshly for his cruelty to just one of his innocents. And even if his cruelty was born out of his own ruined childhood, and his witness of a beloved mother beaten at the hands of a wicked father, it is poor excuse to lay before the Holy Mother and St Peter. I pray time was allowed for that poor soul, before he was snuffed, to ask for forgiveness for his wickedness and so enter the gates of Heaven. And may God forgive me too for my own sins, for they now number more since I have cast my sister's child into a heretic's house.

Chapter XIX

The day was sunlit, warm, and war was stilled. Yet Jack was in poor humour. For even though amnesty had been proclaimed, and plans for peace rumoured, Lord Grey, that very morning, had refused to release Jack from his duty. Jack was unhappy. His commitment to Lord Grey was honoured in his mind, and his commitment to Henri Hueçon and the Guild found wanting.

Jack was keen to return to matters regarding his obligation to Henri, fearing any further delay, even by a day, would cause him further dishonour. He was already many months late for his appointment, and amidst his commitment's discomfort, he remembered Henri's words on the quayside at Newcastle at year's start; *'It is very important… your new commission awaits, and your new master is not a man to be kept waiting.'* Jack winced at the thought of it. Belayed by injury and siege were poor excuses when added to his time spent languishing in a soft bed and weeks of comfort gifted by the generous attentions of a lady. Still, with his new master's documents safe, clutched tight by his secretary, tardiness may be forgiven and promises made to enhance his pay and the standing of his new commission may still be honoured, if haste to Antwerp was his new resolve.

But there was further irritation that weighed heavy on Jack's already irksome temper. It was his recent adoption of the boy. A responsibility that troubled a man without any knowledge of childcare, properly attained from well-tried husbandry.

The boy would not take food from Jack, or Robert, or even the kinder women of the camp. It concerned Jack, for the boy was already pale and thin at his adoption, and a sick and needy child would not aid his goal of urgent departure to Antwerp. But fortunately a trust in Finn emerged, a relationship strange in its birth. One in which the boy took the food that Finn produced, and it was the only food the boy ate, regardless of its poverty or favourless qualities.

No one more than Jack was surprised at the boy's attachment to the mad Irishman; a man returned to a feral skirmishing soldier, on foot, away from the saddle of a horse, and garb of good sense.

'The boy looks to you for food,' announced Jack, watching the boy's hungry eyes follow Finn as he ate a large piece of bread by the side of the road, cross-legged, sword in lap.

'Aye, he sees me as his larder,' replied Finn.

'No, it goes deeper than that.'

'What do ye mean, Jack m' boy?'

'He trusts you like no other.'

'Aye, no doubt he is taken by my handsome appearance.' Finn looked at the boy, tore off a piece of bread and passed it to a grateful hand. 'Am I not the bonny hound that runs afore the hunters to run down their prey?' Finn turned his attention to Jack with a measured pause and words designed to sting. 'The boy perhaps sees me as the true pack leader, *eh Jack?*'

Jack sneered at Finn's reasoning. 'If you were a dog, Finn. You would be the bitch that bore him and not the dog that leads him.'

Finn smiled away Jack's gibe. 'Aye, the boy is fond of me, and I have an affection for him. Like he was my kin. Perhaps ye should give him to me as my cadet. He has good hair, but no *Gaeilge* tongue... but I can teach him that. He would be a better man to know the *Gaeilge*, so he can converse in my beautiful language.' Finn tore off another piece of bread to hold out to the boy. 'The boy learns quick... listen...'

As the boy reached out to take the bread—when his fingers nearly grasped the crust, Finn withdrew it sharply.

Finn threw a roguish smile at the lad, and returning the bread to the boy's hand, said, 'Boy, give thanks in Irish.'

'*Go ro maith agat*,' came the boy's quiet reply.

Jack was impressed. 'Whereas I think you have good bond with the lad, and pleased to hear your offer, I see your mischief with the boy, and see it as good reason for me to take him back home with me. If only to save him from being teased into adulthood.'

'So be it,' replied Finn, shrugging his shoulders with apparent indifference. Finn looked at the boy and wore a frown as a show of sadness. He held the boy's gaze, and saw the familiarity in his eyes that reminded him of his nephew, killed on Leith's fields, and he countered his grief with a quip. 'Just as well... I mean ye cannae teach a Scot to be Irish.' Finn shot a wry look at Jack. 'Just like it's foolish for a Scot to pretend to be English... *Eh, Jack?*'

It was clear to Jack that Finn's apparent easy acceptance of his decision regarding the boy's guardianship was, in fact, poorly received—Finn's eyes shouted it.

Finn continued his taunt. 'What's it like to be a man hiding behind the name of another man. Calling himself a Borderer when it suits him to deny his proper nation. Is it so ye can always choose to be on the winning side?'

Jack took some offence at Finn's comment. Finn's swollen cocksureness, bolstered by his returned Irish garb, irked Jack, but he set it aside for the sake of friendship, co-operation and a sympathy held for Finn's loss.

'Finn, I have a commission for you and Tip. Return to the Marches—to *Hawick*. Take the boy to my uncle's house there. Catherine, my ward, will be birthing soon. She may as well care for two as well as one.'

Finn spat on the ground, his easy demeanour hardened. 'Why can ye not take the boy yerself? He's yer charge. I've too many French to be cutting bloody, to be nursemaidin' a boy not my own kin.'

Despite Jack understanding Finn's nettle, he was finding it hard to deal with Finn's restless temper, it rankled him. So he took a deep breath to calm his composure. 'Because Finn, the rest of us travel to Antwerp. We take up our long overdue commission and return the crippled Spaniard to his master. I think the boy be happier travelling with you to safer places than those to which we travel.' Jack looked hard for agreement on Finn's face. But there was none. 'The fight with the French is over. Have you not cut enough French throats this year and last, to see your blood rested?'

'A hundred more throats will need to be bled before I can stand afore my brother in *Carlow* and smile.' Finn looked to his boots to hide his sorrow from Jack, then he raised his head boldly in strident complaint. 'And what about my commission with ye in Antwerp? My pay? Do you think ye would last a moment more without my fightin' skill to save yer neck?'

Jack held back his temper. It was difficult. He wanted to release his own distress inside him—to shout it out, and strike at something—to kill it. Finn was pushing him, and Robert was nowhere to see them both restrained.

'When you see the boy safe into the care of Catherine, you can travel on to join us in Antwerp… if you can find it.'

'My daddy did not raise me to be a nurse,' countered Finn. 'And I know my east from my west. It seems we set out east for pay… only for you to lead us back west, because you couldn't hold yer own in a fight… Who was it that knocked you down on the French ship? Aye, I remember… was it not the ship's cook? Did he use his peg leg to batter you, and his soup spoon to lay ye out?'

Jack's anger was now apparent to all, and the boy shot a frightened look at Jack and hid behind Finn.

'Your *daddy*, Finn. Do you know your *daddy*, or do you refer to the cuckold that raised you?'

Finn's face grew red. His eyes glared at Jack. Then he dropped his stare and spat on the ground, twisting his mouth as he chewed on his tongue.

But Jack did not care that he was stirring an ember of acrimony into a blaze of Irish fury. He wanted Finn to strike, so he could strike back.

'You talk of a father in Carlow, but what of your mother? Francis tells she was a whore with, I suspect, too many men to assign a face as a your natural father.'

Finn stood up sharply, holding his sword. He flicked it hard to the side, which threw the scabbard clean from the blade. And menace replaced Finn's usual easy demeanour.

Jack stood and did not move. He stayed his hands from his weapons. He gave Finn no reason to strike in defence; no further encouragement to strike in anger.

Finn stepped forward, sword pointing to the side, blade angled to Jack for an easy cut. 'Nae one calls my mammy a whore.'

Jack shook his head at Finn, a gesture to halt Finn's advance.

But Finn took another step. 'What's the matter, Captain? Too scared to draw yer blade? Let's fight. Let's show the boy here the measure of an Irishman against… What are ye today? A Scotsman born, a Borderer bred, or do you be a bluff Englishman? Do ye still think ye too good to be Gaelic?'

Jack stood firm. Teeth clenched. His anger flooded his being. He wanted excuse to strike at Finn—to lay good sense aside for an impassioned rush to cleanse his soul of all its hurt.

'Take the lid off yer pot, Captain… Let blow yer steam… Draw yer sword.'

Jack's hand grabbed the hilt of his sword. But he did not draw it. Instead he pushed down hard, as if the act would bury the blade deep and out of reach.

'Come on Captain. Draw yer sword. Go on. What are ye? Man or frightened mouse? Let me end yer melancholy… be a disconsolate man no more… and get yerself ready to meet the Devil, because men without faith only have one destination in the afterlife.'

Jack snarled through gritted teeth. 'One mair step ye feckless Irish turd… and the bairn will be wearin' yer blood… I swear the blaw I bring on ye will cleave yer foolish mopped head frae yer body.'

Finn just smiled and took his step. 'It seems the Borderer comes out on yer tounge, Captain Jack, and the Scots taints yer words… Finding yerself, Captain, after all these years? Rememberin' whit ye are… are ye? Captain, *Jack.*'

At Jack's back appeared Robert, armed. Finn looked over Jack's shoulder and he cooled a little, and stepped back. He angled his blade away and relaxed his grip on the sword.

'Well Captain, seems *yer* nursemaid is here.' Finn put back on his easy Irish smile. 'Perhaps ye call my mammy what she was.' Finn rubbed the boy's head to cool his temper more. 'My hot blood always get's my mouth into trouble.'

Jack breathed out, as Robert's hand alighted gently on Jack's back.

'Are we settled?' demanded Robert.

'Aye,' said Finn. He looked at the boy as he bent down to

retrieve his scabbard from the ground. 'Boy, yer first sword lesson. Ye can draw yer words against yer friends, but never yer blade. Yer fine blade is fer yer enemies, and curse the blade drawn against yer friends.' He thrust the sword back into its scabbard and placed it with the boy, its weight telling on young arms. 'A gift fer ye. I'd break the bastard blade, but it's a canny sword.' Finn turned to Jack. 'I'll get the boy home. Tip will keep me right.'

Jack nodded his approval and his thanks.

Finn started to walk away, but turned for a final word. 'But after I deliver the boy, I break our bond. I have my own places to go, and a name to make even more feared amongst the French. There is a price to pay fer robbin' the nest of McCuul young'uns.'

ɞɔɔ

The next day, Finn left the camp at Leith with Tip and the boy. He did not say farewell to the others.

Francis was sore he had left without a word in parting, and Robert could only offer a thought shared to sweeten a sour Francis.

'Perhaps he seeks himself. Him lost in his grief. We are all lost men when grief sweeps reason away. Anger changes oor allegiance... at least until oor blood cools.'

'Then Finn will be lost for a long while, for his blood never cools. Methinks he thinks of himself bigger than us now... his loyalty in question. Vengeance and murder his only commitment. His challenge to Captain Jack yesterday confirmed it.'

But Robert shook his head and put an arm around Francis' diminutive frame. 'Perhaps Francis, he, like us, may rebel from time-tae-time, but he is still devoted tae us. Be certain of that.'

But Francis still held resentment. 'I think we'd better be after him before he cuts Tip's throat, and steals the boy to turn into a wild murderous dog.'

'Nah, Finn will see him safe right enough. His dedication will be resolute in this matter. His mind may be fickle when it is unsettled, but he will not foul his promise tae Jack.'

'You apply your honour poorly, Robert. Finn is like the most of us—selfish to the core.'

'Perhaps men are selfish, Francis. Some mair than others, but also we are all steadfast tae a degree. It's simply a knack tae know how tae measure the man, and know his heart.'

'Then your heart is the measure, because you are forever steadfast.'

Robert was startled by Francis' tribute. 'Is that honeyed praise, Francis? Are ye now choosin' tae be a mellow fellow?'

'No, it's complaint, because your devotion to Jack and all your charge, will be the death of us all… some day.'

∞◊∞

Within days, reports of peace were well rooted amongst the camps, with hostilities all but ended. There was little doubt the conflict was over, and Lord Grey found little reason to hold Jack to his commission.

Jack did not delay. He with Robert, Tom, Francis and Peppo were on the road, travelling away from Leith to a better port to see them to Antwerp via a calmer sea, and an ardent oath not to be deflected from their journey's goal again.

'It's been a long road travellin' tae Antwerp,' declared Robert as he sniffed the morning air and rubbed eyes still with sleep.

Jack nodded. 'I only hope it is a road worth the travel.'

Jack leaned back on his horse to stretch out stiffness awarded by a poor bed only left an hour ago. As his face touched the sky, he thought on all those travelling with him, as well as those left to journey on other roads, or lost in war and history along the way.

'This has been a testing journey, Robert.'

'It's nae finished Jack. We've a long way tae travel. But for every trial that tests the traveller, a pilgrim finds a blessin' along the way.'

'Good thought, Robert.' Jack's mind recalled a good friend left at Newcastle; a pilgrim set upon his own passage to a monastery. 'I earnestly hope Edward's journey has had better blessing than ours.'

[The story of the boy continues under the title,
The Mare's Breath.]
[The story of Finn McCuul continues under the title,
Red Wolf.]

Peace

The most mighty princess, Elizabeth by the grace of God, Queen of England, France, and Ireland, defender of the faith, and the most Christian king, Francis and Marie, by the same grace of God, King and Queen of France and Scotland: have accorded upon a reconciliation of a peace and amity to be inviolably kept, between them, their subjects, kingdoms and countries. And therefore in their names it is strictly commanded to all manner of persons borne under their obeisances, or being in their service, to forbear all hostility either by sea or land, and to keep good peace each with other this time forwards, as they will answer there unto at their uttermost perils.

The Proclamation of Peace 7th July MDLX (1560)

Under the terms of the peace treaty, three thousand, six hundred and thirteen French soldiers had left Leith and its environs by the 17th July, and were put on ships, under English supervision, bound for Calais. Another six hundred women and children accompanied them. The defences around Leith were destroyed, and French military presence in Scotland was all but removed, except for one hundred and twenty French soldiers left at *Dunbar* and *Inchkeith*.

Some French soldiers would never return home. They would be laid to rest in the graveyards around Leith and Edinburgh, along with the many more Scot and English soldiers that had failed to remove the French by force.

The fortunate would have their stones and timber markers tended by their women and wives. Their names recorded in glory.

It would be reported by Monsieur d'Oysel that Captain Charles Boulliers was one of the French warriors who fell. *A captain of credit. A captain of France.* It was recorded so. Testimony of his brave action was made. Pension arranged for his grieving widow in Normandy. And his son would carry his sword proudly on to the day he died. His men would fondly remember Boulliers, as a soldier without discredit to that calling, because while he lived, he fought to preserve his country's honour in another man's country. But those who knew the truth of the French Captain could never call him a good man.

Along with broken bodies and broken promises, there are always broken hearts left behind. And many an unwed Scots lass, without a marriage bond, was left on the *Shore* at Leith, as ships loaded their sweethearts to take them back to France.

There was many a wedded wife there too; those with Scottish husbands at hand and lovers leaving; women, who stood Leith's ground and searched the faces of the men departing; forlorn, perhaps looking to hold onto adulterous love already lost, or perhaps simply to offer a fond farewell to their beloved Frenchmen, Englishmen and *Borderers* too.

PART 3
'the Black Merchants' Guild'

Antwerp

Chapter XX

It rained. It had rained for six days. But the wet had not washed the month's journeying from Edward. It only added further discomfort to a man road dirty and travel tired. He looked down to his bundle turned into heavy burden by the rain, and his sadness grew deeper at the sight of woollen robes tied and parcelled, and not worn.

But sorrow had not finished with Edward. The weather found new spite to throw at the traveller, and Edward thought to sit out this cruel new wind, added to even greater wet. He found respite in a shelter from the rain, where the wind's blow may help him dry a little. He thought perhaps a closed eye might gift him kinder thoughts to better take him onto journey's last mile. So he sat in his refuge and shut tight his eyes, and his mind dispelled discomfort and sought the better cheer that comes out of reverie.

It had taken him several weeks to reach his Cistercian monastery. He could have travelled by sea to *Pontevedra*, in Northern Spain. He could have taken the direct route to his monastery. But that would be too easy—too easy for the Guild to track him if they had a want to see their secrets assured, and him quietened by means of a malicious death and a lonely grave. So he had travelled to *Navarre*, to stay a while and lay false talk of heading south to *Valencia* and beyond, in reality to cross the border into *Asturias*, and then into *Galicia*, a land of mountain, moor and forest—to find his monastery… and his peace.

It was not hard travel. Not particularly eventful. He journeyed alone in scholar's robes. But he had made the most of a journey taken for his own reasons, and paid for by his own money, instead of under commission from a master, or employer, or even under covert sponsorship of the Black Merchants' Guild.

He thought of the life left behind. A life made in the Scottish Marches. A life made uncomfortable for a scholar who had outgrown his students, but made comfortable for a man who had found new responsibility and a deep fulfilling friendship. For his tutelage had grown into mentorship of two young people—both with a fervour worth shepherding. But cruel circumstance had killed mentorship, and the Guild's deceitful intent, paying for his place in the Marches, had grown sour. So he had run from the Guild to bury himself deep within another institution, and return to a life long forgotten.

As he thought back to that life forgotten, he pondered on the merits of it. Monastic life was often a poor excuse for a godly one. And a born and nurtured intellect was not always a guaranteed path to more studious responsibilities in an abbey, and he wondered if the path to the monastery was a road badly chosen.

So he searched further back for happier remembrances— schooldays. He squeezed his closed eyes tighter to see them real and not simply as a fancy in a memory grown kinder by the years. Then came better memories of a younger age, and remembrances of new knowledge discovered—*happy learning years*.

Good memories of school days attached themselves to bitter

thoughts of his father. His father, so kind and generous to all, was one who disagreed with his King. A man who stood with others, brave and resolute, to openly take fair issue with Henry VIII's mercenary will of supremacy over the Church and his invalid marriage to the Boleyn woman. Forced publicly to take the *Oath of Succession*, he thought to move his son to the care of friends in the north, to a rich and powerful abbey that would see him safe.

So, even recollections of happy learning days were cut short; when his parents took him from his school at Winchester at the age of thirteen, to find protection in the Abbey of St Mary at Furness.

Edward remembered all. How bitter he felt to be removed from his school. How ignorant he was, at the time, to the cause of it. How a noble man and a gracious father, who gave greatly of himself and devoted to his faith, had refused the final indignation, to take the *Oath of Supremacy,* and agree to the King's self-appointed governance of the Church. And how Henry's men took their pleasure in their King's warrants—foul justice. They saw to it that his father was dragged, and then chained in a public place to starve. His mother disappeared soon after. Edward never saw or heard from her again.

God willing, she is safe.

But like his schooldays, even his life in the abbey was stolen from him. It ended after only three years. Cut short by the long arm of a king—and the suppression of the monasteries. Left with no pension, and only a letter of reference from Abbot Pele of Furness, he sought opportunity to find gainful work when a godly trade was robbed from him by the *Dissolution*.

But it was circumstance, not his condition, which led him into the Black Merchants' Guild. And the Guild was good at creating circumstance—it was very good indeed.

Reward from the Guild could be in many forms. Gold was the

blood of life for many, but rarely guaranteed loyalty. The Guild did not trust those who would sell their loyalty only for gold. So the Guild studied those they desired. They learned their quarry's devotion, their secrets and their passions. It was these they used to subvert the individual—those well placed to serve the Black Merchants' Guild. They gave favours not easily attained elsewhere, but they also used subversion and blackmail—both regularly and effectively.

The Black Merchants' Guild was both powerful and wealthy. It interceded for its merchant members when trade and profit were threatened. It coerced governments, sovereigns and the Church to favour its members' business, and it maintained a route for merchants without a proud patrician face, to attain status in a society that still favoured those with long-established noble birthright. It bought men places of power, whether it was into robes of state, court or even richer robes within the Church.

The Guild was, therefore, most successful procuring its membership amongst those poor born merchants, whose great wealth had been acquired by their own trading prowess.

Those indebted to the Guild could signify their fidelity by the presentation, in their home or establishment, of a bust of *Nikolaos of Myra*, the venerated saint of *Lycia*. Portrayed in bronze, strangely tight-lipped and not holding a gospel, but instead a ledger.

It was said, the origins of the Black Merchants' Guild sprang from the *Varangians*—northern born warriors serving the Byzantine Emperors. Bold fighting men, who once watched over Saint Nikolaos' bones. Shrewd men, who later found themselves displaced from the Emperor's service and forced to find new masters. Ambitious men, who applied their skill and strength of arms to the benefit of new merchant employers, and in turn saw themselves as traders—warrior-merchants, like their ancient Viking forefathers before them.

The Guild was also known amongst its members as *Non dici*, [not to be spoken], for to talk of the society outside its membership was strictly prohibited. It was a rule break within the Guild, and rule breaking meant ruin or death. And death was always preferable, because ruin was complete, and in truth, death was often following close behind.

Edward's coercion, his entrapment within the Guild, was education—the revelation of knowledge not known to him in the libraries of Spain and Holy Rome. He was given access by the Guild and his thirst was indulged. He was employed as librarian to some of the greatest libraries in Europe, cataloguing writings not read for a thousand years. But, even though his tour of the libraries was comprehensive, the contents of one or two libraries remained unknown to him; those with works too great to be read by mere laymen, without direct appointment from the Bishop of Rome himself—books with writings and illustrations too corrupting to be seen by man. These libraries were promised to him by the Guild on completion of simple tasks. His last task was to spy on the household of one of King Henry VIII's knights, sitting in the English Northern Marches, where there was profit in knowledge, and where influencing war or peace was to the Guild's benefit.

The last Guild commission stole too much from Edward. It robbed him of too much time—too much of his true self.

But now he had reached his journey's end and he sat only a short walk from halls of worship, within a temple of devotion. But there was no sound of evening prayers, no chant, no canticles to sing his approach. His arrival and departure from the Spanish monastery in Galicia was a month past, and instead he sat in a doorway of the *Grote Markt*, looking up at merchant housing, warehouses, and the fane centre of commerce; the guild buildings of Antwerp.

Henri Hueçon's name and description, passed amongst people on the street, carried Edward easily to Henri's apartments overlooking the broad market street of the *Meir*. The apartments were in a building most modest, and it surprised Edward to discover Henri's home not to be the palace he was expecting from a man with a show of fine and expensive tastes. But to its credit, it was located in a far better street than others he walked, as he found his way from the quay to the centre of the city.

As Edward looked up to the four floors of Henri's abode, he could not help but notice the strange arrangement of windows on the higher levels of the building's facade. They were larger windows than others fitted to the building, or even the street. Even larger than the rich commercial properties and patricians' housing he witnessed as he traversed the city.

Stranger still, was the sight inside Henri's home. As Edward was welcomed inside by two servants, dressed as princes, he could not help but marvel at the objects and furnishings. It was a glimpse of the world outside Edward's own understanding. The whole world in its finest clothes—the Orient, Persia, Egyptian antiquity and Greek splendour—all were there and placed as if it all belonged together, as if it all was never meant to be apart.

Edward was left waiting in a grand reception room with the large windows he noticed from the street. Except the windows were not only on the façade, but on the opposite elevation too. Edward viewed the scene outside, from each set of windows in turn. The front, overlooking the marketplace, and another set overlooking the rich mansions of the patrician class, built behind the Meir in the open spaces of a crowded city. And, as Edward looked to the windows view into the market street, and around at the splendour of Henri's room, and then to the rear and the grand housing, he thought, *One eye where he's been, a thought to where he is, and another eye on where he wants to be.*

'Edward!'

Edward looked to the voice, to see Henri flanked by his princely servants.

'Good evening, Henri. It is good of you to see me.'

'Ah, Edward… you are wet, *non?*' Henri gestured to his servants. 'A blanket for my guest… at once.'

Edward nodded to acknowledge Henri's show of care. 'Your servants Henri—both handsome boys.'

'You are too generous. They simply fit the poor suits of my last aides.'

Edward smiled at Henri's wit, and asked, *'Poor…* how can that be? You dress them like princelings. *Poor,* is itself a poor choice of descriptive.'

Henri raised his hands in surrender. 'You have caught me. It is always true my servants dress better than their betters.' Henri led Edward to a small table flanked by two large gilded armchairs—thrones. 'Some think, to stay in fashion, it is simply enough to change their collars… I, on the other hand, change the very hue of my accessories.'

'Accessories, Henri?'

'Mes valets, Edward. Now take a seat to rest your legs.'

The servants returned with a heavy brocaded blanket in rich green and red threads, and Edward stood up so one of the servants could wrap him before returning to his seat. Both servants then stood behind Henri's chair, guarding the door, and Edward noticed both men were now wearing swords.

Henri spoke, fingers pointing to each servant in turn, 'This is *Bonetello…* and this is *Francisco…* apprentices from the fencing school of the late *Angelus Viggiani.* Their current fencing master speaks highly of them—in case you have a mind to put them to the test.'

'I do not fence,' replied Edward.

'Perhaps... But you carry a blade nevertheless,' said Henri, earnestly. 'Take an apple Edward. Best use your knife to peel it, so *mes enfants* here may see it gainfully employed... instead of it hidden with foul intent.'

'Do you think I come here to harm you?'

'A man on his way to a monastery does not visit his tailor for advice on what to wear.'

Edward looked away to hide his surprise. *Henri knew his destination*, but then he looked to his bags sitting near the door and assumed Henri had recognised his bundled religious habit. So he returned his head to smile at Henri.

'But it is advice and also help I require.'

'Then I can offer, at the very least, advice. Help on the other hand...' Henri paused, '...well, we shall see.' Henri mimed a cup to his lips and one of the servants left the room briefly.

'I noticed you still wear your scholarly robes.'

'I was robbed of my godly ones,' replied Edward.

'By a thief on the road?'

'No, the robbery was well cloaked. So perhaps they were carried away by a thief in more princely robes.'

Henri's face was illuminated by the hint of accusation, and intrigued by its origins. So he held his gaze on Edward to draw out further discussion. But Edward said nothing more, only returning his stare until another servant, a young boy, entering the room with a tray, broke it.

'Now take a drink with me and let us discuss your current fashion,' announced Henri.

A silver tray with a jug and two glasses was placed on the table in front of Henri. Henri acknowledged the servant, holding his eyes on the retreating boy.

'I will drink better without your men at the door,' announced Edward.

'And I will pour more freely if *mon petits* are close by.'

Henri took the tall, silvered jug and poured red wine into two small etched glasses, giving one to Edward with a smile.

'The wine is a new discovery of mine… A wine previously hidden by those too greedy to see it leave its birthplace.'

Edward sipped the wine and held it on his tongue, swallowing carefully.

'It is good wine, Henri.'

It comes from *Sancerre,* a place birthing many good wines. I have recently secured favours there. Religious intolerances are rife in this world and at times good people need the support of princes to allow them to be who they wish to be.'

'So they give you a good price on their wine?'

'Yes, and gross favours held on account.'

'Favours to you Henri, sometimes come costly.'

'My patronage is reassuringly expensive. But they always find my price fair for the favour they find.' Henri recharged Edward's glass and begged him to take the jug, so he may refill at will. 'How can I help you Edward? Tell me your concerns.'

'My concern is the monastery at Galicia. My godly robes have not replaced my scholarly ones because all was not welcome for me at the abbey—the haven I had chosen for my home. It was taken cruelly from me by, I suspect, the Black Merchants' Guild.'

'The Guild acquires much. Only yesterday we acquired Church interests in cinnabar mines in Spain. But monasteries have no interest for us, except when they have mutual interests in commercial enterprise.' Henri poured himself another drink. 'Let us speak plainly. No riddles. It is clear you have issues with the Guild. You think we strike out at you perhaps… to remove your sanctuary? It is best you tell me your story from the beginning… From that, I will tell you if the Guild had any part to play.'

Edward sat as if comfortable with his surroundings, although he was uneasy with his situation. Henri too, settled in his chair, comforted by a blanket placed over his knees by one of the servants. There was foul reasoning behind Henri's request, and as Edward started to recant his story, he thought it might have been better to refrain from a tale, too difficult in the telling...

Chapter XXI
Edward's Story

'I remember it was mid afternoon when I reached the coast road. It had been a long journey through Asturias and Galicia, walking most of the way. I was unhappy with my shoes and my clothes were better suited to the north than the south. But there was a welcome wind cooling my head—comfort to take my mind off sore feet and weary legs.

I remember the fork in the road—the point at which I could finally sense journey's end, and the end of Edward Hendon, as I was.

I was looking forward to a better life—a monastic one, and leave past deceits behind. I was glad in a way, but sad in another.

It is strange—the mind. The mind that sets its desire on the road ahead—the road unseen, and denies itself... *terminus ad quem*... at a place on journey's travel, rather than at journey's close. Places that show promise of greater comfort and more generous view. Places that, in truth, may be a far, far better rest than the road ahead. It is also strange, the mind that holds onto the comfort and familiarity of the road already travelled, even though prosperity may be lacking, and poorer view exists. Comfort, simply because what is already known holds no surprises to disquiet already troubled thought. But regardless of my musings, I was in good humour on that road.

The walking way clung to the side of high cliff sides, topped with tall trees. The path was cut as a terrace into the rock, with the ocean far below on my right. I remember the sight of the ocean refreshed me. The wind drew patterns on the sea that kept my gaze from my feet, fatigue from my stride, stimulus to my spirit, my hopes enkindled and my dreams revived.

The road was narrow, a wagon width at best, with passing places marked by tall posts at regular intervals. It had good visibility all its length to the point where it disappeared around the headland. I remembered the road would lead to a grand timber viaduct. And I knew I was near my journey's goal.

At the turn of the road, where the viaduct would be normally seen, a terrible sight met me. The massive bridge had been removed. Wiped away, leaving a gaping chasm that was impossible to cross. And in the distance I could see the monastery standing, bathed in sun, and in the harbour, two caravels at anchor.

It was fishing men that told me of the destruction. Hundreds of horsemen killed. How their fishing boats were pulling the dead from the sea for a month after the demolition of the bridge... and how the abbey monks did not come for their fish anymore. And, how the warships stood guard from the sea.

It was by sea, that I approached the monastery. By night. By way of hidden cove and tunnel. A secret entrance situated half a league down the coast. It cost me a handsome purse to procure a local fishing boat to take me there, for the local fishermen feared the place. But I found my way into the secret entrance behind the refectory building. I had been there before. I knew of the monastery's escape to the sea.

The monastery was deserted. No guards at its doors. And I permitted myself a small fire in the kitchen hearth, with dry wood. I considered the sight from the ships too poor to reveal slight smoke to the sentries. Still, I ensured the fire burned small, only on nights with poor sky and no moon. I allowed no window to show a light on the seaward side, and thus kept my presence secret. There was food in the stores—poor choice, but sufficient to see me fed for some considerable time. I would not go hungry.

I had walked an empty abbey before. I had previous cause to walk in solitude along empty corridor, empty cloister, and into empty church. My own in Furness, so many years ago, was emptied after brother monks were pensioned and pried away from their goodly home. It was strange to see it empty. I cannot remember a time before that, when I was in God's holy house, when it was not sated with souls needing medicine and care, alms and sanctuary.

As I walked the empty places, it was the quiet that seemed so wrong. Because there is quiet… and there is deathly silence. The latter is an unnatural soundless world. Too hushed for even a monastery caught in silent meditation. Yet for all the stillness, my imagination conjured up a dozen forms moving about the shadows, all set to do me harm. I am embarrassed to recount that I still have childish fears that conjure up danger, where no danger could exist in such a soundless world.

I knew this monastery. I knew of its library. It was the attraction calling me to its doors from the Marches of Scotland. I knew of its secrets too. Books too lascivious to hold on its shelves were kept in secret places, well hidden. The Abbot knew better than to have such corruption within easy reach. For in the hands of idle men, godly thought was forever tested by the presence of sin, whether it was in written thought or presented of wanton flesh.

I regret the mystery of my brothers' absence gave way to the excitement of having unrestricted access to the great library, and the thoughts of finding new books to be read. Even my daily devotions—prayers, gave way to reading works not writ to save the mortal soul, but to excite febrile thought into ungodly notion.

I remember how I set about, excited, the preparation of a feast of literature—a banquet of books, with new flavours to excite my intellect. How I read through two days and nights until my eyes could not see beyond my outstretched arm.

I did not rest, even on the third night. I did not sleep. There were too many books for me to read. I wanted them all—to read them all. But as I sought out books from the library's *inventorium*—precious volumes on subjects new to me—ideas to challenge my own learned view, I discovered missing volumes. One. Then two. Then five and five more. I looked upon the worktables to locate the books missing from the shelves and I wondered where they were. They would be nowhere else. Tracts to be copied and studied were always done so in the library. No, the books were not there, they were somewhere else, somewhere they should not be.

I thought perhaps the missing books were within another part of the abbey, with other books of ill-repute, or vulgar subject. I do not know why I thought this, because their subjects were science, and of medicine, architecture and fauna. Perhaps I wanted reason to search out the hidden library. Hidden from all but the most trusted brethren.

But to look for that hidden library would take a hundred years, and a hundred years I did not have.

There came a morning when fatigue became too much for me to continue and I found a meagre bed to lie on, to close my eyes. But still I did not sleep. My mind still raged with new knowledge, new thought and new ideas, and an obsession to find hidden books still to read.

So that day I walked the monastery through all doors open, and forced doors that were locked. I looked for clues to the whereabouts of another library, but found nothing except the traces of foreign occupation, and the signs of my brethren moved on without time to make good their preparations for their journey.

I left my search of the crypt for the daylight hours, even though only torch and candle would illuminate it. But the daytime hour gave me some comfort against my fearful imagination, and safety from such ghosts and demons that may have interred themselves into a place of rightful rest and peace, by way of foul deed and iniquity.

The smell was strong in the crypt.

Death, I thought, *coffins disturbed perhaps?*

The crypt was extensive and I was not in a mind to explore the extent of it for sight of a putrid corpse—even for a library full of treasure. But when I examined the records, they showed the last death sixteenth months past. No, something else was dead down there, other than the fated passing of a brother.

For all I reasoned against it, I knew where the answer was—the crypt. But I sat two days in the fresh air of the cloister, before I entered it again.

I took a dozen lighted torches and all the candles I could muster before I could go to the place where the stink of death was the strongest. I quelled the need to leave that place, for the stench was as bad as I have ever experienced. But no sign of death could I find. No tomb disturbed, or rotting corpse.

I looked around for a concealed entrance to a room or vault; markings on the floor, irregularities in the stone, and found nothing. I reasoned, although the smell was strongest in the place I searched, the entrance was to be found somewhere else. My nose was a good instrument and I knew beyond the walls, was death. There was no doubt in that.

I studied each area of the crypt in turn, discounting areas where secret doors would be impossible to conceal. Those areas where floor, wall and low vaulted ceiling showed no signs of fault in the mortar, or break in their construction. For two days I searched, carefully discounting each small area of the crypt; lifting coffer lids to discover nothing but bones; going over each stone and flag in turn.

There was an annexe within the crypt. It seemed to be an addition; later built than the original. It had no door and at its centre, was a large stone coffer, larger than the other coffers placed about the crypt in their smaller anterooms and alcoves. I tried to lift the stone lid, but it was heavier than those I had moved previously. It did not give. I walked around the coffer running my hands over the lid and sides. They were cold and smooth to the touch, until I reached the last side. The stone was not cold. In fact it did not feel like stone at all.

It did not take me long to pick at the slab that formed the end of the coffer to discover it was wood and plaster, painted to look like its neighbours. I could not believe it—the illusion was perfect, and I worked my hands over the panel to find a catch or release. But I found nothing. Then I worked an iron bar into the joints surrounding the timber boarding. I levered hard to dislodge the panel, but it would not move. It took me a while to locate a better tool—one with length enough to apply stronger leverage... Yes, it took me a while longer to split the panel from its hinges.

The panel removed did not reveal a coffin within, but a staircase leading down. I had to stoop to access it, but the staircase led to a tunnel, and the short tunnel led to another staircase, which led to a door, not locked.

Beyond, I found a cave, a *Mithraeum*, with benches on each side running its length to an apse and an altar. Beyond the apse was another door, solid and brute. The smell of death was strongest there—foul, and I knew what lay beyond the door. On a hook by the door the key was at hand, but I did not go further.

I returned to the kitchen store to find strong smelling vinegar, which I soaked into a cloth, wrapping it around my mouth and nose. I returned to the secret passage, and eventually stood before the brute door and unlocked it. The smell from the open door penetrated deep into my nose, and even through the sharp unpleasant odour of the vinegar. The over-note of death was terrible, and I held my hand hard over my face as if to block it out, forcing the cloth to render me light-headed.

I did find a body. I was expecting it. But the room was full of death. Dozens of bodies set about—some sitting hunched against the walls, some lying on the ground. Death had rendered them wretched things, terrible in vision. Terrible it was to me, to see so many of my brothers in such a state of decay.

Many were without sign of injury, or clear indication of the evil that had taken breath from their bodies. Some had wounds. By blade or musket, it was hard to tell, but their faces and their torsos had been punctured, some, many times over. I counted fifty-six bodies and thought it likely most of the brothers were there.

I looked for signs. Indication of who may have murdered so many. There were cups about the place and a small barrel of water at the door, half full. I picked up one cup sitting on the stone floor and pulled down my mask to smell the contents. Death was in my nose now, so I pulled off the mask completely and let it fall to the floor. The cup smelled sour. But I could not be sure. So I blew out my nostrils to dispel the remnants of foul vinegar and fouler decay from my nose, and sniffed again. Yes, the water remaining in the cup was tainted. Evaporation had revealed a ring of white crystals around the inside. I thought, *poison perhaps?*

I imagined the scene. Brothers imprisoned, thirsty. Brought in water to drink by their guards. Its taint may have put-off some brothers of stronger fettle. But most would have supped it regardless, to quench intolerable thirst. And those poor souls interred in that dungeon that did not drink... No doubt they were despatched by blade or bullet... Foul it was. Foul to see. Foul to smell. Foul to think of godly men murdered.

For what reason? Why, and by whom?'

Chapter XXII

Edward's head sank into his hands. 'My thoughts of libraries and books were washed from my mind by the horror of that room—by the murder of so many. I recalled my good providence that I was not amongst them…' Edward paused. '…or perhaps I was meant to be amongst them.'

Edward's story, the thought of it, was too terrible for him to continue.

Henri seemed moved by Edward's tale. His face was sombre, mouth held in frown. Yet his eyes held an emotion not shared by the rest of his face. He held in his eyes, a contemplation—a glint of illumination that only comes by way of profitable new understanding. And behind the frown came a smile. Henri could not suppress it, and when he saw Edward might be finished, he prompted him with a question. 'Which books were missing?'

Edward quickly raised his head, Henri's smile adding fuel to Edward's simmering emotion. 'This… This is all you ask, Henri?' Edward's sorrow had turned into extreme agitation. '*Murder.* Is it coincidence that I fear the Guild will murder me… Coincidence that after a veiled threat delivered by you in Newcastle, seven months and more back, I find only murder at my journey's end?'

Henri's servants stepped forward, hands drawing swords, but Henri checked them both with a raised hand.

Henri contemplated past events and fortuity. 'They are strange beasts—coincidences. Some are fortunate encounters, some are unfortunate occurrences, but fortunately, coincidences are rare. So if one should meet one more than rarity, one can be assured one or more coincidences are false by name, and should be called contrivances.'

Edward's look was not friendly, and although Henri's servants stepped back, they kept hands tight on their swords, ready to draw.

Edward ignored Henri's sententious notion—his diversion, and continued resolutely with his own account. 'I questioned around the area of the abbey precinct. It revealed little. There was no indication of who was responsible for such foul murder. Fear was about the locals; those who may have reason to know more than mere gossip, and I suspected silence had been imposed on them on pain of death. But a fisherman with an eye on events, bought by some silver plate I liberated from the monastery's sacristy, declared one ship left shortly before the destruction of the bridge, as three ships arrived; one flying a flag depicting *Sanctus Nicolaus*, which we know is a Guild pennant. He said that one of the three ships carried a princely man in fine attire. A man dressed like no others he had seen before... My reason thought of you, Henri.

Despite all the silence imposed around the monastery, there was news on the border between Galicia and Asturias. Talk of a local Spanish noble who had suffered considerable loss of men. That fact could not be hidden. The deaths of so many horsemen sent to rescue the monastery could not be quietened. Too many widows weeping at the loss of their men, too many merchants with lost trade. They spoke of the *Beast of Galicia*. A man they called *Malin*, some called him *Kalibrado*.'

Henri smiled at Edward. 'So you come to my door… to accuse me of murder perhaps?'

'Where better to start my investigation than with you, Henri?'

'Investigations, Edward? Are we to turn inquisitor?' Henri smiled. 'But, if I said I was Kalibrado… and I murdered the Cistercians… then you are dead… Because you will never leave this room.'

'For the sake of justice, I need to know the truth of it… For the sake of my soul… For the sake of sleep, I need to know the truth of it.'

'*C'est bon, très bon*… confession is good for the soul.'

Henri beckoned one of servants to come close and Henri whispered something in his ear before turning again to Edward.

'Then Edward… I will tell you the truth of it. I have asked for food, because I suspect you are hungry, and for a room to be prepared, because I can see you are tired.'

Edward let out a deep sigh. His shoulders sank. His head held heavy.

'Forget hospitality, just tell me a truth, Henri, any truth… that is… if you are still able to know what a truth is?'

Henri paused. He hesitated, as if he was struggling to find his words. Then he said, 'I saw Kalibrado better those trying to capture him.' A wry smile grew on Henri's lips, admiration for a foul act remembered, well conceived and well delivered. 'But I saw no monks alive, or dead.'

Henri's admission drew Edward's attention, his head rising and his eyes piercing Henri. But Edward stayed silent.

Henri waited a while for Edward to speak, but his own hesitation was met by Edward's continuing silence and a cold stare. Henri waited and waited, and Edward maintained his silence and his stare—until Henri could not bear to continue the unease.

'I know nothing of the murder of your brother monks, or why

Kalibrado was at the monastery. I was there only to collect him…
To collect *Jan van der Goes*.'

Edward's eyes shone with revelation. 'But he is the Master of
the Black Merchants' Guild—*your master*.'

'*Oui*, but he is the master of many men… not just Guild men.
He is many men. It was Kalibrado that visited your monastery
wearing his *nom de guerre*, and not the name of the Master of the
Black Merchants' Guild.'

'Names… the Devil has a clutch of titles, but he is the same
monster… and you were there, now I know it. A master's dog is
always close by.'

'I collected him from the monastery, this is true.'

'So you knew of the murders.'

'*Non*. I have told you, I know nothing of murdered monks.'

'Why should I believe you?'

'It matters not if you believe me, Edward. One's own belief is
that which one wishes it to be. Not simply what another one tells
you it should be. What matters is, do you want justice for your
brothers… and if you do, will you accept my help in procuring it?'

Edward was surprised to hear Henri's words. 'Why would you
wish to see your master harmed?'

'Because the Guild may wield power, it may covertly control
trade and coerce many to ensure our merchant members see
greater profit… and yes, it may kill to see better commerce. But…
murder without profit is a crime against good sense. And in this
respect, if monks were murdered as you say, the Master hurts the
Guild—*my family*.'

'You speak of institutional sensibilities, but deceit is your trade,
Henri. I suspect you have other reasons to see your master
hanged. I have long known loyalty never knows Henri—Henri
only commits to himself.'

'Put your doubts about me to one side. Do we work together?'

'I suspect I have a choice… to let you manipulate me to meet your own ends… or walk away, only to find an honest wind in my face and a Guild knife in my back.'

'It is a wise man who knows the destination of both roads in the fork… He has no excuse for getting lost.'

'Then I have no choice, if I'm to know the truth of murder and see justice applied to the murderer. I will walk the Devil's road with you; to see Kalibrado… *or his agents*, hanged for their crimes.'

'*Bon!*'

At that moment four servants entered, carrying trays with a feast of cold pork, cheese tarts, figs, grapes and fried fish. Henri and Edward broke their discourse to see to it the food was arranged correctly, so both men could reach all the dishes without difficulty. Whilst directing the servants setting the plates, Henri noticed Edward's hose, and the base of his gown under the blanket he wore to warm away the wet. They were soiled and mud-spattered.

'Edward, your clothes are dirty. You must have your servant clean them.'

Edward was keener to try the cheese tart rather than respond to Henri, and it was with a half mouth full that he mumbled, 'I have no servant, Henri.'

Henri seemed surprised as he refilled Edward's glass and placed more tart on Edward's plate. 'Then I will send you one.'

While Edward picked more foods from the silver platters, to place upon a brightly glazed, blue and green patterned *Maiolica* eating-plate, Henri walked to the other side of the room. His eyes searched a long, richly carved oak table, covered with boxes of great beauty and artisan manufacture. Finally he selected a flattish, gilded, but plain box, and returned to his chair next to Edward, who was still eating.

As soon as Henri was comfortable, he opened the two leaves

forming the box's lid, revealing a lavishly decorated icon portraying *Sanctus Nicolaus*.

'An old friend rescued this from a church in France. The Calvinist malcontent was determined to destroy it. My friend determined to save it. *Idolatry* they shouted, as they broke all the glass in the church, as they beat the monks, as they defaced statue and art. One man braved it all to save what was precious to hundreds in that town.'

Edward raised his eyes from the fish he was devouring, to look upon the icon. 'I did not think you favoured faith, or God?'

Henri smiled. 'Do you think I do not believe in God, because I do not devote myself to one faith or another, because I live my life outside the rules of faith? *Non*, when I look upon the artist's work, I do not see the vanity of man, only the hand of God that lends his skill to man, who in turn creates such beauty. But this icon has more meaning. Not because it is a symbol of Catholic faith, but because Jan van der Goes was the one to risk his life to save it. The Guild Master was not always so cruel. I knew him fifteen years back.' Henri ran his palm over the gilded icon. '*Non*, he was never a kind man, but you could not call him unkind either. Cruelty only took him ten years back. He was bitten by a passion, and this passion has led him foul of the Black Merchants' Guild. He has plotted and planned a secret of his own... He has cleverly diverted Guild funds and Guild ships into this secret project... I suspect it... I know it.' Henri looked into the distance, as if another voice was to be heard—one that chastised him for his reveal, and he fell silent.

'How do we expose him for the murder of the monks?' asked Edward.

'If, as you say monks were murdered, and he was the cause of it, you will find no witness to his murder—no confession from the lips of those who know the truth of it. Jan van der Goes is well placed as Guild Master. The Guild's esteemed council profit, and the Guild's clients are happy. He sits on his throne with many cardinals, princes, and even kings at his feet.'

'Then how do we find justice?'

'Not all the Guild's council are happy.' Henri took up a sprig of grapes to examine them—to remove the best of the bunch. 'There are many outside the comfort of the Guild, who would see Jan van der Goes harmed. But to see him yield to justice will be difficult… It could even take a man's lifetime just to find justice in this corrupt world… But Edward, let us work together and use the half we both have left to find it.'

Edward nodded. Then sank a fill of the wine. His plate clean, the platters empty. 'I thought to look to John Brownfield for his support. Is he here with the Guild?'

Henri hesitated, searching for a guarded, but honest reply. 'Er… he is in Scotland.'

'Strange, when we met in Newcastle…' Edward drew a smile to his lips in fond memory of an absent friend, '…he talked of a commission in Antwerp. I assumed it was a Guild commission.'

'Er… *oui*, but he was diverted to Scotland… Guild matters more pressing.'

'Perhaps it is better he is free of this matter. He has already had much to compound his sorrow.'

'Er… yes, yes… *oui*… He is in a far better place. Better he does not get involved.' Henri composed himself. '*Bon*, then we will poke at Kalibrado where his armour is deficient, and greater evidence of crimes can be obtained. Let me tell you, while we eat, about our Master, his home and his devotion to his wife.' Henri looked to the empty platters, and then to his servants. 'Bonatello, a second course, and more wine… and Francisco, make ready with a third––more fruits, cinnamon and honey tarts… and more sweet foods for me… My guest is still hungry, and I have yet to eat.'

Chapter XXIII

As the evening pushed the sun down, Edward waited for Henri in the vestibule of the bankers' guildhall. The gathering of the great of Antwerp in the splendid guildhall was Henri's suggestion how Edward should best meet Jan van der Goes. How best Edward could apply his beguiling charms on the Guild Master's wife.

Edward's talent was ladies. It was a gift given, for he did not study the art of woo. It was a gift of attraction, given by God for what reason he did not know, for he had taken the vow of chastity when he was thirteen and had remained celibate.

Henri too, knew women found Edward desirable. That he could enslave them with his words and arouse them with his smile. It had always vexed Henri—Edward being so blessed with such a stirring talent and not in the mind, whilst in the Guild's covert employ, to use his sexual draw to better use with women of influence; those residing in the houses of men well placed to do the Guild favours.

Disregarding the past, Henri suggested Edward now use his draw and promise of amour to seduce Madame van der Goes—to charm and coax her into revealing her husband's secrets. He stressed it was the only way.

'A woman will always reveal a private affair, if the thought of another affair, more private, can replace it.'

Edward was much impressed by his surroundings. The façade of the guildhall was decorative, far more than those ornate standing sentinels—the guild buildings of the *Grote Markt.* But even this building's external decoration paled into the mundane, against the decoration of the vestibule within. If a guildhall was an expression of its trade's status, then that hall must have been built to honour the trade of royalty, for it was better appointed than any palace Edward could imagine.

There was a steady stream of well-suited men and well-preened ladies entering. Each in turn presented their invitations to the stewards lining the entrance. Men left their swords and cloaks, women their mantles; all exchanged for ivory disks, marked with numerals etched in gold. Edward clutched his and passed it between his fingers, looking nervously at the gold numeral *XVII* upon it, transcribing the numerals into Latin text in his mind to read as *VIXI—I have lived.*

Death—a bad omen, he thought.

Beyond grand gilded and braced oak doors, held back against the richly carved oak panelling, was a perfect glimpse—an exposure of a grand and exquisite reception hall, more lavish in its execution of woodwork and gilding than the vestibule. It easily swallowed up the eager anticipation of its guests as they all filed in—all, but poor Edward, who stood waiting.

Edward's wait in the vestibule was uncomfortably spent as he kicked his heels in a borrowed suit. He could not help but fidget as he waited. His usual attractive mien displaced as he sweated and squirmed in his clothes. His discomfort worsened in his mind, because the suit he wore was one of Henri's so it was not a creation from a diffident tailor. Light blue damask material, highlighted in salmon silk, excessively embroidered and over-embellished in pearls, may form a pretty dress to make a fine picture of a lady, but the picture of it—cut to a suit, unique in arrangement, was poor for Edward. He better fitted to simpler, more scholarly attire.

He pulled at his jacket's extreme high collar, topped with a ruff of such increased proportions as to render his head caught and buried within its yoke, misplacing his well shaped chin within the ruff's stiff cambric folds. He adjusted the great weight of the stuffed peascod doublet's unyielding hold on his body, so stuffed and quilted across his belly, that its designer's illustration of masculinity shone out enough for two men. He adjusted silken sleeves, tight over his arms. Twisted pinching waist, and pulled down the jacket's skirt, flowing out from his body to barely cover buttocks and groin. He looked to his legs, covered in close fitting fine white hose. No codpiece he wore, but there again, Edward needed no enhancement as show for his virility. He brushed his hands down his suit a hundred times without satisfaction, because each time it remained what it was—a bright beacon to be worn by man of opulent show, wanting to be seen by all.

Edward took a deep breath and tried afresh to shrug off his discomfort. He bowed in bold response to any critical judgment by mouth or eye from the other guests. More courtly when it was a lady's eye, more seductively when the eye was accompanied by a smile. But in between the looks and gazes of the guests, Edward still squirmed—flustered by the cut and embarrassment of his suit.

It was at least half an hour before Henri arrived, even though Edward himself had arrived half an hour later than agreed, in the certain knowledge that Henri would be late. Henri was true to his own doctrine; *at any social gathering it is advantageous to be tardy, so as to view all the opponents on the field of battle before revealing one's own soldiery.*

Henri was not alone, for he wore a strange lizard on his shoulder. It was a foul looking creature, whose eyes rotated and stared independently of each other, as if two separate creatures were conjoined down the middle, nose to tail. It wore a jewelled collar of garnets, and was affixed to Henri by a golden twisted rope.

'What manner of beast is that, Henri?' Edward asked, with a degree of abhorrence stilting his words.

'The Portuguese trader who sold it me called it a *Malagasy Dragon.* He declared it would change colour to match its surroundings… I assumed, naturally, it would match perfectly any suit I chose to wear… However, I believe the trader to be a liar, as the only suits it blends with are suits of darker tones, black being its favourite… and I rarely wear black outside of riding and travel. He also declared, it could see everything back, side and front, and keep the flies from my face, so I assumed it a better guard than a hound, a better fly swat than a fan… But in all these respects it is grossly deficient. I must admit it is a draw for conversation. But alas it is a surly beast, with a diet of detritus, and a manner to shoo those it draws.' Henri pondered awhile, thinking on his poor purchase, before adding, 'I wonder how it would taste in a tart?'

Henri then collected two ivory disks from a steward. One for his sword and one for his lizard, which he reconsidered a poor accessory choice for his fine attire.

The two then walked. Henri talked. Edward listened. Henri, like a tour guide illustrating the decoration of the hall, the walls, the ceiling, talking of the building's sponsorship and the guild that built it, the pain of its execution and the pleasure of its design. He claimed it to be, '*a good work in stone and stucco, brick and timber, gilding and glass.*'

The narration pleased Edward, as the two men covered the length of the reception hall, to stand at two more doors, closed, greater and taller than those before. More stewards in livery opened the doors, and they stepped into the inner reception room and into the great and good—the elite of Antwerp.

Henri turned to Edward. 'Edward, to many, my paramour, Antwerp, is the centre of the World. Home to a hundred thousand souls, mistress to a hundred thousand more. Commerce—the reverence on which the city flourishes. Her devotion is not to the Spanish Crown that thinks it governs it, or the Pontiff who thinks he guides it. *Non*, Antwerp's dedication is to money—finance in all its forms, her trade in cloth and all goods made. She lends money and invests in countries more powerful than her own... and thus she wields greater power. She dictates who can afford wars, and which kings can build palaces. She is the universe for those who prefer their nobility to be built on gold rather than heritage, and piety built on knowledge rather than blind ignorance.'

Lecture finished, Edward and Henri entered the hall. Edward could not help but raise his head to the vaulted ceiling to gaze. Discomfort held his stare. His head restrained awkwardly by his neck attire. But still he studied the magnificent fresco. His eyes traced the ornate plaster, the gilding on the timbers—all softly illuminated and animated by six large hanging gilded candelabra. Then he lowered his head to count the ten statues of Apollo, all illustrating his associations with the sun, prophecy, medicine and music; standing as sentinels that lined the wall of the great hall. Each was furnished with an identical standing candelabrum, gilded and matched to those that illuminated from above. Lights that shone a different life into each statue's face, showing a different mien—animation to cold stone faces, studying and menacing the crowd.

Henri Hueçon watched Edward's head scan his surroundings. He frowned at the sight of Edward, displaying dropped jaw and widened eyes.

'The hall is well lit, Edward, but two better illuminations are, firstly, it is never appropriate to appear awed by your surroundings; you should always present yourself as one whose closet is even better built and decorated. Secondly, you do not wear a collar… you carry it, like a cloud about one's neck… Or in my case, like a slipped halo... Not, as in your case, like a slipped knot.'

'Sorry, Henri. But surely one cannot help but be intoxicated by these surroundings.'

'To you, I suppose this is a treat for eyes—peepers only used to the grim walls and ceilings of the Scottish Marches.'

Edward did not wish to sally out against Henri's unkind observation—his dismissive of a land Edward loved. Instead, Edward diverted his irritation onto a man staggering in front of him, smiling widely, two drinks away from repose on the floor. Edward could not help but bring observation of the comedy in front of him to Henri, with a finger pointed.

Henri shook his head at the crapulent man. 'It is not seemly for a man to be drunker than his guests. Neither is it seemly to appear fresh at a party, drunker than those who leave it.'

'Who is it?' Edward asked.

'Floris… Frans Floris de Vriendt.' Hueçon laughed.

'Humour, Henri?'

'Oui. His name means *friend*. Given by his grandfather. It best describes him, and the nature of generous boys born to another generous man.'

Edward forced a puzzled look, trying to suppress unseemly glee at the man's unfortunate condition. 'Why is he tolerated at this party—in this company?'

'Fabulous wealth. An artist respected by many notabilities in the Painters' Guild. An artist, popular with his students and his workshop… And of course this party is sponsored to promote his brother's designs for the new city hall and his latest architecture pattern books.'

On a large table, in the centre of the room, was a model some six feet in length—a representation of a building. A bold avant-corps dominated its centre, towering over three storey wings either side. Edward walked forward a little, so he may see the model better. But people blocked his view and he struggled to see all the statue detail built into niches on the tower. One statue he recognised—the Virgin Mary. He stepped back to his original position to see the overall composition again. He thought the structure imposing, but not outstanding. So he determined the design was to complement other guildhall structures lining the Grote Markt, more than to stand and shout its own glory.

Henri was restless. He wished to see Edward about his work. He had work of his own. Antwerp's elite were present, and Henri had seeds to sow and crops to harvest—*favours*.

Henri sought out some wine for both men, using the ruse to seek out those guests best to receive his discourse and his company. He returned with two fine silver cups, and both raised their drinks to their lips, as both pairs of eyes scanned the room.

There were many eyes on Henri and Edward. Henri expected it, but Edward was discomfited by it, unless of course it was a pretty woman. One such had caught his eye. She presented a sight to Edward that defied his interpretation of a beautiful woman. She looked and dressed like no other woman he had seen before. Her dress was elegant, in damask, richly, but elegantly embroidered, as if the embroiderer wanted only to enhance the material and not overwhelm it. All was beautifully trimmed with material that shone and sparkled in the candlelight. Spanish cut, but with a V-shape bodice, which did all to compliment her tiny waist above skirts underpinned by a bell shaped French farthingale, which did all to enhance her form.

Edward had not seen such elegance and immodesty presented in the same wrappings. For as the richness of her dress shouted quality, the details were a siren's call to all the poor men in the room who tried not to stare at her. Whether it was her split skirts revealing petticoats below, or her bosom above, exposed by the low décolleté collar, shaded but not concealed by her transparent partlet. Or the picture of desire that sat upon her high collar and small ruff—a plinth to support the artist's sculpture, a perfect vision in *Parian* marble, perfect form, perfect carving, wearing perfect hair, barely covered, rich and red.

Edward's desire shone in his eyes. His thought of it stirred his groin and wetted his mouth. His stare and his want called the beauty, and she came.

'Henri, I see you have an apprentice... I would say he dresses better... but he looks a little uncomfortable in his clothes.'

'Mais oui, I agree, Angeline. He unfortunately lacks the understanding of my tailor's vision.'

'Perhaps your tailor could only see one man beneath his art in cloth, Henri?'

'I disagree. My man here simply has no knack of presenting my tailor's art to the public.'

'Perhaps, Henri... but I think your man does not need fine thread to improve his beauty... I think his beauty is in his eyes, face and...' Angeline's eyes dropped slowly over Edward's form, to his waist, his groin and his legs, well presented in Henri's hose. '...and his dancing perhaps?'

Edward was an old hand at playing women. His vow of chastity may have prevented the pleasure of coitus, but it had not dulled his thought of it, or prevented him the pleasure of procuring it, if only to abstain. He thought of it as a greater act of sacrifice and character to be presented with the opportunity of penetration into a fair, even beauteous woman, and then to refuse—to hold back its lustful call. Nevertheless, Edward had sharpened all the enticement and play around the act. His eyes played a woman, drawing her base thoughts to the fore, and his Romanic words would quicken their breath and rob them of self-restraint, flush their cheeks and even bring a tear or two to their nether-eye. But Edward knew, in this game with Angeline, he was no player; he was but a dullard—a boy in the wake of this woman's sport.

Edward's discomfort was evident, and Henri, who would have normally been the first to cheer on Angeline's game, stepped in to save him. Because he needed Edward's focus on his own game—the wife of Jan van der Goes.

'You are terrible Angeline… leave him. He has no money, no position, and no power for you to bed.'

Angeline frowned. 'A pity… I would count the pleasure of him… pleasure for pleasure's sake, and nothing else.'

Henri bowed, his eyes remaining on Angeline in a show of appreciation of her beauty, and acknowledgement of her sacrifice. Angeline took Henri's cue, and with a telling, teasing smile towards Edward, she parted, to be quickly encircled by a group of men, their abandoned wives and women looking on, spitefully.

'Is Kalibrado here? Is his wife here?' asked Edward, keen to rid his thoughts of Angeline, and satisfy his own game with an opponent less his match.

Henri subtly gestured direction with his cup, adding quietly, '*Oui*. She is over there, talking to her husband, the Guild Master.' Henri gestured again, thinking Edward had not seen his feint. 'There in front of that poorly rendered tapestry of questionable subject, and badly blended colour.'

Edward did not look at the people, but looked to the tapestry on the far wall, comparing it with others that adorned the walls of the chamber. He thought a moment or two away from the thought of women might cool his lustful thought, and restore calm to his body—to still his breath before the game.

All the tapestry, in his eyes, was well woven in fine silk and richly died woollen weft threads. Embellished with a copious use of gold and silver threads and wire.

Fine workmanship, and a fine subject, he thought. 'One of a series, judging by the others, *The Parable of the Lost Son*, perhaps?'

'The scriptures. So *passé*. We live in modern times, Edward. Exploration is opening up new worlds. Science instead of superstition. Invention instead of Inquisition. We should celebrate these things in our arts, instead of ancient texts and religious idolatry.'

'I know you have God in your heart, but are you not a believer in the holy word?'

'*Mais oui*. One would not live long in this world if he declared himself atheistic.'

Edward simply looked upon his perfidious friend, and smiled to hide his confusion. Then he concentrated his attention onto his original focus, Jan van der Goes—Kalibrado, and his wife. Kalibrado was as Henri described. He was an extremely handsome man. Well dressed as befitting a wealthy man. Imposing. He spoke to an equally handsome woman, dressed well as befitting a wife of a wealthy man. Beautiful. She constantly touched him. Her hands in graceful animation, falling on his arms and chest as they talked. The pair were a composition of equal parts. Well framed by the tapestry behind. Well illuminated by the candelabrum above.

As Edward studied the pair, Kalibrado was ushered away by another guest. So his beautiful consort turned her attention to the third member of their party—another woman. But Edward's scrutiny remained on Kalibrado and his countenance. His face said all—disappointment. Dismayed to be parted from his wife, or perhaps frustrated to be pulled into another conversation. Edward could not be sure.

It was without any sense of apprehension that Edward approached the ladies. He considered the other woman to be plain and poor looking. She was modestly dressed, but the clothes were of quality, so she was a woman of some means. However the focus of his design was art in cloth. She had presence and beauty. Her hair, jet-black, worn very extravagantly, ornamented with pearls and diamonds, tied with black silk ribbons and lace. She was of extraordinary beauty—beauty that only Mediterranean women could carry. Perfect complexion and almond eyes. She carried a mole above her mouth, which did not mar her beauty; it simply drew the beholders eyes to her rich red lips. Exquisite.

'My ladies. May I introduce myself? I am Edward Hendon.'

On the approach, Edward had imagined her voice. It did not disappoint. Her voice matched her visage, beautiful. Her accent, Spanish. Her words, warm and musical.

'Welcome to the party, Master Hendon.'

'I am very grateful to be in such company. In such a place, full of beauty—art in all its forms.' Edward's eyes lingered on the woman, falling away to her bust, well framed in dark blue damask.

The lady's eyes followed Edward's gaze as he admired her form. She smiled, and she breathed in, and then slowly out, swelling her breasts and emphasizing her plenteous bosom.

The game was on.

'Well said, Master Hendon. But you add your own beauty to these rooms.'

'You flatter me, madam. But I am a shadow in your light.'

Edward scanned the room for onlookers, and for husbands,

feigning interest in the musicians, busy preparing in a gallery over the entrance to the room. All was clear, so Edward returned to his conquest of the lady.

'If you permit. I would like to partner you... when the dancing commences.'

Her smile grew broader, as she read Edward's pause. Edward's deliberate innuendo. She replied, 'Ah, if only my husband would allow it. But I am afraid he is a very jealous man. With a temper quick to rage.'

'I have heard as much. But he has good sense to be jealous... To protect his treasure, lest a thief liberates him of it.'

'Mr Hendon, are you a thief?'

Edward saw the sparkle in the lady's eyes. He knew she favoured him. Her eyes said it, and so his game was well played, so far. She was not a moral woman—thankfully, and it was no trouble to feign interest in the lady. She was indeed exquisite. He leaned in close with guileful smile and a low voice that pushed out hot breath on her cheek. 'I am the Prince of Thieves, and I would steal your heart.'

The lady lost her breath for a moment, her pupils wide and her cheek flushed.

What more was blooming under her robes? Edward thought to himself, as he lifted the lady's hand to kiss it softly. Leaving his lips on her fingers, longer than was decent.

Edward pressed home his woo and stared deep into the lady's eyes. She held his gaze, deep and lusty. But his look was too intense and she found her breath quickening. So she broke her stare, to drop her eyes, only to rest them on Edward's feet, well shod. She slowly lifted her eyes—to his legs well formed in close fitting hose, and to his groin, again enlarged with want.

The lady recovered herself. She was caught and embarrassed by her display. She thought to bring her companion in—to deflect

Edward's advances and thus save her from the scolding her husband would issue. He was no doubt watching all.

'Mr Hendon. You rudely ignore my companion.'

Edward took his eyes of his lady, to look upon the other woman. Her upper lip had curled in disdain from her witness of their vulgar courting. She was as plain as the other woman was beautiful. Her hair was thin. Ornamentation absent. And her dress, although expensively crafted, was modesty itself.

Edward apologised to the woman, 'I am sorry. Please forgive me. I am from the country... and my manners are rude. I am amiss to forget proper introduction.'

The plain woman nodded her head, in dour acceptance of Edward's apology, and her beautiful companion stepped forward to make introductions to Edward.

'Master Hendon, may I introduce myself. I am Consuela Machuca, and this fine woman who you ignore, because I suspect you think she is dull and plain-favoured, as is the way amongst all her sisterhood, is Madame van der Goes.'

Edward was caught. His surprise was evident. His mistake foolish. More foolish it was to admit it by his look of disbelief. His response was disordered. His thoughts muddled. *How could he have made such a mistake?* He looked to Consuela, as if it was perhaps a joke. *He hoped it was a joke.*

'Er... Er... Forgive me... I thought... I thought you were Madam van der Goes.'

Consuela remained quiet. Silenced by the brutal look the plain woman threw at her. Instead, Madam van der Goes replied, her voice hard and unfriendly.

'Sir. It appears you apply your country charms to the wrong woman... It appears you intend to woo a name, and not a beauty. Well here I am... the name you hoped to wench. Do you still wish to dance, *Master Hendon?*'

Edward's embarrassment sent him into retreat. However, his game, badly played, was not lost on all. Eyes from above, on the gallery, had watched his performance with Consuela and Madame van der Goes with great interest.

Henri Hueçon made his way to the Guildhall's Meetings room, via a courteous bow and a nod of recognition to all he passed. The Meetings room was a place out of the party where quiet conversation could be had, where business could be done. Tall it was. Fabrics lined the walls to suppress din and preserve quiet colloquy. Grand carving covered the ceiling to hold the eye in awe of the artisan's skill.

The room ran long, like a corridor, with tall windows extending floor to ceiling down one side, and great oak booths the other. Each booth, enclosed by a pair of decorated settles, stood with a table. And each settle, large enough to accommodate four people, had oaken backs twice taller than a man, and thick enough to kill sound's travel and preserve private discourse. Great gilded candelabrum stood sentry over each table, and two earnest men, in green felt-cloth robes and caps, stood sentry over all. They guarded the booths well, ensuring those who used the stalls declared their meeting's intent, recording names and safeguarding privacy.

Amongst it all, decorating the work of the artisan, were the works of the artist—sculpture and painting of sublime creation and ethereal thought. Henri enjoyed their company, but only a few works pleased his eye. And none were a match for his own reflected image, framed perfectly in the night-backed window glass. He smiled at it. He held his stance so he could admire the detail of it—a man sculptured by a great artist.

Henri considered himself elite, and so did his guest entering the room, *Cosimo Albissi*. He did not have Henri's show, his word craft, or his presence, but he had greater worldly gifts—he was far richer by his own design, and far more influential through his associations. He had influence over the politics and power that dwelled within the Italian States, within Catholic princedoms and he had leverage over all the seven major guilds that operated in Florence, via that archaic institution, *the Arti Maggiori*, as well as directives over Italian commerce that sailed from Italian ports.

'Does the evening go well with you, Henri?'

'It is a poor party, but your presence makes it bearable.'

'I see you keep your tailor busy.'

'It pleases me to keep him employed, and his six young mouths well fed.'

Cosimo smiled. 'Your charity has no limits, Henri, but I know of your tailor. He has no children.'

'No children, but he keeps boys quietly for his pleasure.'

Cosimo put his large hand on Henri's shoulder and led him on down the hall. 'I am pleased to have an opportunity to talk with you, Henri... free from the formality of the Black Council.'

'I am always pleased to converse, especially with your learned tongue. But you know it is forbidden to discuss matters pertaining to the Black Merchants' Guild outside the formality of the Council. I break the rule just by mentioning the Guild and acknowledgement of our membership... This place is a sea of ears and a wave of wagging tongues.'

'Your sensitivities to the rules of the Guild amuses me. You who break the rules as often as you change your suit... but I will humour you. Let us be cryptic, Henri... Are you game?'

'I am game, if the game will see me on the winning side, and not paying a forfeit.'

'*Paura non*—fear not. Let me share an allegory with you.' Cosimo changed his tone, as if he were reading a bedtime story to a child. 'There was once a great assembly of affluent men who sought the stars and who had a house, and it had a steward. And like all good stewards, he did his work diligently. He ensured his masters' household was well managed, and the business of the household productive. He saw to it that his masters' profits increased, and their privacy preserved. The masters never questioned the steward's methods. They just enjoyed the pleasure of their well-run house and the gold he multiplied. They treated him kindly, and became to look upon him as more a bastard son, rather than a lowborn servant.

But like any good servant on a long leash, without close control, he began to look to his own pleasures and profit—even strike foul those who he saw as threat, and his masters saw as friends. He acted with gross impunity. He thought the injurious secrets he held about his masters would keep him safe from harm. And so he thought, he could commit to his own wicked ends, in his own name and in names of invention, in the belief his masters would turn a blind eye to his own sins.' Cosimo paused, discomfort on his face, angered thoughts in his head—irritations to taint his narration. '*More so,* our proud steward, his arrogance well nurtured by some masters of the house, sees his future as householder, and not as house-server. Our *good* steward now writes his reports as a politician does. He holds a crooked tongue, and applies it to the page. Frankness is absent and deceit is present, and hidden amongst the platitudes and sincerities is not the truth, but omission.' Cosimo paused again, to counter his anger and return to calmer delivery. 'Now our steward has an assistant... an able man. Never content to stand in the shadows of the steward, he has earned his enmity. But he is better favoured in the house by some masters who appreciate his talents, if not his show.' Cosimo looked Henri up and down. 'In fact he would do better to sacrifice his time at his tailors, and take the yarns; the threads of suspicion cast at the steward, and weave truth from them.'

Henri was made uneasy. Not by the direction of Cosimo's

discourse, but by the poor method of its travel. His meaning was not well hidden, and perhaps an easy decipher for intrigued ears. So Henri looked to his surroundings, to see four guests too close for comfort; two with eyes on Henri and Cosimo.

And why not, with Cosimo so rich and Henri so richly dressed.

'Come to a booth, Cosimo. The party crowds us even here, and ears come closer.'

Henri led Cosimo to one of the booths, and waited to be seated. A green-cap approached, took their names and title of their discourse. Henri declared to the green-cap, *'In matters of chess'.* Both were seated, and offered a tray of fruits and wine, brought by a second green-cap.

The green-cap poured. Henri spoke, ignoring both the fruit and wine offered, leaving the green-cap to serve Cosimo alone.

'In matters of chess, I will have my knight covering his king, and my bishop covering his queen. But I sense his rook is about the game, and will shadow both my bishop and my knight, to take them both from the game, and even perhaps hold my own king in check.' Henri moved his hands around the table as if it were a chessboard, moving imaginary pieces. 'Although I must admit my knight is slow to play, and my feint with my bishop on his queen may be wasted. My bishop may even block my play... and I may need to sacrifice it… It is a dangerous game. My chess opponent does not trust me… and I am certain, I am only in the game whilst he ponders how to steal it from me.'

'I will pretend to understand your moves. But be careful you do not lose the game, Henri. Reward comes only to brave souls…. Be brave.'

Both rose to leave the booth. Cosimo looked about. No one was near. The booths were empty, and the two green-caps too distant to hear. Even so, the green-caps would keep confidence. It was their first rule.

'I wish to be clear, Henri. The steward's actions are bringing Catholic complaint against the Guild. And good commerce transcends Faiths' discord, only if we do not provoke it. Whilst gold and power are the principle dedications of the elite in our society, and we are in place to secure it for them, we are assured progress. But that progress can easily be regarded as a tumour, if we are seen to favour one faith, one doctrine over another. Faith, after all, is a comfortable banner for the poor to shelter under, and the poor will unseat their elite if they have the numbers at hand. Remember, Henri, the Guild has its enemies. Many with an ear in high places.'

Henri nodded his understanding. 'Cosimo, with regards to the house in your story. Who in the house doubts the suitability of the steward's assistant?'

'The Dutch banker recently married to that Spanish beauty, Consuela Machuca. That proud beauty who does not take the rich banker's name, for it is poorer than her own, but enthusiastically spends his gold as his wife, for he his richer than her rich family name. The banker whose wealth has grown by the gift of Jan van der Goes steering hand. He and Salomon Beeckman, are principal amongst the dissenters. There are others.'

'Ah Beeckman, a moral man, pious, sinless, God fearing. He has a much loved only son I believe.'

'Yes. It is said Antony Beekman is his gold—his treasure. Salomon has seen six sons and twelve daughters dead in infancy. It is no wonder he treasures him so.'

'How are you, Angeline? Who is your escort tonight?' asked Kalibrado, wiping the soiled edge of his cup with gloved hand, his eyes counting the guests, sorting them in his mind; patrician, plutocrat, and pretender.

'The son of a Medici.'

'A rich client… Or should I say a well connected client?'

'He does for favours.'

'And what of my favours?'

'Yours, or the Guilds?'

'The Guild's of course. But you discriminate carelessly. Remember my favours and the Guild's are the same.'

'I doubt that. But I continue to do as you ask. But your man continues as he is. He snorts and ruts like a hog.'

'But my dear, he is my hog, and he roots out for me treasures from the earth. Secrets only a good snout will reveal. Rooting them out even better than you. And the hog will find truffles. And truffles are like secrets, most delicious when they are fresh… My hog, *Furet,* will work better, be less distracted, and hopelessly loyal, if he is happy. I only ask you to keep him happy, and keep me as his only key to your *devoted* attentions.'

Angeline was always an attraction to be stared at. Desired by men. Envied by women. Despised by some who hated what she was, and what she had attained for herself in a man's world. She acknowledged them all. Never too haughty to give a poorer guest her smile, to make a man happy to have her attention, even for a moment. For they knew to have her attention for a moment more, would be more than their purse would allow.

But while she scanned the room and met her admirers' eyes and countered their smiles, she kept her conversation with Kalibrado in her mind.

'I do not know why I accomodate you.'

'I will remind you why. You are a courtesan with a desire to be called noble.'

'I walk in noble society, and could marry any noble I desire.'

'I doubt that. But even so, everyone will still know you for what you are—a scented whore. But I have a place in mind where you will be a noble amongst noble people, with slaves to do your bidding and your fellow countrymen will not see you for what you are, or what you were. This is what you most desire, and I am the only one to grant this boon.'

After an unpleasant thought, she said through gritted teeth and smile, 'Then I will continue to entertain your man—as if he were my true love.'

'That is all I ask… and of course continue with your reports on him to me.'

Angeline's smile wavered, and she patted her lips as if the action would return it. But it was catching the eye of a rich man leaving the Meetings room, talking to the star guest of the party in matters of attire and presentation, that restored it to its sensuous best.

Kalibrado saw the two men as well. 'What does Hueçon want with Cosimo Albissi in the Meetings room, I wonder? It cannot be to play cards, but private discourse, too private to be proper, I wager.'

'Do they not share in membership of your Black Merchants' Guild?' replied Angeline, her eyes scanning the room. 'Then it is plain they will have secrets to serve out to each other.'

Kalibrado smiled at a group of guests, his words directed towards Angeline, while his eyes nodded recognition to each guest in the group that caught his eye, including Cosimo, who had attached himself, away from Henri Hueçon.

'Cosimo, he smiles at me while he schemes.'

'Yes, I am afraid he no longer holds you in high regard, Guild Master.'

'You mention the Guild too freely, Angeline. It will be your undoing. As will be your friendship with Hueçon.'

'Henri is no threat to you. He enjoys playing at being Henri too much to scheme against you.'

'You either do not know Hueçon well, or you know him too

well. I think it is the latter… Do not protect Hueçon, Angeline…
Do not be so foolish.'

'Do you trust anyone, Kalibrado?'

Kalibrado stared at Angeline, surprised to hear his secret alias
used so indiscreetly. 'Not even myself.'

'Not even God?'

'Not even God. God is the rod used to beat the back of the
beast—the whip to tame the lion, to make it compliant against its
own nature. Does the lion trust the whip? I accept the lion for
what he is. He mounts at will. Kills without remorse. Fights to
maintain his pride and place. And the lioness is no different. It is
her nature to shun the lion, in preference of care for her cubs. She
will kill all to protect that which she truly loves—her young, and
rarely the mate who sires them. All mankind are lions, kings of the
earth. It is the Church that makes them sheep, against their nature;
bends God's own holy word to meet its own aspiration. I have
read the blessed word in Greek, Angeline, words written a
thousand years past. Words the Church turns into new meaning.
Man's devotion is misplaced in the Church's rule, hidden within a
fiction. Sin is man's true nature, deceit his real essence.'

Angeline was irked by Kalibrado's words. His poor view on
mankind—of Church, of God.

'You will burn.'

'Perhaps, but I have a dream to make real first. And when it is
real, faith will be sustained once more, and I will make peace with
God… Yes, we all may burn; we who sin daily without regret.
You and I are the same in this respect. We show our devotion in
the proper place, at the proper time… We both hold the hand of
God, but not the God of the Church's corrupted creation, but the
God of our own knowing. The God that dwells in our own
remorseless hearts.'

'Do not set my devotion to faith—to the Church, against your corrupt measure. Do not measure all men by it. Surely those of God, free from base temptation and committed to day-long devotions are free from sin?'

'Are there such creatures?'

'Coenobites—monks.'

'You are naive for a whore. How many monks, priests, cardinals and even Popes has your kind serviced? They are the worst of sinners, because they are greater hypocrites. They deny themselves as men. God made man, and man cannot dip his wick in one heifer; he needs to ply his appetite. Hence why you and your ladies profit so. But it is a fools fancy, because man mistakes his pleasure and denies his real need—to spread his own seed, to ensure his own line. Monks are no different… They are men after all.'

Angeline's vexation grew into reckless counter. 'Is that why you murdered so many?'

Kalibrado stared at Angeline. His mouth formed cruel shape, and his eyes narrowed in displeasure. 'It seems my hog squeals in his sleep, or do you tease the truffle from him as you pleasure him?'

Angeline's face held its calm, its beautiful countenance. 'It is my craft to separate a man's secret desires and dreams from his soul. How else can I hope to best pleasure him? If secrets fall from him during the act of pleasure, how am I to ignore them?'

Kalibrado spoke his displeasure to Angeline. 'It seems you do not fear me.'

Angeline turned to look at Kalibrado. 'I am frightened of no man, or even the devil dressed as a handsome man.'

Kalibrado smiled to hide his anger. 'Well said Angeline. You put me in my place.' He bowed deeply and smiled again. 'Now can a humble man ask a favour?'

'You may,' replied Angeline, keen to appease the danger in

front of her.

Dangerous to provoke such a man, she thought, *foolish even, without a clear aim to profit from it.*

'When you see my hog, give him this message.' Kalibrado passed a sealed note to Angeline. She studied the note and the seal upon it. She knew not to tamper with the seal, and even though she had many of her noble clients' seals copied, none of her metal-smiths would dare to copy a Guild seal.

৪০৪

To call Angeline a mere courtesan was perhaps an injustice. She was much more than that. Because in a world with rules shaped and governed by men, where women had little influence other than by the coercion or cajolement of their kindred, she was a woman with power. Even queens, with all their sovereign power, were often only permitted their rule by the will of men. Even wealth, by way of inheritance, was no route to liberty in a man's world, so long as laws were made by men to profit men. But Angeline had her own wealth, well hidden, and a power over men. It was true that her wealth was amassed by the gifts of men, but she was not subject to their will, only their supplication.

She had entertained bankers and rich merchants well that night. Her *sisters* had presented themselves as delightful company, convincingly adoring and attentive to their suitors. More money earned, more favours acquired, and new information to sell to the Guild, to make its Council stronger in a city, perhaps the richest in Europe, and intent on becoming the largest north of the Alps.

Ever since the decline of Bruges, Antwerp had provided a rich source of new wealth. Money grew from sugar, spices, textiles, new world silver, and everything else that could be bought and sold from all over the emerging world. The city was a hub of trade, with hundreds of ships and carts laden with goods passing through the city daily. Its well-established bourse, attracting financers and moneylenders from all over Europe. Traders from Spain, Germany, Portugal and Venice added to the diversity. Even Jews and Muslims were tolerated in a city devoted to commerce, rather than commitment to the rule of kings or the bondage of the Church.

In this great cosmopolitan city, people grew rich and people became poor as the shifting fortunes of economics dictated success and failure. Many saw the decline of Antwerp coming—many more with foresight moved their commerce to Amsterdam. Amidst it all however, was the enterprising souls that serviced the beast of Antwerp—its commercial heart.

Angeline's commerce was immorality. Her trade was sex, and her skill—the flattery of men. She was cultured and a favourite amongst the aesthetes. A model for many a fresh new Italian artist with affluent backers, looking to make more money from their art in a city of wealth, governed by an oligarchy of banker-aristocrats.

✂

After the party was over, Angeline retired to her extensive rooms. They were richly decorated, even more so than the richest palaces of Rome. Gifts were everywhere. Sculpture, bronzes, and even gold statues adorned alcove and tabletop. Paintings; gifts from artists, hung on every wall; portraits of her fashioned as *Artemis* and *Andromeda*; images of her ruling over *Bacchus* and *Pan*.

Furet sat on a fine upholstered chair, watching Angeline, drinking wine from a finely decorated glass.

'I am devoted to you my love.'

'You are obsessed with thought of me, *Furet*. You do not love me real, because you do not know me real. I am a painting—an

323

image enhanced by the skill of an artist; an image created in the mind, not real in the earth.'

'I am devoted to you my love.'

'I am only a thought that haunts your mind—one that gives you no peace, *Furet*.'

'I am devoted to you my love.'

'*Furet*, infatuation is not devotion. It is torment that destroys, or is destroyed when true love comes along. Keep your devotion for God... *Furet*.'

'I will repeat my devotion forever, simply to hear you say my name. You say it so sweetly.'

'I release my words like a rehearsed song, *Furet*. It is merely good composition, and careful delivery.'

'You try to deter me, Angeline, and it simply escalates my devotion to you.'

'Then, Furet, you are lost, because you are in love with a sculpture, and art is cold to the touch.' Angeline pulled a paper from a small silken bag she had attached within the folds of her dress. 'Speaking of cold things, Jan van der Goes gave me this to give to you.'

Furet took the small square of paper, bearing the Guild's seal, and placed it carefully into his shirt.

Angeline smiled softly, but her mind was troubled passing the message to Furet. *No good came from the pen of Jan van der Goes.*

'Why do you work for the Guild, *Furet?* '

'I work for Jan van der Goes, and he is the Guild.'

'He is the Devil, *Furet*. You would be better off without him.'

'I am richer than a poor man should be. Jan van der Goes pays well. And when a man has more money, he eats better, dresses finer, and can surround his inner walls with colour, whilst he builds his walls higher to protect his wealth. I have been a carpenter, a soldier, a beggar, an actor on the stage, but none paid as well as my current role.'

'And what *is* your role, *Furet?* The Devil's hands perhaps? Murderer? Spy?'

Furet bowed his head slightly, and a rare moment of remorse shaded his face. 'My thought of you washes the filth from my hands.'

Angeline saw Furet's head dip, as a sign of hurt requiring her healing hand—her practiced hand, that made men forget their sins by flooding their mind with greater sin, sweetly proffered.

Angeline walked over to him and knelt before him, cupping her scented hand to his cheek. His cheek fell into the deep aroma of roses, and he closed his eyes to the sweet sensation of it.

'*Poor Furet,*' she whispered. *Stupid Furet,* she thought.

Chapter XXIV

The day after the party, Edward called on Henri Hueçon. He was not at home.

On the second day, Henri was *engaged* in meetings of importance and unavailable to receive visitors.

On the third day, Edward was kept waiting from mid-afternoon till the evening hour. He did not see Henri.

On the fourth day, Edward protested, but Henri's secretary only announced further delay.

On the fifth day, Edward thought to find another way to see Henri. So he remained outside Henri's home, in the hope of seeing Henri leave, and to bring about a meeting on his own terms. Even at knifepoint if necessary.

But as Edward waited, the summer rain drowning his discontent, he replaced frustration with a more measured understanding of Henri's sponsorship. Edward knew. Edward understood. Henri would not be his route to truth or justice.

Edward looked up at the gabled peaks, at the tall buildings of the grand façade that ran the street. He looked beyond their show, to the poor and plain construction of the buildings behind— beyond the dressed stone, corbel and endless window glass—their show of wealth. And he knew. Henri too was simply show. And behind his velvet façade, was a man like most other men—a man of deceit, avarice and self-service. Henri's own ends were met, and no further help would be offered, none that is, that would not help Henri.

Edward could not believe any master of the Black Merchants' Guild could be involved in events that would surely harm it. Henri knew of Kalibrado's guilt or innocence—that Edward knew. However justice would be whatever Henri wished it to be. Justice designed to benefit Henri Hueçon.

The truth sometimes is spoken from within; it is the only words to trust. Edward did not need confirmation from outside himself—accusation from the lying tongues of deceitful men. Jan van der Goes in the guise of Kalibrado *had* ordered the murder of the monks. Their bodies disposed badly, because he had no time to wish away so much death, so completely.

Still, Edward waited and waited, but Henri did not show. And Edward thought on the point of it.

Waiting for what? More lies and deceit?

He thought on it and thought on it, and because of it, Edward delayed his return to his lodgings. It was his mistake. He could have pondered thought on thought within the security and comfort of his own walls, but instead he remained in the shadows to the late hour, when the city streets are taken over by miscreants. So when it came time to retire and walk the wet streets back to the security of his room, huddled against the rain, past the timber skeleton of an empty market and greater shadow, he felt unease. He felt watched.

Hard rain is far better cover against mischief than dark. In the rain, people close their eyes to their surroundings. They do not deliberate, or examine that which goes on around them. They lower their heads, and only seek that which brings them respite from the driving wet. So from wet shadows, three pairs of eyes easily stalked their prey unobserved. *Furet's* eyes were the brightest, mean intent shining out. And like all good predators, the men waited until their prey was an easy strike away.

Edward had no warning. Their cudgels rained down hard. How many he did not know. Two? Three perhaps? He was too concerned protecting himself with arm and folded body. The blows were hard and remorseless. Edward tried to stand up, to seek a better defence, but they concentrated on his legs to keep him down; on body, to keep him winded; on arm, to keep Edward from defence and possible retaliation.

Then the blows left as suddenly as they arrived, as German sounds were made in the distance. Then he heard sounds of footsteps receding, and new footsteps entered Edward's pained mind.

'Lass mich dir helfen.'

Edward grimaced from a dozen hurts, from a dozen blows, and through gritted teeth he pushed out his pain.

Again the voice called out, *'Lass mich dir helfen.'*

Edward opened his eyes to the world, indifferent to the rain, to the filth and wet that covered him. He focused on his saviour; the broad shadow that stood over him. He could not make a man out of the shape. No feature. No face. So he looked past the silhouette, to the street and alleys on both sides.

'Where did they go?' asked Edward, his face twisted, his words forced on his breath.

'Are you *Englisch*? Let me help you,' replied the shadow.

Edward ran his hands over his body, where it hurt. Feeling the stabs of pain, where the blows had hit hardest.

'Y…Yes… I'm English.'

'Are you well?'

'If you mean… am I unharmed?' Edward sat up. 'Bruised… but nothing broken… I think.'

'You do not bleed… They steal your gold, *ja?*'

Edward pushed his hand down his side to locate his purse. It was still attached to his belt. 'It appears they left me in funds.'

'Lucky that I come by this way.'

'Yes… thank you.'

'*Ja. Grothmier* walks this street every night to return home… From his building work, *ja?*'

'Thank you, Groth—mier?'

'*Ja*, Grothmier. Like my *Papa,* and his before him. Are you fine to go onto your bed, *Englisch?*'

Edward stood up. But the blows had left him weak in the legs and pained in the ribs.

'I may need some assistance.'

'Then I will help you. My *Mama* would wish it. She says a good deed is one more step to Heaven.'

Grothmier ran his hands down Edward's sides and lifted Edward's arm over his broad shoulders. He took his weight and helped him walk a little to regain movement in damaged legs. He gauged Edward's movement and the degree of pain issuing from Edward's face to his exertions.

Grothmier shared his diagnosis. 'Your ribs, bruised but not broken. Legs, bruised but not broken. Fortune smiles, *ja*. They did not knock your head and break your skull.'

Edward responded, pain still punctuating his speech, '*Fortune smiling*… is a poor choice of sentiment, Grothmier.'

'Sorry *Englisch*, I do not understand.'

'Neither do I, Grothmier… I would have given up my purse on the first blow. Strange thieves, who spend their time thumping rather than thieving.'

℞☣℟

Two days, and Edward rested. Grothmier called on him daily to check on his progress. Bringing food and helping Edward as best he could. Thirty more steps to Heaven he earned in those two days. Edward thought this man not destined for Purgatory, but would be hastened to the gates of Heaven.

Along with jugs of beer, he brought food; fresh bread, pork, and half a pie rich with herbs; all wrapped in cotton cloth. Grothmier also brought news of Antwerp, and a broom to sweep out Edward's poor lodgings.

Edward lay on his room's bed, as Grothmier swept. Edward grumbled and twisted, and tried to thump life back into the bed's poor mattress, barely a horse's fill of hay. But Edward thought his mattress long dead, and thought better than to inflict further violence on whatever dwelled within the sacking.

Amongst old straw, creatures do dwell—and bite.

'Could you not rent better, *Englisch*? Is the landlord blind, to offer his guests such dirty lodgings?' Grothmier's words flowed with his broom. His concentration fixed on his labour. His labour intent on filling the air with dust. More rubbish to send into the street, half the dirt to settle back into Edward's room.

'The lodgings suit me fine, Grothmier. Besides, better lodgings cost more… and I prefer less auspicious surroundings. They will draw less attention in a city teeming with guile.'

'I do not understand.'

Edward smiled at Grothmier as he swept. He studied a man busy in his work. It took his thoughts off his bed's discomfort and into mind's acute analysis. Edward saw a man not suited to the broom, but fitting well into worker's clothes. He wore a face of a seasoned soldier, with features common to the Low Countries. Strong jawed. Dark-haired, not greyed. But he wore his hair long, contrary to the local fashion, and in Edward's mind this marked him possibly Swiss, from one of the predominantly German speaking cantons of that area. Eyes brown, more black. His eyes and hair declared a younger man. He was strong through his whole body, and Edward thought his labour probably varied and hard. Well fed. Resolute. Dirty. But fresh dirt… not ingrained. Thus he bathed periodically. A worker yes. A peasant no. He seemed fit for more than mere labour work.

Edward could have simply enquired to Grothmier's origins, but intellectual vanity stayed his tongue. Ignorance applied was often a better policy. It avoided exchanging histories and maintaining deceit between those, who perhaps wish to become friends.

Grothmier caught Edward's stare and pondered. He read Edward's gaze, and said, 'I sense trouble in you, *Englisch*.'

'That does not surprise me. I suspect you seek troubled souls. Perhaps that is how you make your living—*Samaritan*.'

'It is easy to find sorry souls in this kingdom. I offer help to the troubled, if there is help required. The untroubled rarely require the hand of Grothmier.'

'So what is *my* trouble, Grothmier?'

'*Skandal.*'

'I do not understand.'

'*Skandal.* Is it not the pastime of the rich and poor alike? Gossip fills the alehouse, kitchen and market. News of the infidelity of a wife is good gossip, *ja*? It ignites the imagination and brings smile to the mouth. Your conquest of Lady Consuela Machuca is already well known. You, I am afraid, are one of many to try their plough on that field. Many have dug nothing but rocks, and sown seed only to see it wither.'

'My plough did not till the field… Simple flirtation. And anyway it was the wrong field.'

'Sorry, *Englisch*. I do not understand.'

'I thought she was another. I did not think to check the ladies name, before I proffered her my passion.'

'Poor manners, *Englisch*. Who did you think she was?'

'Madame van der Goes.'

'Is she not the wife of another rich banker-merchant of Antwerp? I hear she is plain and very ugly.'

'Not ugly. But I did not think Jan van der Goes would be paired to someone as plain as she. Her family must be rich and well placed to benefit the banker-merchant, to see him wed such a homely woman.'

Grothmier seemed excited. '*Ah Englisch, ja, ja.* Gold *und* power is a wondrous pairing…much good reason to marry, *ja?* But beauty is seen different. Some see beauty in pigs, some in horses. And Madame van de Goes is the daughter of a poor butcher… no money… no power… I think he marries her for love… *Ja?*'

Grothmier's broom never skipped a beat—the composition of his sweeping, regular and endless. And the floor was swept once, twice, and twice more.

'So *Englisch*. You sought out the lady because she was the wife of Jan van der Goes?'

Edward frowned. Not because of his actions with regards to Madame van der Goes, but because he talked too much to a man, as much a stranger as he was a Samaritan. *More fuel for ale-house gossip*, he thought. So Edward remained silent.

Grothmier continued to sweep and overlaid a tune to the beat of the broom. His mouth was a keen instrument. He whistled it well—*The Carman's Whistle*. But after a while, Grothmier rested his tune and cast his line again.

'Why do you wish Jan van der Goes harm?'

'Harm, Grothmier?' replied Edward.

'*Ja*. Harm. I understand Jan van der Goes is devoted to wife.'

Edward lifted himself off the bed. He stretched and stamped feeling into his legs.

'And no doubt, being so devoted, his wife is well acquainted with her husband's secrets.'

'I doubt many men trust wives with secrets, *Englisch*. Those are for their confessors.'

'Yes… trust and secrets… Siblings born from the same womb, only to live in disquiet.'

'You talk a *gute* riddle, *Englisch*.'

Edward's eyes widened. 'Hmmm… riddles, yes. A bigger riddle, Grothmier, is why do you sweep away the floorboards with the windows closed. The dust simply settles where you sweep.'

Grothmier laughed, his smile broad and friendly. 'I never said my services were capable, only well meant.'

∽∾

'*Englisch*, a man calls on you… He claims he is a servant, sent from the house of Hueçon to assist you.'

'Send him away Grothmier… Servant, spy, whatever he is, he will only have one master.'

'But surely a servant is a gift worth the taking?'

Edward was in no mood to receive emissaries from Henri, or his gifts. A week had passed since the party, and nearly two since Henri offered him a servant. Whatever assistance Henri offered now, it could only be to profit Henri.

A servant indeed. A poor gift indeed. Armed guards would be better.

Already half hiding from another beating, or worse, Edward was wary about the immediate world around him, or leaving his room without good reason. He fretted over his possible exposure to further mischief at the hands of those discontents unseen; jealous husbands, the Black Merchants' Guild, Jan van der Goes, Henri Hueçon, or even the man in the street with no reason to harm him, other than it suited him to do so. Edward was at a loss to decide what course of action he could take. But a reassurance sprang to mind.

'Grothmier, I have a thought. Will you take his place?'

'*Nein*, I am no servant, I'm no valet, no cook… and he is paid, I am not. I am certain even the good *Samariter*, did not make a living out of doing the good deeds.'

'I will pay you more and worry less, if you would take the place of Hueçon's man.'

Then my purse thanks you. My wife thanks you… *und meine kinder* thank you. But if this man of Hueçon's is a spy, would it not be better to keep him close?'

'Close?' replied Edward.

'To feed him false report, if deceit suits better than truth.'

'A risky strategy, Grothmier.'

'Perhaps, but I will stay… to keep watch on the spy.'

'Thank you, Grothmier—good man of Antwerp.'

'Good, perhaps not, but a richer man for the extra gold you will put in my purse. God save you, *Englisch*.'

෫෧෬

Hueçon's servant was a good servant. Grothmier said it. Edward knew it. He was polite and attentive, circumspect and punctilious. All things a good servant should be. But whatever his instructions were regarding Edward's care, he certainly gave better service to his master—Henri Hueçon. For as easy as he wore a smile for Edward, he also hid his disdain from him. For all the personal and domestic chores he undertook, there was also hidden mischief in his service.

His name was *Felix*. He spoke well in English, Spanish, French and German, as well as all brute dialects associated with Flanders. Edward cleverly tested Felix in Italian and Latin, to check his understanding and determined, in Romanic languages at least,

334

Felix was deficient. Grothmier understood a little Italian, the language of Antwerp's master builders and architects, so when Edward and Grothmier wished to converse privately, they did so in Italian; always at distance from Felix, in case his ignorance of Italian was simply a clever feint.

Felix politely took Edward's messages asking Henri for another meeting, and politely gave reasons back as to why his master was unavailable. He returned Henri's party suit, his eyes cursing Edward's poor care of it. He even took Edward's own clothes, while he slept, to have them washed. But they never returned, and thus Edward found himself a prisoner in his lodgings, in his underwear.

Felix fed Edward poorer than Grothmier. Food, Edward thought, that was poorly chosen from questionable market vendors. Food, which had a taint Edward found unpalatable. Some food was so bad that he sent it into the street through his window to feed the dogs. Food, the street dogs sniffed, contemplated, pawed and pushed with their noses. But ate it in the end they did. Pigs did too, those on route to the meat market. All on four legs ate it, except the city's cats; they would charily sniff and run from it. Some on two legs ate it as well. Some even ate it only to immediately purge more dung into the streets of Antwerp. Some even to throw it back towards the window from which it came.

Grothmier followed Felix to the market, the laundry, brewers, butchers, herbalist, apothecary, and to his master's house. He kept him in his sights whilst Edward remained in his room. And Edward slept and slept, as if a lifetime of misplaced rest had chosen to reconcile their disunion. And in that begrimed room, on that lumpy bed, he slept without dream, or without break. He slept longer than even the dogs did in the street outside.

Felix did not knock at the door. He did not display politeness when he entered the room. He did not excuse himself, or apologise to Edward for his curt interruption. Edward's engrossment in a poetry volume, *Songs and Sonnets, by Lord Henry Howard [Earl of Surrey] and Thomas Wyatt*, was going to be rudely interrupted, and Felix did not seem to care.

Felix' delivery was breathless and urgent, 'Monsieur Hendon… *The Banker* has sent his brother-in-law with a note… A demand for satisfaction… An honour-contest… *A duel.*'

Edward did not listen. He did not take his eyes off his book. It was too delicious to leave. The prose too good—too absorbing. To remove one's eyes would be a discredit to the author. So Edward read through the intrusion into his concentration.

'You should be careful running stairs, Felix. Men with a poor vocation for exertion have broken their necks, or broken their hearts undertaking such a strain.'

Felix, seeing Edward's indifferent response to his news, started to repeat himself. 'The Banker has sent his brother-in-law with a…'

Edward raised his hand to stop Felix talking. His eyes remaining affixed on his book. 'If you refer to the Banker with a Spanish beauty as his wife, but not with his name. Isn't he a little too old, a little too fat, to be duelling, Felix?'

'Monsieur Hendon, The Banker doesn't…'

'I would of thought the Banker a little too… mmm… *rich* to risk his life.'

'Monsieur, please listen.'

Edward was finding it increasingly difficult to finish his page, and maintain his response to Felix. So Edward ignored Felix' pleas for attention, completely.

'Monsieur.'

Edward was lost in prose.

'*Monsieur!*'

Wit formed a smile on Edward's lips, and he chuntered, 'Is not his wife a little too lusty, a little too alluring to keep her chaste and from being chased by suitors?'

Felix, vexed that Edward's response was still lingering in the direction of his own observations, slapped the table underpinning Edward's book, *hard.*

'*Monsieur Hendon!*'

Edward raised his head to look at Felix, red faced from his outburst. Felix had finally broken Edward's concentration—his battle lost to read-on the prose that had delighted him so.

Edward placed a ribbon on the page he was reading and very carefully closed the book. Treating the tome with the reverence it deserved.

'Sorry Felix, what were you saying?'

'Monsieur Hendon, it is not the Banker who submits you to the duel, but his brother-in-law who commits to the duel in lieu of his sister's husband. And he is an excellent swordsman. No equal I hear.'

Edward could handle weapons, and could apply them to good effect. He had even killed before, but he was no duellist, no expert in swordplay. This was a problem more pressing than his textual education. Edward thoughts turned to alarm.

'Does he wait outside? Have I time to prepare… or flee?'

'Here.' Felix handed Edward a note. Edward unfolded it. It was written by a Flemish hand.

'I do not read Low Dutch.'

Felix took back the note. 'It sets a date… Ten days time, at five of the clock before midday. Outside the *Maaden Huis*… the orphanage for girls.'

'*Ten days… the orphanage.* It seems our duellist intends to make me sweat first, and then impress a few maids whilst he makes me bleed. Perverse it is, honour—to provoke fear, prick flesh and stain his sword with blood, and then to stain his prick with the blood of a few virgins' honour... Perverse it is.'

Chapter XXV

The light flickered in the palace's chamber. Draft made it so. It was a surprise to many how wind found its way to the lower levels, through a dozen doors, to pierce the brick and windowless walls.

Jack barely had time to adjust to his new surroundings. Two hours off the ship, and his men billeted in the Guild's dormitory. The sights of Antwerp deprived for a sight more memorable, but less than worthy of a prodigious city.

'I do not believe in torture, only the example it can bring. My men know what is expected. Failure is not punished—mistakes can be made. After all, we are all human. All imperfect. *Do you not agree, Captain Brownfield?*'

The poor man was hung from a beam, hands tied. Not so high, that he could not support himself a little on his toes against the pressure applied to his throat by the noose, but high enough to remain in serious discomfort.

Kalibrado nodded to his guard standing by, who then walked to the poor hung man. He stood before the hapless fellow, only to kick away the poor man's feet, so he swung and choked. The man, desperate to steady himself, stretched his toes to find the floor, to dance a grotesque jig, whilst sounding terrible choking noises.

'I would normally keep a man this way until he had learned his lesson.' Kalibrado's voice was calm and measured; neither pleasure nor concern tainted it. 'I suspect the lesson here was learned many hours ago.'

'Yet still he hangs?' asked Jack.

'Yes. He is a short man. The guard here, needed to cut a new, longer rope for the task. I wished to see it well used... I dislike waste.'

Jack held his tongue at first. He suppressed questions desperate to be asked. But as Kalibrado turned to leave the room, curiosity won over good sense, and Jack asked his question.

'What was his crime?'

'I do allow mistakes in my guards, my clerks... my foot soldiers... But never in my captains, my factors, or any of those who directly manage my affairs.'

'And this poor soul?' asked Jack.

'Ferdinand Bure is the former captain of my guard. He performed poorly.'

Kalibrado studied the condition of the hung man. His tortured eyes were red and drawn. His face strained. Days of beard-growth showed on his dirty face. His hose stained with urine and excreta. Disgust formed on Kalibrado's face as he raised his hand to his nose, to hold out the stink of the cell, until he left it behind.

'My confidence in this man was well wasted, although I have to admit his endurance of the rope is... *impressive.*'

A question asked. A lesson learned. Jack regarded his new commission with certainty. *It was a short route to ruin for him... and his men.*

Kalibrado walked Jack through the corridor, past doors and more cells guarded by the red and black liveries of his guard, until they entered another door of another cell.

'Here is your test… Commitment to the Guild—*to me*, requires action without question. I am the Guild… now kill her.'

Jack looked on a wretched form in rags, standing, tied to a post. The grubby bag covering her head, the cleanest garment she wore. Jack's heart was sour, for he knew what Kalibrado expected. Jack had killed. He had executed prisoners before, both in France, for reasons of war, and in his homeland, for reasons of justice. But he thought this to be different. She was perhaps an innocent, a poor kinless woman, snatched by Kalibrado to test Jack's compunction for killing—his attitude to murder without reservation. Or perhaps a petty thief saved from the hangman, to become practice for Kalibrado's cruel art of torture and test.

Kalibrado shook his head. 'Already you delay. You are far from suitable. Hueçon is an ass to recommend you.'

Jack walked up to the woman and removed the hood. She was a girl, and in poor condition. His examination of her was brief. Jack's knife did its work well. The girl's death was swift, quiet and absolute.

Kalibrado did not see Jack's muted action. He was too far into his castigation of Hueçon to notice Jack's knife thrust into the girl. He also missed Jack turning away, to walk to the door. But Jack soon felt the eyes of the Devil on him and he turned to face Kalibrado.

'Do you want me, or should I go?'

Kalibrado glared at Jack. Annoyed he would dare to leave without being excused. Then he turned his head to see the girl slumped, her tattered gown showing blood around her chest. Kalibrado raised his deep black eyebrows in surprise. He studied Jack's face, the look in his eye. And for the first time since the tour began, Kalibrado smiled.

'Your efficiency surprises me, Captain Brownfield. But you do not smile.'

Jack's face was stoic, his voice calm. 'Killing is not an act for smiling.'

'Ah, but it is. A man who does not smile, does not find pleasure in what he does. Do you not agree, Captain Brownfield?'

'You enjoy killing?'

'No, but I smile whenever what is done is right. Two kinds of men smile after killing. The wanton man who enjoys the cruelty of it, and the wise man that is happy with prudent and proper action. I distrust one and trust the other. What do you say?'

'Am I retained as Captain of the Guard?'

'Ah… a man intent on keeping his thoughts to himself. I will have to watch you closely. Test you a little more perhaps? Report to me tomorrow. I have a task for you. Further opportunity to practice that smile.'

Two flights of stone stairs took Jack back up to the hall, where men and women were about their labour. Kalibrado's palace was busy. Clerks ran the corridors. Guards stood the doors. Women and girls in plain blue dress hurried by, blinkered to their surroundings. It was hard to keep a steady track through the crowded corridors as Jack traversed over the marbled covered floor and down the marbled columned hall.

Through it all, Jack returned to the Great Room, where Kalibrado's tour began. It was a grand centrepiece in a great house, topped by a dome, inspired by *Brunelleschi's* celebrated dome of *Santa Maria del Fiore*—the great cathedral of Florence.

In the centre of the vast room, was employment; ten desks long, by ten desks wide, each with a clerk on duty. Amongst the desks, men stood dictating letters. The clerks copied, magnifying the quiet sound of solitary pens scratching paper, into one hundred pens grating the senses. But regardless of poor noise, the sight of it all was a picture of order and efficiency. And directing it all, from the corner of the room, behind a larger desk, aloft a grand dais, was the master of it all, Peppo; restored to his proper place, administering the affairs of the Master of the Black Merchants' Guild.

Jack caught Peppo's eye. But any friendliness displayed by a man rescued, and brought to Antwerp in good company, was now absent from Peppo's expression. Jack was now in Peppo's world, where he was prince, and Kalibrado was king—a reversal of fortune for those who knew the truth of it. But all those poor souls were long dead. So their secret was well kept.

Jack thought to leave the palace, and make good the remainder of the day in a city, yet unknown to him. To tour and see its facets and faces. To become acquainted with its distractions and dispositions. He wished to clear his mind of deed done, and the dread of deeds yet to be asked under a foul commission. But in the corridor that ran to the entrance vestibule, Jack met the procurer of his new contract, Henri Hueçon, flanked by two tall Swiss-German Guards.

The guards were *Landsknechts*, by their bright garb. Dressed in cut and slashed suits. Topped with large hats wearing feathers of four colours. Big men, supported on monstrous feet and footwear. Tall halberds by their side; weapons of polished metal, from spear tip through blade, down through metal shaft to form three spikes at the base.

Jack's observation was accompanied by a shallow nod. 'Your guards are impressive, Henri. Big and colourful, like ox in silk.'

The two guards looked to each other, confused, mean intent glowing in their exchanged gaze. *Insult or ignominy?*

'They serve good their purpose,' replied Henri, 'They are *Doppelsöldner, Brothers of Saint Mark*, masters of the long sword… and thus *reassuringly* expensive to keep.'

'I have seen their like fight in France, and run away in Scotland.'

Jack's words pricked at the two beasts and they brought their halberds sharply forward in defence of their honour.

'*Arrêtez.*' Henri raised his hand against his guards. 'Not ox, *Jacques*, but *Lions of Alsace*. Poke oxen with a stick, *Jacques*, and they will walk on. Poke lions… and they will eat you.'

Jack drew a knowing smile in response at Henri's diplomacy, admiring his uttered caresses on the bruised egos of his German guards.

'It is good to see you, *Jacques*, safe and well. Acceptable journey I hope. It was indeed a slow ship that brought you. Did Peppo come alone? Or did he bring something for his master?'

'Yes, we were delayed somewhat. And Peppo brought folios back to his master. Maps I am certain.'

'Did you see them?'

'No, Peppo insisted the seals remain intact… and in truth, I do not think even he knew their contents.'

Henri smiled with his knowledge of Jack's trials. 'I hope you made good use of your time, *Jacques*?'

'Time is good coin. But when one has abundance, it is rarely spent wisely.'

Henri nodded his head wistfully, 'So true, *Jacques*.'

'But friendship is better coin, Henri. And I'm afraid you have wasted a great deal of it bringing my men and I here to service the Devil. This is no soft commission.'

'*Mais non, Jacques.*' Henri smiled. 'He is not the Devil. He is the Devil's master. The Devil is merely his apprentice.'

'Aye, I wonder who is the true devil here… Henri. False report of the nature of this commission you gave to me. A short life you gift me… and an unworthy service you have offered to my men.'

'Ah, *Jacques*, in a world of deceit you need friends. Let us keep good rapport and strengthen our camaraderie over some excellently conceived wine—the best my suppliers can offer. My home here is modest, but comfortable. You will not see better visions of the artist's work outside of Rome.' Henri leaned into Jack's ear to hide his next words from his guards. '…and for the sake of better comfort… I will put my oxen here in the cowshed, where they better belong.'

Jack was not for Henri's show of conciliation and purposed hospitality. His face held a disappointment that Henri could not fail to notice. And Jack's mind held desire to be free of Henri's self-illumination, and his ill-conceived notion of selfless cordiality.

'My apologies, Henri, but I think I prefer to spend the evening with my own men over much badly brewed beer.'

Henri raised his hands in sad acceptance. 'So be it. Your desire is my desire.'

Jack sighed at Henri's response—earnestly delivered, with spurious sentiment. Jack turned. He nearly escaped Henri's net, but Henri had another line to cast.

'Our friend, Edward Hendon is in the city. He is in great peril. He needs our help. A favour best supported by yourself and two more with your trust. Will you help?'

'In this respect, Henri, for my old tutor, I will help. But I will state it now, clear, so I do not offend later on when you ask it… I will not help you in your campaign against the Guild Master, who I suspect is your opponent. If this is your plan, you have thought poorly of me to employ me so… Jan van der Goes is a man not to be played like one of your games, Henri. I will not betray my commission to see you profit, and my honour pay the price of it.'

Chapter XXVI

The Banker was a punctual man. He maintained his place of business in the *Grote Markt*, a walk away from his rich home and Spanish wife. His route was well planned. Not short and direct, but one to pass the market at a place where the smells pleased and the sights of his city were kind to his eye. Never alone, he walked with his escort—two men good with the sword, keen-eyed to mischief and well paid to protect a rich man from those with a fancy for his purse, or more ambitious designs on kidnap and ransom.

It was a good day for the Banker. His status was assured. His wealth was increasing. And his hand reached out over a great number of lives, some made better by his care, some richer by his alliance and some made envious by his success. He was praised for his philanthropy and known for his enterprise.

His commercial interests were wide and varied; copper, silver and coal, all exported and imported through Antwerp. His merchant fleet was substantial, his warehousing extensive, his holdings in manufactories numerous.

He produced trade goods destined for Asia. He sponsored exploration and innovation. He developed arms and architecture—his foundries producing peerless weaponry, his architects the newest building. He set about replacing old ideas with fresh thinking, inefficiency with order, old stone with new vision—new forms more fitting the revival of classical thinking, inspired by classical art.

Art, he collected, and the art market in Antwerp benefited greatly by his enterprise. He was a collector-dealer of great renown. His collections were his expression, they reflected his tastes and his appetites—paintings, countless icons and sculpture from antiquity. Patron to many; he was the artists' favourite. Especially favoured by those moneyless initiates with new concepts to exhibit.

He was noted amongst academics for his studious learning. Admired for his knowledge of the sciences. He collected instruments, both mathematical and optical, and books covering alchemy, medicine, theology and subjects both cosmological and geographical.

His library was extensive and he opened it generously, without notice, to any scholar, philosopher or preacher.

Through his library, he fostered education. He established academies and contributed to universities. He ensured his servants' children had access into learning. Indeed, many said he helped not only his own, but any he thought worthy of a helping hand into a better life.

His house, they said, was much a comfort for those who served it, as those it served. He was both rich and modest in his way, and for all he was a propertied man, his house was his only home—his haven. He did not see the need for palaces as a mark of show. But his home had seen lavish extension, not for a growing family, but for his growing collection; rooms to house it all. He insisted his architects only brought new design. New idea born out of private commission. His architects often broke their clients confidences to share designs never seen before—strange new buildings and cities for a strange new world.

His charity was boundless. His generosity immeasurable. He provided, without earthly reward, hospital, orphanage and almshouse. He supported his guild, and gave without restraint, aid to the needful. His servants and workers had little to concern them. Good pension. Good care. The Church too held him in high regard. With provisions well made for his soul's receipt, via donation to bishops and cardinals, new chapel and church and even cathedral, built on the stone of his endeavour.

All in all, a good life was well made by the Banker, and his own reputation was all. It stood him tall amongst the other high citizens of Antwerp. He was well known to princes and kings for the money he lent and the power of his industry.

This day, a third joined his walking party, Consuela's beloved younger brother and thus brother-in-law to the Banker. He was a well-tested duellist. Veteran soldier. Celebrated fighter. The Banker was happy. He found great reassurance in the company of Consuela's brother, *Diego*. His wit was perfect, and his Spanish show of affection warmed even the coldest heart. And while he was present, those courtiers with an appetite for his beautiful, flirtatious wife were stayed at a distance. They feared dire retribution by a husband with honour to safeguard and a lady's brother, both keen and well able to uphold it. It pleased the Banker to think on one foolish dressed courtier, soon to add to Diego's tally of victories, for he had heard Henri Hueçon's guest was no swordsman, and the Banker owed Hueçon no favour.

The Banker's good humour was made all the better for a joke shared on the way. But the joke was curtailed. Smiles abandoned, and their procession halted. Their way was blocked.

Thirty paces ahead, a solitary man stood before the Banker's party. Sword drawn. Malicious intent in his eyes.

The Banker's guards stepped forward to shield their charge.

Diego took the lead, standing proud and sword drawn in response to the threat. He replied to the solitary swordsman's foolish play, by shaking his head disdainfully. Disappointment shaped his smile. He was vexed that the swordsman had not recognised, *Diego Machuca, his 'reputation with a sword—unrivalled north of Salamanca'.*

But the swordsman did not move or cower in the face of Diego's self-assurance, and Diego's ease of mind with his own skill became unsettled. He thought the man before him too confident to be standing so bold without some protection unseen, and he turned to look to his brother-in-law to ensure he was safe.

All was clear.

Diego confirmed three stood against only one. Diego would need no support to kill one man and his confidence returned, bolstered by a lone swordsman with no pistol. Diego thought to simply draw his own, to let loose lead at the villain, to save his fine clean shirt from the sweat of exertion. There may be no honour in such a kill, but the swordsman before him dressed poor, probably no more than luckless scoundrel looking for parlous pay, so no honour to accrue in his heart pierced by Diego's rapier. And it was, after all, *his favourite shirt.*

Diego turned away from the swordsman, to hide his hand pulling back his cloak, and smiling to the guards to show them his intent, he started to draw his pistol from his belt. But no sooner than the smile had left his lips, Diego saw the two guards behind him twist violently—bolts of steel piercing their flesh. He looked urgently to where the attacking crossbowmen may be standing, ready to counter a second volley. But two men came out of the shadows, each with two pistols. Shots rang out. One from each man to ensure the guards were stilled. Then immediately they turned their second pistols on Diego and killed him.

The swordsman, seeing his comrades succeed, began his march up to the Banker. The Banker's eyes were wide. His hands held in horror at the sight of dead men on the ground. Eyes darted from each corpse in turn, then to the swordsman, closing fast— greater horror to come. He backed up to a wall—no escape.

The swordsman's stride did not falter and the blade reached the Banker's chest in a moment, to pierce the silk of his doublet, and prick the flesh beneath.

'Nee-nee. Dood me niet!'

The swordsman cocked his head and screwed his face slightly, as if he did not understand the Banker's tongue, or was surprised by his words. Either way, the swordsman replied, his words calm and measured. 'The world is the Devil's dominion. On Earth, all flesh is his. Only through release can one's soul find salvation…either through death, or through earthly revelation… *Have you prepared your soul, Master Banker?*'

The Banker's actions were involuntary. He pushed his arms out as a shield against sword. Dutch words were forgotten. English words found. His heart pounded and breath quickened. Urine running his leg.

'Don't… don't kill me… I have money, *take it.*'

The swordsman shook his head. 'Gold is not my pleasure… But my friend, Edward Hendon is.'

'*The Englishman.* I forgive him. It was my wife's mistake, a slight misunderstanding. *Please don't kill me…*'

'Your celebrated devotion to your own honour shows badly in the face of your own death.'

'No-no…*please, I beg you!*'

'You've had your duel… and you lost.'

The swordsman pushed hard on his sword, face twisted with exertion. The blade found resistance. So he applied greater pressure, negotiating blade's journey past rib, into heart's home. He watched the blade disappear deep into the Banker's chest, to find the brick wall beyond. Blood ran the wound and blade. And life left the Banker, his eyes stilled.

All three men walked into the shadows, leaving the alarm call behind, leaving *five* bodies on the ground in their wake.

A lifetime of earnest commitment, hard work, and a rich life robbed. Snuffed easily in a wink of another man's whim.

Chapter XXVII

Henri Hueçon had procured entertainment. And amongst his guests was young Antony Beekman, beloved only son of Salomon Beekman, merchant and member of the Black Council, governing assembly of the Black Merchants' Guild.

It was not unusual for Henri to invite those he thought well connected to better placed men, to events of spectacle and social gathering. It was his way. And as Salomon held high-placed position within the Black Council, Henri courting his young son was no less than those in the know expected an ambitious Henri to do. Even more so, as Henri was seen as no favourite of Salomon, ingratiating himself with an influential son seemed an able strategy into Salomon's favour. In all, the notables around them reported, 'It was less than a raised eyebrow's worth, but perhaps worthy of a wry thought.'

The theatre was surreptitiously installed in a building meant for daily commerce and not meant for dramatic spectacle, because the makeshift theatre was outside respectability, for its plays were entertainment of a different sort—vulgar humour. They were not the rhetoric and poetry of the amateur societies that performed with zeal in Antwerp. Chambers of theatre, loving amateurs delightfully named, *The Olive branch, The Gillyflower and The Marigold.*

Their plays and rhetoric were what the City would prefer its citizens and transients to see and hear. They were the fair spectacle. But the performance Henri invited Antony Beekman to enjoy was a play designed only to enliven the hidden sodomite's fancy.

'The play is delightful, Henri. Do you just love its show?'

'I'm afraid delight will be the last line, of the last act, Antony.'

'Why so, Henri?'

'The wit is misplaced, well lost by the writer's wayward pen. And his ill-conceived contrivances are masquerading as folly rather than farce.'

'But isn't all farce absurd and improbable, Henri?'

'Yes, but the skill in the writer makes it probable…' Henri broke his dialogue and cast his eyes from his companion to the stage, and to the three daughters of the apothecary, fluttering their obscene eyelashes at the hero; his stance shouting all his role, 'And the *ladies* could have shaved before the performance.'

Antony laughed. 'You are too critical, Henri. You can hardly tell they are boys, they wear their dresses so well.'

'True, they make better show of womankind. More so than the kind of woman here tonight, who are indeed more hairy than the boys on the stage, and manlier than the hero, whose stance is more placed to counter the weight of his codpiece, rather than his actable performance. The codpiece's enormity is beyond the realm of humour, and into deformity that would render our hero a clown, or a freak for show.'

'No, no, Henri, you are too, too critical. Our *maids* do well, and our hero looks well… Well capable of keeping the apothecary's maids smiling.'

'If boys are to play maids, then their countenance should suit. It would enhance the spectacle, and convince yon dullard hero to treat his *maids* as maids, and not boys dressed as maids.'

'Yes, the actor seems confused. But caution, Henri. Lets not

353

wish for prettier boys, lest yon actor forgets himself, and in a moment of fervour, forgets his act and ravishes the maids for real, and prick does find arse instead of quim.'

Henri nodded his agreement. 'Ahh… If only those boy-maids were so easily found in this moral world we build in Antwerp.'

'I am lost to your meaning, Henri.'

'In antiquity, boys were readily available for men. The Ancients thought of boys as simple pleasures, more giving to a man's gratification than ladies, because they understand a man's pleasure more than ladies.'

Antony hesitated to reply. But self-suppressed desires found an ease of release in front of such an amoral show, in enlightened company. 'Do you legitimize sodomy, Henri?'

'No, of course not… But one should not deny himself his sins… Sin then repent. Our Lord loves a sinner that repents… but how can we repent if we do not sin?'

Antony held his eyes to the ground in shame. 'But sin such as that, will see us in damnation.'

'Sin is between the sinner and the Saviour… It is better to spite the Church, which is indeed full of sinners… Believe me… our fair maids on the stage have fumbled beneath the cassock of many a priest, and many more a bishop, whose sins are denial and a blind eye to their own proclivities. Repent, that is the key to everlasting salvation… but one must sin first.'

Henri's young guest found more than a crumb of comfort in Henri's words, but not enough to feed, to satisfaction, a soul tortured by denial of its sexuality.

Henri studied his neighbour's face. Abhorrence was still in the young man's eyes, so Henri feigned retreat in his discourse. 'Ah Antony, *mon bon ami*, forget my musings… A foolish man who wishes he were born long ago in a better time, within the Roman, or Greek *Aristokratikos*… better nobility, a better time… Yes a better time for men, *oui?*'

'You think it noble to love boys?'

'No, I think it noble to be pleasured by boys… Do you not wish to be noble, Antony?'

'Yes, but…'

'Yes, but the King must be wrong, and all those noble men and high-born women who can afford to hide their pleasures from the Church's piety.

'Are you saying King Philip, the noblest of noble Catholics, is a sodomite?'

Henri, who did not know if his fiction was false, could not refute it. 'He is a handsome man. A man who is gracious, courteous and who dresses very tastefully. A slight man not given to physical arts, but who is susceptible to the ethereal ones. He, who surrounds himself with handsome young valets to attend his bedchamber, what more can one surmise, when it is the way with nobles and gentlemen, who often only have the company of willing boys and chosen wives of little attraction? But enough discourse, I say sin and be saved. Let live and not lambaste.'

'You have a way of bringing logic to chaos. A devil's tongue for persuasion. Perhaps, Henri, we need to discuss your philosophy more… it intrigues me… And perhaps you can tell me who else, noble, has a fancy for boys. Perhaps a quiet supper after the play?'

'I would like that… but alas I cannot stay long. But for your pleasure, in my absence, I will invite some of the players along for a…' Henri offered a wry smile. '…*private performance.*'

'That would be amusing, Henri, but expensive?'

'*Mais non*, leave the trifle of arrangement and cost to me. However we must keep such a show private, otherwise it will not be… *special.*'

'I am in your debt, Henri.'

'*Mais non*, forget it.'

The act concluded. The loud and boisterous ovation from the audience hailed it. So Henri raised his own hands in applause, looking to the audience and their pleasure, nodding his head gracefully in agreement. But in his mind their applause was not for the actors on the stage, but for Henri Hueçon, the greatest player of them all.

Henri bowed to them all and looked upon his young guest, with a roguish smile. The seed of corruption was sown—the shoot of sin to grow, the shame of the father to reap, a favour won, a favour to wear up his sleeve, an ace ready to play at cards, when a winning hand was required.

As the applause died, Antony turned to Henri to see him still raising his hands in his show of appreciation.

'So you enjoyed the play after all, Henri?'

'This is merely the first act my dear boy.'

Chapter XXVIII

The books in his room spoke. They used to speak to him only in the evening hours. But as the days passed, they filled his afternoons. Then eventually he read in morning's light, until the books had no more to say.

Grothmier had not visited Edward for eight days, and he was missing his company and the better victuals he brought. He missed the better exchange that exists between men of deeper insight into the world; discourse that was forever absent between Felix and himself—a sham master and a loaned servant, whose platitudes and politeness did not provoke lively conversation.

But most of all, he was missing the advice Grothmier may bring to temper his own disquiet—apprehension of an impending duel, and unease regarding those agents that meant him harm. He needed a friend—good counsel. But in his solitude, Edward simply waited the days out, as if some great wonder would take pity on him, and save him from hurt. But as days passed by, fear of death became real and the fantasy of miracle faded away.

Without reasoned discourse, or new learned text to fill his mind, Edward's isolation was reinforced. And as he sank into seclusion, conscious reason gave way to subconscious fear. His bold cause lost to his own uncertain thought. His confidence misplaced somewhere in the perceived security of his room. Avoidance found. Poor excuses created. Blame cast on tiredness attributed to hard journeying, long completed, injuries long healed, clothes stolen and perpetual stomach cramps courtesy of food and drink brought by Felix, or even the lack of it eaten, for Hueçon's servant had not been to tend him for three days.

Paranoia stalked Edward, or was it a man hiding in the shadows of the street below?

Do perfidious eyes watch me at my window?

Edward studied all. He considered the faces of those who walked by, or rested in sight of his lodging. He looked into their eyes for foul intent, past their hoods and hats to study hidden stare.

Do I watch the world, or does it watch me?

He looked to men of fighting cast. He looked to those in shrouds and cloaks—to anyone uncomfortable in their clothes.

Men concealing arms; pistols?

Edward watched the shadows. He looked hard into the dark of window space, door and alley. He imagined watchers, spies and assassins—all with muskets pointing.

While I watch, they will not reveal. Will they kill me as I sit at window's light to read?

Then he imagined thieves, beggars, boys; all those who loitered—malevolent forms, scheming. And in his fancy, he drew out their misdeed for his mind to picture their mischief against his life. To see it play out—to see him murdered. Foul imaginings.

And with deep breath, Edward saw it real again, and sane reason brought him back to see nothing but people on the street.

He sighed, and wondered, *why do they wait?*

Calm befell Edward.

Then suddenly—a noise sharp and loud. Commotion. Men fighting. Voices raised. People crowding on the street. And Edward panicked.

A feint! Distraction! The time is here. Edward away from window… Hide from bullet… Quickly now… before it's too late!

Anxiety gripped Edward hard. It flushed his body with heat, his skin with sweat, his mind with racing fevered thought. He took a breath. He held it long. He closed his eyes. He sought lost reason to shut out found alarm.

'Be strong… Mind be still,' he said aloud.

'Be strong… Be strong… Mind be still,' he said again, louder still.

Edward rubbed hard his face to draw out his madness. He wished away his mind's conflict—alien thinking. He put in his mind that his thoughts were the result of sickness, fever, or perhaps something he ate.

So he turned to a faith long overlooked, neglected in the living of life without proper order, absent of the influence of an attending priest and Church's regime. He gently put his hands together in earnest supplication, and prayed.

'I renew my devotion. I pray to you blessed mother of God. Help me clear my mind of fog. Let me see clear the way to a better road; a path of blessed choice… For I am lost. For Christ's sake. Amen.' And Edward made the sign of the cross, as if it was his last act of living.

He stayed still, eyes closed for two hour strikes of the church bell. He kept tight his eyes from seeing the world as he walked Elysium in his mind, and remembered all the good of his life, amongst all the bad. Held them tight until his heart relaxed and his mind was eased, until he fell asleep again.

Edward had clothes, not his own, but replacements brought by Felix in lieu of his own not returned, apparently lost at laundry—or stolen. Edward stared at the suit as he raised the coffer's lid. His eyes could not hide his incredulity. The clothes certainly cast-off by Henri Hueçon, for only Henri could wear them. But even Henri would have discarded them as too gaudy for respectable attire. So Edward thought perhaps they were a costume of sorts, for carnival or masquerade, and therefore clothing unsuitable for the pitiable streets, in a modest quarter of the city. Hose of fierce red, decorated with birds—stuffed humming birds, attached as if they as if they hovered ready to take nectar from invisible flowers sewn about the leggings, a red doublet of a size to fit a child, a bright red velvet jerkin complete with hood decorated with pearls and a bird of fantastical form, colourfully feathered and wearing a crown of many jewels, boots in bright red leather, adorned with golden bells and threads, designed to catch the light and announce the wearer's steps. All in all, a suit better suited to the stage—to dress a jester or an odious sodomite prince. But the silk shirt was modest enough, and its fanciful collar removable. The birds pulled from the hose, and from the folds of their red velvet nest, rendered the suit wearable. And mercifully Edward had his own shoes. Edward dressed and looked himself over.

Still a clown.

He pulled on the hood, and sat in a chair, first to think on his woes, then to think on himself and how he looked.

Foolish man… Foolish fears. My fate is predetermined. Accept it Edward. Welcome it.

He rubbed his chin and felt beard's growth. Edward was in need of a haircut. A month without a shave was not his way. Clean face he normally wore. He preferred it that way against any local convention, or princely guided fashion. He wished a good shave and tidy hair, a clean chin and pate to bring freshness to a dull mind. He again ran his fingers over his throat to feel bristle.

Yes a good shave from another, not by the hands of Hueçon's servant, whom I can only trust to cut deeper by gross miscalculation, or deliberate design.

So it was. Edward took the wool blanket from his bed and wrapped it over his shoulders. Worn, it was long enough to lessen the show of the suit, as well as good covering to keep out unseasonable summer chill. And he opened the room's door and broke free his prison to join the world again.

In the next building, on the first floor, was the barber-surgeon. His rooms were reported as dirty, but other tenants in Edward's building claimed him to have a good eye, a steady hand and a keen price.

Edward's entrance confirmed it all. The barber-surgeon's room was indeed dirty. The walls unwashed. The floor unswept. Tools of trade scattered around without good order or proper place. In all, a room ungroomed, and not a room to have any malady of wound or blood comforted.

'Good morning, sir,' came a voice from the corner.

Edward smiled. It was good to see the barber-surgeon busy washing his hands, to see a smile on a face—a face happy to find a new customer in his shop.

'Good morning, Master Barber.'

'How can I serve you?'

'Shave me clean and cut my hair neat if you please.'

The barber was standing on a box-stool. He was a short man, barely five foot tall—stool and all. Head shaved, his cheeks glowed and a plentiful beard flowed to curl around to his chest, unkempt and wild—a poor endorsement for a barber's trade. He stepped off his stool, wiping his hands on a cloth dirtier than, no doubt, the hands he just washed. And throwing the rag over his shoulder, he kicked the stool to slide over the floor to rest next to a tall chair.

'Take a seat, sir.'

The barber-surgeon finished drying his hands by wiping them down his hose, now showing fresh stains of dirt.

'We've seen you... my wife Anna and me. We wondered if you venture clear of your room and come into my place. Hiding away, we'd say. From whom, we'd ask.'

'Well your wonderings are over, Master Barber. I am a murdering pirate king. Fugitive for reason of killing ninety-nine barbers and their wives and steeping myself in their rich red blood... So now you have one less surprise to hold.'

Edward walked over to the barber's chair, dropping his blanket to the floor, fully revealing his red suit. He leaned into the barber's ear and whispered, 'Let us hope you have wonderings left to keep life's mystery alive.'

The barber smiled nervously and showed Edward to his chair, replying, 'G-Good jest... sir. It is good to hear humour in these trying days.'

From another corner of the room, a woman appeared and began to dust the paraphernalia of a busy barber and insanitary surgeon. Dust, but not dust, as her eyes were not on her work, but on her husband's handsome customer. Her cloth was not hard tasked and all remained dirty.

Edward had long understood the need for cleanliness where bloodletting was concerned. Sciences learned in his days at the Abbey of Furness, and through books read, including more recently, *De Contagione et Contagiosis* by *Girolamo Fracastoro*. It recalled to Edward's mind Fracastoro's newly published collective works, and how they too were missing from the monastery's great library at Galicia, along with better translations from Islamic medicine.

The barber beckoned to the woman. 'Hot water if you please, Anna... This man has good growth.' He turned to rub his fingers through Edward's beard. 'Sir, may I suggest a good beard may frame your face better. A good portrait deserves a handsome frame... what say you, Anna?'

The woman was caught staring at Edward. She flushed pink, and turned her head to bury it in her hands. But she did not retire. She simply moved to another part of the room, to fiddle with objects and rearrange them, only to move them all back to from whence they had just been removed.

'Women are a mystery. I never see her in my shop, unless it is to bring hot water or new cloths... yet today... there she stands.'

The barber looked to his wife, adjusting her dress, her hair and the line of her bodice.

'What do you say, Anna... you are mystery, *Ja?* Now please stop preening and bring some hot water.'

But the woman did not answer. She was too busy smiling at Edward.

Edward sat in the barber's chair, and the barber wrapped a cloth around his shoulders. But after ten minutes wait, ten minutes barber-prattle, the razor gave way to scissors for the hair, because no hot water was coming by way of his distracted wife. His wife was missing, instead an attentive *woman* stood in her place—wanting and dreaming.

The barber busied his hands on Edward's hair. 'I think you are a learned man, a disciple of learning. I've seen your man bring you books. We have good book sellers and printers, don't you think? Ah, *ja* the best of everything we have... A rich city she is—Antwerp. Anna and I love her so. Nowhere in the world can you go and walk a street alongside a Catholic and Protestant, Jew and Muslim man, atheist and conformist, Hindu and Buddhist, Italian, French, German, Swiss, Dutch, English, Spanish, Greek, and Turk. All walking without too much fear, and with little restraint. It is Heaven's example on this good earth—a lesson in human charity to the World. Are you in Antwerp for business? Everyone is these days. This is true, *ja*? What do you think of the weather? The weather is cool is it not? One hundred days of cold, eighty days of dark, sixty days of snow, forty days of rain… all for twenty days of sun.'

The barber's voice was strangely soothing, and Edward found himself slipping into daydream. Then half-eyes. So he fought drowsiness with a question, to break the barber's monologue and lead to better, mutual dialogue.

'How long have you lived here?'

'Twenty years. I know everybody in this city. Everyone gets their hair cut here. I have let their blood, set their bones, pulled their teeth. Is that not the way of it, Anna?'

'*Ja*, husband. You spill good their blood,' replied the woman, standing three steps closer. Eyes fixed on Edward, wide and wanting, above a smile wider still. Broom now in hand, but not sweeping.

The barber flicked the scissors towards his wife to break her gaze. To let her know her lustful stare upon his handsome client was no longer to be endured by a too tolerant husband.

'*Ja*. I spill their blood, but no one dies from it, eh, *Master Pirate*? Well, not yet anyway.'

The barber let out a laugh, best kept in, for it was disturbing in its delivery. It did, however, bring Edward out of somnolence, for a moment at least.

'Do you know Jan van der Goes, the Banker-Merchant?'

The barber stopped cutting while he thought. Then after a moment returned the scissors to Edward's shrinking hair. 'Er, no…'

Edward tried again. 'Do you know Henri Hueçon, the merchant?'

'Er… no. I don't recall the name.'

'How about his servant, Felix, or Grothmier, the builder?'

'*Nein*... I don't know those fellows.'

'Then, *Master Barber*, either I've stepped out of my room into another city, or you boast beyond your knowledge.'

But the barber protested, '*Nein, nein*. I know everyone of my clique. It is the way here. Catholics stick with Catholics, Protestants with Protestants, The wealthy and the poor... Patricians, trade, and the serving class... Jews, the French, Spanish, Dutch... Even you *Englanders* stick to your own... eh?'

'Not quite,' replied Edward.

'I stick with my family and those of my country. We are everywhere in Antwerp. Is that not right, Anna?'

'*Ja*, husband. We have much family from *Basel* and *Bâle* here, we know all from our country... *all*.'

'Yes, I have fought alongside my countrymen. Bloody work it was. My amputation saw cut more limbs on my comrades-at-arms, than my comrade's blades laid cuts on the enemy. *Ja*, bloody work it was. Eyes gauged out, limbs lopped, bones broken, arrows attached. Have you seen the mess a barbed arrow does to the body? In too deep, and you have to push it through. A mess it makes of flesh. Bone too... if it strikes and splinters. Blood... more I have never seen... *Ja*... Blood... Blood enough for this surgeon... Wounds awash with blood... blood... blood...'

And all the time Edward's eyes were closing—closing—closing. The barber's voice serene. *Blood*, he thought.

Wake up Edward.

But his eyes were closing—closing—closing—sleep.

'*Englisch*, the Banker is dead.'

Edward was shook violently. And his eyes sprang open.

'*Englisch*, the Banker is dead.'

Edward shook his head, and took a moment to fix himself in

his surroundings.

'*Englisch*... Can you hear me?'

Grothmier stood over Edward, still sitting in the barber's chair. No one else was in the room. Edward rubbed his face. He was shaved. He ran hand over head. His hair was cut. And he looked at Grothmier and smiled.

'*Englisch*, the Banker is dead.'

'And so is the baker, tanner and shoemaker, Grothmier. I warrant you each day a banker dies somewhere.'

'No, *the Banker* is dead. Murdered behind the Grote Markt. The Spanish lady's husband and her brother killed too.'

Edward focused his eyes and regained his wits. 'Then I am spared a duel.'

'*Ja*, but you are suspected... There was no robbery, only murder... Come, *Englisch*, back to your room and pack. I find you somewhere else to stay... keep you from trouble. *Ja?*'

'Where's Felix?'

'I have not seen him.'

છાલછ

Grothmier took Edward to another part of the city—to rooms significantly poorer than his last lodgings. Where secrets were better kept and miscreants better hidden. Edward was lost again. Locked away.

Edward, despite new found resolve, could not help but fret over his situation—a duel avoided, only to be replaced by warrant; saved from death, but placed again in jeopardy; Henri Hueçon's assistance and then avoidance. Edward knew that he likely be hanged or murdered more than find the truth of the events at Galicia. Edward knew his fate was being determined by another's design—to some end unseen. And worse on worse, while he waited out dilemma, even poorer was his bed, and dirtier was his room. Yet despite all this—*he was still alive.*

Serendipity or misfortune?

All the logic and circumstance lead to one conclusion.

Misfortune.

Edward cursed Henri and looked to the kindness of Grothmier. At least Grothmier maintained his company, so sanity and reason remained Edward's shield, and further gross disquiet was therefore likely parried. He raised his face to look beyond the timbered ceiling, to imagine the clear blue sky above. He closed his eyes and blew out his angst. He prayed. He sat. He watched the narrow street.

The *Oude Werf* was busy. The scent of fish filled the air. And, once again, boredom kept Edward at his window. His eyes searched the crowd, hoping to find interest amongst the throng of townsfolk and travellers walking from the quay. He hoped to see a pretty wench walk the street. But the memory of *Angeline* made the few worth the look, poor to see. Then he spied a friar. Then a boy with three books bundled. The friar was rushed, and the boy felt his anxiety more than once by way of a hateful hand lashed about his head. Twice the boy dropped the books, and the friar kicked the boy until they were retrieved. Edward shook his head, and under his breath chastised the friar for such poor temper and for the cruelty inflicted on the boy. The act brought remembrance of himself as a boy, and saw him on the street in the poor boy's place, under the lash of his betters.

Were the books worth the kicking and the company of the friar worth the beating?

Edward recalled his brother monks; murdered. He imagined the library at *Galicia* emptied of books—cleansed of the very temptation that had been his bewitchment. He wondered if his quest for truth, merely a quest to satisfy his own vanity—to have answers for questions for knowledge's sake, and not for sake of justice for strangers murdered. Perhaps his quest was for the sake of misdeed carried out against himself, simply hateful retribution against the Guild for his life wasted—for another prospective future robbed.

He thought on all those demons unseen—demons that should have been long forgotten—those who stole his father and mother, school and sanctuary.

What am I doing? There is no justice in this realm of base greed and foul sponsorship. The truth of murder will simply become another burden on my soul. Another thousand nights of sleep robbed. Why do I need to know? Is my quest for knowledge, my gross sin? Just to satisfy my intellect? Why appoint myself inquisitor? My brothers are with the goodly Father, and thus in a better place. They need no justice… They are above base requital.

God, who is greater than all this, will punish all murder committed on earth. No immunity can be given to those that kill, regardless of reason or right. They will find better justice as their souls depart the earth. Jan van der Goes, will find crueller punishment by God's fair judgement.

He prayed. He hoped to receive direction to leave his quest. Premise to forget his sense of misdirected justice, and to run. But other voices spoke to him—his own anger at the cruelty of men, his own fear of them, and *Grothmier.*

'Why does Jan van der Goes, trouble you so, *kamerad?* My mama would say, share your food Grothmier, and two will not go hungry. Share your troubles and… er… two will be troubled… er, no… two troubled heads are better than one…. er, no…*ach schwein…* I don't remember. Never mind *Englisch.* Tell me your troubles and they may seem lighter.'

'My troubles are best not shared, friend Grothmier.'

Edward smiled at Grothmier. A smile to hide his thoughts.

Troubles Grothmier asks. Justice dictates I find the truth of foul murder. Good reason dictates it's better to lose justice and lose myself.

'You know, *Englisch*, if Jan van der Goes troubles you so. Why not raise it with him direct?'

'Because even if I could procure a meeting with a man so private, would he admit to a crime so freely?'

'Crime, *Englisch*? What crime?'

Edward wondered if to answer.

Leave Grothmier out of this, Edward. He has done enough… it is not his burden.

'No crime, Grothmier… nothing… affairs best left.'

'What has the Frenchman, *Hueçon*, to do with the affair?'

'Nothing I hope… but there again… probably everything.'

'You talk in riddles, *Englisch*. But perhaps Jan van der Goes, may talk freely of crime at the point of a pistol?'

'Perhaps, Grothmier. But perhaps pistol's point be hard to achieve against one so well protected.'

'Often men so private, live in privacy deep within high walls. Guards kept at distance. Breach the walls, steal past the guard… and perhaps you have your private discourse.'

'Steal past the guard? Fanciful thought.'

'Perhaps not, *Englisch*. I know a man who smuggles meat out of his palace kitchens… he may smuggle us in for a few coin more.'

'Us, Grothmier?'

Ja, Englisch, us. Your trouble is shared whether you wish it or not. My mama would wish it.'

Edward thought to argue, but then he thought again. Henri was not his ally. Kalibrado was not his friend. He had no home. No place to go. The authorities would seek him out for murder. Innocent he was. But if the Black Merchants' Guild wanted to see him guilty, the noose was only a bribe away. But a man not known to him, not kin, had taken up his cause without thought to know its reason, without regard for his own safety. Perhaps that was enough.

Grothmier was purposeful. 'First I will find you new clothes; a less attractive suit. Have you a sword, a pistol?'

'No weapons have I outside a knife. But no sword, Grothmier. I can use a knife, but a sword, no.'

Grothmier looked at Edward's knife on the table, and shook his head at its meagre blade. 'Then a good pistol I will find… Give me your gold, *Englisch*.'

'I will let you help me, but I will not allow you to accompany me.'

'You will need a strong accomplice, *Ja?*'

'I do this alone, or not at all.'

'Very well, *Englisch*, but at least let me equip you as a soldier. Let me sharpen your knife and load your pistol. Let me see you safely within the Devil's walls.'

Chapter XXIX

Edward was wet with blood. It soaked his shirt. His discomfort was gross and unbearable. He closed his eyes and settled his breath. He emptied his mind of his predicament. Placed his thoughts in good green fields and his body under clear blue skies. But soothing thought is hard to hold, when the stink of blood fills the nose and the weight of dead meat weighs heavy on one's bones.

'Not long now… do not move.'

The low voice reassured Edward. *Not long now. Not long now. Take comfort… Rest easy.* Edward steadied his mind and calmed his thought.

The wagon passed into Kalibrado's palace without incident—past the guards to rest at the kitchen block. The wagoner and the butcher unloaded the sacks of meat; carcasses of beef, pork and mutton—a day's provision for the kitchens of a great house.

'Be still… Be still. For the love of life, sir… *Please be still!*' The butcher's voice was louder than before. Fear was about it, and it rattled Edward.

Danger of discovery, Edward thought, and he considered where his knife lay about his body—to ready himself to draw it, if need be. His pistol too bound within his clothes to be readied in haste.

Edward surrendered to the voice, and held himself ridged in his sack. He was still. Difficult it was, as he was carried to the store, to act like a body of meat. But, with muscles taut and breath held, he held himself stiff. He thought his lungs would burst, or his limbs would shake under stress. But he calmed his mind, disconnected his body from conscious thought and the discomfort of his hold, and eventually, he was placed to rest on the cold stone of the store.

As agreed, Edward waited for two hours, until all sound had gone. But as his knife pierced the sack and cut free the covering, he realised he had not waited long enough. The door to the meat store was open and staff still inhabited the kitchen.

The store was large, with recesses and dark corners—*places to hide*. Edward crept around feeling his way, until he was far from the best of the stores, until the sweet stink of forgotten meat and rotten vegetable filled his nostrils.

The stench kept Edward company, as he sat in the darkest shadow, watching the door and the light beyond. The cold was fierce. More so, as Edward sat unmoving in his bitter corner, arms folded and head kept low. Edward wished he had thought better to have worn more clothes, an extra shirt perhaps.

The cold played hurt on his arms, legs, feet and hands. He could find no comfort against the pain. He was too frightened to move leg, stamp foot, or adjust arm to find better comfort against the bitter air.

The discomfort of his silent crouch was unbearable, as muscle ached and shook. Fear took hold, born out of cold mood and colder circumstance, and in panic, he thought to run free of the cold, out of the store and find his way home. His mind fought body's self-saving instinct to move—to run. His mind fevered in its fight.

Where is home? All was too late. I am where I am, to do what must be done. Foul smell. Foul act to do. Think of better. Think what a hero would do? I am Achilles. I am Odysseus. I'm inside the Trojan Horse. Must not disappoint my generals. Wait, have courage Edward… Think what lies beyond the Horse—beyond the store.

So Edward directed his mind to the remembrance of Henri's description of Kalibrado, and his palace described by Felix, who knew it through a period of service there.

His mind became calmer, and pain subsided a little. But in a moment, fear was upon him again. His heart stopped. His breath stopped. His body ridged again. Still. But his heart's arrest was but a moment, and now it pounded hard and relentless. The kitchen maid was in the store, laughing loud, and a guard was muttering sounds in dialect indiscernible to Edward's ear.

Edward's eyes were fixed on the couple, and he prayed for them to leave. For a moment it seemed they were going to find a place amongst the sacks, boxes and barrels, to enjoy lusty exchange. The guard had pulled away the girl's top. His hands firm upon her breasts, but as his hands moved to raise her skirts, she called out, '*Zu kalt,*' and ran free of the store with the guard in hot pursuit, closing tight the door behind him.

Edward slow counted to one thousand after he lost sight of light under the closed door. He rubbed feeling back into his legs, and quietly stepped to the door, opening it only enough to peer through. All in the kitchen was quiet. Edward could not understand why the store had no lock. But it was as the butcher had advised, and Edward concluded, no one dared steal from Jan van der Goes.

The fire in the grate was low, banked to keep it alive. Edward saw no one. So he stepped free of the store and entered the kitchen, closing the store door carefully. The kitchen was empty.

A fire, free from servants? None wanting warmth and comfort?

Straw filled sacks lay on the ground, close to the hearth. Places for people to seek sleep's rest. There were even smaller sacks for children, or dogs.

Thank God—no hounds, he thought, and he moved to the stairs beyond the barrels and boxes that littered the far side of the kitchen.

Well-worn steps used daily—constant traffic of a busy house. They could only lead to the palace proper, he thought.

Edward picked a candle from a wall sconce and lit it from the fire's embers. He then pulled free his wheel-lock pistol from his jacket, winding the lock slowly with a key carried on a chain about his neck. He primed the pan with a small fill of gunpowder from a slim silvered flask carried on the same chain to prime its fire. He closed the cover carefully. He thought to pull back the dog on the pistol, to ready its fire, but thought again.

Nerves will discharge the pistol before it finds its true target. Best not cock it.

Instead he pointed it, to lead his way. He climbed the stairs, through unlocked door. He crept the servants' corridor, and climbed more servant stairs. For a long while he sidled in the dark and gloom, edging his way cautiously along unfamiliar ways. Forever fearing his light would catch a draft and lose its flame. He travelled until he came upon a series of grand doors, oddly ornate against the plain rendered corridor.

These will lead to palace corridors, private rooms and bedchambers.

All was quiet.

No guards yet. Time to choose a door.

Edward chose a door and held the door's latch firmly and twisted carefully. The door groaned a little, and Edward felt it resist—its hinges wanting to scream. So Edward carefully put down his pistol and held his candle up to the walls, to trace back to one of the unlit oil lamps that the lined the corridor. He reached up and hoped they were charged. The first one was empty, but the second had a good fill of oil. He freed the bowl from its bracket and carefully carried it back to his door, to pour the contents over the door's hinges.

The door opened easily and silently and Edward peered around the door into the empty corridor. His candle was poor light in such a vast space. He could barely make out decoration or doors lining the opposite side of corridor. Then Edward heard noises in the distance.

Guards perhaps?

The sound resonated around the hall. It filled the space and echoed around the walls. It unsettled Edward's reason and his hand trembled, shaking his candle, stirring his torch into brighter flame and his environ into brighter flickering light.

Edward hesitated to enter the corridor, with people so close at hand. He thought to walk further the servants' way, and away from the noise of the guards. So he turned to re-enter the corridor behind him.

Horror came in three faces, made into grotesque forms by the light of the lamps they carried. Three masks, sneering and cruel. Blade points held towards Edward. Vile purpose shone in their eyes.

One of the grotesques spoke. 'This palace is the Devil's dominion. Here, all souls are his. Only through God's good care, can you find salvation. Have you prepared your soul to meet the Devil?'

Edward did not think to pull back the dog on his pistol and let go a shot, or draw his blade in defence. Or even have clever words to reply. He had only a thought.

I am caught.

'We thought we were stalking a rat. But boys, the rat turns out to be a blood befouled mouse—but a learned one.'

That voice.

He found the resolve to cock the dog on his pistol—to present his arms in defence against the three.

'Calm down mouse.'

Then Edward recognised the voice. 'Francis, is that you?'

'Well if it isn't me, I should be killing a thief, instead of greeting a *friend.*'

Edward raised his candle high to illuminate the scene better. And Edward was confronted with three to be seen with relief, and not three to fear. Although it disturbed him to hear Francis use the word '*friend*'. Francis being so surly, such a word could only be used in irony, or insult.

Jack too raised his light to throw better illumination. 'Henri told me you were in Antwerp. He said you were in hiding from the wrath of the Guild Master. And by the sight of you, it looks like you've found hard times too. I've never seen you so dirty.' Jack studied the stains on Edward's clothes. 'Is that... *blood...* are you hurt?'

'No,' replied Edward. 'I travelled in by way of a meat wagon.'

'What of your monastery?' asked Jack.

'Taken from me, by way of slaughter. The abbey was pillaged of life...' Edward's voice cracked. 'No one alive.'

Francis broke in to save hearing Edward's sorrow. 'We've been looking for you in the city... We expected to find you in the last inn, not stalking these foul walls.'

'Aye, lad. Lost yer way tae the beer? There's precious comfort in these halls,' added Robert.

Edward smiled and relaxed his grip on his pistol. 'I'm pleased to see you all... Are Tom and Finn with you?'

Robert answered, 'Finn's nae wi' us, and Tom's still beddin' a woman he met off the boat, at Antwerp's quay.' He formed a grin that Edward was pleased to see on the big Scot. 'He'll nae be finished fer a good few days yet. Once he gets his blood fired, he'll keep at her, until he cannae lift his pike nae mair.'

Jack interrupted, 'This is no place for reunion. By my commission, as new captain serving Jan van der Goes, I should arrest you... So what, against all good sense, are you doing here?'

'To see Jan van der Goes,' replied Edward.

'Usually, an appointment with his secretary is the best way to meet him. A letter of introduction is better than the point of a pistol.'

'I'm afraid John... my appointment is one Jan van der Goes may not wish to keep. I have difficult questions to ask.'

'What I understand of the Guild Master, they'll be difficult questions concerning murder, I suspect. Are you here to judge him? To execute him perhaps?'

Edward did not wish to answer. So a different question was offered. 'Can I ask, how are you captain for the Master of the Black Merchants' Guild?'

'By way of Henri Hueçon. But it's a commission to test my mettle. This man, Jan van der Goes, pensions men poorly. And Henri wants me to spy for him, against my employer. Henri even told me you were in peril, to coerce my allegiance in his quest against the Guild Master. But I am afraid I cannot take either man's gold without dishonouring myself. So Friday is my last day as Captain of the Guard.'

Edward looked to the door still open, and to the voices still to be heard in the distance. 'John, will you help me find Jan van der Goes?'

Jack wanted to help Edward, but his honour fought with his conscience. 'Go back and hide Edward. I will seek you out in five days after my commission ends. And together, we will seek your audience with Jan van der Goes… at sword point if necessary.'

Francis stepped in. 'Aye, and in six we'll all be dead… I'm told no one leaves the Guild Master's employ—*breathing*.'

Edward curled down his mouth and looked to the floor. He contemplated Jack's offer, and Francis' fear. 'Five days. Methinks I will not be alive in four… because I think events transpire to see me dead, John. There has been foul act. I cannot bear the thought of standing in God's divine realm without the knowledge of who is judged for the murder of brother monks.'

'It is a strange tutelage you seek. And in truth, it would not surprise me to hear that Jan van der Goes is guilty of such a crime. But I cannot help you murder my employer.'

Robert stepped forward. 'I will go wi' Edward.'

'I cannot allow it,' countered Jack.

'I will stand wi' Edward, in the name of yer friendship. I will only guide him tae the door of Jan van der Goes.' Robert threw a glance at Edward, with a wink. '…If Edward promises nae tae murder the Guild Master.'

'I only want the truth of the matter,' replied Edward.

Jack shook his head at Robert. 'We are commissioned to protect the monster. Edward will likely kill him. I would, and I do not even know the true nature of his crimes. But I know the nature of this man. If Edward points his pistol at Jan van der Goes, he must pull the trigger, because the Guild Master will surely kill him if he does not.'

'Help me, John,' pleaded Edward.

'I cannot.'

Edward shook his head and gritted his teeth to stifle the displeasure raised in his voice. '*I cannot*. I cannot believe our meeting is not a gift from God, directed by the Holy Mother to see my quest to completion, and me safe in its delivery. Why else would we meet? What other fate could bring us together? Who else could destine two distant parted friends to join once more, two different journeys to converge at a common point… if not God working for the common good? Does not all the reason of chance and logic I taught you, not lead you to this conclusion?'

'I am sorry, but this is your journey alone, my friend. Your reasoning concerning the good fortune of our convergence is misplaced, by both its poor timing and my duty.' Jack looked away. He held tight his countenance, lest his thoughts betray him; kept fair reason from eroding his own twisted sanity—his sense of duty. Because his adherence to duty was his last defence in a troubled mind. His duty in many ways had become his only reason for being. And for all he wanted to help Edward, without his devotion to his duty, *what was there?*

'I cannot join you, or let you continue.'

'Then if not for God and for predestination, John… then for our friendship?'

'Our friendship is eternal, but my duty exacting. My devotion to these two earnest moralities cannot be shared… One must yield to the other… I hope you understand.'

'Let me help him,' pleaded Robert.

But Jack was not for turning. 'I forbid it.'

'Enough quarrel,' growled Francis, 'Even we should not be here. If we are all caught, we are as likely to be put to the sword as trespassers and assassins.'

'I do not understand, why should you not be here?' asked Edward.

'We had last minute release from duty tonight,' replied Jack.

'Aye, it looks like most of the guards are free from duty, the servant's too,' added Francis.

Jack stared at Robert. He knew his will was lost on the Scot. Robert had made it his mind to help Edward.

'If you go with Edward, to help him befoul my responsibility, you leave my service, Robert.'

'Tae save Edward, and protect both yer honour tae yer employer, and yer devotion tae yer friend, then I desert yer service gladly. Think of me how ye please. But yer conscience will likely be the end of ye, if Edward here is harmed, hung by the Guild Master's rope.'

'You think me a poor friend, Robert?'

'I think ye are in conflict, even now, tae where yer duty lies. One's honour is nae easily assigned tae righteous decision, when allegiance has already been sworn tae a perfidious path. Let me stand with yer tutor, Edward, in the name of yer constancy of friendship with him. I will be yer conscience. Turn away Jack. Be blind to his presence. Leave me tae it, and let yer honour be maintained tae yer strange allegiance tae yer iniquitous master.'

Jack held his head low, and put a hand on Francis' shoulders to lead him away.

'Walk on Edward. Count four mair doors then ye'll be at the door tae see ye into the Guild Master's chambers—two rooms, connected. There is a bedchamber and a study beyond. The talk is, he dwells alone, his wife and children sleepin' elsewhere. But I cannae guarantee he will be alone tonight. I understand his secretary, Peppo, often works with him until mornin's light.'

Edward nodded his understanding to Robert and moved forward. Robert remained standing still.

'Are you not coming, Robert?'

'This is as far as I go. To go further would mean I dishonour Jack.'

Edward grimaced, then sighed. 'I understand. Will I encounter guards?'

'The halls are strangely quiet. Guards strangely missin'. There should be guards here, Edward. Be careful. It feels foul. I will walk the halls aboot, tae see if I can find where they are, if only tae distract them.'

Edward thanked Robert and counted four more doors and entered. The room was well lit, better lit than other rooms in the palace where finances were without restriction. And it was warm. Edward recalled Henri's description, and it confirmed he was in Kalibrado's bedchamber.

'...*The Guild Master prefers light. He does not feel easy with shadow and darkness. His bedchamber is well fired summer and winter, and always with a hundred candles burning throughout till dawn. He willed it, and woe betide the servant who allowed only ninety-nine candles to burn against the darkness...*'

Edward walked through the room, searching for clues to confirm the nature of the man for himself. He saw books about, and examples of needlecraft, executed by both skilful fingers and young ambition—works of family craft. Portraits of his wife and children hung the walls—one, two... four. The largest was a family group, with himself painted harshly—a poor representation of his attractive mien, whilst his wife was painted most elegantly, and again Henri's words came to the fore.

'...*It is difficult to reconcile the monster with morality. A man capable of murder without compunction, but with such moral virtue towards his role as husband and father, as to place him the most virtuous man in all of Christendom. His love displayed for his family is an example to all husbands and all fathers. Indeed, it is difficult for those who mix in social discourse with his wife, to think of Jan van der Goes as anything but a moral man. So those in the know, and who know his family, think them ignorant to his purpose—to his deeds. Perhaps his family chooses ignorance and wishes it so...*'

Edward stood before the door, and listened. Sounds of movement within.

Is he alone? No discussion, no other footsteps.

Edward waited. He waited for the sounds of discourse to help him render the scene of the room in his imagination. He remembered Henri's description.

'...*He is like you, Edward. He loves books, or should I say the learned texts within them...*'

Edward pictured the bookshelves and piles of books then shook his mind clean and thought on again, Henri's portrait of a monster.

'...*He is an ordered man. Ordered to the point of insanity. Everything is ordered with him, and that which offends his order, is plucked from his sight...*'

Then Edward heard a voice from behind the door, muted by the thick wooden portal.

'One, two, three, four, five books in azure leather. One, two, three, four books in red leather. One volume, *Iliad*, in green leather. I must tell the *amanuensis superior* to have that volume rebound in red. Three books tall, ten books short. Sixteen volumes of songs and sonnets, but seventeen are its number. One short. Curse the man who spoils my order, a bigger curse on the man who compiles his volumes in odd numbers. *Do you not agree?*'

Edward imagined two people within. He took a deep breath and cocked his pistol, and slowly and carefully tried the door. It was unlocked. He opened the door, hoping eyes already inside the room were engaged on sights away from his entrance.

Kalibrado stood with his back to Edward. He was at his bookshelves, counting. Edward searched the room for other people. There were none. Bookshelves lined the walls, and only a desk, stacked with portfolios, and a chair furnished the floor. Edward could see a sword on the far wall, on a rack, but no other weapons on desk, or shelf. And Kalibrado was without a dagger upon his person. Edward slipped in and locked the door behind him.

'Who is that? Who enters without polite knock, or leave to enter?' Kalibrado turned to face Edward. '*With a pistol too.* Are you a robber sir, or an assassin?'

'My name is Edward Hendon and I visit to ask you questions.'

'An interview. Put your questions to paper and give them to my secretary. That would be polite action… *do you not agree?* Kalibrado raised a finger to his lips in thought. 'There again what questions I wonder require the coercion of a pistol to answer. I suspect questions I would not answer if cordially asked. So I say to you sir, I do not answer your questions. Take your pistol and retire, before I call the guard and have you beaten.'

'If you call out, I will kill you. If you do not answer my questions… I will kill you.'

'What have I done to warrant such cruel behaviour? By your bloodstained clothes and smell of you, you are a butcher perhaps, or are you a pedlar of rotten meat? Have my merchants sold you poor flesh, or has the market for your pork waned? Do you blame me for the poor commerce that sees Antwerp on its final years?' Kalibrado smiled and gestured to the door. 'Take it from me, pedlar, move to Amsterdam… It is the next golden city. Go now. Do not delay. And do not target me because I am simply a better merchant than thee. Because I am, it is true. But I deal in much more than meat. I am so much more. So much more, that it is your mistake to threaten me so.'

Edward was unsettled by Kalibrado's misplaced discourse and conspicuous confidence in the face of his pistol. And to emphasis his advantage, and Kalibrado's peril, he raised his wheel-lock to point at Kalibrado's head.

'This is a pistol sir. Not a sword to fence with. You use words to parry my intent. You babble as defence. Perhaps to steal time from me? Perhaps to give time for your guards to reach your door? So I ask you only one question. Are you *Kalibrado, the Beast of Galicia?*'

'A name I have heard. A poor epithet. If I am… *the beast*, what is it to you?'

'I found much death at the monastery at Galicia—murder.'

Kalibrado's confidence was lost for a moment, only to be replaced with enlightenment, 'So the mystery is revealed. You are here to avenge the death of some monks?'

'Only to discover the truth.'

'And then to kill me, I suppose.'

'I am here as your confessor.'

'A priest? A priest with a pistol… How inappropriate.' Kalibrado's tone was mocking.

'No, I am a man who took up the calling of a monk again… Only to have it stolen, by foul act—again.'

'Even more unfitting… A monk with a gun… *Oh how foolish it sounds!* And it sounds by your declaration, you care more that I steal your abbey from you, rather than the murder of a few monks. If you kill me monk… is not your soul damned?'

'I have killed before.'

'So it is already damned. Do you wish me to confess?'

'Yes, on paper, signed and sealed,' ordered Edward.

Kalibrado seemed resigned to his fate and he took a piece of vellum and a pen. 'Then let us get on with it… But before I write my confession. May I ask, what is your connection with Henri Hueçon?'

'I have none.'

'Come, come, Brother Edward. If truths be the only thing told here, as I write my own death warrant, then tell me the truth. You were his guest at a party. You even wooed my wife. Sorry, not my wife, but my wife's name. I wonder, is Henri, with all his sins, a patron of your order? Perhaps he is a monk himself?' Kalibrado raised his face to the ceiling laughing. *What amusement to think of it!'*

'The truth of Galicia. *Write.'*

'Now let me think… I did not kill them. But I did personally supervise their entombment. But I have to say on remembering such a trifle. Although none were dead when I locked them in, their fate was sealed by my action. So on second thought. Yes I killed them.'

Edward held his hate tightly. His whole body shook with the strain of it. He begged it to leave. He pleaded with it to subside. But his anger had him, and it shouted to be heard. And he screamed, *'Murderer!'*

'Quiet, Brother Edward, or you'll have my guards at your throat. *Murderer* is a poor description of me. I am many things. I have many capacities. But only one dream to fulfil. Murder simply another tool to achieve it. And like the craftsman, you do not name him for the tools he uses.'

'You can write your confession, or I can pull the trigger.'

'*Furet* said you are studious man—a man who is well read; a lover of libraries. Did I take the monk's library in Galicia away from you? He said you were a good man. Furet would be disappointed to think on you as an executioner.'

'I do not know this Furet. Enough talk. Write.'

'Very well.' Kalibrado sat at his desk and arranged his sheet of vellum, square on the desk. He inspected his pen's nib, and then he reselected another, with a nib in better condition. He wrote. '*I, Jan van der Goes…*' Kalibrado raised his head, and said, 'Shall I date it?'

'Write.'

Kalibrado nodded compliance. 'Furet is a good man. A little over complicated perhaps.'

Edward's patience was tiring. 'Write!'

'Why would a cock covet my hen? I am no fool. I know my sweet hen has poor feathers. She is far more than show. I suspect Hueçon is behind it, and it is me his cock pecks at. Furet thought perhaps he could use the cock to my advantage against Hueçon, and obtain his plan. He is very complex in his thinkings. Perhaps a little too elaborate... but with Hueçon, subtlety is a better tool to separate him from his secrets... and obtaining secrets by torture is a poor tool to obtain truth... but a good one to both punish and deter poor behaviour. And after all, one does not simply pluck a stranger off the street, to torture the truth out of him—without knowing who the cock is, and who his patrician connections are.'

Edward's fear grew. Kalibrado was toying with him.

Perhaps he stalls for time. Perhaps a secret signal has been sent to the guardhouse. They are on the way.

Edward flustered with the thought of it, then composed himself, and growled, 'I have no connections to Henri Hueçon... *Write.*'

But Kalibrado put down his pen. 'Come, Brother Edward. You appear at a party as Hueçon's guest. You, with no eminence in court, or trade, or good house of Antwerp. You wear his jester's suit, and perform woo on my good wife. Why?' Kalibrado folded his arms. 'Hueçon sponsors you. You are an agent of his. Enquiries have revealed it. You seek to compromise me through my wife. So what is his plan?'

Edward's brow furrowed, heavy with concern that Kalibrado was not at the end of his pistol, but some how, he was at the end of Kalibrado's. Edward thought to pull the trigger, to put a swift end to Kalibrado's life and his rhetoric. He thought on it, even though the noise of the pistol would surely invite Kalibrado's guards to end his own life. But curiosity won over fear.

'He wishes to discover your secret... He thought your wife the best route to it.'

'Ah secrets. I have many,' replied Kalibrado.

'The secret that drives you to foul the Guild.'

Kalibrado thought on Henri's play to seduce his wife. 'I think your fallacious French friend plays you false. My wife is devoted to me, as I am to her. No, that route to my hidden thought is well guarded…. Her bed would not share you, and my secrets are well kept by her. Hueçon knows this. But you have gone to some trouble to trespass my home. And I know Henri is not behind your foolish attempt at intimidation. So why does Henri…?' Kalibrado pondered a moment. 'But of course. Yes of course. Hueçon, the clown. But it is I, who is the fool. For a jester's suit does not cloak the clown, but hides the fox. I should always place that truth foremost in my reasoning. *Yes!* He is a cunning weasel, to send a handsome cock into my henhouse, to harass my hen, simply to divert me while the fox steals my eggs... *No!* He steals the whole henhouse. Yes… my devotion to my wife… my undoing. My thoughts are always on her. She is my prize. I have committed considerable of my best resource to the cock, because he attends my hen, and neglected the fox.' Kalibrado raised his face into the air, remembering his own dreams and aspirations, and then returned his head level to Edward and his pistol pointing steadily at him. 'It is good to have faith in one's future, Brother Edward. To know exactly one's destiny.'

'Then you should know you have no future on earth.'

'I think, Brother Edward, your reasoning is muddled. You think to pull the trigger. You wonder if you are prepared to die for it. For my men will come in and likely kill you.' Kalibrado stood up and walked towards the wall, towards a rack where a sword sat. 'Pull the trigger, Brother Edward. Pull it well and do not miss.'

As Kalibrado reached for the sword, Edward steadied his pistol in his right hand to point square and true into Kalibrado's back, cradling the heavy weapon in his left hand to assure its aim. He stared at the back of Kalibrado's head, and he thought to kill the monster immediately.

Edward's face told his story, a tale with no happy ending for Kalibrado. A story sown with its roots in anger, and growth fuelled

by angst and blood. Fuelled by absolute hate and now a total greed
for the revenge of all those injustices he endured by men of power.
Kalibrado was all those he hated, and Edward's eyes shouted his
hate. His teeth clenched to hold back the obscenities he wished to
spit at the monster. But he waited for the monster to turn so he
could look into its eyes, the window to its soul, and the condition
of the good and evil that dwelt within it. And he knew if evil wore
its face, it wore it well, and those who looked upon it could expect
no mercy from it.

Kill him, Edward.

But Kalibrado took an age to turn. He was in no hurry, not
even moving as though he was in any danger. Edward's aim was
steady, his intent true. Good aim from a good man, and for all of
Edward's hate, he was a good man. But there are no good men
without evil, the good hide their evil deep within their soul, locked
away. But even the good can dig deep into themselves to find it,
and use it well to destroy that which fuels their anger. So Edward
was ready to pull the trigger, and send the shot into Kalibrado's
chest, or as he thought, better still into the very face of evil, and he
raised his pistol accordingly.

But in a moment Edward thought on his soul, his promise to
Robert, and his heart in God's hands. He thought on all his
promises to God already well disregarded and his devotions poorly
applied. So he took his vengeance and threw it away, and gave it
up for his love of God—*anger had no place in it.* And Edward
pointed the pistol to the bookcase, to the books, and squeezed the
trigger. The gun flashed, but no recoil. Then Edward looked to the
pistol, and then to the books that showed no damage, then to
Kalibrado, who had turned to face him—and Edward looked into
the face of evil.

Kalibrado was smiling, sword in hand.

'I was irked by the conundrum. I wanted to know who held

your leash, and your master's intent. I wanted you in front of me.' He raised his sword to point at Edward. 'Furet is a good agent, is he not? Or should I call him by his alias? Call him *Grothmier*. Furet is indeed a good actor.... *Do you not agree?*'

But Edward found no surprise in Kalibrado's words, instead he thought on his fate, the forfeiture of life. Most likely, after not a little torture perhaps? But he had chosen his future, and reignited his devotion to God. Still, he thought to throw his pistol at Kalibrado, then to rush him, but he thought better of it. He looked again at the pistol. The pistol Grothmier said he had loaded, and Furet had not. He felt the heft of the pistol in his hand and placed it carefully on the desk in front of him.

Kalibrado walked to a bookcase behind his desk. To grasp a broad vertical carving, that formed the shelf support. He opened it, to reveal a broad red silk rope, which he tugged downwards.

'My guards will be here in a moment.' Kalibrado moved to a position near the door and unlocked it. 'They will be a while. They are lodged some distance away. I did not want your entry to be too difficult.'

Edward smiled. There was little else to do. His time was up. He would be with God soon, and he would need to be ready to confess his sins before the ultimate power on earth, the ultimate power in heaven. Torments to be soon at an end. Soon he hoped to be forgiven.

Kalibrado, though, was not finished crowing. 'I do not like to have an itch I cannot scratch. When it was clear you did not trust Grothmier enough to tell him all your purpose, I asked him to send you on to me, on what you believed to be *your* terms. I fear Furet may have failed in his own ploy, because perhaps he grew fond of you, and did not press home his own plan with enough vigour… Yet he still betrayed you. Sent you here to reveal yourself and your purpose to me.'

'I should have known. Where the Guild exists, to trust anyone is folly.'

'Now I know the truth of it, Brother Edward… The Italians call it vendetta.' Kalibrado laughed. 'But enough. I have wasted my time on you. Now I will have to act quickly and discover the real mischief Henri has brought to my door. He covets my seat, and I suspect he has plotted well to remove me from it.' Kalibrado held an ear to the door, faint sounds he heard. 'My guards… I will have you tortured a while, only for my pleasure. I will have to ensure all is true, and you are really who you are, and Hueçon is not playing more tricks at my expense.' Kalibrado shook his head, rebuking himself for his paranoia and blind concern. *'Stupid.'*

Six guards came in, hurried, dressed in red and black livery, all but one with swords at the ready. Edward looked at the faces of each, hoping to see one familiar—to see Jack, or Robert, or Francis… but all were strangers.

Kalibrado addressed the lead guard. No sword did he carry, but a thick black cudgel. Edward thought on the cudgel. He raised an eyebrow to it and expected a beating at the very least.

The six guards turned their hostile attention on Edward, and he sighed deeply. The lead guard weighed up Edward, running his eyes up and down the man and asked, 'Are you Edward Hendon?'

Edward was puzzled to be addressed by the guard, but replied nevertheless, 'Yes.'

The guard turned to Kalibrado to address him, and leaned into his ear. Whatever was said it provoked anger in Kalibrado's eyes, and Edward stood uneasy. He wished he had thrown his pistol when he had the opportunity. His best, but poor chance lost. Edward was less resigned to his fate now, less reconciled to meeting God. The guards meant business, and the thought of torture was not something a man could shrug off so easily.

Kalibrado was annoyed at the guard, and the guard backed off a foot or two. But it was not to maintain a distance from Kalibrado's anger, but to allow him room to swing his cudgel, which found its arc terminating on Kalibrado's head, with a sickening thud.

Edward stood astonished at the turn of events, at the sight of Kalibrado's unconscious body on the floor. He stood and stared. Reason left him. Words evaded him. But Edward was roused from his world of disbelief by the guard's voice.

'Master Hendon. We have orders from the Guild Master to hand over Kalibrado to the Guild Council, to do with him as they deem proper.'

Edward fell back into his state of disbelief. 'But *he is* the Guild Master.'

'Was, Master Hendon, was.'

'I do not understand.'

The guard looked about the room and spied the pistol on the desk. He knew it was not Kalibrado's—it was too plain. He then picked it off the desk and placed it in Edward's hand, saying, 'It is not our place to understand, only to take orders.'

The guard's words did not ease Edward's troubled reason, and he pressed his questions on. 'But Kalibrado gives you orders.'

'No, sir. The Guild Council issues my orders. My orders are to serve the Guild Master. The Guild has a new master—a Frenchman I am told.'

Chapter XXX

The ornamented palace was as fine a residence as the Guild owned. The Guild had its members in high places, and those in turn had influence over princes, lords and high men of creed. So the Guild was provided with many fine houses. But the absolute grandeur of this particular palace was the reason Kalibrado had selected it for his home in Antwerp. It was already a perfect masterpiece of the builder and stonemason's art—a vision in brick, marble and stucco. But Henri Hueçon wasted no time ordering the improvements, to better present the character of his newly allocated home. He called it, 'a modest dwelling, with modest improvements required'. Although in order to suit his sensibility towards colour and texture, the *modest improvements* would be considerable and expensive.

Henri would seek to convert some of the considerable funds, from the sale of Kalibrado's assets, into new art for wall and niche, hall and gallery. His rooms would feature the very newest abstraction, from the very best furniture makers in both the Low Countries and Italy. All in new, exotic woods, richly gilded, and upholstered—fine furniture and elegant seating, without any adherence to outdated conceptions of hierarchy or traditional pattern. Clothing chests, reconsidered. Handsome they would become, to better display beautiful clothes, with banks upon banks of drawer and cabinet, built to house accessory, linen and silks. Designed like exquisite oversized jewel boxes; created to house the finest jewellery—Henri's attire. All built, all bespoke for a gentleman with a vision into the future, and scorn thrown at the past. A beacon to illuminate the fashion for the next century.

He would order extensive remodelling of the gardens, which had seen many seasons of care committed by Kalibrado's wife. The green would be wiped away, and the order of stone and marble decoration put in its place. Statues that reflected Henri's exquisite and eclectic taste of life.

Deep inside the palace, within extensive apartments set out for Henri's personal accommodation, stood richly adorned rooms newly created to house his suits. Henri stood in front of a series of large mirrors created in Venice, at a price beyond reason. A wall of reflection installed to fill the space before him—magnifying the large room, so it appeared as a vast space.

Peppo was allowed to serve Henri in his private chamber. A privilege lost on Peppo, a man *promoted* from his weighty administrative duties to a new role as *assistant without office*—a mere lackey to the new Guild Master. Henri thought Peppo, with invaluable contacts and knowledge of the palace, too useful to be wasted, too dangerous to be thrown away. Henri did not seek to wipe away the sense of the old Guild Master in every aspect. He reasoned some of Kalibrado's bequest was better kept close at hand and in front of eye, lest it bit him from behind.

'…and Peppo, will you serve me as well as Jan van der Goes, the former Guild Master?'

'I serve only the Guild Master.'

'I am glad to hear it, even if it does not, I suspect, answer my question.'

'My loyalties are clear.'

'So they are', said Henri pensively, 'What of your former master, do we still have him, or have his disciples already freed him? I know you follow his progress. Please do not deny it.'

'He is still held. But arrangements to transfer him to the fortress of Sancerre have been delayed.'

Henry tried to hide a wry smile. 'I suspect they find difficulty assembling enough guard to escort him. No one wants the responsibility of transporting Kalibrado. What of his wife and children, do we have report of them?'

'They remain hidden, *Monsieur Hueçon*. The trail cold.'

Peppo's use of name instead of rank was not lost on Henri, but it surprised him that Peppo dared to be so derogative. 'Strange… that they disappeared so quickly. Within the very hour of my order to seize Kalibrado in fact… It was as if someone in the palace had good reason to protect the family of Kalibrado, more than warn Kalibrado himself.'

Henri worked his hands over his outfit, straightening any line of his costume that was at odds with the perfect picture in the mirror. He sighed, and announced to his reflection, 'I think I will add my tailor's name on the list of potential enemies of the Black Guild. He disappoints me, like those who seek to maintain kindness to Kalibrado.'

Henri waited for a response, and he watched Peppo in the reflection, apparently indifferent to Henri's disclosure, tidying the new suits that Henri had tried and discarded, brushing each one ready to return it to its wooden dress-stand. Henri waited, and waited. But it was not until Henri took his eyes off Peppo, and returned them to the vision in a pale red suit before him, that a reply was given.

'Jan van der Goes has as many good friends as bad enemies, *Guild Master.*'

Henri took his eyes off his reflection and rested his eyes to the floor in contemplation, and Peppo knew his remark was not a welcome sound for his new keeper.

Henri's face showed disappointment, a show for Peppo to chastise him for his careless words. But Henri returned his gaze into the mirror. He thought his reflected face did not suit such fine attire, and he replaced it with a smile upon an imperturbable visage.

'Perhaps I keep the tailor, and lose the valet. The dresser who presents my suits so badly…' Henri waited a moment until he was sure Peppo's unease was well rooted. 'You can go now.'

Peppo turned to leave, knowing his service under Henri Hueçon likely to be short. He could only hope that brevity would be confined only to his employment, and not to his life. So he walked the corridors of the palace, performing Kalibrado's count in his head. He turned into rooms, once his master's rooms. And when he reached the room he called his own, he pulled from his purse a pair of black gloves; the last gift presented to him by Kalibrado; his only master; his only true devotion.

An hour had passed from Peppo's departure, before a secretary entered Henri's room to break Henri's deep scrutiny of the fine picture before him.

'Captain Brownfield and Edward Hendon have arrived and await your pleasure, Guild Master.'

'Are they alone?' enquired Henri.

'They arrive with three other men.'

Henri thought awhile, before he replied, 'Send them up to my study in half the hour… No… make that three quarters of the hour. An hour may try their patience, already well tested.

'As you wish, Guild Master.'

'And ensure they leave all weapons with the courtyard guard.'

'Yes, Guild Master.'

The secretary bowed and left the room, but Henri maintained his scrutiny on the mirror. The news was welcome and Henri did not think further on Peppo. He concentrated instead on the majesty of his new apartments. He was happy that the chamber was with proper light, with as many candles as Peppo could purchase, so that no smudge or speck of dust could attach itself unseen to tarnish his attire, and with enough mirrors so he could study all aspects of himself carefully. He adjusted the cuffs of his shirt and inspected every inch of his form for perfection. The beads around his neck he arranged so the stones lay perfectly on his chest. Then he took his mind off the absolute devotion of his life—himself, and thought on Edward and then Jack.

'*Pauvre Jacques*,' he said to himself with a smile.

In the courtyard, the secretary had, after purposed delay, announced the Guild Master's availability. He had the courtyard guards search and remove all weapons from Jack and Edward. The secretary then beckoned the two to follow him.

Standing clear of Tom and Francis, it was Robert who was the one to put a hand on Jack's shoulder, to check him from following the secretary. Robert's concern was clear.

'Dae ye really need tae go in there?'

'I am afraid so.' Jack's reluctance was poorly hidden, and he turned to Robert, removing his hand. 'If we are to turn our backs on the Guild, better they know it. If we do not come out, do not come in, because we'll be long past helping.'

But Robert stepped boldly forward, to clamp his hand on Jack again, firmer and harder. 'No, Jack, I dinnae trust that Frenchy. It feels foul. He twists all tae see himself secure. He's a far, far fouler demon than the man he replaces. Come away. Let's be gone. There are more honest commissions tae be doin', and better places tae be.'

'I cannot simply ride away, Robert, and hope the Guild leave me to it.' Jack's smile was for Robert. 'Edward here knows the truth of it… It is not their way.'

But Robert was not for calming, even with Edward's nod of agreement to Jack's reasoning.

'No, Jack,' pleaded Robert, 'Come let us go… leave now.'

Jack's reply to Robert was earnest. 'Go… Go with the others. I brought you, via sea battle to siege, to bloody intrigue in a moated city. A poor picked assignment indeed. Now I must free you from it. If you fret so about safety—see Tom and Francis safe. We will catch you later under the shadow of the cathedral's tower.'

'They will go. I will send them on,' announced Robert, his voice broken, 'But I will stay. And if I dae not see ye back with me within the hour, I will rain bloody retribution on this place.'

'Then Robert, steadfast friend… stand your guard. And *we* will see you, either within the hour back in this courtyard, or within the day, in Heaven's green fields.'

Two guards opened the doors to Jack and Edward, to allow their entry into Henri's study. Two beautiful men; slight of build, deep black dressed and brightly jewelled. No weapons, nor fighters' craft possessed—men only of show. Jack and Edward paid little heed to them as they approached Henri's desk, free from paper or ledger, but adorned with fine objects of marvellous curiosity and pleasing form.

'I understand you killed a girl,' said Henri seated, not lifting his eyes from a carved ivory roundel, toyed with between his fingers. 'Killed as a test of commitment to Jan van der Goes, or Kalibrado, if it pleases you to call him such.' Henri's eyes lifted to Jack, his fingers continuing to caress the smooth ivory, carved on opposing sides with interpretations of life and death.

'I did. I killed her quick, and did it with a clean heart,' replied Jack.

'A clean heart, *Jacques... mais non?*' Henri raised the ivory roundel, presenting it in his palm for Jack and Edward to see. 'I am told this carving is six hundred years old. It depicts the beauty of life on one side, and the vileness of death on the other. It is from a culture that sees no afterlife for the soul, only decay. They see no blessed release at deaths hour, only demise. So how can you declare a death clean with assurance?' Hueçon spoke with incredulity in his voice. 'Was she not alive? And then was she not dead at your hand...? Did you not steal her life?'

'I did it to spare her further suffering. She had already been beaten bad, and subject to worse agonies—tortures that I could only imagine. Her eyes invited death.'

'But still, *Jacques... to kill a girl.*'

'Kalibrado would have killed her regardless. I had witnessed the science of his cruelty, I simply saved her from further suffering.'

'Ah well.' Henri turned the ivory in his hand to view both sides in turn. Then he flipped the roundel in the air to catch it, and placed it on the back of his hand. The depiction of life was uppermost, and Henri smiled. Then he threw the roundel into a box by the side of his desk. Discarding the antiquity without care or consideration.

'Like life and death, *Jacques*. Death and the Devil are also two sides of the same coin. Where one is called, the other is close behind.'

Edward shifted on his feet, and Jack looked on his former tutor for guidance, but none came. Instead, Henri stood up from behind his desk and walked free of it, to stand in front of the two men.

DEVOTION and the DEVIL

'Ah well,' announced Henri, 'I am a little happier, *Jacques,* to be wiser to your motives in so foul an act.' Henri then approached Jack to put his hand on the side of his arm, squeezing it gently. 'I have to admit, I was little disappointed with you. Favours to me are rarely refused, and it stole my cheer for you to refuse me, your good friend. And then for you to carry out such a murderous act for Kalibrado—*le monstre.*'

Jack was irked by Henri's sensibilities, and he pulled back his arm, to free it from Henri's hold, returning harsh delivered words. 'I was under commission. A commission sponsored by you... to the monster. I am bound by my poor honour to fulfil my commissions, and not to betray them with deceit.' Jack turned to face the window, to support his mind's eye view of the larger world. 'The world is full of monsters, Henri—and only a few good saints. Rarely are my duties invoked by saintly doings... *Do you not agree, Guild Master?*'

Henri's face lost its glow—it had found chastisement. Jack's words made it so. They had pierced his ego, and wounded his pride.

Henri retreated behind his desk, and affability left his tone. 'I suppose you are both here to question what role you have? Now your *commission* with Kalibrado is at an end.'

Jack turned back to Henri. 'We are here only to request that we part from the Guild, and I from the Guild Master's employ.'

'*Mais non, Jacques.* You think you have no stomach for the Guild. But you are simply sickening a little. I will give you five hundred ducats to pay for your pleasures. Then come back to me. I have work for you here and there, but mostly there. Edward will never be free from the Guild, he knows this from last we met in Newcastle. He can go wherever he pleases, I have no further use for him. But the secrets he holds will never leave the Guild.' Henri walked over to the window, and Jack's eyes followed him, until he was only a silhouette against the window's glare.

Henri continued. 'No one walks from the Guild with its secrets in their hand. To do so would mean their hand would need to be cut off. And to hold its secrets in their head... well you can see my dilemma.'

Jack looked on Edward, his face stolid. He waited for Edward to speak up against Henri. But Edward remained silent. So Jack spoke in his stead. 'Sorry, Henri, but I take my men on to more honest work. Even if it is murder for gold, it will be honest murder, free from intrigue. Edward is one of my men in this respect. You foul him, and you foul me, and I will make you pay for it.'

Henri smiled away the rebuff. '*Jacques*, you remind me why I like you. Why I have liked you since we first met as friends on an English riverbank. When your boyish face was covered in snot, and your clothes were as poor as your childish manners. When you were swordless and charmless.'

'I have appreciated your friendship, Henri. Even though it was one born out of deceit, as you moulded me to serve the Guild... As you have done with so many others. But it is an alliance that sits uneasy with me. And with you now Master of the Black Merchants' Guild, I have no place calling you friend, only employer... and in truth I do not care to call you friend any longer.'

'*Non*, do not say these things. Am I so different, *Jacques*, to the man who helped you when you were a boy, to the man who took you under my gracious wing?'

'You are a man full of deceit. Even now you still maintain your pretences. Friendship with me is one of them.'

'I will forget these hurtful things. You are displeased with me for placing you in Kalibrado's guard... and it may have been careless of me to suggest you for such an... *unpleasant commission*. But you came to no harm—so no harm is done.'

Jack fired his reply, 'What of Edward here…? You placed him in harms way, and he is lucky to be alive.'

Henri took a fig from a sliver tray, sitting on a table next to the window. He studied it then returned it to the tray, to pick one with a more pleasing form to his eye.

'*Jacques*, you charge me with deceit. So I will prove you wrong. I will be fair with you and Edward. Although I agree he was placed in harms way. I did not leave him there. Felix was a good servant in respect of this service, in terms of keeping Edward safe and asleep in his room.' Henri turned to Edward, solemn faced. 'He paid dearly for his brave service to you Edward, and to me.'

Edward finally spoke. 'What has happened to Felix?'

'Furet murdered him I suspect—because poor Felix was suspicious of Furet's poor show as Grothmier. I'm surprised, Edward, you did not see through Furet's act. Kindness blinds you—*it always has*.'

'I cannot deny I liked the fellow,' replied Edward.

'Perhaps he liked you too,' announced Henri smiling, 'After all, he saved you by killing the Banker and, of course, his brother-in-law, before he had opportunity to kill you in duel. Although, *peut-être*, I suspect Furet saved your life by design rather than desire. He even left poor Felix's freshly killed body at the scene of the Banker's murder to implicate me in his foul act. Although I must confess I am perplexed by the Banker's death. The Banker was one of Kalibrado's most ardent supporters. To have Furet kill him to implicate me, or Edward, or even you Jack, had little real value. *Non*, he had a greater reason to murder such a man of greater value to himself and the Guild.' Henri hesitated and smiled as he discovered new delicious reasoning. 'Murder is such a useful tool, it can serve many masters… Perhaps a master unseen directs this play?'

Jack interrupted, 'Henri, are we to walk free from here, or is murder on your mind?'

'I will allow you, Edward, and all to leave free of the Guild's employ, with a boon and without enmity, if you complete one more task for me.'

Jack looked on Henri with nothing but doubt. 'I suspect the cost of our discharge to ourselves, will be more costly than any boon you offer.'

'Gold to the value of a year's employ for each of your group,' said Henri, 'But I will not lie to you. It will be hard earned pay for the assignment I ask. You see, *Jacques*, the Guild have ordered Kalibrado to face inquisition. To interrogate him to the reasons behind his actions that has brought the Guild into dispute with its more influential Catholic patrons… All I ask is… that you free Kalibrado.'

Jack and Edward could only look at each other, momentarily lost for words.

'Why do you want him free?' asked Edward.

'I am now Master of the Black Merchants' Guild, with influence over one third of the world's trade. It is a prize to be worshipped. A devotion to die for. Yet Kalibrado risked it all for another dream. What could be so fabulous? I need to know.'

'Then let the inquisitor's sadistic tools unlock his secrets,' replied Jack.

Henri shook his head. 'He will stay silent. His secret is his, and no one will share it. No perverted device will open his locked soul. No, *Jacques*, I need him free to pursue his dedication, to allow me to find that which he has risked all to pursue.'

'But even if we free him, he will be caught. Caught easily without the Guild to protect him.'

'*Oui*, but he is a very resourceful man. Perhaps he will stay at liberty long enough to reveal his secret to me.'

Jack stood, and thought hard on the offer, *Freedom from the*

Guild by way of a deceiver's contract, with likely death whilst freeing a monster. Or refusal, and likely death by the hand of the Guild. Poor choices indeed.

Henri studied Jack, and he saw a man in dilemma—a man who was mulling over choices in his head. A man who *would* decide a path, but be reluctant in its choosing, and unenthusiastic in its travelling.

After a while Jack answered, 'I alone will seek to free Kalibrado. If Edward and my men are still free to go their own way—with the pay you promise.'

Henri shook his head. 'You will need your men to free *le monstre, non?*'

'No, Henri, I will find a way on my own.'

'The odds are too poor, *Jacques*... I think you sacrifice yourself to save your comrades. Alone you will die. You know this. Your honour will not see Kalibrado free, or your friends safe.'

Henri walked to another table, a one with a richly embroidered cloth covering it. He reached under the covering and drew his sword.

In all the years Jack knew Henri Hueçon, he had never seen him draw a sword in threat, or defence, only in tutelage. But now the point of Henri's sword was at Jack, and Jack did not know whether to take it as a serious threat.

'*Jacques*. Bring the smile to my handsome face. Take my commission to free Kalibrado. You must take your men too... Self-sacrifice is for martyrs. You will not save your men by forfeiting your own life.'

'I do not understand... You threaten my men?' said Jack, looking for any weapons placed around the room, in case Henri's intent was to cut with his sword.

Henri looked flustered. He looked at his sword and regret coloured his face. He relaxed his guard—his grip. '*Non*... That would only bring only sadness to me... *Mais non*, my wording is poorly applied. Do this small favour for me… And all favours are paid… You will be free of the Guild… and I will pay your full boon in gold now.'

Jack had known Henri, and had called him friend. He understood well Henri's foppish behaviour, and he knew he was a man devoted to himself and that which he thought would glorify him further in the eyes of others. This was without doubt his dedication. But however deceitful Henri may be, Jack knew his intention with regard to gold and freedom from the Guild may be true.

Jack mulled over his options. He voiced the first of his thoughts. 'I could take your gold and run.' Then he voiced his second thought. 'I could take your gold and report your intention to the Guild Council. Let them deal with you as they see fit.' And then his final thought, 'Or I could simply kill you now and have done with it.'

'One could do all those things. Even though your word with the Guild Council would have little sway against me. *Non*… If you take the gold, you will take the commission. After all, you are *nothing* but a man of honour.' Henri turned to a mirror, hanging on a wall, near to where he stood to look at himself. '*Pauvres Jacques*. To think you would kill me is unthinkable. I am all that I love, and to kill me… is to kill all that I love.'

Jack simply shook his head at Henri's perverse and self-adoring view of himself. 'Then I will take your task and fail—perhaps deliberately. It would not be surprising if I fail such a difficult task.'

'I think you will be diligent… It is your way.'

'It seems, Henri, I must do what you ask to safeguard reason.'

'*Bon*.' Henri seemed happy to break his guard and put away his sword. 'Peppo will go with you. He has all details and knowledge to help you free Kalibrado.'

DEVOTION and the DEVIL

Edward asked, 'Is it wise to share your plans with Peppo? He will undoubtedly inform on you to the Guild Council. They will be very unhappy.'

Henri wagged his finger, as he picked up a brush from a nearby table to remove a spot he had noticed on his suit. 'Peppo too wants to see Kalibrado free… For his own reasons I suspect. He will help you, I am sure of it.'

Jack nodded to Edward. 'Then we take our leave from you. Send Peppo to me on a horse with the gold.' Jack beckoned Edward to follow him, and they turned to leave Henri's study. But Henri spoke again, and Jack and Edward turned their heads to hear his words.

'*Jacques, mon ami.* I am glad you choose my commission… I will trust you will be successful and we see each other soon. To share good wine and good tale.'

'From this day forward, Henri, we are not friends… Do not call me such. I will fulfil my commission. You see to it that you keep to our contract. And my name to you is, *John*, John Brownfield. But you may address me as Captain, Captain Brownfield.'

Hueçon smirked at Jack's declaration. 'You give yourself everything, *Jacques*. A rank without commission, a name not your birthright… and a self served honour that sits uneasy with your soul. Honour without allegiance, *Jacques*, is pride. You abandon honour when you turn away from your family's name, and your country's calling. You are a *condottiere*, and mercenaries do not have honour, *Jacques*. They are only devoted to themselves and their own pleasure. Your self-esteem comes only from those base, ignorant men, foolish enough to see you as their leader—a bigger man than themselves. Without them, or true name, or country, or faith, or any devotion greater than your own self… you are nothing. We are the same person, *Jacques… Brownfield* and *Hueçon* are pseudonyms for deceit—the same men in different suits. Except you are a bigger deceit than I, *Captain Brownfield*.' Henri then turned his attention on Edward. 'Oh, and I should warn you Edward. Furet will probably be seeking Kalibrado as well… Not to free his master, but to revenge the death of his sweetheart, *Angeline*.'

Edward looked puzzled at first. Then he thought on the red-haired beauty at the party. As recognition of the girl's name illuminated Edward's face, Henri turned to Jack.

'He may decide to kill you too, *Jacques*… After all, it may have been Kalibrado's order, but it was your knife that stilled her life.'

Chapter XXXI

The men met under the great spire of Antwerp's grand cathedral. Hidden in the teeming mass of the faithful waiting outside its doors to demonstrate their devotion within the halls of worship. The throng was busy. Noise filled the square. It was a place of ten thousand people and more, gathering. Bells rang their call. Their sound cloaked twenty-score conversations between both the worthy and the wicked. Noise enough to hide the discourse of men not there for reasons of worship, but for hidden meeting. Jack, Edward, Robert, Francis, Tom and Peppo—all were present, but few were happy to be there, and none but one with thoughts of atonement and godly devotion.

'Where dae we go?' asked Robert, keeping his voice from the ears about him. 'Dae we have a commission, or are we runnin' from the Frenchy?'

'Not running.' Jack thought on Robert's words, and cast an ironic smile at Edward. 'Edward and I are *free* from the Guild,' casting another sideward glance towards Edward in wry confirmation.

'So we have no employ from the Frenchy?' spat Francis, bitter.

But Robert read Jack's countenance, and shook his head. 'No, Francis, I suspect the Frenchy still has Jack in his perfumed grasp.'

Jack smiled at Robert's discerning eye. 'If you are all game, we have another commission... To free our former employer, Jan van der Goes, from the Guild.'

'That sounds like a game for fools,' countered Francis, looking to Robert and Tom for support in his condemnation. 'Who but the foolish would want to snatch that devil called Kalibrado? Let him rot where he is, I say.'

Peppo remained quiet, and Jack observed his abstinence from defence of his former master with suspicion.

'I can only agree with you,' replied Jack. 'For it still sounds foolish to me as I utter the words. But there it is. Good gold if the Devil goes free.'

'Good gold?' asked Tom.

'A year's pay,' replied Jack, and Tom nodded his approval.

But Francis was still unhappy. 'I'll need ten times that to see me risking my life. Storming prison walls indeed.' Francis paced his agitation out. Three steps forward, and three back. 'We'll only end up in them walls, never to get out.'

'No walls, Francis. Peppo tells they'll be escorting Jan van der Goes to another prison deep in France, away from his allies, sponsors and agents... Chance to free him on route I think.'

'And his escort?' asked Robert.

Jack turned to Peppo, inviting him to answer.

'There will be no fewer than sixty,' offered Peppo.

'Men ten times oor number,' replied Robert, eyes wide.

'Aye, and maybe ten times more,' added Francis, spitting to the floor, still pacing, but now in steps of four.

'Peppo, do we know who will transport Kalibrado?' asked Jack.

'Yes, an able French gentleman. A veteran of many battles, with no favours owed to Henri Hueçon.'

Robert looked to the ground, to look for some sense in the

dirt, because his ears only heard calamity. He took a deep breath and lifted his head to Peppo. 'And his men?'

'They will be seasoned troopers. The Guild will accept nothing else.'

Robert said nothing. Francis heard all and said nothing, but his face shouted his discontent, his steps increasing with every return.

Robert cleared his mind of the folly proposed, and instead looked around to the crowds preparing to enter the cathedral. He was in awe of their numbers, impressed by their constancy to their Catholic faith. He looked to his own fidelity, tested by life, and formed by the nature of his own spirit. He thought on his duty to his men, his protection of his friends and his devotion to Jack. He thought on proper action and he scanned the crowed a second time, but this time to confirm he and the others were not being watched, or overheard.

Robert's eyes remained on the crowd as he sidled close to Jack, his voice low for only him to hear. 'The Frenchy tasks ye wi' a grand difficulty, Jack… It's as if he wants ye tae fail.'

'Perhaps,' replied Jack. 'But he pays us in gold… in advance of the commission as inducement.'

'And my master will pay you gold again to free him,' added Peppo.

Jack narrowed his eyes at Peppo's declaration, and turned to Edward. 'Walk with me.'

At distance, away from the group, out of inquisitive ear's reach in a noisy crowd, Jack halted Edward.

'I am not comfortable with Peppo. I have observed him since Scotland. He has a loyalty to his former employer, Kalibrado, that unnerves me… Devotion even to the death, I suspect.'

'Yes,' replied Edward. 'Dedication to his employer, even though Kalibrado no longer employs. Yet Peppo's devotion to his former master remains. I sense something far greater than mere duty, or the pay it brings, binds these two men.'

'At least we can be certain he is not Henri's spy.'

'Who knows certainty with Henri,' grumbled Edward, 'When he wears blue, I challenge my view and call it green. When he says yes, I hear no.'

Jack looked to the open doors of the cathedral. 'This is no game for you, Edward. Take up your monk's garb and return to your religious devotion. Leave this to me.'

'My business with Kalibrado is unfinished. Justice is still wanting. Truth still hidden. Also, I know Furet's true face. He will hide it well from you. He is a bigger fox than I have ever encountered... Besides, Henri's gold is as good as any, and I'm short on funds and may need to buy my way into another monastery.'

'I have to say, I would welcome your help, Edward. It will be wits and wiles that free Kalibrado, not sweat and the sword. But it's Henri I fear more than the sixty that guard our goal.'

Edward placed his hand on Jack's shoulder. 'Yes, to Henri, we are old vestments to be thrown away—accessories that have lost their shine. I cannot believe Henri would risk his position within the Guild to free Kalibrado. I suspect Henri will not rest easy, even if we succeed, so long as we have tongues to wag witness of Henri's deceit at his Guild masters... They will not be happy with him.'

Jack nodded his agreement, and thought more on Robert's words. 'Why send us, if he expects us to fail? Freeing Kalibrado may scratch Henri's itch, but I agree, alive we become an irritation that he will find little comfort from. He has other plans for us, not to our benefit.' Jack threw a glance to Francis, his now dozen steps or so of agitation bringing him ever closer to their position, and in conflict with the crowd standing about. 'We better return to the others, lest they think we plot.'

'Yes Jack—*plot*.' Edward smiled at Jack, embracing him, squeezing hard. 'We have known Henri far too long. Intrigue has infected our reasoning—paranoia our fever.' Edward released Jack and raised his face to look upon the tip of the cathedral's tall spire, standing four hundred feet above them. 'Give me leave for a while. I wish to enter the cathedral. It may be my last time to cleanse my spirit.'

Jack nodded agreement, and Edward disappeared into the crowd flowing through the open cathedral doors. And Jack returned to his men.

Tom moved forward as Jack approached, so his hand could ruffle Jack's blond hair.

'Jack m'boy. Me and Robert have decided. Forget the Frenchy and his gold. Let's away. We'll be able to hide ye and Edward better in a land we know. There's many a Cumberland forest, hill and valley where the hunters' dogs will be hard pressed to track ye.'

'Aye, Jack,' added Robert, 'We would follow ye into the depths of Hades, sober and withoot a blade of protection between us, if ye asked it. But forget ye this commission, and let's be goin' back tae the Borders. Enough of this nonsense. We should expect nothin' but death from the Frenchy... Aye death, or even worse things I cannae imagine.'

Francis halted his pacing and stood in front of the men. 'Yes, we'll all die if we try to free the Devil from a hundred men— perhaps two hundred. All none too keen, I wager, to be having him bound amongst them in the first place. We have gold enough.' Francis' mind's eye looked to his stabled horse and his stuffed saddlebag. 'Aye we've gold enough and spoils even to sell. Treasures to see us well fed.'

Jack stood and thought. He looked to each man in turn and studied the men's faces. He considered their protests and their advice. But it was Francis who had lit the fire under his reasoning, and fanned it into flame. And a smile formed his face. 'Yes, Francis is right… They'll be riding hard to be rid themselves of Kalibrado… Which gives me a notion…'

[The rescue of Kalibrado continues under the title, *Sancerre*]

Epilogue

The evening was all the better for the rain that fell on the city that afternoon—*strangely clean*. The waters of the sunken city refreshed, the cobbles washed and the green that dotted balcony and terrace, windowsill and entranceway, was verdant and bright.

The boatman was discrete. He paid no attention to the women chatting in his *battella* as he stood its deck and rowed the canal. His eyes were fixed on the way ahead. And he filled his thoughts, lest an idle mind be tempted to listen into his customers' private discourse. He chose to think on the balconied ladies that lined his route—women more his fit and fancy—women of questionable repute, spending their evening hours standing their verandas, and spying the traffic below on the waterway as it passed. So the boatman held good his posture, and held high his head so that his handsome profile may catch the fancy of a wench, keen perhaps to separate him from his day's earnings. And a secret smile shaped his lips, as pleasured thoughts filled his brain. But his fancy that night was not of wenching, but of a hot meal before well-deserved rest and the pleasure of his wife's face at the sight of good day's take, her company better for a good yield, and his good children's song sweeter for their mother's better humour.

Within the boat, the four ladies were dressed in dark blue mantles, ciphered with a large cross in white—*Sisters of Avalon.*

They had two children in their charge, but no servants, nor baggage, nor anything that marked them out as travellers, or women of wealth and substance. Except each wore a gold ring, an extravagant example of the goldsmith's craft, bearing a bull emblem—*a snorting bull.*

One woman was senior to the others, as demonstrated by the three other women's respectful observance of the fourth's discourse and actions. The three listened intently to their senior, as initiates might listen to a sage.

The sun was receding, still yet to hide, as they reached their landing. The four women disembarked to the jetty with help from two men, liveried as stewards from the Tirabosco-Priuli Company of Merchants. A third and fourth man stood by. One dressed well as an important official would dress in order to meet important people. The other dressed only to impress those with an eye for cheaply bought show.

The official stepped forward to welcome the women, his greeting courteous and audible, 'Benvenuto *signore.* I hope our weather has not spoiled your transit through our city?'

From the group, only one woman stepped forward to reward the official with acknowledgement.

'Thank you, *Principale.* Our journey has been acceptable thus far. My companions and I are keen to continue on without delay.'

Luca da Mosto smiled. 'Everything is ready. Your ship awaits your gracious presence. Supplies, including your book boxes have been aboard for three days. I have to say madam… I applaud your collection of books.'

'Thank you, *Principale.* Have our other ships sailed?' asked the woman, looking to her senior, as if she had directed the question herself, and was anxious to hear a favourable response.

'Five days ago. The captains, as instructed, were not given charts to the final destination until the fourth day at sea.'

'Good.'

Luca da Mosto then stepped beyond the woman to address her senior. 'I have kept my tongue madam, but I must ask again. Where do you go?'

The senior woman replied, 'To my dream, *Principale da Mosto . . .* to my dream and my devotion.'

'Will your husband be joining you?'

'No. He was lost to me twelve months ago.'

'I am sorry to hear it . . . He was much admired amongst my fellow merchants . . . and my master, the *Monsignor el Doxe*. He has much to thank him for . . . Election to *Doge* of the *Most Serene Republic of Venice* is never cheap, and never achieved without the procurement of influential friends, and the silence of influential enemies. Yes, difficult to achieve, even with a brother preceding him as *Doge* to grease the cogs of election. The *Serenisima Repùblica Vèneta* is certainly a prize, do you not agree?'

The senior woman did not reply, or demonstrate any interest in Luca da Mosto's declaration of praise for her husband, or of his beloved Venetia.

Luca was forced to retreat a little, and rethink his cultivation of his client's favour. He thought perhaps his comments were misplaced, and perhaps she knew nothing of her husband and the Guild's sponsorship of his master. *But she knew everything.* His recollection of events proposed another scenario, and perhaps his master had another to thank—another agent of the Guild; one who had dispossessed the lady's husband, and therefore was not a name to prick at a grieving widow.

'How, may I ask, did your husband die? I would like to offer my prayers for his soul, and light a candle to his memory?'

'I did not say he was dead . . . only lost. He was a good husband—a good father.'

'Then I am still sorry for your loss, madam.'

'I am not sorry. My husband was already lost, because of his devotion to me. What else could he do but sacrifice all to give me my desire? Is it not the mark of the truest devotion, for one to sacrifice their own dreams to embrace those of the entity they love? *Do you not agree?'*

'Then madam, your dream must be Heaven... Will you not share your dream with me?'

The senior woman threw a withering look at Luca that killed his enquiry dead on his lips, so that a new direction of discourse he had to find.

'Er... this is your ship's captain, my brother... *Giacomo da Mosto.'*

Luca's brother stood forward and bowed sharply, raising himself in a flourish to announce his Italian style. 'Ladies...'

Luca quickly stepped forward before his brother could say more, and thus save himself further embarrassment; his brother was without polish; his seafaring nature stunting his subtlety in polite society.

'I am sorry the coach can only take four,' announced Luca da Mosto. 'May I suggest I travel with three ladies and the children? My brother can escort your remaining lady on return of the coach.'

The senior woman nodded in reply.

Giacomo da Mosto held his tongue for half the hour while they waited. But his eyes had already stripped the lady in his charge naked and his prurient mind had debased her into a bitch to be covered.

'I see you travel without husbands. It is not safe for ladies to travel without male companions. It is a long voyage, and my men are men, and men being men... *well you understand my meaning.* In which case my cabin is always open to you for your... *protection.'*

The woman glared at the captain. She knew all too well his meaning of *protection.*

The Italian captain, seeing the woman's face, countered in feigned retreat, 'I apologise if I insult you.'

The woman continued to glare at the captain, his smile a telling reveal on his face—a sign of his true lascivious intent.

'May I make a point, Captain da Mosto? Because I think good manners will be too blunt to pierce your dull head.'

The captain nodded and bowed in polite, but insincere compliance.

'There was a certain Spanish lady called *Consuela*. She thought herself beautiful, and because of her good fortune in marriage, she held great eminence in her circle of society. She insulted my sisterhood once at a party… The offence may have seemed trivial, but as a consequence, Consuela's rich husband, an esteemed banker of Antwerp, died by a blade, and his death removed all her good fortune… They say, in poverty, she was forced to remarry and now sweats in the Americas, her face pocked by disease.'

The woman studied Captain da Mosto's face to ascertain if he had found true contrition for his insult. But his lecherous smile remained. The captain thought it time for him to speak, but the woman raised her hand to halt him.

'Some monks insulted my sisterhood once. They thought my *Sisters of Avalon*, being mere women, unworthy to study the books in their library. Then they died, and we were able to read and take the books without censure. Their offence, in the world of men, was slight, but their chastisement, in our world of women, severe.

Now I have delivered my point. What I need to know, Captain da Mosto is… *do you understand?*'

[The story of the Sisters of Avalon continues under the title, *Two Crows*.]

417

Author's Note

Although *Devotion and the Devil*, its stories and principal characters, is a work of fiction, the settings are real (with the notable exception of the Monastery of Galicia), as are the majority of the main historical events and issues surrounding Sixteenth Century Europe. The circumstances surrounding Newcastle, Edinburgh and Antwerp, and particularly events around the Siege of Leith, are recorded histories, and only the existence of the Black Merchants' Guild is a fiction.

The siege of Leith, a not particularly well known history, had its own cast of characters, of which only a few I have borrowed for the tale; Lord William Grey, Sir William Winter, Sir Richard Lee, John Knox, Henri Cleutin; titled Monsieur d'Oysel and the Queen Regent, Marie of Guise. These are just a few of the real protagonists who took part in the siege, represented fictionally by my hand, or simply mentioned in order to tell the story of the *School of War*. The natures of those people are surmised from the situations they actually found themselves in, but of course their opinions and actions are an invention for fiction's sake.

I have attempted to adhere to the history of the siege as detailed in histories and contemporary reports given as account of the action by observers and politicians of the day, regardless of their own bias and competencies. I have to thank works both modern and antiquarian. Works of record, research and even Sixteenth and Seventeenth Century fiction, including *Thomas Churchyard (The School of Warre)* and *William Sampson (Vow Breaker)* for their own dramatic portrayal of the Siege of Leith, either in verse or performance—their own fictions no doubt colouring my own work.

The language throughout the story has been greatly modernised to give only a hint of flavour of dialect and rhetoric. One must understand the complexity of Sixteenth Century forms of English used and spoken, as well as the difficulties with the multiple dialects and languages spoken across Europe at the time, especially within the commercial hubs of trade. So for reasons of accessibility, modern English is used throughout, with only slight reference made to the protagonists' native tongue. So I offer my apologies, to both scholars and readers well versed in archaic language and text, for the alien tongue used by my characters at a time when language had very different phrasing and delivery.

There are countless reference sources used, and many commendable authors have contributed to this work. Many to thank. Many to applaud. Many to laud for their own devotion to history that in turn has embellished my own fiction. But alas, there are too many to list, and too many to praise.

The *Borderer Chronicles* are written as a saga, purely as an entertainment; a series of novels written without allegiance to genre or even devotion to history, but as a signpost for readers to perhaps seek out a greater understanding of the time, and the wonderful places and natures of the peoples included within the tales.

It is work enjoyed by its author, who through reading countless well-researched and penned reference works, has enriched his own knowledge and understanding of events long past. As a writer it has given me opportunity to visit new places, to meet new people and make new friends, to walk the old ways and imagine the sights and smells of half a millennia past, to imagine a life of a man; a Border Horseman, from birth to death, neither Scot nor Englishman.

Mark Montgomery, Author, MMXIII (2013)

Historical Note
The Siege of Leith

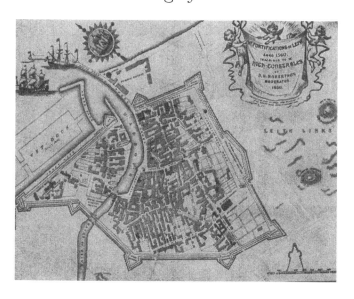

Leith 1560

Chronology of events surrounding the Siege of Leith

1542:

After incursion by the English into the Scottish Borders, James V, King of Scotland, marches on Carlisle with intent to punish the English, but is defeated at the battle of Solway Moss. James V, dies soon after and leaves his newborn daughter, Mary, as Queen of Scotland. James Hamilton, Earl of Arran, is appointed Scottish Regent, and with the captured Scottish nobles, promises their infant queen in marriage to Henry VIII, King of England's own son Edward, in order to create a union between England and Scotland in Henry's favour.

May 1544:

Henry VIII, angry that the Scots renege on the agreement to marry their infant Queen to his own son Edward, invades Scotland, landing at Granton and capturing Leith in order to assault Edinburgh Castle. The English are forced withdraw after three days, burning Leith and Holyrood Palace.

July 1547:

The English invade Scotland again, and defeat the Scottish at Pinkie Cleugh (10 September 1547). Lord Grey heads the first charge, and is injured by a pike trust into his mouth. Leith is reconnoitred at this time by Sir Richard Lee.

16 June 1548:

French troops arrive at Leith, invited by the Scottish Court to strengthen their *'Auld Alliance'* against the English.

August 1548:

The infant Scottish queen, betrothed to the Dauphine of France, is removed secretly to France. During 1548, work begins to fortify Leith.

1549:

The English occupation of parts of lowland Scotland and the Borders wanes in the face of cost to the English Treasury and increasing numbers of French troops.

1554:

Marie of Guise, Mary Queen of Scotland's mother is appointed Regent in place of the Earl of Arran.

1558:

Mary, the young Scottish Queen marries Francois, Dauphine of France.

10th July 1559:

Queen Mary's husband becomes King of France, his father, Henri II dying in a jousting accident.

1559:

Senior Scottish nobles, disaffected with Marie of Guise's policy of appointing Frenchmen into key positions within the Scottish Court, joins with an anti-French protestant party, first established in 1557 as a protest against Mary's marriage to the Dauphine, *'The Faithful Congregation of Christ Jesus in Scotland'*. These *Lords of the Congregation* raise an army of 12,000 to remove the French from Scotland.

25th July 1559:
A truce is drawn up between the Lords of the Congregation and Marie of Guise (*The Articles of Leith*). The Lords promise to withdraw from Edinburgh, in return for protestant religious freedoms. The treaty is strained when disagreements emerge regarding the increase in the French garrison and when Catholic freedom of worship is compromised.

January 1560:
An English fleet, under the command of Sir William Winter, arrives in the Firth of Forth, landing artillery at Figgate, to help the Scottish Protestant Lords. English diplomats falsely claim Winter has no commission to act on behalf of the English Crown.

27th February 1560:
The Duke of Norfolk, on behalf of the English Crown, signs the Treaty of Berwick, and takes Scottish Protestants under Elizabeth 1's protection.

6th April 1560:
The English lay siege to Leith.

15th April 1560:
The French sally out of Leith and overwhelm the English trench line, sabotaging three artillery pieces (by driving spikes through the guns' gunpowder touch holes). Sir James a Croftes manages to oust the French attackers. Lord Grey's son, Arthur Grey, is wounded in the counter-action.

1st May 1560:
An accidental fire burns the southwest quarter of Leith.

7th May 1560:
Large-scale assault fails to take Leith by force. Five thousand

Scottish and English soldiers, in two waves, attack the western ramparts. A further 500 troops are landed on the seaward access to Leith, and a further 1,700 attack from the south as a feint. The action lasts only a few hours and reports (disputed) cite 1200 English and Scottish dead, with only 15 French casualties.

13th May 1560:
The English kill a large number of civilians and French soldiers, forced through hunger to pick cockles on the shores outside Leith.

15th May 1560:
Sir Richard Lee sends a map made of the fortifications of Leith to London, as part of an enquiry into the failure of the attack on 7 May.

19th May 1560:
Marie of Guise, regularly receiving secret intelligences regarding the detail of English dispositions, has coded letters regarding the English mining operations intercepted by Lord Grey. Grey manages to block further messages.

28 May 1560:
The French are reported to have had no meat for three weeks. The ration is daily bread and a salted salmon between six men per week.

11th June 1560:
Marie of Guise dies of oedema at Edinburgh Castle.

17th June 1560:
Armistice agreed after French become disheartened by the death of Marie of Guise.

20th June 1560:
French and English soldiers share a meal together on the beach outside Leith.

22nd June 1560:
Armistice broken, but no fighting follows.

4th July 1560:
A brief skirmish becomes the last fighting of the siege.

7th July 1560:
Peace agreed (*The Treaty of Leith*) between Elizabeth and Francois (King of France) and Mary (Queen of Scots).

17th July 1560:
A total of 4,195 French troops with their families are evacuated from Scotland, under English supervision, with 120 left to remain at Inchkeith and Dunbar. All Leith's defences are removed.

1561:
Lord Grey, heavily censured for his poor action with regards to the Siege of Leith, retires from active service, his governorship of Berwick and Warden of the Marches. He dies within a year (14 December 1562).

March 1561:
Marie of Guise's body is smuggled out of Edinburgh Castle and eventually interred in Reims, France.

Main primary references and sources for further reading:-

- The History of Leith from earliest accounts to the present period, Alexander Campbell (1827)
- Port of Leith; Its History and its People, Sue Mowat (2008)
- The Fortifications and Siege of Leith, Stuart Harris
- The School of Warre, Thomas Churchyard (1560)
- The Vow Breaker, William Sampson (1636)
- Edinburgh and the Reformation, Michael Lynch (1993)
- The History of the Estate of Scotland, 1558-60, The Wodrow Society (1844)
- Two missions of Jacques de la Brosse, Gladys Dickinson (1942)
- Annals of the first four years of Queen Elizabeth by Sir John Hayward, Camben Society (1840)

Solution to the Cipher

IJ VCKPY VQ ASL SLKTLD VQ HGHWVY, ASL
IPHCLC VQ ASPD SPAELC OLZ HWS YTNSAD
VGLC KZJFTPUEZ

BY ORDER OF THE LADIES OF AVALON, THE
BEARER OF THIS LETTER HAS ALL RIGHTS
OVER DOCUMENTS

Made in the USA
Lexington, KY
09 August 2019